Not So Human

a novel by

THOMAS J. FREEMAN

Cover design by Thomas J. Freeman
Interior design by Thomas J. Freeman
First Edition

ISBN: General – [979-8-9944487-0-0; 979-8-9944487-1-7]
ISBN: Amazon – [979-8-2735119-1-0; 979-8-2735659-5-1]
ISBN: Barnes & Noble – [979-8-2603555-2-7; 979-8-2603577-6-7]
Printed in the United States of America

Published by Thomas J. Freeman

This is for my amazing mother, Nancy.
Without you, I wouldn't have these wonderfully
horrific ideas.
Long live horror and the love of creative demise.

Preface

The story you are about to read is not merely a tale of survival, nor is it simply an account of collapse and conflict. It is a reflection on what it means to be *human*. Not in comfort, but in crisis; not in victory, but in the space between surrender and hope.

I began writing *Not So Human* as an exploration of how fragile our understanding of the world truly is. We assume we know what lies beneath our not-so-metaphorical feet, what lives beside us, and who we are in the face of challenge. But when the world shifts, literally and philosophically, we are forced to question everything: our origins, our values, our dominion.

This novel is a layered account. Beneath the science fiction and apocalyptic backdrop lies a story of deep connection: between friends, between ideas, between civilizations. It asks whether humanity's intelligence is truly its greatest strength or its most fatal flaw.

Some elements of this story were inspired by real scientific limitations: our inability to explore more than a few miles beneath the Earth's surface, the mysteries of evolution, and our cultural blind spots to unseen life. Other parts emerged from my fascination with resilience, the kind that doesn't roar, but *refuses* to die.

Not So Human is for those who wonder what lies in the darkness we've never dared to dig into. It's for those who believe humanity is both flawed and full of promise. Most of all, it is for anyone who has ever asked, in silence or pain: **Who are we when everything falls apart?**

— *Thomas J. Freeman*

"Man is not made for defeat. A man can be destroyed but not defeated."

— Ernest Hemingway

The Old Man and the Sea

Not So Human

BOOK I.

RISE OF THE

HIDDEN

I. EARTH

The scratch of ink against aged paper cuts through the forest silence; the only unnatural sound in this reclaimed world. I wonder if anyone will read these words, or if I'll survive long enough to finish them. The rising sun gives a light I don't strictly need anymore, but habits of old tend to stick around. Even with enhanced vision, there's comfort in honest daylight as I work. If you find this, tell the world what happened. How we faced what forever changed humanity.

Sitting motionless among these ancient trees, I hear what others couldn't: a low thrum beneath the Earth's surface, the planet's slow machinery. At shallow dawn, it drops below the range that rattles the leaf mold, roughly ten Hertz worth of quiet, our best hour for moving or writing. I take a measured breath of air so clean it would have been unimaginable in the before-times, when pollution choked our skies. The purity should be a blessing; instead, it carries the weight of what we lost: billions of lives, entire civilizations, the illusion of human supremacy.

My eyes scan the horizon for threats, for any sign of movement, human or otherwise. A thread of soil unzips down the side of a stump, then stills. I hold my breath for seven counts. No clicks in the sub-sonic, no ripple in the leaf litter; I return to my task. The weight of this message presses against my chest as I begin to chronicle how everything changed, how we discovered we were never alone on this planet.

Dear survivors,

I know the landscape that greets you now. You wake into it; I keep watch inside it. This is no longer the world your history books described, nor the one whispered about in pre-collapse tales of human achievement. You've awakened to a raw, unforgiving vista stripped of comforting illusions. Here, every dawn is a renewed fight for survival's most basic elements.

Nature has reclaimed what we thought we'd conquered. Trees grow wild and twisted, their branches reaching toward skies finally free of industrial poison. The air carries a purity that should inspire hope; instead, it serves as a constant reminder of the civilization we've lost. This new world, beautiful in its terrible honesty, conceals dangers in every shadow. The pervasive silence that now defines our existence makes threats easier to detect, but it also allows our minds to dwell endlessly on what was destroyed.

Survival has become humanity's sole occupation and daily primal struggle. We hunt, we scavenge, we search constantly for shelter and sustenance, living closer to our animal ancestors than to the beings we once believed ourselves to be. This transformation from civilized citizens to desperate fighters reveals the fragility of everything we built. Yet even as we claw for each day, we remember who we were. We refuse to become mere prey. We continue our fight for the right to call this planet home.

You may understand what shattered our world. Perhaps you lived through the initial tremors, heard the screams as reality reset itself around us. Or maybe, depending on when these words find you, the true nature of our catastrophe remains unclear. Either way, begin with this: a question that challenges everything humanity believed about its place in existence. If I told you that throughout the final decades of human civilization, when we believed ourselves more advanced than ever, a war was being meticulously prepared, a conflict designed to eliminate ninety percent of its target population, what would your mind conjure? Mushroom clouds? Engineered plagues? Lights descending from the stars?

But none of those familiar catastrophes occurred.

What if the enemy that systematically dismantled human civilization, stripping us of our perceived dominion and forcing Earth into this violent reset, emerged not from the stars above or laboratories, but from the very ground beneath our feet? From the foundational depths of our existence, the place we believed we had conquered completely?

What would you say then? How would you reconcile a threat so fundamentally alien, yet so intimately connected to the planet we called home?

This war, this subterranean assault on everything we understood, defied every framework humanity had for conflict. It didn't simply push us toward extinction; it held us at the edge and made us look down. Our assumptions of species dominance became weapons turned against us. This enemy didn't just destroy our way of life, but it forced us to witness our reflection in the dying eyes of our companions.

Thrust into this new reality, we had no choice but to fight. Not simply for survival, but for our right to exist as humans, to prove that our millennia of evolution and achievement hadn't been meaningless. We had believed that our technological advancements were humanity's triumph. That we had transcended daily survival and achieved something that separated us from mere animals. That belief shattered like glass against stone.

Natural selection, raw and immediate, favored resilience and adaptability over intelligence or strength. I've witnessed the precise moment a survivor's will broke, their eyes going empty as hope died. I've also seen the sudden clarity that strikes others when they realize the old rules no longer apply, when they understand that survival demands a fundamental transformation of self. Sterile diagrams of the human psyche never screamed... the people did.

This vulgar, uncompromising reality changed us all.

The battles that followed, wars fought on scales from continental strategy to personal and desperate skirmishes, carved scars into both landscape and soul. But I sit here as living proof that humanity's story isn't finished. I will tell you how we fought back from that first moment of understanding, how we began proving ourselves worthy before we even grasped the full scope of our situation.

Life as we knew it may be irrevocably lost, likely never to return to its former state. But I guarantee you this: we won't surrender easily. Not while breath remains in our bodies. This enemy, whatever its true nature, believes itself faster, stronger, more intelligent than humanity. Yet even the most carefully crafted plans, the most overwhelming advantages, inevitably crumble when perceived strengths become fundamental weaknesses.

Humanity, though transformed, continues learning how to exploit that truth.

Despite this resolve coursing through the veins of humanity's remnants, I would lie if I claimed this war has been anything but devastating. It has been a tapestry woven from ingenuity and sacrifice, brilliant victories snatched from impossible odds balanced against countless losses. We cling to those small triumphs: moments when the human spirit defied mathematical impossibility, when cleverness overcame brute force, when cooperation achieved what individual strength could not.

But for every gain, we've suffered losses that cut deeper than mere death, though the dead number in the billions. We've lost innocence, hope, the very fabric of the world we once knew. Layered over everything are the quiet sorrows: whispered goodbyes, silent burials, and the despair that settles over refugee camps when rain falls and the future seems uncertain.

Yet we endure, driven by stubborn hope for something better.

I pause in my writing, dabbing the pen tip against my tongue, an old habit to revive a drying instrument. The forest silence no longer comforts; it feels vast, ancient, watchful. It feels like *them*.

A pebble ticks against my boot from nowhere. I freeze, count to seven, and let the ground count me back. Nothing. For now.

From the Earth we come and to the Earth we go.

As we found ourselves fighting for the right to continue inhabiting this planet, we awakened to a fundamental shift: for the first time in 2.5 million years of documented human existence, we had become the hunted. We were prey, navigating survival in circumstances that activated ancient instincts buried beneath layers of civilization and technology.

In those initial days, many clung to fading religious hopes, as if divine intervention might protect us from these pursuers. We huddled like sheep in a pen, surrounded by wolves, waiting for shepherds who never came, too overwhelmed to flee into the unknown.

This war, I now understand, was destined to be humanity's last as the societies we had constructed, built on the ideology that humans were Earth's sole proprietors, began to crumble. We considered ourselves untouchable, too advanced to be genuinely threatened by anything terrestrial. Our confidence was, in retrospect, a profound delusion.

Perhaps this is human nature at its core: the drive to conquer and control any threat inside our perceived domain. However, we failed to account for what ultimately sealed our fate: we were being observed. Studied. Every defense, every pattern, every reaction meticulously analyzed by an intelligence we couldn't fathom.

Nothing remains hidden when the watcher's eyes stay unknown to the watched.

This truth undermined everything we'd built, mirroring the predators we thought we'd mastered. While we remained oblivious, believing ourselves apex, they catalogued our hubris and the weaknesses that came with it. They learned our patterns, our essence, turning our strengths into traps.

In chilling contrast to their intimate knowledge of humanity, we remained ignorant of their existence, let alone their survival methods unfolding in the realm we called our own. For eons, since intelligent life first emerged, they have thrived unseen in the dark, intricate spaces beneath our cities, farms, and oceans.

Ironically, our understanding has never been clearer than it is now. Our minds, once dulled by illusions of safety and dominance, will never again fall victim to the naivety that led us here. As I finish this thought, watching true dawn paint the ruined landscape with golden light, I know that vigilance, however exhausting, remains our only chance for survival.

The Earth was formed 4.6 billion years ago through violent collisions that sculpted this sphere and its lunar companion. In its earliest epochs, our planet was a molten fireball; a superheated core collapsed in on itself. Over eons, that fury cooled, settled, and shifted. Lacking a beating heart, yes, but changing with a living thing's patience. It grew, developed, and evolved until it reached a kind of stability.

In humanity's late, arrogant blink of the timeline, we dissected our bleeding planet with textbooks and sterile diagrams. We memorized the layers, inner core, outer core, mantle, and crust. We recited that seventy-one percent of the Earth is water. We bragged that we'd explored five percent of the oceans and drilled to a maximum depth of twelve kilometers, 7.67 miles. At our proudest depth, we still barely scratched the paint. These days, I time my crossings to the mantle's breathing; still, when the thrum rises, I move when it falls.

The implications were staggering, yet we ignored them. We left the vast majority beneath our societies, our mines, and our foundations unexplored, unknown, and unheeded.

I share this not as a lecture, but as a stark reminder of the limits of what we previously called truth. We behaved as if every process existed to enable human dominance over land, air, and water.

Our understanding, painstakingly assembled, was superficial. We grasped only what we could touch, what instruments could measure, what our imaginations allowed. We dismissed the possibility of intelligent life originating within Earth itself, considering it primitive, alien, and beneath consideration.

But what if our method of survival, sunlight, surface air, and predictable cycles, wasn't the only path to intelligence? What if Earth's true inhabitants chose differently, burrowing deeper, becoming one with the planet's heart, patiently observing as we operated on their ceiling?

What if we were never rulers, but temporary tenants, unaware of silent, ancient residents beneath our feet?

Despite warnings from rare voices with similar ideas about Earth's hidden possibilities, humanity kept its eyes outward. We scanned distant galaxies, certain we'd exhausted our own world. We convinced ourselves that no existential threat could originate from within our sphere.

This belief was so misguided that its absurdity now reveals itself in every discovery of life we still fail to understand, in the humbling knowledge that infinitely more exists on Earth than we can fathom. This oversight blinded us, leading us to champion the false truth that our systems were the pinnacle of evolution, our communication the most sophisticated, our might absolute enough that we couldn't be humbled, not even by an army of ants, should they organize into a weapon.

We catastrophically underestimated what other life forms could do if they evolved along different paths and coordinated their efforts.

Perhaps modern humans believed we'd never need to fear pervasive threats from Earth itself. We had no precedent saying we couldn't defend our ground against planetary dangers. Even though our drills barely scratched the surface, even though we knew countless species and civilizations vanished into forgotten depths, we maintained faith that our generation possessed what it took to call this planet home, ours alone, unchallenged.

What I've laid before you is the truth I've come to understand about our former humanity. Enlightenment came after the world transformed beyond recognition.

I write these words ten years after the first irreversible events changed everything. My perspectives, once naive and later siloed, were tempered by survival and loss. Everything I know now, I learned through blood; it might have saved them then. These words echo constantly: Maybe if I had been more independent in thought, more focused in my research, and more rigorously prepared for situations that most people would never dream of confronting, they would still be here.

I see their faces clearly, hear their laughter, feel their presence, and imagine them waiting for my return with news that we had won. That we had proven our right to call this planet home. Forever.

A tremor, not of Earth, but of memory, shakes my hand, making ink dance momentarily across the page. I wish I could claim that these past ten years have mercifully faded into obscurity, that pain and vivid memories of life before the end have grown dim with time. But I'm afforded no such luxury.

I remain here, mobile and functional, cursed with perfect recall of everything we've lost. Every scar on this landscape marks my soul. It's been exactly ten years since I learned the truth, since my purpose was forged in fire, since I lived my last days of simply being human without question or qualification.

My name is Dion Hammond. I am currently thirty years old in human-measured time, though the years since the Collapse feel like centuries.

Now, as true dawn breaks and casts long shadows across this wounded world, I invite you to follow my recollection. We will journey backward. Back to the days before everything began to end, back to May 2025, when I was twenty years old and believed I understood both myself and the world beneath my feet.

Back to when we all believed we were safe.

II. ROOTS

On Thursday, May 15th, 2025, I stood two days away from a milestone that felt like the culmination of everything I'd worked toward. I was poised to graduate from Clear View University with a bachelor's degree in geological engineering, specializing in tunneling systems. The registrar said no one my age had crossed that stage before, though I didn't bother to verify it. My path to that moment hadn't been driven by conventional ambition, but by an obsession that had consumed me since childhood.

From my earliest conscious moments, I'd harbored an unshakeable fascination with planet Earth; not just its surface beauty, but its hidden architecture. I was captivated by its construction, from its molten core to its atmospheric boundary, constantly questioning how it supported human civilization and what secrets lay buried in its depths.

Earth could have been entirely covered by impassable mountain ranges, fundamentally altering how societies developed, or preventing their development entirely. Massive structures could collapse into hidden cavities or shifting plates, causing catastrophic loss of life. Yet, these disasters occurred far less frequently than my analytical mind calculated they could. These geological inconsistencies sparked the kind of focused curiosity that becomes a life.

My primary goal was comprehensive understanding, to learn everything conceivable about our planetary home. I devoured old news articles, technical textbooks, obscure research papers, documentaries, and even archaic VHS recordings. I sought to understand humanity's interaction with Earth's subsurface, and more critically, to comprehend why everything functioned as we believed it did. How did we humans play our role without disturbing the forces that had sustained our species?

This pursuit drove me to excel in every arena. Mastering subjects rapidly, often completing years of curriculum in months, maintaining peak athletic performance; everything was calculated to free maximum time for research. The side effect, standing out, never felt like a burden; it felt like a clearance to keep going. I was pursuing what fulfilled me, what provided genuine purpose.

I had reached this level of awareness early on in life, not from any desire to fast-track adulthood, but because of my innate ability to adapt quickly to any situation and leverage that adaptation toward my true passions. I never intended to excel academically as I did, despite what others might assume. Instead, I preferred spending unfocused time with friends, though I rarely had any, or competing in sports like lacrosse and volleyball, where I became team captain in high school alongside my geological pursuits.

This drive to participate fully in life outside academics paradoxically made my abilities more pronounced, creating larger gaps between my peers and myself. I simply couldn't tolerate inadequate performance in anything, and my parents recognized this trait when I was three years old. That early recognition led them to place me in accelerated programs where I excelled at unprecedented rates.

By age twelve, I was a freshman at prestigious Brookhall Senior High School and predictably at the top of every class. My achievement drive was intense as I pursued everything learnable within academic domains, but I intentionally avoided external recognition to escape the politics of scholastic success. My intellectual and physical abilities at such a young age made my parents view me as humanity's ideal specimen. I, however, considered myself simply someone who grasped concepts and strategies more quickly than others. I recognized my differences but had no desire to publicize them; I only wanted to be myself.

Despite these achievements, I decided it was time for my parents and everyone championing my academic gifts to understand my humble self-assessment. With quiet stubbornness, I chose to take the full four years to complete high school, focusing explicitly on understanding myself and forming genuine connections, rather than demonstrating superiority through human interaction.

My parents didn't appreciate this decision, constantly reminding me where I could be, what I could accomplish, as if I were destined to save the world.

Although they didn't realize it at the time, they were completely correct. However, I wanted to experience humanity more traditionally while remaining true to myself. I had finally found my niche, a group of students similar enough that we could become genuine friends, something I'd experienced fleetingly before but could never maintain as I advanced beyond my peers. Previous friends often grew to feel as though they were a burden on my time or intellect, though I never encouraged this perception.

Reflecting on this period, I often wonder if I should have simply listened to my parents and finished school early.

Developing friendships and "normal" experiences proved helpful for later survival, but perhaps not as much as I'd hoped. If I had continued my isolated path, focusing solely on research into Earth's hidden mechanisms, perhaps I could have foreseen what was coming.

I cannot say with certainty, but I know that graduating from college in 2021 would have provided four additional years to prepare for the challenges ahead. I was strong, intelligent, and, unbeknownst to me then, capable of far more than I understood.

Despite these regrets, I can only address what occurred and continue forward with what is.

The friends I made during my first year of high school became lifelong companions. More than that, they became family, and I feel that bond even now. Without them and the lessons they unknowingly taught me, I wouldn't be here to share this account. They deserve proper recognition, and their stories need to be shared alongside mine.

However, before delving into those high school experiences, there's someone who holds a special place in my life, an undeniable presence. The only person who truly knows me, and whom I will continue searching for until I find answers.

I met Abrial Alavar, Bri, at age four. Though we hadn't known each other since birth, it felt as if I'd known her forever. A bond we would understand better over the years.

My first clear and interactive memory of Bri dates to kindergarten. I'm uncertain why we had never spoken before, especially since we lived only houses apart in the same quiet suburb. We never interacted, never acknowledged each other's presence. I hardly noticed her until one specific moment, though I could tell she was different from my observations of other children. Bri, like me, possessed awareness and intellect that made childish games a low priority. However, she paid more attention to those low-priority tasks than I did, and significantly more than most children.

Looking back to the last day before Christmas break, the classroom walls were lined with maps and platitudes, and the air was thick with the scent of gingerbread. While the others glued candy to collapsing houses and compared Santa lists, Bri and I, still strangers, were independently mapping the most optimal route for Santa's global journey, assuming he existed.

The precise moment our silence broke was when I noticed her Santa route began in Northeast Russia, while I, with my developing understanding of global time zones, believed he should start in Kiribati.

"Your route doesn't make sense," I stated matter-of-factly. It wasn't a taunt; it was a diagnosis.

Bri looked at me with surprise, not at my words, but at the fact that I had spoken to her at all. Her dark eyes, usually placid from my passing glances, showed something I couldn't yet identify. Though they were still as ponds in late summer.

"Kiribati is furthest ahead in time zones. Start there and work westward until you reach everyone on their Christmas day," I explained with characteristic directness as Bri slowly processed the first words she'd ever received from me. She simply stared, calculating.

"Russia makes more sense," she countered, her voice precise. "Clear Asia, Africa, and Australia first, then hit the Americas. Less ground to cover as the day progresses. More efficient present delivery per time unit."

As I examined her logic closely, realization dawned. This was the first person I'd encountered who was similar yet different enough to be an intellectual challenger, a true peer. This was friendship.

Although this was our first conversation, an immediate mental connection was established. I realized my previous sense of isolation hadn't been complete; she had been there all along, parallel to my existence. I began questioning Bri about her thought processes, her interests, and why she always remained on the sidelines when other children napped, snacked, or engaged in what I considered pointless conversations. Her answers broadened my understanding, and I immediately recognized a kindred spirit.

We were both intellectually advanced, both possessed premature maturity, and both were instinctively seen as "different" by classmates. I was perpetually the outsider regardless of group participation, and she was identical in this regard. By age four, we had established a shared understanding of our realities, laterally existing until these inner truths connected.

After a passionate discussion about Santa's optimal routes, where I considered her circumstances and found her logic genuinely challenging, I made a decisive statement.

"You're like me. You're not running the base model like they are. That has to mean something." I gestured toward our classmates, who remained oblivious to our conversation mere feet away. "We should be friends and continue exchanging ideas. I'm Dion, but my family calls me 'D.' What's your name?" I extended my hand with an oddly formal ceremony for a four-year-old, though the gesture felt natural.

"My name is Abrial. You'd know that if you ever checked the seating chart our teacher posted, but I suppose that wouldn't matter to you," she replied flatly, arms folded, ignoring my extended hand with a hint of amusement in her eyes. "You didn't ask my opinion, but I've decided to accept your friendship terms. I look forward to our continued alliance. I've been observing you for some time, as I assume you have been observing others. While we're not identical, we're similar enough. Maybe you'll provide the intellectual engagement I lack compared to these other children." Bri looked at me directly, her gaze unwavering.

From that moment, Bri and I became inseparable. For years, it was just us, a singular unit navigating the world together. We remained faithful to our Christmas break promises, encouraging each other's curiosity about everything around us. Though our primary fascination remained Earth itself, since she harbored similar interests in planetary formation and mechanics, we engaged in other activities as well.

Given that she was also the type to excel academically primarily to pursue personal interests, we often embarked on exploratory adventures in our local area. This included sneaking into abandoned mine shafts, charting the deepest sections of public parks, visiting mountain rock extraction sites where our parents took us, and occasionally diving into video and board games. We even shared similar birthdays; hers fell two days after mine on July 5th, making those three days of celebration relatively exciting for us.

I didn't realize it then, but Bri was everything to me; my confidante and intellectual partner. I believed myself equally essential to her, since we represented all either of us knew regarding profound human connections. However, when ninth grade arrived and we both became the young "prodigies" navigating Brookhall Senior High, the rest of our eventual family joined our story.

Advance to the midpoint of our first quarter, first year. Bri and I would convene, as always, in a quiet, unused corner of the science wing to discuss geological theories, debate scientific paradoxes, or simply decompress after intense varsity volleyball practices; another area where we excelled, though with different approaches. While she was physically capable, her direct demeanor and lack of conventional enthusiasm made her unsuited for captain roles, since she wouldn't provide the morale-boosting support team sports required. This left her unperturbed as she never desired such positions and preferred being the independent force that emerged when "teamwork" failed.

On a particular Friday, after an exceptionally demanding practice, Bri broke our established pattern by not meeting me as I waited patiently in the deserted hallway connecting the gymnasiums. The fluorescent bulbs ticked like insects in the ceiling, adding to the strange theme. As minutes accumulated and I waited for her post-practice appearance, I observed a subtle shift in atmospheric tension. Something was wrong.

Following instinct, I rose and moved to peer around the corner, hoping to glimpse her or understand the disruption. As I began looking stealthily, I noticed Bri walking away from the exit toward home, which was immediately odd behavior. Even stranger, she walked with two other people, an occurrence that genuinely surprised me. These individuals looked vaguely familiar from bustling hallways, but I'd never paid particular attention, dismissing them as background noise.

Rapidly analyzing the situation, I asked myself: "Who are these people, and how did they convince Bri to accompany them, especially in this direction?"

Curiosity and slight concern that anyone besides me could withstand her directness and intellect drove me to follow them through school corridors, remaining as silent and unobserved as possible. Bri maintained an undefeated record against me in any cat-and-mouse scenario, always seeming to know precisely where I was, possessing heightened environmental awareness that detected nearly every presence through minimal action.

As I trailed them through the long, dimming halls lit only by aging fluorescent fixtures, they abruptly disappeared through a side door toward the athletic fields. Approaching cautiously, unable to see clearly beyond the exit, I stopped just before stepping outside, my hand hovering over cool metal.

My environmental awareness, while not matching Bri's level, still exceeded average capability. This advantage gave me the distinct impression that Bri was no longer nearby. Deciding the situation was becoming more complex than I preferred, and knowing Bri could handle herself in any scenario, I chose to exit through this rear entrance.

Walking around the school's corner toward the front, the corridor hum followed me out; tired light clinging to the air. That's when I saw her.

A girl in a black and green tracksuit sat perched atop one of the building's side ledges, staring directly at me with a spreading grin. Simultaneously, I noticed the other stranger who'd been with Bri emerging from nearby bushes, dressed in a black polo shirt and khakis. Observing them both, I couldn't interpret the situation; their planning, how it involved me, and why they were concealing themselves.

Before anyone could speak, before I could formulate questions, I felt a firm hand grip my shoulder from behind. Warmth through fabric. A familiar pressure.

"How did you get behind me? I saw you exit through that door, then lost track," I questioned, rare surprise flickering in my voice as I began turning toward her.

"Just because I'm not the physical specimen you are doesn't mean I lack speed," she replied in her characteristic direct tone, though I detected microscopic amusement beneath her words, a rare expression from Bri. It was the half-smile she rationed to emergencies and private victories.

"You two can approach. Our friend here is sufficiently surprised," Bri announced calmly, addressing the newcomers as the tracksuit girl jumped effortlessly from the ledge, landing with soft precision. The other guy casually approached from the vegetation.

"Since we're here, introductions are necessary. This is Dion, though you may call him D—"

"My name is Dion. 'D' is reserved for family," I interrupted, cutting off Bri mid-sentence, unwilling to let these new acquaintances become familiar too quickly.

"As I was explaining," Bri continued, completely dismissing my preferences with typical nonchalance, demonstrating her general coldness, "this is D's first opportunity to encounter people outside sports or academics. He's developed the belief that others aren't worth his time, which is why he never noticed our communications until I arranged this moment."

As Bri introduced me with characteristic bluntness, I finally had opportunity to observe these two without distraction from unfolding events. The girl in the tracksuit had long, curly, dark hair that flowed past her shoulders. The athletic wear suggested track team membership, but her demonstrated speed and kinetic energy confirmed it. Though high school remained new for all of us as freshmen, I assumed they shared our grade level. I began recalling seeing her in the school newspaper, though I'd never truly noticed her in classes. From her effortless descent from the ledge to her apparent ease in reaching that position initially, I understood why Bri had selected her for our group.

The guy, conversely, seemed unremarkable at first assessment. Nothing indicated athletic prowess, nor did he appear exceptionally gifted academically or otherwise. But Bri had brought him here for a reason. As I observed more carefully, letting my analytical mind process surface details, I discerned something in his expression that demanded attention. He didn't possess Bri's direct demeanor; in fact, he seemed genuinely friendly and open. But something about him stood out, a hidden depth beneath the surface. The person wearing a black polo and khakis, with a short, dirty-blond fade, who seemed to hide behind an amicable exterior, was who Bri truly wanted me to meet.

Standing in the overgrown grass beside the school, the late-afternoon sun casting long shadows, Bri continued with the formal introductions.

"D, to my right is Auxiliadora Tudwrig, 'Auxi' for efficiency. First-year like us. Shares our interest in Earth's mechanisms, though from a more biological perspective. She's worth your consideration, D, if you're willing. She's also physically capable, which I don't state lightly," Bri explained with rare warmth as Auxi regarded me with a half-smile, her wide eyes radiating active energy.

"To my left, Kendry Rainer. I call him Ken, although he adapts to whatever greeting he receives; flexibility seems to be central to his nature. You'll soon understand why he's here. While not extremely athletic or particularly passionate about studying our planetary home, he possesses attributes that will prove beneficial," Bri continued. I noticed genuine brightness in her eyes, the expression she wore when truly fascinated.

As I tentatively shook hands with these new faces and conversed until we eventually walked home in gathering twilight, I had to trust Bri's judgment. We weren't identical, she and I, but we shared perspective to the extent that she understood what I needed even when I didn't. This shared awareness, which we accessed daily, was precisely why I accepted her introduction of these new characters into our lives. Denying her would have meant denying myself, and I had never denied myself in my twelve years of existence.

III. GROWTH

Accepting these people into my life was a luxury I only later understood represented survival itself. In my youth, I viewed it as a beneficial arrangement, a logical progression from solitary existence. I couldn't yet comprehend that this small, unconventional group was actually the blueprint for enduring what was coming. Though they differed from Bri and me in outward expressions and immediate interests, Auxi and Kendry proved themselves not merely engaging companions, but essential components of our emerging collective.

Their academic strengths, our same-year cohort with staggered birthdays, and the diverse perspectives they contributed weren't just enriching; they were raw materials from which our future would be forged. They helped me understand myself beyond rigid intellectual confines, demonstrating how effective individuals could become when they abandoned isolation.

Bri, ever the keen observer, had located these two through methodical observation, waiting for the optimal moment to act. This made me reflect on what I, in my logical isolation, might have overlooked. I used to question why people gathered into groups, believing that additional individuals simply created more vulnerabilities. Now, a world removed from that naive reasoning, I see the truth: a collective becomes a force multiplier for effectiveness, while isolation represents ultimate vulnerability. No individual can truly operate in a world devoid of others. When the door to alternative perspectives closes, improvement becomes impossible; a lesson learned through experience and seared into my soul by the fires of our fallen world.

Over the following four years, our quartet grew closer. We discovered balance in our dynamic and developed through inevitable adolescent experiences, albeit with more intense debates and higher stakes for recreational activities. Through countless local adventures, passionate disagreements that sharpened our minds, spirited debates that forced articulation of complex thoughts, and occasional sporting competitions with Kendry as impartial judge, we thrived as a unit.

I had always believed myself destined for solitude, a singular intellect. Then Bri arrived and transformed that outlook. This deepening understanding of human connection marked the second time she had revolutionized my perspective, and daily, I began recognizing more clearly why our paths had intersected.

Our bond felt unbreakable. Bri and I remained inseparable, constantly improving each other through shared focus and, now, through additional friendship's value. Where I had once considered her merely direct, she repeatedly surprised me with unexpected actions and subtle gestures of care. She consistently reminded me that I always had more to learn, not just about Earth, but about human interaction itself.

This friendship, this collective pursuit of intellectual and personal achievement, continued through high school and supported our shared ambition for collegiate alignment. Though Bri maintained her direct demeanor, a sharp, analytical edge that rarely softened for casual acquaintances, she did adapt over time, allowing glimpses of dry wit and fierce loyalty to emerge. I, too, remained selective about people beyond academic obligations, not pursuing additional close friendships outside this core group. Despite this selectivity, I grew noticeably more relaxed during those years, influenced by Kendry's calm, informal approach and laid-back attitude. He demonstrated that practical intelligence reflects more than outward presentation.

Auxi and Kendry maintained other friendship circles, so we often found ourselves in situations requiring interaction with their associates, group gatherings, and social activities. I slowly realized these events held genuine meaning and connection for others. To preserve these peripheral friendships for Auxi and Kendry's sake, I attended their events, interacting with their friends through carefully crafted superficial engagement. I was never seen as an outcast among their groups, solely because of my ability to convincingly feign enjoyment and interest. Though Bri, with her lack of pretense, couldn't manage this performance and often appeared overly direct, I could make nearly anyone believe I cared deeply about their mundane stories when, in reality, I remained mentally disengaged. This was my method for staying faithful to internal priorities while maintaining group harmony. I could withstand social discomfort for what I perceived as the greater good of preserving our collective unity.

Again, I interrupt this story, which leads to our world's current state, to pose a question: Do you consider my past behavior "human"?

My youth feels like a different lifetime governed by different rules. I examine that person and question whether I was doing what humanity, in its purest form, would recognize as 'human.' The most fundamental concept of "us," of being human, builds upon individual understanding until, perhaps, tentative consensus emerges. Throughout our existence, humanity operated on foundational opinions championed by individuals, influential groups, or entire societies. Each held local truth; none survived every test.

Ultimately, "human" was never clearly defined. It was simply a designation we assigned ourselves for categorization among other planetary life forms; a form of self-proclaimed relevance within the animal kingdom.

That kingdom has fallen.

I continue questioning you, survivor: What do you believe it means to be human now, in this fractured reality?

For us, the answer has never been more precise than now, as we live through life's complete restructuring. However, definitions crumble fast, and the answer is yours to forge from your path.

Despite that fact, I believe certain elements make us human. The ability to truly comprehend others' lives, to grasp their struggles and joys, even when you can't relate to their specific circumstances, remains fundamentally human. So let us relate to one another across our vastly different times through shared experiences of tragedy and endurance.

As our friendship flourished and we learned more about each other, I glimpsed what these associates would become by college's end and, as it developed, by the world's end.

Our "games" and playful competitions were never mere entertainment. They were training. They were moments when essential natures revealed themselves; skills that would eventually determine life or death. An example of this is Auxi's athleticism, combined with an adventurous spirit, that would surprise many. Though not as fast or physically powerful as I, she was undeniably more daring, a force that often provided crucial advantages in difficult situations.

The best example of her daring behavior and speed comes from tenth grade, when our quartet, in a moment of combined youthful ambition and strategic foresight, decided to enter an elite-level airsoft tournament. This highly competitive event was unlike anything Bri and I would typically pursue, and certainly unlike anything Kendry, with his non-athletic build, would naturally join. Auxi, however, was determined.

"I want to test ourselves. Build our collective ability to react under pressure," she declared with characteristic enthusiasm, her eyes bright with anticipation. "There's an elite tournament next weekend that I think would be the perfect opportunity. There's a one-hundred-twenty-five entry fee, which is steep, I know. But... there is also a five-thousand-dollar prize for MVP, which I'm sure one of us could win." It wasn't a weekend rec meet; this was a sponsored regional milsim qualifier, with one hundred per side, cash on the line, and marshals checking full-seal eye protection and the approved training blades.

She wanted to test our limits and, more importantly, develop our group's capacity for decisive action in stressful situations. With typical audacity, she aspired to enter elite-level competition despite having no real firearms experience. When tournament organizers questioned her inexperience and advised against participation, she found their concern exciting, a determined gleam intensifying in her eyes.

I, being pragmatic, figured I'd played sufficient shooting games and watched enough action films to operate mock weapons adequately, even without real experience. Most of all, I was curious about how far this drive to dive into unknown challenges would take her. Regardless of my reservations, I supported her initiative.

After patiently explaining to our parents why we needed five hundred dollars for this tournament, we confidently promised to recover the investment if one of us didn't win the five-thousand-dollar MVP prize, knowing our skill sets made earning five hundred dollars through odd jobs relatively simple. They reluctantly agreed to let us participate.

Upon arriving at the tournament site and collecting our military-themed gear, a strange happening to those who brought their own, I immediately noticed everyone staring at us. Some looks conveyed pity, but most radiated competitive intensity. They seemed eager for engagement. I retreated into analytical thought, categorizing the various types of opposition. Kendry tensed visibly, Bri appeared unaffected, and Auxi had an entirely different reaction.

"Auxi, how are you feel—" I stopped mid-word.

Auxi's entire demeanor shifted, showing intense excitement and a desire to address our perceived disadvantage. She was completely focused, her usually playful eyes now wide with predatory awareness.

"How am I feeling?" she repeated, her voice dropping to a low hum, eyes locked on the crowd. "I feel good. Challenged. Confronted in a way that's never existed before." She stood perfectly still, radiating controlled intensity, waiting for combat to begin. "My focus right now feels exceptional, almost as if I'm on the track against an Olympic sprinter. I'm ready for conflict and everything it brings."

This was the same expression I would see years later as our world collapsed around us.

Though calm and composed externally, a demeanor I'd witnessed countless times, I could sense her desperate need to begin, to engage these people who assumed superiority over us. Witnessing this aspect of her made me question what other abilities she'd been concealing.

The buzzer to enter the playing area rang loudly, a harsh metallic sound cutting through the tension. I glanced at Bri, who met my gaze with a slight, knowing smile;

understanding passed between us. We entered the battlefield slowly, driven to our starting location in a mock bunker to await commencement.

After being divided into opposing teams across a mile of playing field littered with rust-eaten buses, rickety structures, derelict vehicles, crumbling tunnels, and other post-apocalyptic scenery, we arrived at our team's starting position. The day's game mode was "capture the flag." Seize the enemy's banner and return it to base, a two-mile journey symbolizing victory.

During transport to our starting point, I observed the terrain. My brain, trained for efficiency and competition, focused on surveying the landscape, using the surroundings and provided maps to determine optimal routes. I attempted to communicate with the "adults" on our team about possible strategic approaches, but they showed no interest in my analysis.

"Don't think we need strategy from a kid," one muttered dismissively.

Auxi was too focused for conversation. Bri, with a simple wave, had plotted her independent path. Kendry decided to follow Bri, believing he could maintain her pace better than

Auxi or me. Realizing I was alone in my planning, I quietly developed the most effective approach to win this game mode, even as a potential solo effort.

Once both teams were equipped and prepared, a tense countdown from ten began, echoing across the mile-long battlefield. Hot summer breeze prickled my skin as I controlled my breathing, forcing it into a steady rhythm. With five seconds remaining, I took one final look at my friends, hoping for their success in our first real test of strategy and survival.

As the clock reached zero and the starting buzzer sounded, Auxi seemed to vanish, bolting forward with blinding speed I'd never witnessed from her, simultaneously surprising me and piquing my intense interest. Without time to consider her other hidden capabilities, I immediately sought cover, moving low and fast, beginning work along my planned route with the expectation of encountering enemies around the midpoint between respective starting positions.

I watched Bri and Kendry disappear deeper into the field, a blur of strategic motion, and found myself alone again, relying on personal capability to navigate the challenge.

Navigating the simulated societal wreckage, with overgrown grass and weeds adding practical atmosphere, I found myself enveloped in profound silence. It wasn't just game-quiet; even the birds had ceded the field. Realizing all of this, the quietude felt unnatural given the supposed battle raging around me. It was silence I now recognize as harbinger; a warning of things to come.

This fleeting peace shattered when a sharp airsoft pellet whistled past my face, grazing my protective mask. Not knowing the shooter's location, relying purely on instinct, I sprinted into a nearby dilapidated building, barely outrunning the sudden barrage of gunfire trailing inches behind me.

Inside, I pressed against a crumbling wall and cautiously peered through what had once been a window, now just loose boards haphazardly nailed over a gaping hole on the second floor. Using the midday sun as a reference to detect potential scope glare, I noticed one adversary crawling stealthily toward my building. At the same time, another remained farther back, partially concealed by a gnarled tree.

I assumed they couldn't determine if I was alone, but assumptions were dangerous. I had to act decisively. Aiming precisely at the tree-hidden target, I gently squeezed the trigger, hearing the satisfying thud of pellet meeting target.

"Hit!" they called out, eliminating themselves from play.

In a moment of brief celebration, I smiled beneath my protective mask but failed to track the second person quickly enough. They had vanished upon hearing their teammate's elimination call.

Recognizing my tactical error, I shifted into reactive mode as distinct footsteps echoed within the building below. These fast, determined steps weren't from one person; it was approximately three sets, each with different rhythms and coordinated movement.

Deciding to maintain position and counter-attack rather than retreat, I quickly formulated a strategy. Waiting patiently for them to ascend the creaking stairs, I discovered a baseball on the dusty floor near the barricaded window. The upstairs layout allowed for positioning behind the railing in an adjacent room, which would provide clear sight lines of ascending attackers, and was my chosen ambush point.

Three players moved upward slowly, heavy boots thudding against worn wood. As the last one ascended, their back momentarily toward me, I hurled the baseball with a sharp crack into a far corner, creating a distraction, while simultaneously slipping into the connected room. Two of the three predictably split up and rushed toward the noise, while the third, more cautious, remained by the stairs guarding their retreat. I capitalized on the moment and swiftly shot the stair guard, hitting them cleanly before concealing myself again.

"Hit!" they yelled in frustration as I initiated my plan's second phase.

With the remaining two players now on high alert, their forms dimly visible through swirling dust, I had to move more fluidly, prepared for immediate combat. Years of critically analyzing action films and playing tactical games with Bri, dissecting strategies, proved valuable as I maneuvered through the upstairs arena with natural agility.

Spotting one remaining player with their back briefly turned, their guard momentarily dropped, I shot them cleanly.

"Hit!" came another frustrated call.

The third member emerged from around the corner, blindly firing their reserves in a desperate, spraying motion. Using agility and now-familiar terrain, I darted into the next room, circled through a nearby door, executed a low, precise forward roll, and landed directly before my unsuspecting enemy. Given this unexpected positioning and my opponent being completely caught off guard, I managed the final shot cleanly.

"Hit!" came the last call.

"Yes!" I shouted, the sound echoing through the empty structure, pleased with my accomplishment of eliminating four of their hundred players single-handedly.

In my brief moment of satisfaction at removing four percent of the competition alone, I let my guard down, overlooking environmental awareness. I failed to detect the fourth intruder, the one I'd missed, as they aimed from just below the stairs' top.

Before I knew it, sharp pain struck my back.

"Hit," I called out, focusing immediately on what I needed for survival in the next round.

My instincts and lifelong preparedness had failed for the first time. Emotions, completely surprising me with their intensity, had compromised my performance. I was a child playing a game, and for the first time, I felt the consequences of being genuinely human.

Walking back to the tent, where the eliminated players awaited the next round, my mind raced as I plotted an improved strategy. I realized I hadn't been sufficiently careful, as clinically detached, as necessary. My attention to detail and dismissal of seemingly minor elements, things I'd always deemed irrelevant, had affected my performance, demonstrating how everything could gain critical significance within seconds.

From that moment forward, I prioritized maintaining awareness of all factors, never wanting to become victim of false security that led me to believe in inherent superiority, especially when unaware of others' true potential or unfolding situational dynamics.

Upon arriving at the waiting area, which took longer due to my preference for walking over the "dead player" transport, I saw Bri and Kendry already seated patiently, composed, watching various television screens displaying live field footage.

"When did you two end up here?" I asked, slumping beside them onto a metal bench.

"Got back just in time to watch your John Wick impression," Kendry said with characteristic half-smile, his relaxed tone carrying subtle appreciation.

"You performed better than Bri and I managed, but it wasn't quite there. You can do better," he continued, his voice maintaining that casual analytical tone I'd grown to appreciate. "Too much in your head, not as aware of surroundings as usual. Work on that. It would make you more formidable against superior numbers. Or put simply, get your head on straight and think clearly."

Kendry's relaxed articulation, a calm analytical breakdown, was refreshing.

"You weren't as effective as I expected, but we didn't fare better," Bri stated, her eyes still scanning screens intently. I noticed her subtly listening to game plans being discussed by nearby players, displaying her awareness and ability to transform observation into opportunity.

"Since neither of you mentioned what happened, you're either embarrassed or want me to ask. So what landed you back here so quickly?" I questioned skeptically, sensing an untold story.

"Simple. We were ambushed by ten players. Two from our team got in my way and forced me into defensive positioning," Bri explained calmly, her voice devoid of emotion, as if reporting weather conditions. "I wanted to address the situation, but Kendry was too absorbed in analysis to move effectively. I didn't want to leave him exposed, so I took out three from twenty yards with precise shots, then heard two more approaching our flank. From there, I couldn't reload fast enough; which landed us here."

Her focus had already shifted as she continued mental preparation for the next round through rapid analysis of information gathering from screens and conversations.

I remembered Auxi's eager determination to test herself in challenging situations, the very drive that brought us here. Asking Bri and Kendry if they'd seen her, we noticed a small crowd of players from both teams huddled around display monitors, their murmurs escalating into excited shouts. We moved toward them, hoping to locate Auxi, when one of the opposing team members looked at us in shock.

"Wasn't she with you?" the man asked, jaw slack, pointing a trembling finger at live footage being displayed.

My eyes widened in disbelief and awe as I watched Auxi sprinting through tall grass, a green and black blur, eliminating opponents with surgical precision. We witnessed her racing throughout the enemy base, her image flitting from camera to camera as the outdated system struggled tracking her speed. At one point, she apparently ran out of ammunition. Not missing a beat, she utilized the approved training blade included in our gear, executing a flurry of efficient motions. As enemies scattered and fled, I could see her eyes were wide with exhilaration, even through quick movements on the blurry screen.

As my interest piqued and excitement about her capabilities grew, I noticed she had completely forgotten the objective, the flag. She was focused solely on engaging maximum opponents, experiencing the pure release of potential. Many observers muttered complaints about teamwork, but I wasn't among them. Her determination to place individual power above team objectives, executing it with such ferocity, fascinated me completely.

This was the same intensity I would witness years later, unleashed against an enemy that wasn't playing games.

I was observing her true nature. I wanted to see her add to the almost fifty eliminations she had, nearly half of the entire enemy force.

However, before I could witness her continuation, the piercing siren signaled game termination, and our team was declared defeated.

"What? How can they end the game and call us losers when our team was winning?" I said aloud, confusion evident as my mind struggled reconciling the chaos with established rules.

"Got to play the objective, kid. Kills only matter if you eliminate the entire opposing team before someone captures your flag. You failed at that. While little Miss Ninja lived out her action fantasies, our guy grabbed your flag and brought it home," explained a gruff veteran who'd clearly played this game extensively, his voice carrying the wisdom of vast airsoft experience.

Auxi arrived at the losers' tent approximately ten minutes later, chest heaving, appearing upset not by defeat, but by the activity's cessation.

"That was one of the best feelings of my entire life," she gasped, voice raw with exertion. "Winning would've been nice, but I wish I'd had more time to continue." She lifted her head slowly, eyes still blazing with focused intensity. "Truth is... I don't care if we win the next round. I want, no, I need, to get back out there and pick up where I left off."

Her unapologetic declaration sharpened my senses and focused my intent as we prepared for round two, beginning our journey to the starting position.

As the remaining team reloaded ammunition and worked in groups developing respective strategies, Kendry, surprisingly, devised his own distinct plan. He, too, must have been inspired by Auxi, or at least had come to understand the unique team dynamics he was working with. Outlining his strategy, he revealed another unexpected aspect of himself I hadn't previously witnessed: the strategist who would one day orchestrate our survival.

"Listen up. I have a plan for this must-win round," Kendry began, his voice calm, clear, stripped of usual sarcastic undertones. "I know I'm not as physically gifted as you three, but I guarantee this'll work. D and Auxi, you're the fastest and most combat-skilled, based on what I know and observed today. You two will push forward individually from the flanks, eliminate small teams, then converge three-quarters through for a direct assault on their flag. Auxi," his voice gained authoritative edge, "make sure you follow the plan. I see your burning desires, and I understand them, but this five thousand won't win itself; you gotta coordinate with D."

His words, direct and precise, cut through ambient noise with unexpected command presence.

"Bri and I will defend our flag from enemies penetrating the center. Bri, I need you to stay mobile while you keep an eye on everything. You are much more mobile than I and everyone else here, other than D, so let's use that to our advantage. I'll guard the flag within the room and whistle if more attackers arrive than I can handle on my own. Hopefully, other players won't interfere with our plan, but we'll adapt as needed. We need this victory, and I refuse to contribute to another failure."

Kendry's explanation, delivered with an analytical mindset now applied to battlefield tactics, carried direct authority that rivaled Bri's own commanding presence.

Upon hearing these precise instructions, we all quietly agreed, a testament to Kendry's unexpected leadership capacity, and Bri gave me another rare half-smile, acknowledging the approach's soundness. This was my first time witnessing Kendry speak with such sharp strategic ability, using analytical skills to transform defeat into survival blueprint.

This must have been what Bri recognized when they first met, that hidden potential she'd mentioned. I finally began understanding why he'd been brought into our world. She knew he was capable of controlling complex scenarios, but this was confirmation, witnessing his strategic mindset under genuine pressure.

Whatever the case with Kendry in that moment, he and Auxi had triggered my analytical processes as I pondered their capability limits. I'd never realized inherent boundaries could be pushed so dramatically, could bend and break in such unexpected ways. Seeing what they could accomplish in simulated conflict, I knew their potential ceilings were expansive, perhaps even comparable to mine, each in uniquely formidable ways.

As the match prepared to start and we returned to our original positions, we lined up in pairs, waiting for the signal, the tension almost tangible. Auxi and I nodded understanding, our roles clear. Simultaneously, Bri looked subtly amused by the developing drama, a faint smirk playing across her lips, while Kendry wore a serious, keenly anticipatory expression, eyes sharp and calculating.

The game signal rang. Auxi nearly vanished as she bolted up the left flank toward enemy territory, a green blur in the dappled light, and I followed suit, moving to the right. Time to test whether Kendry's bold strategy would succeed.

For the first time in years, I was genuinely interested in the outcome; a welcome yet unusual sensation.

Sprinting through the constructed forest and dystopian landscape, I found myself instinctively choosing my knife over the gun, relying on close-quarters combat to eliminate opponents swiftly. I began experiencing a sense of peace similar to what I imagined Auxi felt, discovering focus in the hunt itself. Before I knew it, I'd arrived at the central convergence point where I was to meet Auxi.

Reaching the center, I saw her sprinting toward the same location, arriving moments after me, eyes showing pure exhilaration.

"Twenty-three down on my side," she reported breathlessly, grinning.

"You?"

"Eighteen. Ready to finish this?"

We immediately combined our forces into a single, coordinated effort, rushing straight through the middle toward their stronghold and swiftly eliminating the few remaining guards outside. Quickly clearing the building of lingering threats, our movements flowed with practiced efficiency.

Silently agreeing that I should carry the flag back, as Auxi was better suited for rapid combat and could cover our retreat more effectively, I grabbed the brightly colored banner. Without hesitation, we sprinted toward our base.

During our return, we passed multiple groups from our side, their faces showing surprise as they struggled to comprehend the speed and precision with which we'd completed this task. Upon arriving back at base, we noticed Kendry and Bri waiting patiently, composed, appearing to have seen no action; meaning Kendry's strategy had worked to perfection.

After just twenty minutes, our team had secured victory and advanced to the third, final, winner-takes-all round. The remaining player total was ninety-five for us, fifteen for them, with nearly half of all outs, by our count, belonging solely to Auxi and me.

Preparing for the decisive round, we approached with an identical mindset and planned strategy, confident in our execution capabilities. Though the opposing team might have recognized our approach by now, we believed their chance to adjust quickly enough was minimal.

When the buzzer sounded for round three, Auxi and I bolted up the sidelines with practiced speed. Immediately noticing a reduced enemy presence in our usual paths, it was apparent that something had changed. The flanks felt thinner than logic allowed, a gap with intent hidden in it. My unease about the situation not proceeding as planned was confirmed as we both reached the opposing team's base much faster than before, each eliminating only five enemies along the mile-long stretch, a significantly lower number than in our previous engagement.

Approaching their shelter, we eliminated approximately five remaining exterior guards and rushed inside to capture their flag. Upon doing so, almost no resistance remained, with only two unconcerned individuals guarding the objective.

"Something's wrong," I muttered, my instincts screaming warnings.

"Yeah... that was way too easy," Auxi agreed, though her usual intensity was diminishing. She believed the opposing team had practically surrendered.

While she showed anticlimactic emotions, I knew something else was happening. No team would quit this severely in a winner-takes-all situation, especially after their previous aggression. Suddenly, we noticed player counters displaying a rapid decline in active teammates. Our side was being eliminated systematically while we remained a mile away, deep in enemy territory.

"They set a trap and we took the bait," I realized grimly.

Racing back straight through the center of the playing field while carrying their flag, Auxi and I passed many teammates heading to the losers' tent, their faces grim with defeat. About a quarter-mile from our base, Auxi abruptly stopped me, her hand gripping my arm firmly.

"There's a bunch of them up ahead, a pretty large group from what I can guess," she warned, her voice sharp with tactical awareness.

Placing their flag down for combat readiness, we both dropped into low crouching positions and expertly navigated the vast overgrown vegetation, using it as concealment. Then I saw the truth: around fifty enemies moving in a disciplined, coordinated formation through the woods toward our base, possibly twenty more already assaulting our flag room.

Rather than accepting slim chances of sneaking around this force to engage them later, we made a decisive choice. We would strike immediately, eliminating as many as possible before they spotted and overwhelmed us.

Taking aim from nearby trees, Auxi and I quickly eliminated three players each with precise shots before the rest reacted with professional speed, dropping prone and deploying multiple smoke canisters around the area. They had prepared for us, learning from their mistakes in the previous round. Thick smoke leveled the playing field, reducing our superior senses to educated guesswork.

As they spread throughout the cloudy, disorienting environment, I moved silently through the clearing, relying on sound and intuition to eliminate anyone I could approach undetected. Thinking I'd isolated a single target, four players suddenly emerged from outside my vision, approximately three feet into the thick, swirling smoke, attempting to eliminate me with tactical knives.

Recognizing an immediate threat, I used my reflexes and athleticism to eliminate the first attacker with a swift strike, then flipped my knife backward to spin under the second, landing a precise cut on their leg for insurance. The remaining three closed distance, but using newly opened space, I burst into fog and circled behind them, landing eliminating strikes as I slid behind a nearby tree.

"You should have kept running," said a low voice directly behind me.

Before I could turn around, I felt the unmistakable barrel pressure against my back. Silently admitting defeat with nowhere to escape, I waited, bracing for the trigger pull. As time decelerated, I felt a powerful force, and the player behind me seemingly vanished before they could fire.

Whirling around in surprise, I saw my attacker on the ground, calling "hit" while raising their arm in defeat. Standing over them, Auxi appeared with her protective mask removed, breathing heavily as she flipped wild hair from her face with a single motion.

"What? Don't you see we're at war?" She stated with characteristic hyperbole before instantly sprinting back into thick, swirling smoke.

Recognizing this second chance and understanding how seriously she was taking this moment, I refocused on the battle and pushed forward against the remaining enemies with renewed determination.

As I efficiently worked through the next five players I encountered, avoiding previous mistakes, the smoke began lifting, slowly revealing the landscape. Realizing our team's player count continued to decrease rapidly, I knew a separate enemy force existed elsewhere, executing a pincer movement. We had to break free from this engagement and return to base.

Locating Auxi, who continued to eliminate enemies efficiently while rolling from tree to tree for cover, we instantly combined forces to eradicate the remaining ten players huddled together, attempting to bolster their defensive strength. We charged them at full speed, not allowing further communication, our only thought being elimination and return to Bri and Kendry.

Using myself as the spearhead of the initial striking force, I quickly eliminated the first five enemies, then dropped to a low squat so Auxi, without breaking stride, could propel herself from my back. While she was airborne, heading directly toward three opponents, the enemies were caught off guard, their faces frozen beneath protective gear. Using this advantage, I sprinted to eliminate the other two who were positioned several feet back, aiming at Auxi.

As she landed, she swept one player down with a fluid kick and eliminated another with a precise strike. The third had raised their weapon and taken aim before I could reach them, but Auxi was prepared. With sudden, fluid motion, she grabbed the enemy she'd swept down and used them as a shield before hurling them at the remaining attacker. At the exact moment she threw the first enemy, she pulled an airsoft grenade pin from their belt. It exploded with a sharp CRACK when they collapsed together, eliminating the competition in that sector.

Recognizing the quarter-mile remaining to our base, we had no time for recovery before retrieving the flag and sprinting toward the objective room. Auxi's endurance, a quality I was beginning to recognize as formidable as her speed, held perfectly. She was Maryland's 200-meter state champion with a sub-24, which proved beneficial in multiple ways. This conditioning required minimal recovery time upon arrival, allowing an immediate perimeter assessment, which revealed no exterior presence and an empty battlefield.

After checking the active player counts, I noticed that our team had six active players, while our opponents maintained eight, an imbalance that defied the logic of our recent success.

"How could the numbers drop like this?" I whispered, voice controlled, as I raised my weapon and placed down the captured flag.

"Sounds like there's a standoff. I can hear the yelling from our flag room," Auxi observed with stern focus, eyes narrowing. "I'm gonna go check that out."

"Wait, I think we should—" I couldn't finish before she slipped into the building.

Not wanting to separate at this critical juncture, I crept toward the door Auxi had entered, senses on maximum alert. At that moment, I heard sharp, unmistakable airsoft gunfire and noticed a sudden, rapid change in active player count on my device. I pressed against the wall outside the entrance, flattened, waiting, trying to discern what had occurred: two enemies eliminated, one of ours down.

I rose from my crouch and entered cautiously, weapon elevated. Scanning the dim interior, I noticed Auxi peering intently through a cracked door at the stair's top, her body uncharacteristically motionless. Curious about what could possibly make her pause, I silently ascended.

As I approached the door, the tension in the air thickened by degrees. The sense that something transcended usual gameplay felt more potent than outside in the battle-torn field. The sun had begun setting, casting elongated shadows, the air growing stale, and Auxi's uncharacteristic stillness indicated a unique situation. I continued, compelled by the need to understand.

Upon reaching the door, I leaned slowly, peering through the narrow crack to visualize what captivated Auxi. That's when I witnessed it.

The scene was unexpected within the confines of an airsoft match, an image I would remember for the rest of my life. Bri stood perfectly composed, looking straight at our door with an even bigger smile than usual, radiating a sense of satisfaction. Our last remaining teammate stuck their rifle barrel through a half-open closet, frozen with wide eyes. And there was Kendry, pistol held loosely, pointing at six remaining enemies kneeling with raised hands, pressed against a grimy wall in surrender.

The situation itself wasn't what made this moment memorable, but how everything had defied logic to reach this point. I couldn't understand how players in an airsoft game, something with no real consequences, would simply surrender. But somehow, it had happened. Whatever they had witnessed, whatever presence they'd encountered, had left sufficient impact to reduce them to pieces on Kendry's strategic board.

As I finally pushed the door open, hinges creaking in sudden silence, Kendry spoke.

"About time you two joined us. I've been waiting, but I appreciate you handling the trouble downstairs, Aux," he said, voice calm and casual yet carrying an underlying current of absolute authority. "These people were more challenging than I'd prefer to admit, but I'll explain more when we've won. Can you grab the flag from outside? I'd really like to get this over with."

His tone had shifted completely. Not like he had different personality, but as if a mask had been removed, revealing capabilities he normally kept hidden.

As I retrieved the flag from outside, my mind processed the impossible situation. I quickly returned it to our base, securing a decisive victory.

Returning to the flag room, the enemies Kendry had somehow neutralized remained in shock, and I couldn't help but notice the transformation in his demeanor. It wasn't as if he'd become a different person, but rather as if the critical moment had passed and he'd reverted to the Kendry we knew. Though understandable given the stress of the situation, it nonetheless remained a pivotal moment that embedded itself in my memory.

Back at the original staging area, our quartet collected our winnings, with Auxi claiming MVP for her aggressive performance. As we moved through the crowd, we found ourselves regarded with a mixture of admiration, fear, and resentment. Some of the very people who had initially looked down on us, the high school kids, were now, in their defeat, acknowledging our tactics, our ability to recover from overwhelming odds, and the physical prowess we'd displayed.

However, those who feared and resented us represented the other side of this reaction. They were questioning among themselves exactly how a group of freshman high schoolers could outperform adults in an airsoft competition; something many had been playing for years, if not decades. This left many believing, their eyes wide with suspicion, that something about us wasn't right, that we had cheated, or disturbingly, that we weren't even the same species. The word "human" slipped through more than one whisper, stretched thin between praise and warning.

A stretch perhaps, but their behavior suggested exactly that.

Regardless of their dismay with the results, we had won and quickly made our way to Kendry's house to clean up and recover from our mentally and physically demanding day.

IV. HUMANITY

At this point in my recollection of events, I have reflected on the moments of light, memories untainted by the blood, death, and daily hardship that define our new world. But I must not digress. The past is not a luxury; it is a lesson. Even in this fractured present, I remain in pursuit of understanding human nature. This pursuit has often led me to examine my own development, searching for the moments when we began becoming who we needed to be.

That first test in simulated battlefield conditions, the airsoft tournament, demonstrated a truth I carry with me today: every person harbors an unexpressed aspect. Whether it was Auxi's unleashed intensity or the expressions of our defeated enemies that day, it became clear that people are not always what they initially present themselves as. We all possess deeper, hidden facets that manifest under specific conditions; conditions we did not choose then, but conditions that would choose us later.

Under the right circumstances, our nature adapts, fundamentally altering our understanding of what it means to be human. That day, amidst the shouts and mock gunfire,

I recognized my own areas for improvement. I understood that regardless of my skills, I must remain committed to constant refinement. There was no point where I would be "good enough," no plateau of perfection worth reaching. My momentary lapse in vigilance might have cost us that first simulation round, but in a world where stakes would inevitably rise beyond mere competition, such failure could cost everything. This was critical practice, a rehearsal for future challenges and the brutal realities that lay ahead.

That day, I also noticed something else about Bri. Her behavior, her composed attitude amidst chaos, felt familiar yet revealed new depths. Her ability to remain unflappable while others, even adults, showed signs of pressure added another layer to her character I hadn't fully recognized. She maintained perfect composure, and her quiet patience and confidence in Kendry, her subtle support, displayed leadership qualities I had never witnessed before. Her unspoken permission, her acceptance of his unorthodox strategies, allowed him to take command and ultimately led to our victory. Her awareness, confidence, and serenity revealed another truth about humanity: not every inner response releases under tension. Some require significant losses to activate.

Bri had assembled us for a specific reason, a purpose still forming in ways we couldn't yet comprehend. The airsoft tournament was her method of demonstrating a piece of that design. She had orchestrated the situation, expertly revealing Kendry's previously unseen potential. She knew how to allow others to excel, how to guide them without seeming to exert direct influence. Bri possessed an understanding of human nature's flaws and strengths, subtly steering individuals toward common goals. This skill, I would soon discover, would prove essential during the increasingly challenging months ahead.

As I conclude this reflection on our past, I must emphasize the significance of Kendry. To this day, Kendry remains one of the most intriguing individuals I have ever encountered; a mind as complex as it is brilliant. His actions and strategic thinking during that final airsoft round offered a glimpse of his true capabilities. They demonstrated that when our backs were against the wall, we could count on Kendry completely. His unexpected transformation in that field served as evidence of the untapped potential we all possessed and a promise of what we would become capable of when the games became real.

I understand that discussing Kendry's abilities presents challenges in explanation. The best way to introduce them is to recount the evening after the tournament, when we finally addressed what had transpired in those critical final moments before Auxi and I arrived at the flag room.

"Is anyone going to elaborate on what happened in that last round?" I asked, curiosity edged in my voice as we circled Kendry's dining table and his father's spaghetti. The sauce was sweet with basil; steam fogged the cheap glassware.

"That... you're still stuck on that game, man?" Kendry said, wearing an expression I couldn't read. "Honestly couldn't tell you. It just... happened, y'know."

"How do you mean?" I said. "You directed a defense under pressure, and now you don't recall the sequence? Give me the bones."

"Sure." He twirled noodles, stalled with a sip of water. The silence stretched until Auxi's fork began to tap out a metronome.

"They rushed center. After you and Auxi split wide, they gambled we'd repeat. They ceded the sidelines, pooled their numbers in the middle, and sent a wave all at once straight to us."

He swallowed, finally committing. "Bri saw it breaking and went out to thin the crowd a bit. While she was doing her thing, a few slipped past and got within feet of our building, which I think she let happen." He glanced at Bri.

"I might have intentionally left them a seam," she said, calm as a level. "When they came inside, it felt like time thinned. My chest tightened, almost like I was underwater. Every nerve felt bright. I told the closest three on our side to make noise at the far stairwell while we shifted two to the catwalk to cut angles. We nudged the bookcase six inches to narrow the landing, attempting to use the furniture as a funnel. Then out of nowhere, I had an upstairs defense drawn in my head: choke points, sightlines, who trades, who revives. I know I'm not the strongest or fastest in our group, but damnit, I needed to contribute something meaningful to make this work..."

"Language!" his father called from upstairs.

"My bad!" Kendry yelled back, a brief, sheepish grin flashing across his face before he continued. "As the situation escalated, my brain shifted into overdrive to read the dynamics. I pulled a rubber training blade from the kit and let one of the enemies know what it could do. Not to tag him, but to signal the stakes. He hesitated; I stripped his wallet and used it as leverage. People respect rules even when they're losing, so this must have started a chain reaction. After that, circling them with the teammates I had remaining, fear did half the work. I'm fuzzy on the rest, but I remember winning before you two arrived. It felt good to adapt, to conquer, and to finally contribute meaningfully to the team."

Kendry took a reflective pause, his eyes growing distant.

"We should do this again sometime, though. I wanna see how far this capability extends if I can focus on it properly. I need to understand this new aspect of myself and figure out how to manage it deliberately. Like you guys have learned to do with your abilities, I wanna have a specialty too." His voice carried genuine earnestness as he finished his plate and rose to collect ours.

Bri gave me that knowing smirk from before, while Auxi seemed content for him to finish speaking, her restless energy already anticipating the next adventure. I saw precisely what Bri wanted me to see. Although his vague account didn't sound extraordinary, the implications were significant: he had adapted without our direct intervention, altered the game's dynamic, and bent the situation to his will. His abilities deserved further exploration.

"Interesting. So this transformation happened completely without warning? No prior situation or specific motivation comes to mind?" I asked, maintaining a calm exterior while my analytical mind processed the implications.

"Nope, just sorta happened and feels weird thinking about it. But hey, we won, man," Kendry said with a casual shrug, continuing to scrub dishes while seemingly dismissing the event's significance.

"What about you, Auxi? I knew you possessed intensity; we've all witnessed glimpses before, but this time felt fundamentally different. I found it impressive, but I'm curious how it developed or what it truly felt like from your perspective," I asked, turning my attention toward her.

"I don't know how to explain it, to be honest. But it felt natural, like breathing the cleanest air when time slows down," she said, her eyes brightening with remembered exhilaration.

"I was also really focused and motivated, which added to the vibe of it all. That feeling of domination, of winning, of being able to just unleash, that's something I need to experience again. It was a euphoric release I didn't know I was capable of. For lack of better words."

Naturally, we were all exhausted after dinner and the demanding day we'd experienced. We moved to the living room to watch one of our preferred slasher films, and slowly, inevitably, fell asleep before reaching the movie's midpoint. Auxi and I claimed opposite ends of the same long couch around 9:30 PM. Bri curled into the reclining chair in the corner, looking deceptively small for someone who had orchestrated so much. Kendry, characteristically adaptable, simply took a pillow and blanket to sleep on the wooden floor before the television, seemingly able to find rest in the most unlikely circumstances.

Our first real challenge, our initial opportunity to observe what we could accomplish under pressure, proved to be a revealing experience. We gained a deeper understanding of ourselves and our cohesion as a unit, gaining insight into how we would respond to the greater challenges yet to come.

Those outings, those tests of our evolving abilities, continued throughout our high school years. They became our private academy, our specialized training ground. We advanced our understanding, consistently increasing the complexity and stakes of the challenges we undertook. Though not all these tests were physical in nature. We often examined our mental acuity through chess matches, battles of intellect, and strategic foresight.

But Kendry, driven by his need for mastery, took this pursuit several steps further. Since he wasn't actively involved in organized school sports or clubs like the rest of us, he began secretly entering top-level chess tournaments, seeking out grandmasters and seasoned professionals to test different, unconventional strategies. He could have pursued national and even international recognition, but he remained content operating under the radar, preferring to cultivate his skills in anonymity so he wouldn't be pressured into a predetermined career path. He valued his freedom and the pursuit of his own interests, a quiet calculation I now understand was more valuable than any trophy could have been.

In addition to our chess activities, we participated in various martial arts tournaments, with a primary focus on Brazilian Jiu-Jitsu and kickboxing. That became my particular passion, a method for honing physical prowess and strategic thinking in close combat situations. However, we all participated at different times, and we even managed to involve Kendry despite his initial reluctance. Everyone cultivated individual strengths, but always toward something we would eventually achieve together. Our personal pursuits contributed to our collective strength. Whether attending Bri's elaborate scavenger hunts through forgotten areas of the city or free-climbing sheer rock faces with Auxi, using nothing but hands and feet to cling to stone, we ensured each activity taught us something while remaining genuinely enjoyable. We never settled, never became complacent, constantly pushing the boundaries of our capabilities.

As we matured, developing through adolescence into young adulthood, we began considering next steps and what the future might hold for us, our lives having become increasingly intertwined. Understanding that our academic and athletic achievements would provide access to any school in the country with full scholarships, we compiled a list of what truly mattered to us moving forward. Upon reviewing those priorities, we concluded that none of us wanted to travel farther than necessary, and that perceived educational quality was valuable primarily through institutional reputation, since our own efforts and desires would ultimately forge our career paths. Using the criteria we developed, we collectively set our sights on Clear View University, a prestigious private institution along the Maryland shore, making it our unanimous top priority.

The envelope was thick enough to be a promise. Kendry waited until we were all in his living room, the TV paused on a chess stream, his hands steady except for the twitch in his thumb. He slit the paper, scanned, and for a heartbeat, nothing moved. Then his shoulders dropped and he laughed, quietly, unbelieving. "Full ride," he said, and then, softer, "College of Engineering. Early admission." Auxi tackled him from the side; the letter bent but didn't tear. Bri only nodded once, as if the universe had finally caught up to a plan she'd written long ago. At the bottom was a note about the chess team. He didn't smile at that part, just folded it away like an enigma.

Although we had grown concerned by the prolonged delay of his results, since ours had all arrived over a month prior, we knew this university wouldn't make the mistake of rejecting one of the most promising minds and natural problem-solvers they would encounter. Kendry's abilities weren't widely known outside our small circle, but his intellect and connections within competitive chess communities spoke volumes about his potential.

As high school concluded and life's next stage approached, the world had already begun its slow evolution toward something darker. The following four years of college were memorable, a period of growth and shared experience, but no one could have anticipated the shocking surprise awaiting us at the very end: the termination of the world as we understood it.

Throughout the four years of college that followed, life continued as expected for our collective; a purposeful bubble of ambition amidst a subtly changing world. Although we weren't traditional college students in our approach, we nonetheless had an exceptional time, meticulously pursuing what we truly desired: our own unique forms of gratification and intellectual challenge.

Kendry and I began college as roommates, a natural pairing, while Bri and Auxi shared accommodations. Our university, being somewhat traditional, maintained separate dormitories without co-ed visitation past 8 PM. However, given our collective problem-solving abilities, we always found methods to gather together indoors when we didn't prefer outdoor activities or when weather conditions were suboptimal. Since no subjects or classes presented particular difficulty for us, even though we were all clustered under the demanding engineering umbrella. All but Auxi, who, with her characteristic practical approach, chose to major in microbiology with aspirations of becoming a trauma surgeon. Despite her being in a different college from the rest of us, and Kendry majoring in mechanical engineering while Bri pursued the same field as me, geological engineering, but with a specialized concentration on influencing natural geological developments, we maintained ample time to excel outside classroom requirements and test ourselves in different, higher-stakes arenas.

Bri never bragged. On nights she trusted us, she let me stand in the lab's hum and watch a rig whisper sand through a clear column while acoustic sensors clicked like beetles. "We're mapping how faults activate," she said, "and how to make them stop." She didn't look at me when she said it.

Bri, demonstrating her exceptional capabilities, swiftly became lead researcher for a prominent program in the College of Engineering, with recognition extending across the East Coast. This research focused on geological structures and explored how humans could influence them to benefit society. Her work remained largely secretive, but she would occasionally share information or daily tasks with us, just enough to pique our interest and provide glimpses into the kind of world-shaping knowledge she was accumulating. Knowledge that would one day serve a very different purpose than initially intended.

Meanwhile, I continued excelling in performance, becoming the nation's number one attackman in lacrosse for four consecutive years, constantly pushing myself to test new techniques and take strategic risks on the field. I wasn't necessarily popular among my teammates or coaches for this approach, but it proved effective enough to lead us to four perfect, undefeated seasons; proof that my methods, however unconventional, consistently produced results.

Auxi, channeling her boundless energy and natural athleticism, performed exceptionally on the track, consistently breaking records. Although she had declined an opportunity to compete for Team USA in the Olympics, a decision that surprised many observers, she nonetheless dominated all national competitions, rarely finishing lower than first place in any race shorter than 400 meters. Her drive, her need to excel, was never about recognition or medals; it was always about the raw feeling of being the best, the pure power of her own capabilities unleashed.

As for Kendry, although he didn't compete in collegiate sports or participate in secretive research programs, he leveraged his connections within the mechanical engineering department to work on graduate-level projects. This opportunity enabled him to become lead creator for the university's private autonomous vehicle program, developing the first fully functional system of its kind. His innovative ideas and designs significantly contributed to the project's success, resulting in a safe and effective fully autonomous vehicle the world had never seen before. It boasted a range of one thousand miles and required only thirty minutes to charge from zero to one hundred percent. This was an achievement he attributed to a stacked solid-state pack on a high-voltage architecture and brutal thermal management; engineering he would later adapt for survival rather than convenience.

All these individual successes and personal goals demanded enormous time investments, and we found ourselves busier than we'd ever imagined possible. However, amidst demanding schedules and personal triumphs, we always made time to gather, reconnect, and continue sharpening our skills through activities that pushed us beyond comfort zones. Where many people would show pressure or feel compelled to change their fundamental nature to fit in, we, with our shared understanding and unwavering resolve, stayed true to course and remembered who we were and why we existed on this Earth. Despite accolades, awards, recognition, and our collective power to elevate our university to among the world's top institutions, we never lost sight of our core identities. In fact, the pressure and drive for excellence made it clearer that we needed substantial challenges to prepare, to provide necessary friction and resistance so we could survive when the inevitable time came.

We didn't recognize it then, but the drive to improve and work harder originated from somewhere deep within us, a part that knew with absolute certainty that we needed these capabilities to survive. We didn't lead uncomfortable lives, nor did we consciously avoid rest, but we knew with unspoken certainty that a day would come when we'd face challenges we couldn't easily overcome; problems that would defy both intellect and strength. Just like that day on the airsoft field, you never truly know what a situation can become, regardless of how thoroughly you prepare or how meticulously you plan.

Despite college representing a time for growth and personal improvement, we found ourselves entering a world where our very adulthood was inducted into an era of sinister occurrences and unraveling empathy, a slow descent toward the end times. A pervasive sense of dread impacted the world. Not so much my friends and I, insulated in our purposeful bubble, but it created effects impossible to entirely escape.

Most people in my generation were raised on steady exposure to conflict that invaded every corner of existence. When they weren't witnessing events directly, television screens and social media platforms extrapolated them into their psyche. Shootings, wildfires, hurricanes, accidents, protests turned violent riots, inhumane acts, and instances of mass violence became occurrences people witnessed daily. The news transformed into a relentless parade of human suffering. These traumas, these experiences, affect people profoundly, subtly twisting their perception of reality. We watched it happen all around us, even as we told ourselves we were different, that we were somehow immune.

Even the people we were meant to respect, the leaders, no longer maintained any semblance of moral standards. Politicians and public figures of the past would at least attempt deception or performative appeals to people's better nature, even if insincerely motivated. But now? They barely bothered hiding their true, malicious intentions and bigoted perspectives. To make matters worse, many people, in a horrifying display of societal decay, actively approved of this open depravity and even encouraged it further, demonstrating how far society had fallen. Humanity, it seemed, consistently chose hatred and destruction over the challenging paths of sacrifice and genuine development. An occurrence that appeared to be acknowledged by the Earth itself.

During these times, there was planetary turmoil extending far beyond what I've shared. Strange phenomena began occurring that defied natural explanation. Instead of investigating properly or heeding these warnings, humans, in their collective folly, chose to dismiss them and act as though they were mysterious, unexplainable happenings, turning blind eyes to the truths being starkly displayed.

A prime example of this willful ignorance occurred when a clear day in San Francisco suddenly erupted into a lattice of lightning, sending a commercial airliner crashing into Montara Mountain, its very shoulder seeming subtly shifted, ensuring no survivors. Another: the widespread collapse of homes throughout Southeast Asia. Structures that had withstood countless storms and seismic events were suddenly falling into the ground, crumbling from their foundations. These homes, which had survived so much, were reduced to rubble. Yet no one cared to investigate beyond sending condolences.

The news turned feral. Blizzards froze hot climates in a day. Inland towns drowned in the remnants of storms that ran out of coastline. Wildfires jumped four-lane highways without wind. In Bri's lab, spectrograms began to show a low, persistent hum under places that shouldn't hum.

The warnings only grew more frequent and severe over time. Humanity's collective reaction continued to dissipate, reaching a point of complete numbness. Society became entirely desensitized, only reacting when immediate threats of total annihilation or significant monetary losses were at stake. This apathy meant that when children were killed in stores or world leaders forced specific populations to starve, it barely qualified as front-page news. Society and humanity as we knew them were collapsing, and the very meaning of "human" was becoming more blurred, more indistinct, than ever before.

Despite all this, some of us, a resilient few, continued forward and attempted, in our own small ways, to create positive change. My friends and I, clinging to our shared purpose, continued enjoying life, not dwelling on worldwide sorrows we couldn't immediately alter, making the most of college while creating a haven of meaningful ambition amidst global chaos. All we ever wanted was to help people and make the world better in the process, leaving a positive impact. Although this remains theoretically possible, too much has transpired since these idealistic thoughts first formed, and I'm uncertain anyone will have that opportunity again. Perhaps if a sufficiently significant crisis had united us and pulled humanity together before the ultimate end, that could have been the case. Unfortunately, however, there's no time for what-ifs at this stage. Only what is.

The world as we knew it continued experiencing decline, but the signs of approaching the end had become largely ignored until society could no longer maintain a pretense. Cold fronts, unlike anything previously documented, destroyed cities and countries that had never experienced freezing crises. California was inundated with unprecedented rainfall and tropical systems, resulting in devastating impacts far inland. Wildfires scorched the Earth with supernatural ferocity, sometimes appearing to ignite through impossible means. None of these, however, were worse than the relentless earthquakes and tsunamis that began ripping apart cities and shorelines with indiscriminate power. Entire committees and organizations were hastily created to combat these devastating effects and prepare people across the US for every imaginable natural disaster, as they no longer seemed constrained by geological location, striking anywhere, at any time.

Although these events fell outside the scope of natural disasters we typically experience, they still, for a time, appeared to follow recognizable, albeit intensified, historical patterns we could classify as "normal." However, nine days from graduation, the pattern tore. Ominous, inexplicable holes began appearing worldwide, right where the hum had been. And this time, no one could pretend not to hear.

V. FINAL DAYS

WEDNESDAY, MAY 7, 2025 – EIGHT DAYS

It was officially our final day of classes. We had completed all coursework, performing well enough to bypass final examinations, and had delivered every end-of-college project and presentation with our customary excellence. At that point, all that remained was the ceremonial crossing of the stage, a transition into the planned future. A future we now know was never meant to unfold.

"Hey, guys! I hope you're all as ready as I am to get out of college," I announced, stepping into my apartment. The scent of Kendry's latest engineering concoction mingled with the faint aroma of cleaning supplies. Kendry had already invited Bri and Auxi, making our living space the natural gathering point.

Anticipating this celebration, I had picked up carryout on the way back. As we settled in, surrounded by the steam of mambo sauce-covered chicken and bowls piled high with fried assortments, we ate, savoring the simple pleasure of good food. We recounted our college years, each sharing our respective journeys.

Auxi and I discussed our athletic paths, highlighting that we both had opportunities to pursue professional careers. Yet, with shared understanding, we declined. We instinctively knew there were more significant issues to address in the real world than those found in sports arenas. We recognized our abilities in athletics, competition, and physical prowess as natural talents, but we had both independently reached the same conclusion: it would be more prudent to hone and wield these skills as tools to aid our developing careers, or to remain sharp for emergencies, rather than damaging our bodies for entertainment.

Bri discussed her realization that most people, despite outward projections, lacked substantial inner depth. This assessment, delivered with typical honesty, was the clearest answer she could provide. Her ability to analyze almost anything and peel back layers of pretense was invaluable. After observing this emptiness, she realized that seeing someone beyond their initial façade required extraordinary circumstances to determine if they fit into her specific categories for human nuance.

When Kendry began reflecting, he expressed how he had built upon his ability to adapt and solve complex situations with limited information or resources. Ever since that first day at the airsoft tournament, when he'd discovered this new aspect of himself, he had worked to make it stronger, more efficient, and more valuable, ensuring his back wouldn't need to be against the wall for him to succeed. This drive felt increasingly crucial as every passing day seemed one step closer to mass destruction, a shift threatening to upend society's fragile fabric.

In summarizing our collective college experiences, we agreed that they had been relatively uneventful, outside of our organized "outings." We had all developed in our own unique ways, contributing to our significant bonds and a deeper understanding. This has the unintended effect of reducing the value others seemed to add beyond team obligations or competitive arenas. Though this was nothing new for Bri and me, Auxi and Kendry, who had naturally felt more at ease with others, had developed this same sense of disconnect. This isn't to say others were inferior, but no situation or conversation felt genuine, and it often became an intellectual burden to be present. Our perspectives needed to be understood beyond those of "regular" students; our goals and chosen paths seemed to exceed their comprehension. Above all, we thought more strategically and with greater urgency about the future than most peers.

To fulfill our purpose means practicing purposefully, honing every skill, and sculpting your mind into the most optimal state achievable for your goal, leaving no room for unnecessary distractions or complacency. We didn't fully understand what was approaching then, the scale of impending catastrophe, but we all felt premonition that we should remain constantly aware, perpetually alert, and focused on our objectives, as everything around us seemed liable to collapse at any moment.

The night drew to a close. Growing tired, our bodies heavy from the weight of our achievements, we watched science fiction horror films late into the night, flickering images on the screen mirroring anxieties that gnawed at the edges of our minds. As we finally allowed the reality of freedom from college to settle in, we couldn't have imagined what the next few days would bring. Our celebration of life to come was, in fact, a final, unaware farewell to the world we had known.

THURSDAY, MAY 8, 2025 – SEVEN DAYS

Waking the following morning, I found Auxi stirring on the sofa's other end, Bri curled into her corner armchair, and

Kendry sprawled comfortably on the floor, just like old times. Our sleep-heavy eyes collectively landed on the television screen. Confusion pierced through morning haze as we saw scrolling headlines: massive, inexplicable holes had begun appearing throughout the West Coast.

Staring at the headlines, we watched as a Los Angeles anchorman pointed to a ten-foot diameter hole that had appeared in a busy intersection's center. They stated this might be due to subsurface sinkholes. But that explanation felt insufficient; it didn't account for three other similar chasms that had appeared in California, nor the two more materialized in Washington state, all within hours. Despite this growing phenomenon, no one had yet succumbed to panic. Streets outside still buzzed with morning traffic, a normalcy that felt increasingly discordant.

I didn't know what to think initially, so I turned to Bri, her analytical mind my usual compass.

"Any ideas what's happening?" I asked.

"Assuming no malicious factors are involved, it could plausibly be true that these holes are, as reported, some form of geological anomaly," she stated, face unreadable, sharp eyes dissecting every nuance of the news feed. "It could be due to accelerated climate change and erosion, previously used then forgotten man-made subterranean holes, or... something else entirely."

"What could that 'something else' be?" Kendry asked, voice low, mind beginning to consider hypotheses.

"I'm not completely certain, Ken, but my research has revealed things about Earth we hadn't previously conceived," she replied, severity etching itself onto her features. "I can't share details, as this is highly classified work I'm completing with a private entity, but the Earth may not be what we once believed. Its very core is... changing. We have been logging short bursts of very low-frequency and ultra-low-frequency noise along with radon spikes and brief piezoelectric electromagnetic surges in granite belts. That is all I can risk saying."

"What? Why are we just hearing about this now?" I demanded, unwilling to remain misinformed about something so potentially significant.

"Because it's classified. That's precisely the point," Bri responded, irritation coloring her voice. "I'm not fully aware of the overarching research scope, and was brought in purely for my geological expertise. Although I can't share everything, I can say we've found similar instances scattered across the United States, along with other geological inconsistencies. Based on available data, I believe they're natural and relatively harmless unless someone is directly above one during opening. However, I'm unsure if these particular holes, these sudden, expanding openings, are identical to what we've documented."

Understanding any further conversation would be futile, that Bri had reached her sharing limit, we dropped the topic. The silence that followed was heavy with unspoken questions. We continued our day as usual, returning to increasingly delicate normalcy. As everyone departed for respective obligations, part of my mind remained focused on Bri's words.

I found myself at the local engineering firm where I worked part-time, analyzing tunnel roadmap proposals for viability. A note on my monitor read: 'You are not building bridges; you are buying ten seconds.' Kendry's line had a way of sticking. My attention was focused on this arena, where I continued working with my team to design improved tunnel concepts, laying solid foundation as I prepared to graduate and accept a more significant, clandestine opportunity.

Consequently, I heard nothing else about the holes for the rest of the day.

At that time, Bri had returned to her secretive research, attempting to gain deeper insight into West Coast occurrences; her efforts, she later confirmed, proved fruitless, as the data remained elusive.

Kendry, meanwhile, continued with his research program, focus sharp. He hoped to prepare his autonomous vehicle design for critical road testing, ensuring his work could continue seamlessly after he departed from university. Auxi had an upcoming track meet in Ohio from the 9th through 11th, a competition for which they were preparing, and her team was departing that very night at 8 PM.

Unfazed by the televised events, the world continued its usual, frantic pace, convinced that everything was under control, a collective delusion. Even we, with our insights, didn't consider it too concerning, not yet. Humanity, in its overconfidence, couldn't have been more incorrect. The holes were warnings, a prelude to the world's final act.

FRIDAY, MAY 9, 2025 – SIX DAYS

The following day brought new information regarding the strange holes and their increasingly frequent appearances. They opened with a newfound speed, spreading West to East, a creeping geological phenomenon. More concerning, they had begun appearing in other countries, ignoring all borders.

Holes suddenly opened in Mexico, swallowing small buildings, cars, and significant portions of houses, leaving gaping wounds in urban landscapes. Holes appeared in the UK, tearing sidewalks and buckling concrete, killing bikers and pedestrians with surgical precision. They began growing wider, their diameters expanding rapidly, creating an occurrence too obvious, too pervasive, to simply dismiss as natural geological shifts. No holes in recorded history had ever randomly opened with such capacity and overwhelming range as those spreading across the globe.

For the first twelve hours of Eastern Standard Time, much of the world experienced this phenomenon, except for the extreme poles and frigid environments that were largely uninhabitable for humans. It was as if the Earth itself was reacting to our existence, a sentient being tearing at its own skin.

Realizing that whatever was happening, whatever force was tearing at the planet's crust, would undoubtedly reach our university within days, I began working with Bri and Kendry to devise immediate protection for those at school. Given that the government had still not declared a state of emergency, we knew that the daily routines of attending finals and other tasks would continue, placing more people at risk.

We implemented our improvised plan swiftly, utilizing campus resources, materials, structural knowledge, and willpower, to create reinforced beams connecting the main walkways. By designing these beams to extend the full sidewalk and occasional street width, securing them in multiple locations, we figured we could reduce the chaos and casualties. Half of the bolts stripped under torque, we could not measure, so we improvised: a jack handle through a wrench for leverage, a ratchet strapped to a bench to steady it, and shear connectors scavenged from a lab rack. We ran load straps between nodes to share the weight if one anchor failed. It was not elegant, but it was a promise of ten more seconds.

As we worked on this, several trusted classmates and teammates, their faces showing a dawning comprehension of the impending peril, joined us. We worked relentlessly through the night and into the following day, the metallic tang of sweat sharp in pre-dawn air. Our preparation wasn't for final exams, but for survival in a world already crumbling beneath our feet.

SATURDAY, MAY 10, 2025 – FIVE DAYS

Around eight AM, a sudden cacophony of screams tore through the morning air, a sound that would become all too familiar in the coming days. We looked up, startled, and saw waves of people running toward us, faces contorted with panic, as we wrestled with the last beam supports.

There was no warning sound, no tremor, no tell-tale ground movement indicating its pending arrival. Seeing this hole form, Kendry and I, our minds instantly processing the threat, ran perpendicular to everyone else; a calculated risk, hoping to elude the rapidly expanding opening while simultaneously avoiding the stampeding crowd.

Running along provisional beams we had connected throughout campus, we noticed with grim satisfaction that they were holding. We also saw an older professor, face bewildered, seemingly unaware of the event, and unable to move quickly enough. Recognizing the relentless advance of the widening hole, which consumed everything in its path, I ran to her, voice sharp with urgency, and told her to get on my back. Rebar twanged like plucked piano wire. A stop sign skated past us like a red coin. The air tasted like a battery on the tongue. I felt like the world itself was becoming a blast of sensory triggers moving in slow motion.

Reluctant at first, eyes wide, she saw the void growing closer, dark edges swallowing ground. Then, with a desperate sound, she latched onto me, her grip strong. We immediately pivoted back onto the beam system and kept running, ground trembling beneath our feet. Buildings began crumbling around us, foundations groaning, and glass shards flew everywhere as we fled the collapsing scene.

Although we were quicker than most, some fragments struck us before we reached an open, relatively untouched area we had presumed safer. By the time we made it to the safer location, gasping for breath, I had several superficial cuts on my face. Kendry, with a wince, pulled a larger glass piece from his hand while loosening dust from his clothes, appearance now grimier. The professor I had carried wasn't seriously hurt, save for dust and minor bruises from cascading debris.

Looking back toward the chaos, I saw enormous dust clouds billowing into the sky, obscuring much destruction. People wandered around disoriented, many with injuries, some covered only in dust, while others were streaked with blood, not knowing if it was their own or where it was coming from.

Returning to the heart of the matter, our primary objective was to locate Bri and offer assistance where possible. On the way toward the hole's ragged edge, we spotted several people who had helped construct our beam systems, faces grim but resolute.

"Have you seen Bri anywhere?" I asked Aaron, an engineering student.

"Yeah, she was heading that way," he said, pointing directly toward the newly formed hole's center. "That system you designed held up nicely. You saved a lot of us, and I'd be more than happy to help if you have another idea."

"Thanks, Aaron. I'll let you know of anything else we think of," I said, voice tight with urgency, as Kendry and I immediately turned and headed toward this new hole's origin.

As we approached the center, the ground slowly faded away beneath our feet until nothing but narrow, intersecting beams remained, suspended over a void. Looking out into the open hole's dark emptiness, I noticed Bri standing on beam sets even further into the region, hovering over the abyss, yet still close enough to the solid side where she could, theoretically, jump off if they suddenly failed.

Wanting to know what she was studying with such intense focus, I told Kendry I was approaching her.

"Yeah, B, go ahead. I'll just stay here. You know, where the ground is more solid," Kendry said, stepping back toward solid ground, shaking his head with a mixture of apprehension and amusement.

Arriving at Bri's side, the unstable beams swaying slightly under our combined weight, I asked what she was looking at, her gaze so absorbed in the abyss.

"Do you feel that?" Bri asked, voice a low murmur, as she intensely studied the churning, dark depths.

"Feel what? I don't get any sensation from this hole other than potential for an untimely demise," I replied, sarcasm a shield against growing unease.

"It feels like something is down there, something visceral, something immense... like it is calling me. No, calling to everyone," Bri said, eyes fixed on the darkness, voice holding resonance that rose through the noise.

"I understand I haven't always been as aware of my surroundings as you, or as attuned to subtle energies, but you sound like you're losing it, Bri," I said, skepticism rising, rational mind fighting against the sensation now beginning to prickle at my own skin.

"Just focus, and listen carefully to the ground, to the very air around you. Feel for anything that may not be normal, anything that resonates with this presence," Bri instructed, voice calm but insistent.

While balancing myself on vibrating beams, I closed my eyes, forcing myself to shed distractions, and listened closely to the hole. Although I couldn't hear anything initially, except for distant cries and the creak of settling earth, I slowly began to feel that there was something more to these openings, something beyond geological shifts.

Surely everyone had figured by now that something extraordinary was occurring, yet no one had any clue what it could be. Listening and feeling more intently, pushing my senses to their limits, I felt everything: from subtle air currents around me to the acrid, metallic smell of blood from injured civilians nearby. Even more so, a sub-sonic pulse wavered at the edge of my senses, a bass note someone forgot to stop.

Something was down there, something massive, stirring from ancient slumber. For the first time, I felt chilling certainty that humanity was not alone.

At that precise moment, a sharp, sudden jolt coursed through the beams. Bri tapped my shoulder, touch firm, and said, voice barely above a whisper, "It's coming."

Feeling the same sensation she was, a wave of cold dread mixed with a strange exhilaration washed over me, and I prepared for what was about to emerge from the ground's hole. I leaped back to solid ground, Bri mirroring my movement, bracing for impact. Anticipating some creature or monster from Earth's core, I instinctively got into a defensive position, one quickly adjustable to a full sprint if necessary.

Sensing the creature inching closer to the surface, its presence a palpable weight in the air, my heart began pounding faster. Time slowed as the unknown entity reached just under the abyss's edge. My imagination ran wild for the next half second, conjuring every conceivable beast that could be about to expose itself to our world.

Just then, a delicate, iridescent butterfly, wings shimmering with improbable color, flew out of the darkness and climbed into the open air. The hum stopped. The air went ordinary. A faint scent of ozone and brine lingered where it passed, and a dusting of metallic grit clung to my forearm like glitter that refused to fall.

Although something strange was happening, demonstrably worsening daily, we had no clear understanding of what it would truly become or ultimately unleash.

Heading back toward everyone else and the campus, our mission to check on Bri was accomplished, and we looked back one final time at the gaping hole. Out of my peripheral vision, a fleeting image, I believed I saw something move within its depths with speed comparable to Auxi's, if not closer to my own. Unsure what had happened and attributing it to severe sleep deprivation and the day's stress, I turned my attention back to the injured students and partially damaged campus, a more immediate and tangible problem.

Upon the day's completion and the occurrence of miscellaneous deaths among the damages, the university, finally acknowledging the danger, decided to administer finals online, thereby protecting students from unnecessary travel and gathering. Many students had already gone home by this point, fleeing the impending chaos, but many more planned to leave within days of the announcement, hoping to be with their families during trying times.

Fatigued from our night of work and the day's events, Bri returned to Kendry's and my apartment to rest for the next unpredictable day. We didn't know what was coming, but we wanted to ensure we were close together, united, and ready for anything.

Now, I pause my recollection of events leading to the end.

A loudspeaker cracks: "This is a designated seismic shelter. Remain calm."

Calm is a verb that no one performs well.

"Cots will be assigned by number."

Numbers make people feel arranged. Order is a costume you wear to a funeral.

"Do not congregate near exits."

We congregate anyway, because wanting the door is older than language.

We tell stories about what humans are: resilient, generous, impossible to break. We post the words and buy the mugs. But stories do not hold weight; beams do. Plans do. The will to look at a hole in the ground and say, "We are still crossing here," does.

We had time. To shore, to signal, to warn. We used it to pretend we had more. That is not evil. It is a habit. Habits kill you slowly, then all at once.

I am not condemning us. I am cataloging what failed so we can stop failing in the same direction. Call it survival etiquette. Call it a list I should have written sooner.

SUNDAY, MAY 11, 2025 – FOUR DAYS

Somehow, in the span between this day and the previous one, the world had succumbed to widespread panic. We were now forced to take occurrences seriously, as severe damage and other unprecedented incidents had begun occurring with regularity. Bridges collapsed into churning rivers. Airports lost the ability to safely operate, their runways scarred, their control towers silent. Wireless systems jittered as timing references slipped. Wideband noise bursts and ionospheric scintillation chewed at signals, so cell towers and radios could not agree on time, which meant nothing else could either.

In the wake of these occurrences, the government, with belated urgency, finally decided to take the situation seriously and call a nationwide travel ban, something generally unnecessary, as only the most stubborn or ignorant people would venture out. However, some people, attempting to cling to semblances of everyday life, thought they could circumvent this. They found themselves driving into newly opened holes or being involved in more catastrophes, their lives extinguished instantly.

As for how we were impacted, the shutdown was more of a shelter-in-place order. However, this meant that Auxi, with her team, would have to remain far away, immobilized by the unknown, trapped in an Ohio hotel.

This day, Sunday, brought more than just a government shutdown and failing internet connections. Earth itself had begun trembling like never before, a deep rumble from beneath the crust. Earthquakes now seemed more potent, more intentional in their destructive force, laying waste to many remaining cities worldwide and seemingly using gaping holes as vacuums to erase evidence of their violence.

Mountains shifted, their ancient peaks groaning, and vast oceans poured into lands, waters churning with fury, as Earth began cracking from the immense pressure of relentless tremors, further showing us how quickly what we had learned as life could be altered.

Despite these disastrous effects occurring worldwide, none had more striking destruction or implications than those in Monaco. This city-state, situated along the French Riviera, has long been recognized as one of the world's safest places from natural disasters, a testament to its geological stability. Although the occurrences we had been experiencing that week did not discriminate in their impact, striking across the globe, no one would have expected Monaco to crumble as it did.

While attempting to watch the news through static at our still-undamaged apartment, a small bastion of normalcy, the station, flickering with interference, began covering Monaco's plight. There, they had experienced larger-scale earthquakes than in their modern history. The broadcaster, voice strained, informed viewers of the quakes' rapidity and steadily increasing strength throughout the hours.

In the middle of their live broadcast, the ground cracked behind them, deep fissures splitting the street, and buildings shook, concrete skeletons moaning. The camera tilted, then fell, showing a jag of sky and a blur of legs. A power flicker rolled across the frame, and a thin carrier howl rose, the sound a radio makes when it is being unmade. Then the channel went to static.

Our prior research and relentless pursuit of knowledge had helped us be more mentally prepared than most, with sharper minds and sturdier wills. But this escalating situation was still uncharted territory, pushing even our limits. Not knowing what to do, we began preparing for the worst and sent delayed, garbled texts to our families, urging them to do the same: stock up and prepare for what was ahead.

Although none of us were far from home, as our families lived two hours west of our university, we figured it was not the best time to attempt travel. Instead, we put immediate emphasis on stocking up on whatever food and water were still available at rapidly dwindling stores. Though it wasn't much, we had enough to keep up sustained and mobile for the time being.

By this point, the United States was consumed by panic, meaning all food, every roll of toilet paper, and other essential items were becoming thinly stretched, fiercely contested commodities. This scramble for survival quickly led to acts of violence, further showing how the stress we had been under for so long finally came to a head, exploding outward, as the world around us fell apart.

In all this chaos and amidst our preparation for the coming days, we relentlessly attempted to contact Auxi, who was stuck with her team in an Ohio hotel. They were on day three of their track meet when the shutdown went into full effect, stranding them there for as long as the shutdown lasted or until vital resources were depleted.

We called her periodically throughout this time, constant worry for her safety weighing on us. Nevertheless, we were unable to establish contact for the entire first half of the day, the silence a heavy burden. Not wanting to lose track of her situation, we continued our efforts until a call from Kendry, a clear line in the static, finally made its way through.

When she answered, voice surprisingly steady, she explained that everything had been relatively okay for them, despite locals being erratic and everyone on edge. Although they were in Columbus, people there seemed to possess more self-control than in many major cities and had not yet resorted to extreme violence. This made it slightly safer for them to make quick store trips for food, ensuring they had enough to get through this unpredictable streak. She told us she was running the hotel stairs to burn anxiety out of her body, and that she had spent an hour in a dark hallway talking a freshman teammate through a breathing count when the lights cut again.

I had unwavering confidence in Auxi that if things truly went south, if the situation became untenable, she could handle herself to get out or at least let us know somehow. She could have likely returned to school without the team's help, given her formidable abilities, but she decided, with trademark loyalty, to wait it out with them and ensure everyone was safe.

Despite the world seemingly coming to an end, things went as well as we could have hoped for my friends and me. The circumstances were undesirable, even apocalyptic, but the university remained largely unaffected by direct physical destruction, and Auxi was doing fine, as much as we could possibly have asked for in such a situation. Utilizing this brief respite, we pondered how we could truly understand what was happening and, more importantly, how we could prevent this descent into chaos in the future.

We didn't know it yet, but the events that we, humanity, believed to be side effects of Earth's reaction to human actions would soon reveal themselves to be much more complex. A problem we could neither simply prevent nor adequately prepare for, a force beyond our current comprehension.

With nothing else we could do to help or prepare for the coming days, we packed our belongings and headed to a local shelter, a designated safe zone supposedly safer from earthquakes rattling the entire world. The structure was angled strategically into the ground, providing a relatively safer space for most. However, Bri, Kendry, and I mainly went to ensure others' safety and to remain under the radar as we secretly prepared for what was next.

While many around us were left praying and hoping this would simply end, we, with our unique burdens, got much-needed rest and prepared, with grim resolve, for what we assumed would be another long day.

However, the truth would be something no one had expected.

VI. IT GETS BETTER BEFORE...

MONDAY, MAY 12, 2025 – THREE DAYS

The following morning, communication lines were clear and cell service was crisp, almost too eager to pretend the world wasn't cracked. The earthquakes had seemingly ceased. None had been reported for hours, the most extended break since their onset. A quiet, unsettling calm settled over the devastated landscape, a pressure in the air that felt like a held breath.

Proceeding with caution, many people slowly began emerging from their shelters, eyes wide with disbelief and fragile hope. News coverage, now clear, captured the pause. Wary of what could happen next, the government didn't lift the travel ban. Instead, they suggested people reach out to loved ones while maintaining social distancing as an option. Additionally, they urged civil servants and emergency services to take advantage of the calm to aid those injured or trapped under rubble.

Arising from our temporary safety, our trio stepped out into the morning light. We all stared at the pervasive destruction around us. Although our immediate area on the university campus wasn't as severely damaged as some other places seen on news reports, the gaping holes, fractured streets, and skeletal remains of crumbling buildings provided a stark reminder of how fortunate we were.

Some televisions in the shelter remained functional, their screens flickering with coverage of damage around the world. Many places had flooded, with vast swaths of land transformed into muddy lakes, and countless iconic landmarks reduced to debris. Monaco was worst: streets swallowed by harbor water, windows brimming with oil-slick brine, and a coastline turned into a slow, obscene drift of debris.

As a single, distant helicopter circled the area, the world became enlightened about what had truly taken place after the camera crew fled. The once-vibrant coastal community had become wholly submerged, entirely flooded, and irrevocably destroyed, its façade transformed into a waterlogged, silent graveyard. Bodies, bloated and grotesque, floated in dark, viscous mixtures of oil and blood. Homes drifted aimlessly, their foundations ripped away, and the remnants of life were now putrid filth to be scraped away.

Staring, transfixed, at that screen, I pondered how little was known about Earth's raw, untamed power. Throughout my research, I never thought something like this could happen in our lifetime. Looking at Bri and Kendry for shared understanding, I noticed dread across Kendry's face; his usual pragmatic calm had been shattered. As for Bri, she maintained her expressionless gaze, then turned from the television and faced me directly.

Looking at me, her eyes, for a fleeting moment, held a deeper glint. Sweeping across the crowds of people slowly appearing from our safe place, their faces drawn with defeat, I gained an immediate, intuitive sense of what she wanted me to do. It was an unspoken command, a subtle nudge toward action. Facing the sea of people, their shoulders slumped, I took a deep breath and began to speak.

"It's beautiful, isn't it?" My voice, unpracticed in public speaking, began to find its timbre, growing stronger and ringing with urgency I usually keep buried in my actions. "I see that you're all confused by what I mean, at least those of you paying attention. Regardless, we've survived the night and lived to see another day. Not only that, but it's a day where we can see the world, speak with our families, and take a moment to gather our thoughts so we can be prepared for the next wave..."

I paused and let the quiet work. Confusion is a lever; I felt it slip the pin.

"I wish I could say this is over, but the truth is that it can start just as abruptly as it did before, so we need to make the most of this time to prepare. Sure, I'm tired, you're tired, and we're all a bit hurt, but would you rather lie down and wait for another surge or go and claim what's ours? There's a break in the turmoil. An opening. An opportunity to do something with this stillness."

Staring at me, many faces were still blank with shock, with a few showing signs that my words had taken effect. I tried once more, voice dense with determination. "There are people around us who need help. We can provide that. Step back from your emotions and recognize the severity of the situation. This is your defining moment, the moment where you look back and smile or frown in regret. Don't make the wrong decision."

In that moment, it was almost as if the crowd, a paralyzed, traumatized mass, awoke from a deep, debilitating trance. A ripple of recognition, then purpose, spread through them. Their eyes, once vacant, filled with newfound resolve. They sought out various emergency services in the area, their movements becoming more purposeful, and began, with tentative yet growing energy, searching for survivors and life amidst the rubble.

Kendry, ever observant, questioned my motives, brow furrowed, recognizing this sudden outburst as fundamentally out of my controlled character. I explained that Bri must have wanted me to do it, a silent communication of necessity, but likely didn't expect how I would approach it, given the directive and militant style of my words. I was surprised by myself, too, at the depth to which I expressed my inner emotions, regardless of how they came across. Bri may have been surprised as well, based on the subtly less expressionless, almost impressed look on her face.

"That was... something. Slightly strong for some of their current mental states, but effective as long as you got them to move," Bri said, her usual blunt assessment softened by a hint of approval.

"You know how college students are these days. I could have taken a softer or more dramatic approach, but sometimes you need to convey the severity. If they hadn't moved, I would have told them the truth; that they were all going to die if they stayed motionless. Thankfully, I didn't have to resort to that," I said, a wry admission.

As we walked away, leaving the slowly stirring crowd behind us, I turned to see more people emerging from the shelter we'd been in, a steady stream now joining the effort. Witnessing students and faculty, once lost in their own despair, now moving purposefully toward the rubble and chilling silhouettes of bodies, I could clearly tell the profound difference in their mindset. They seemed more driven, more deeply rejuvenated, even in such a grim, hopeless scenario. They had found purpose.

As others came together to help, organizing into small, effective groups, our trio met to strategize, our minds already seeking the next challenge. We decided we could be of greater use in more densely populated, heavily damaged areas of the city. We quickly gathered a few trusted volunteers from our beam-building crew, their faces etched with newfound determination. Those able to come with us, those with strength and will, would help the injured or trapped; a more efficient use of our collective resources, given the relative lack of immediate destruction in our university's area.

Making our way to the crowded, devastated area of the city, the air grew thick with dust and the acrid smell of burnt metal. We didn't know what lay ahead. But we were sure that, under our focused leadership, this small, chosen group might prove useful and, more importantly, prove to itself that it was more than simply survivors; it was an agent of adaptation.

After carefully navigating a few surviving vehicles through the devastated area, where tires crunched on shattered glass, we found a surprisingly large number of people and various organizations already attempting to coordinate, with many people still in hiding. We quickly helped less severely injured civilians get to makeshift medical tents, where they could be seen professionally after the more critically injured were given priority. After getting them situated and leaving a couple of students and professors behind to provide support, we located a small, overwhelmed team of professional rescuers and gathered essential equipment to begin our own targeted search.

As we meticulously searched for missing and injured people in the labyrinthine wreckage, carefully moving debris, my thoughts drifted to my parents back home. I hoped they were doing well, though we'd remained in sporadic contact throughout these events. Although quick phone calls and garbled messages allowed connection, they didn't let me fully understand their fear or the extent of their survival. I assumed that since they were sheltering with Bri's parents, they were fine. Bri confirmed her parents were doing well, hunkered down. I was waiting for things to be undeniably clear, for the threat to fully recede, before making the dangerous trip back. As the government shutdown was still in effect, no one could travel far, which limited the possibility of going home and, paradoxically, added to the sense of duty I felt toward my university and the people directly around me.

Continuing my relentless search through jagged rubble, mind still on my family, I was suddenly yanked into the present by a discovery Kendry had made nearby. He was clearing debris, movements precise, listening for a child he'd sworn he'd heard yell for help. He called Bri to help, as she was closest and, unlike me, not lost in thought.

Removing heavy, splintered wreckage of a collapsed building, they found the child, small and terrified, quickly clearing space around his head to ease his labored breathing. The kid, voice a reedy whisper, said he couldn't feel his arms or legs and had been stuck since the night before, an unthinkable ordeal for so small a body. Being no more than ten, he had astonishing awareness and presence of mind, saving his voice to yell only when he heard the faint promise of help.

Realizing the devastating situation, their faces grim, they called to me, voices sharp, snapping me out of my trance. I signaled for a nearby medical team, my mind already assessing the dire need. The boy would require immediate, specialized help we couldn't provide.

When everyone was there, a huddle of grim faces, we continued clearing the remaining rubble. Bri wedged a beam, I levered concrete, and Kendry kept the boy talking and counted breaths. In that process, as we began clearing his lower body while Kendry and the medics were near his head, a foul, sickening stench filled the air, growing stronger as we got closer.

Assuming the smell was a ruptured sewage line or rotten food, I forced myself to keep going, my muscles straining. Bri slowed, her movements hesitant, and I found myself doing most of the heavy, repulsive work. Feeling close, I looked to Bri for help, and she, her face a mask of disgust, reluctantly assisted me in removing a heavier, jagged piece of concrete directly over his legs.

Once the concrete was clear, we knew, with sickening certainty, that something was profoundly wrong. His lower body, revealed in harsh daylight, didn't match his upper body. His legs were clearly broken, twisted at unnatural angles, but there was something else far more horrifying. His jeans were soaked in dark, congealed blood, and his legs were impossibly, unnaturally flat, appearing two-dimensional, like a macabre paper cut-out. A low-pressure throb passed through my palms on the stone, the same skin-deep pulse I'd started to notice since the shaking stopped.

As we recoiled, backing away to let the medics take a closer look, his legs, with a subtle, horrifying shift, began to move. "Hey, kid, are you moving your feet?" asked one of the medical team, voice strained. "No..." said the kid, weak and terrified. "I can't feel my arms or legs."

Unsure what to make of it, the medic carefully reached for the boy's shoe to pull it off slowly. The smell worsened, becoming a suffocating cloud. The shoe fell, clattering against concrete, and the medic yelped as dozens of rats ran from the boy's pants and shoes, from the putrid area of rubble he was buried under, scurrying into the shadows.

His now exposed legs displayed blackened, shriveled stems that looked like half-eaten licorice sticks. The boy, in his innocence, was merely curious about what was happening. The medical team, faces pale, didn't want to tell him, avoiding an inevitable, traumatizing freakout. "Wrap and shield. Watch for crush syndrome," one medic said, already hanging fluids. "He's hypovolemic but responsive. Keep him engaged."

Working toward his head, we saw that the rats had, thankfully, stopped at some point, likely due to our intervention, but everything below the knee was useless and rotten, consumed by gnawing darkness.

This was sickening to see, a violation of natural order. My skin crawled as I continued to free the child, actions automatic, mind reeling. Bri and Kendry were equally disgusted, although Bri, ever stoic, showed it less; her focus stayed locked, her hands efficient.

As we moved further up his body, his arms were finally released, covered with small, jagged bites and a few signs of infection, but nothing untreatable. We wrapped his ravaged legs in a blanket before he could see them, shielding him from the truth, and carried him toward a medical tent for critical attention. He thanked us in a thin voice, then broke into heart-wrenching tears as searing pain in his upper body finally reached him.

We didn't know how that kid had survived, how his small body had endured such a horror, or what to make of it. Regardless, we were shocked and silenced. None of us had seen anything like it in person, not in our structured lives, and we didn't know which emotion to grab.

The brutal reality of what was happening worldwide had begun to set in, and a grim, suffocating dread had settled deep in our bones. Although we continued our work for the rest of the day, mechanically searching and not finding any more half-eaten people who were miraculously alive, my thoughts were filled with the boy and his devoured, blackened legs. I imagined the same would go for Bri and Kendry.

The day went on, a blur of motion and grim discovery, and no more earthquakes occurred. As things calmed through the long, shadowy night, we decided, exhausted, to rest in one of the nearby cot areas; a temporary, uncomfortable haven. The haunting sight of distant smoke rising into the bruised sky and the unsettling movement of unseen aircraft remained noticeable, a reminder of unseen forces. Yet, none of it seemed close to us. Under it all, that faint pressure beat in the ground like a learned second heartbeat.

Processing all that had happened, the terror, the revelations, the boy, I watched the sky until I finally drifted into heavy, dreamless sleep.

TUESDAY, MAY 13, 2025 – TWO DAYS

We woke to the percussive thrum of helicopters slicing the air overhead. My eyes snapped open, adrenaline jolting me upright. I braced for the next catastrophe.

Instead, our area was the same as yesterday: injured and deceased, and the weary faces of those helping them. Bri was already up and moving, her quiet efficiency unnerving. I shoved Kendry's shoulder to wake him. He groaned. The day was already in motion, though it was only 5:00 AM.

After a brief wipe-down with what little water we could spare, the rest saved for drinking or triage, we sat to eat. "Canned pineapples and spam... crazy how quickly things can go downhill," Kendry muttered, poking his plate. "Agreed," I said, forcing down the last bite, the metallic taste lingering. "Not ideal, but it's something."

"The helicopters, they keep coming," Bri said, gaze tilted toward the unseen sky. "Aren't you two curious where they're headed?" "Perhaps," I said, listening to the constant hum. "They could be helping people. They're military, sure, but we don't know."

"How many have you seen coming back?" Kendry countered. "I know Bri has a hunch. Why not go see? Better than staying in this rancid graveyard. Not that we're useless here—" "He's right," Bri said, cutting in, voice low and firm. "Let's check it out. The ground has been trembling, faintly, like heavy equipment is moving nearby."

"Alright," I said. "But we need to be back here if the chaos resumes. Keep an eye on your phones for updates from Auxi. Emergency use only. We don't know how many outlets are functional right now." We grabbed a few emergency supplies and headed out.

Following the helicopter path, we ran into others; small, anxious groups, all drawn in the same direction. Motives differed, mostly morbid curiosity, but ours were sharper. Given Bri's clandestine research and her immediate recognition of the organization's logo on a military helicopter, she figured following might yield something crucial. However, she didn't say it out loud.

In any sane situation, you go away from military helicopters. Today we went toward them, deeper into the battered city.

On the way toward the city's scarred center, where the largest local hole yawned, we passed televisions showing similar scenes across the country. Identical helicopters. Scientists in blue hazmat suits were surrounding holes, stringing bright yellow tape, and raising massive, fast-built walls to keep civilians out.

Understanding this would happen here, Bri and I ran. Kendry did his best to keep pace.

Closer to the hole, the ground vibrated underfoot. Helicopter noise rose to a deafening crescendo. Other machines powered up. We slid through a narrow alley and peeked, not ready to step into whatever waited.

A camp was rising, the kind that doesn't want you to ask questions. A few civilians argued. Soldiers forcefully directed them away, some drawing weapons when people refused. Most soldiers were measured, giving warnings before escalating, but it was clear we wouldn't get close. We waited in the shadows.

Kendry, panting slightly, arrived and whispered that the larger group of survivors we'd passed was five minutes behind him. A window.

We scouted for a vantage point. A three-story store with intact windows and upstairs offices would give us a view. We slipped alley to alley, avoiding patrols.

The back door was secured with a simple key lock, lacking modern security features. Bri picked it with a jagged piece of metal, and we were in.

Inside the abandoned clothing store, the air was thick with dust, and we saw a dead security system, the wires dangling uselessly. We moved upstairs to a window with an unobstructed view and eased a curtain aside. Then a sharp argument erupted in the alley we'd used.

I slid to the next window. The survivor group met a wall of soldiers and were told to leave. "It's classified," wind-amplified voices shouted, and the crowd, after a long moment, backed off.

Once the scene cooled, I returned to the other window. "What are the scientists doing?" I asked. "Analyzing for something specific," Kendry said. "They're using scanners, I've never seen. something crazy high-tech." "Those are called Biological Residual Readers. A BRR for short," Bri said, clinical as a lab note. "I've read about it. It scans for biological DNA or excreta, traces of life, primarily used in deep caves."

"So they think something is down there," I said, a chill along my spine. "Something alive. Or whatever made these holes was... biological."

We watched the methodical activity for the rest of the day. Hazmat-clad scientists dropped small drones into the hole. They either didn't return or didn't show anything useful. Frustration grew. One tech tried a tether; the line snapped slack, then went still too fast, like the hole had no bottom and also too many edges.

Hours passed. Bri was thinking hard, brow wrinkled. I didn't ask. Something tugged at me, too, a whisper at the back of my mind. I chalked it up to stress and plotted escape routes in case we were caught.

Kendry found more food and water in the abandoned area. We saved our rations and ate what he scavenged. Stale crackers and dry tuna aren't ideal, but they're better than the mystery items from earlier.

As night deepened, machines hummed in the distance. Activity dwindled. It seemed like a good time to sleep. From the hole came a small rockfall that ended too cleanly, like a breath cut short. We closed our eyes anyway.

WEDNESDAY, MAY 14, 2025 – ONE DAY

We woke to silence where the generator hum had been. An unnerving quiet, thick and suffocating.

At the window, we saw that everyone had vanished. Equipment remained, abandoned, like a stage after the actors fled. Trying to understand how an entire encampment could leave without us noticing, especially Bri, we surveyed the area from multiple angles.

The internet was down again. This time it was total. No handshake, no negotiation. Just a dead screen.

A heavy silence filled the air, broken only by the wind. The hole exuded an ominous presence, as if daring us to learn what it withheld. My teeth felt that same low pressure I'd started to recognize, like weather that wasn't on any map.

We decided to investigate what had happened to the soldiers. We stepped outside, cautious.

The wind whistled through the empty area. Scientists' equipment and computers remained untouched, screens dark. Soldiers' gear lay scattered, a testament to a hasty, unseen departure.

In the sleeping tents, we noticed signs of struggle. No shots fired, nothing we would have missed, but small, dark streaks of blood smeared as if someone had tried to erase them and only made them worse.

Bri called us to the hole's edge. Her voice was low, urgent. We approached through the remnants of a military operation gone wrong.

A thick trail of blood led from one tent to the hole. It was different from the small stains we'd seen. A viscous smear, as if someone had been dragged. The line was too straight, too clean, like a ruler had been laid from cot to rim.

In the tent, a pool of drying blood began on a cot. No body. No remains. No answer.

Minds reeling, we followed the thick trail back to the hole. It went straight down the slick wall into blackness. Looking more closely, we saw other streaks along the entire edge. Many more.

"Guys, we've seen enough. Whatever happened here, I don't want to be present when it happens again. Wouldn't you two agree?" Kendry said, his voice tight.

"I couldn't agree more," I said, gaze fixed on the streaks, turning to leave.

"Wait," Bri said, surprisingly calm. "They have a BRR here. We should see whether this was human or something else." She was already reaching for the scanner.

"How do we know it will catch anything? Maybe this leaves no trace," I argued. "Perhaps," Bri said. "But I need to know. You can go. I'm checking." She walked toward the device.

We followed, our concerns tabled by her resolve. If danger moved, one of us should have felt it by now. We hadn't. That made me wonder even more.

She set the wand near the blood. The tablet woke to a display of bars and numbers. The progress line began to crawl. As we waited, we heard the rumble of heavy vehicles approaching, their engines growing louder. We needed to leave soon.

"A sizeable force," Bri said, eyes on the screen. "We'll be fine." The bar reached eighty-five percent. "Thirty seconds," she said.

The trucks stopped hard. Doors slammed. Soldiers spread across the area. Shouts rose as they found the blood.

"We go now," I hissed.

"Ten seconds," Bri said without blinking.

The bar stuttered, then leapt. A dialog popped: UNKNOWN GENETIC CODE. Below it: CLASSIFIED. ACCESS REQUIRED. The tablet chirped completion.

Looking back, I'm still not sure why we didn't run the instant it finished. Maybe the raw shock. Maybe Bri needed one more confirmed line of data. Maybe she calculated the odds, and I trusted her without admitting it. That question stays with me.

We slipped into the alley that had brought us there and quickly, silently grabbed a pair of pistols, extra ammunition, and a few useful weapons from abandoned stock. It wasn't full chaos yet, but it was headed that way.

Sprinting through the alley to safer ground, we saw soldiers swarming the area, flashlights cutting the gloom, checking the very building we'd used. Whether they'd seen us or not, we kept moving.

Back at the campus shelter, the space was empty. Assuming everyone had migrated to the city center, we went there. Along the way, we saw more survivors in small clusters, a faint thread of hope that whatever happened to the soldiers hadn't happened here.

At the larger shelter, the group we knew was huddled, grim-faced. Relieved when they saw us. They asked what we'd seen.

We told them. Dread moved through their faces like a shadow. Bri pulled out the BRR and explained, briefly and clearly, what it did. She loaded the results and compared them against its library. The screen read: "non-human genetic code detected." Then: "classified. access required."

We assumed whatever was classified was what had attacked the soldiers. Confusion fought fear. A few clung to hope, a classification that meant someone knew what it was and maybe could control it. Others said that more soldiers and helicopters had arrived elsewhere, and since no one had noticed any mass disappearance, maybe this was isolated. Contained.

We hid our new weapons under our clothes and cleaned up.

Understanding that the situation had changed, we planned to head for Auxi the next day. We had hoped to cross paths if she were to move back from Ohio. With phones dead and news down, everyone stayed in the dark, clinging to fragile hope that normal would return.

Things hadn't completely fallen apart, not yet. We preferred to be prepared for when they did. We loaded every scrap of food, every drop of water, and every emergency supply for the trip to Auxi.

A student approved the use of their abandoned vehicle. We filled a gas canister, packed, and forced one last rest before venturing into the unknown.

On our way out of the encampment, we'd checked one generator: switch still set to ON, panel dark, fuel line neatly pinched off as if someone had made time for tidy work. The drag marks at the cots began, not ended, inside the tents.

As I reiterate the story, I find it almost amusing how humanity behaved in those times. Death and uncertainty everywhere. The world had already begun to crumble, piece by piece, and now something was confirmed, undeniably, going around killing people, making them vanish, and leaving a chilling streak of blood.

It was an enigma to us, yet a one-off to others, dismissed and rationalized. Another lapse in humanity's vision. Although you now know what this was, assuming you read this in a time not far from my own, you have to imagine the initial shock it held for us.

We were young, still finding our way, clinging to remnants of comfortable lives. We thought we were preparing to take on the world, to outdo rivals in trivial competitions. Then we had to use those skills to fight for our lives.

The training, both physical and mental, along with the discipline, paid off in dividends once it was completed. But that, I see now, was chance. Not everyone acts. Not everyone becomes a master of their reality. Yet we can. That's a flaw in us; untapped potential. We can do anything; there are no limits to human capacity. Many of us choose not to try.

In a sane world, that isn't life or death. From that confirmation onward, it was. A cleansing process began. It wasn't about who was lazy, a morning person, or who we followed. We had a responsibility to ourselves and our loved ones to get up and fight.

Fight the destruction. Fight the demons that keep you still. Fight for your right to live. I knew the fight wasn't in us all when we ignored warnings and let society be ravaged by an unknown enemy. Humanity didn't fight for our planet. How would it fight for itself?

Despite the despair, there's a reason I can write this while so many are gone. Not everyone is meant to win or survive. The world learned that, brutally, when this began. Humanity is flawed and tragically beautiful in its flaws.

There isn't much left of the world I knew, and I don't know precisely what that means anymore. I hope you can answer the one question I haven't: What does it truly mean to be human?

VII. IT GETS WORSE

THURSDAY, MAY 15, 2025 – RUIN

Our pursuit of Auxi began in the pre-dawn chill, an urgent race against a world spiraling further into ruin. At precisely 4:00 AM, we climbed into the loaned outdoor-style SUV, its rugged frame a practical tool for the grave journey ahead. The path promised eight to twelve grueling hours, duration dictated by the perilous state of roads beneath us. Before taking off, as sky bled from black to bruised violet, I had Kendry double-check our supplies.

"Food, water, gas, paper map, firearms, clothes... It's all here, man. Why am I crammed in the back with this stuff anyway?" Kendry grumbled, voice thick with lingering exhaustion from the previous day.

"You're back there to catch some rest. You're up next behind the wheel in a few hours, so make the most of it," I replied, gaze fixed on fading lines of highway. My tone was even, a constant against rising tension.

Exiting the city was like stepping into a macabre gallery of chaos. The carnage was impossible to ignore; a sprawling monument to a world that had convulsed and bled.

Makeshift efforts had cleared just enough debris for passage. Still, gaping holes punctuated the road every few miles, transforming our drive into a challenging slalom. Worse still, desperate souls, or perhaps merely reckless ones, drove along shoulders, conjuring needless traffic from wreckage. Two drivers traded places in the middle of the lane, doors open, like the rules had evaporated with the asphalt. Traffic laws felt like relics of a forgotten age. I took liberties, driving on the wrong side of the road and even venturing off-road when terrain allowed, all in an effort to maintain momentum.

Yet, despite our progress, the sights were constant assault: skeletal remains of cars, abandoned possessions strewn across asphalt, ghosts of lives upended, and figures sifting through detritus, searching for anything salvageable. We even passed those who seemed in dire need, faces etched with silent distress. Every fiber of my being acknowledged their plight, but we pressed on. They would find aid, I reasoned, prioritizing our primary objective. It was a calculated decision, leaving them to their fate, but our mission was paramount, and in this new, brutal world, misreading intentions was a luxury we couldn't afford. People, I knew, did extreme things when opportunity presented itself.

Two hours in, at exactly 6:00 AM, we reached the bridge; the precarious artery connecting our peninsula to the mainland. The road across it was surprisingly clear, most abandoned vehicles having been shoved to the sides. But the bridge itself was a skeletal ruin, barely clinging to life by a few tattered supports.

A third of the way across, Earth convulsed. The deck heaved; the handrails sang. Wires screamed as the span tried to remember what "bridge" meant. I shoved the accelerator. We weren't outrunning a quake; we were racing a failure curve.

Cars scattered; some nosed under others, some jumped the curb, and some drivers just ran. Halfway to safety, an old taxi slid broadside across our lane like a rusted door slamming shut.

"Out!" Bri was already moving. Kendry white-knuckled the wheel, slewing the SUV to keep us from skating into the barrier.

We hit the taxi's bumper. The deck bounced underfoot; a slow, sick vertical bob that made my teeth buzz. Metal shrieked. The cab gave an inch. Two.

"Again." We set ourselves and shoved. Bri ducked, hand on my collar, and yanked. A main cable parted with a sound like a giant's guitar string snapping. It sliced the space where my neck had been and unzipped a parked sedan's roof before the car pitched, slow-motion, into white water.

"Thanks," I said, clipped. She nodded once. We pushed harder. The cab grudged over far enough to carve a slot a vehicle could slip through.

The bridge lurched sideways, mean this time. Bri pinwheeled into a windshield. Another car knocked me toward the open air. My left hand found rebar, jagged and wet. Pain ripped along my ribs. I tasted copper.

Kendry was crab-walking the SUV toward the gap we'd made, tires squealing, the frame groaning like it resented living. We sprinted. Then the taxi started to slide back.

I threw my shoulder into it. My side lit up, white fire, and my grip faltered. The slot sealed an inch. Two. "We're done," I said, already scanning for another path.

"Push it once more!" a voice barked.

He came from nowhere; ten years older, glasses catching grim light. Wrong time to add variables. The right time to accept leverage.

We heaved. Kendry punched through. We dove in, doors still open. He floored it. Behind us, the span unstitched itself from the far end and folded, clean as paper.

Looking back at the collapsing nightmare, we drove a few more miles before questions started to emerge.

"Who are you, and why did you help us?" Bri asked, eyes sharp, scrutinizing him in the rearview mirror.

"Well, you're welcome," he said, wiping his glasses with slow, deliberate motion. He didn't look at the lenses; he watched our mirrors. "And I appreciate the gratitude. My name is Axel Johnson. I'm heading to Pittsburgh, hoping to find my family. They were fine, then the network crashed, so I need to see for myself. I saw you guys in trouble back there and figured, 'Why not help?' And, it crossed my mind that you might be able to help me along my journey. Chipping in seemed like a good way to sway that thought."

Healthy skepticism still clung to us. We listened as Axel recounted his story: a contracted engineer in Maryland, separated from his team during the quakes. His motives seemed straightforward, understandable even, but in a world like ours, caution was constant.

As we continued our drive toward Ohio, another wave of heavy earthquakes struck us. This time, the ground fractured even more quickly, great chasms ripping open the Earth. The decision about Axel was tabled; Kendry swerved and maneuvered with practiced ease through skeletal remains of cars and throngs of people running for cover. Passing DC and Baltimore, we came upon another gaping hole, surrounded by people and even military personnel, who stood fixated despite Earth's violent tremors.

They seemed mesmerized by the abyss, waiting for some horrifying spectacle to unfold. We had no intention of waiting for the ground beneath them, or us, to collapse into Earth's maw. Kendry veered onto side streets, skillfully bypassing the stunned crowd. Looking back, a chilling sight unfolded. People cried out, scattering from the hole as distant gunshots rattled the air. And then I saw it for the first time.

It climbed out like it had been practicing. Clear slime lacquered its hide, warm enough to fog in cool air. The skull read bear until it opened its mouth; tongue too broad, teeth too uniform. The torso was amphibious bulk on wolf-lean legs set too close together for streets built by humans. It didn't blink. It tilted, a small, surgical angle, then chose.

Claws worried the soil. Then they worried people. When bullets landed, it seemed as if the pain was a non-factor; they kept attacking.

I glanced at Bri; she seemed focused on the road, her attention on our escape, hearing only screams and gunfire.

That fleeting glance was enough. We weren't dealing with anything standard. Before I could even voice my horror, we passed another cluster of people. My eyes scanned windows, searching for more, and then I caught it: some of them looked up, pointed, and cried out. One of those things lunged from a nearby building, a blur of unimaginable speed, and began to attack.

Its speed and reflexes were a terrifying impossibility for an average human, leaving a trail of bodies in its wake, at its mercy; if it had any. Bullets, when they struck, seemed to merely break the creature's skin, revealing thick, almost black liquid I could only assume was blood. Unamused, the monsters continued their slaughter, more surging to the surface, overwhelming everyone in their path. As I counted their steadily increasing numbers, a few of them began to turn in our direction.

The horrifying scene had momentarily fixated us. "Drive!" I commanded, voice sharp. Kendry floored it. We sped away, monsters in relentless pursuit, some smeared with the blood of their victims, others oozing their own tar-like fluids. They were gaining. Kendry pressed harder, the SUV screaming to 80 miles per hour before we finally began to pull away. Even then, they chased us until we passed another group of unfortunate individuals. One took the roofline instead of the street, learning elevation fast; the rest pivoted to the denser cluster like hunger had a compass.

"There were more of them," Kendry said, voice strained as he gripped the wheel. "What the hell was that? What did I just see?!"

"I... I wish I could tell you. That thing... whatever monstrosity that was... it must have burst from those holes and attacked immediately. It moved so fast; I didn't even register it. It went completely under my radar," Bri murmured, her usual calm now stretched thin, though still remarkably composed. "That... that had to be what attacked those soldiers."

"Whatever it was, we need to avoid it if it strikes again," Axel said, with a slight tremor in his voice. "Bullets didn't seem to do much. Running's our best bet."

"Look—" he reset, "distance buys time."

Still vigilant and assessing the new passenger, we asked Axel where he needed to be dropped off. Our mission was Auxi, and we maintained focus, not wanting additional variables in this volatile situation. We explained our destination, Hartford, Connecticut, our hometown as far as Axel was concerned, and informed him we'd have to part ways.

Axel seemed to understand, though a flicker of frustration crossed his face. He suggested we separate at the Maryland border, a compromise that aligned with our route to Auxi. We agreed, continuing our drive, alert for any more encounters with those creatures. Since the initial attack, we hadn't seen any. Yet, a pervasive sense of paranoia and unease lingered along the oddly deserted roads.

The full extent of destruction across the United States was terrifyingly unknown, and with it, the mental state of society at large. Axel seemed collected enough, but caution was paramount. Attempting to bridge the silence, I sought to build a fragile layer of familiarity.

"I can't help but notice the ring on your finger," I began, striving for a casual tone. "Any kids?"

Axel looked down, rolling the ring around his finger. "Not yet, but my first one's on the way. It's partly why I'm in such a rush, and why I hoped you guys could help. My wife's at her parents' house now, but I'm not sure if the situation here is the same as there. I'm trying not to dwell on possibilities too much, you know?"

"I'm truly sorry this situation has erupted at such a monumental point in your family's lives," I said, meeting his gaze, trying to gauge his internal reaction, allowing Bri a chance to observe him too. "I hope everyone is safe. We also need to get back to our families, but in times like these, you have to be equipped and prepared before walking into danger. It feels like anything and everything will go wrong at once, but it's up to us to survive, to capitalize on our circumstances, to make it out alive and back to our loved ones."

Our conversation continued for another hour, a functional exchange over the chasm of the unknown. Finally, we arrived at the Maryland border. It was time to part ways. The highway rest stop was unnervingly empty, a chilling lack of human presence.

We circled the parking lot, sweeping for potential threats, until we found it: an older vehicle, in surprisingly good condition, thankfully free of excessive technology. We let Axel out, then helped him into the car. Bri, with her uncanny knack for all things mechanical, quickly disabled the alarm; not that she was a carjacker, but rather, her exquisite know-how extended to nearly everything, and starting a car was no different.

The engine sputtered to life, but the gas tank was dangerously low, nowhere near enough to reach Pittsburgh. Not wanting to drain our own precious supply, we began searching for a siphon tube among abandoned vehicles. We eventually found a work truck with some plastic tubing that would do the job. I grabbed it and hurried back to our SUV.

Our only gas container was already filled with our fuel. To avoid a messy transfer, we quickly filled our SUV, then prepared a container for siphoning from other cars. Since the gas was for Axel, we all agreed he should be the one to do it. We selected a vehicle that sloshed with sufficient fuel to justify the effort, opened its tank, and inserted the tube. Older work trucks don't fight a gravity siphon; newer return valves can. This one cooperated.

The tank wasn't large enough for gravity to start a flow, so Axel quickly sucked air from the tube. Gasoline rushed in. Though he pulled away instantly, some of the foul liquid found its way into his mouth. He spat it out, rinsing his mouth, grimacing.

With enough gas siphoned and his vehicle refueled and drivable, we ventured into the central area of the rest stop, hoping to find a map for his journey. The main area and offices were the scene of ransacked chaos; papers and trash were strewn everywhere. There were bloodstains, too, but not the grotesque, abundant stains we'd witnessed at the hole where the military had been.

Lost in thought, I heard others call out. They'd found the map, tucked in the drawer of the central desk in the main office. As I headed back outside to meet them and see Axel off, a pervasive sense of unease settled over me. The air felt stale, and my nerves began to hum as the setting sun slowly surrendered to the absolute darkness of the wilderness. I looked at Bri; her face mirrored my apprehension. Kendry and Axel, however, seemed relatively normal, given the circumstances.

Not wanting to unnecessarily heighten tension, we remained calm, yet keenly aware of our surroundings, refusing to succumb to the delusion of safety just because nothing was immediately in sight. We ensured Axel was ready, providing him with some of our stored food and water. Then, with likely final words, we prepared to send him into encroaching night.

"Axel, before you go," I said, leaning into his window, "I want to thank you again for helping us, and for not attempting to rob or kill any of us. I know that sounds extreme, but the truth is, the state of the world is unknown, and there's no clear guidance. I wish you the best on your journey to your family. And no matter what, keep going."

"You know, you guys weren't bad yourselves," Axel replied, shifting into drive. "I wish we could've gotten to know each other more. Although, depending on how things turn out, we might just see each other again. Hopefully, all this crap will be over."

He waved, then began to pull away into deepening twilight. Just before he vanished, I gave his car one last tap on the roof. As I pulled my hand back, I felt something sticky, warm. Looking down, my hand was coated in clear slime, like thick drool from a dog, or something far more unsettling.

The warmth of it confirmed my immediate concern: something was near, or had been here very recently. I moved quickly back to the SUV. Darkness had fully descended now; staying was not a practical option. We grabbed our guns, keeping them close, ready. Wiping my hand on an old shirt I found on the ground, I noted the sticky residue it left; it would need scrubbing.

Unwilling to be hindered, I went directly to the rest stop restroom, straight to the sinks. As the water gushed, I registered an anomaly: Water still works. The pressure was weak, but the grid hadn't bled out yet.

I swiftly washed my hands. The vent over the far wall ticked; a soft rasp that stopped when I stopped. I waited. The room held its breath. Grimy lights and stained walls of the restroom framed a scene that could have been straight out of a horror film, but that was irrelevant. A potential threat lurked just beyond these walls, far more pressing than aesthetics.

After a few more seconds of careful listening, I heard nothing but the increasing whisper of the night breeze. Deciding to leave, I reached for the door. As it swung open, my eyes locked on it: one of the creatures, stealthily creeping up on our SUV, about thirty feet behind it.

I had to act. How many were there? I needed to prevent an attack on Bri and Kendry. Bri was alert, I could tell, but the creature had bypassed her natural perception, moving with eerie silence. I understood I could outmaneuver one of these things, based on what I'd seen earlier, and their attacks didn't seem strategically complex. I yelled loudly, a deliberate shout that drew its attention.

Bri and Kendry snapped their heads my way as the creature sprang into a monstrous sprint, directly at me. I wheeled, darting back into the restroom, slamming and locking the door. Then, I began kicking at the vent leading outside. The creature hit the door sooner than I expected, its bulk shaking the frame. Realizing escape through the vent was not feasible, I moved to the last stall, standing just outside it. The door exploded inward, and the creature burst in, drooling, its head tilted, its sight locked by angle, not by eyes. It paused for a single moment before pouncing. I plunged into a stall, sliding under the door into the next one, and then made a break for the exit before it could recover.

As I sprinted toward the SUV where Bri and Kendry waited, another nightmare materialized on the roof of the rest stop. Knowing I wouldn't make it to the vehicle directly, I frantically gestured for them to drive in circles around the building. Bri instantly understood, the SUV lurching forward. Meanwhile, Kendry was in the passenger seat, pistol clenched, knuckles white, scanning the darkness, ready for immediate action.

The roofline creaked. "Second one. Above," I shouted, already moving. Bri yanked the wheel and carved a tight orbit around the building. I dove under a burned-out sedan. Claw marks raked metal like foil. The creature lifted the car I hid beneath and threw it. I rolled clear and sprinted for the opposite door.

"Duck!" Kendry's voice cracked the night. I dropped. Five shots stitched the dark. Two went wide, one punched meat, one hit an arm, and the last went through an eye and into the cavity behind it. The thing sagged like someone unplugged it. Not dead. Slower. Enough.

Adrenaline blurred the pain in my side, and I ran at my absolute fastest. I flung myself into the backseat. We sped away into the night, the second monster standing there, watching, while the first twitched on the ground.

We drove for a few more miles before pulling off the road into a thick patch of woods. We called it prudent; exhaustion made the decision. We were all utterly drained from a long, treacherous day. Far off, something pinged like a cable under strain, and the woods answered with nothing. We lowered the back seats, grabbed blankets from the trunk, moved our rations aside, and quietly lay there, below the windows, doing our best to secure some sleep as the next day prepared to dawn.

The next morning, we awoke to muted sounds of people walking by our makeshift SUV campsite. Tucked behind a line of trees, unseen, we observed, needing to understand the current social state of the United States, at least in this area. The group passing by looked haggard, as if they hadn't slept in days. There were about ten of them, far too many for us to consider traveling with. Two were teenagers, six were between twenty and forty, and two appeared to be over fifty. They didn't seem to be family, but in these times, one could never really tell. Beyond their rough physical state and minor injuries, they were visibly armed, reinforcing our preference for the solitude of our small group.

Watching them fade into the distance, we prepared for the day, then continued our journey toward Auxi. With another four hours estimated for the trip, we wasted no time, alert to the potential presence of creatures in Ohio. Along the way, we noticed fewer broken-down cars on the road and a striking absence of attack signs. It was unnaturally clear, quiet, and tranquil, a chilling contrast to the world's uncertainty and destruction.

After about an hour, we came across a couple of bodies, apparent victims of monstrous attacks. Clear slime glazed the wounds and shone in tire ruts, pooling, warm. Though these were the first we'd seen on this leg of the trip, it wasn't surprising; we were passing through a small town. Creatures seemed to favor attacking towns over roaming the wilderness. The rest stop, of course, was an exception, but it might have been populated enough at some point to attract them.

Surveying carnage, ensuring we didn't drive over mutilated corpses, some with limbs scattered grotesquely, a faint crackle emerged from the silent radio.

As Bri continued to drive, seemingly unburdened by the previous day's pain, we adjusted the radio, tuning it repeatedly until the voice finally cut through the static, clear enough to understand. It was a young woman, tone confident, yet edged with desperate urgency. Unsure how long the transmission would last, or how it was even working, we leaned closer, tuning in. Then, a voice began to speak.

BOOK II.

SURFACE

WAR

VIII. ROAD TRIP

"Hello, I don't know if anyone can hear me, but I'm alive. Who I am isn't important now, but where I am could be of great value to you. This message isn't pre-recorded, and I'll go live on this channel every two hours. If it stops, that means I'm either dead or the radios are silent; in that case, the choice to travel here is solely yours to judge. However, today, I'm alive, and I have a place of solitude where you can all join me. The military seems to have lost control over the situation. Although they're not completely defeated and remain defensive against the creatures around the U.S., the head of state is no longer here, and every major city is being torn apart. If you'd like to escape this madness and join my group of survivors, make your way about eighty miles northwest of Minneapolis, Minnesota. Here, we have a safe place for you all with food, water, weapons, and shelter. I understand that this may sound like a hoax or a trap, and you're more than welcome to seek refuge elsewhere. Nonetheless, we need more help, and in times like these, we need each other. Please, stay alive and do your best to fight back against these creatures. We cannot lose."

The woman's voice faded into static, leaving us to absorb the implications of her transmission.

"The plan to get Auxi doesn't change," I stated, voice firm. "We need to find her, and then we'll determine our next steps."

"I agree, but can we trust this person? I mean, she just randomly comes on the radio after days of silence and then offers a place to go. I know I'm no genius, well, maybe a bit, but this smells like a trap. All those movies we watched didn't show us this stuff for dramatic effect," Kendry said, a skeptical glint in his eye.

"Listen," Bri began calmly, her reasoning sharp as always. "I say we find Auxi and learn as much about the broader situation as we can. These monsters lack fur, and fewer holes have formed in colder climates than warmer ones, so I believe moving north would be generally more advisable. I also understand that we've been under considerable strain, but don't forget what we're capable of. As long as we stay aware and rely on each other, we can handle an ambush if it proves to be one. I don't think this is an outright trap, but there is potential for it. Regardless, we need Auxi's input to make a full decision. Not to mention our parents, who I'm sure are fine. They raised us, and we're still alive."

"Sounds like that settles it," I affirmed. "We should be in Columbus soon. I know the situation is fluid, but let's proceed with caution and assume these things are widespread... Maintain vigilance as we go. I can see smoke on the horizon ahead."

About two hours from Auxi's location, with ample daylight remaining, we arrived at a scene of burning cars and erratic people running on the road. These were the first civilians we'd seen since that morning, and as we watched their movements, it was clear their flight wasn't merely from the flames. More of the same disturbing monsters appeared, blank glares fixed on us, and they seemed to pivot, darting directly our way, disregarding everyone else in their path.

The one sprinting at us didn't veer like the rest; it locked on us and ran as if we were the only warm thing left on Earth, trampling bodies without breaking stride. We'd stopped. Bri's knuckles whitened on the wheel. A second creature stood in the lane ahead, motionless, as if it had been placed there.

"Break left-right, use the cars," I said. "If they chase one of us, the other gets the SUV." Bri nodded once. Kendry swallowed.

The sound hit, not from a mouth, but from seams along their ribs, a kettle-high shriek that made the air feel thin. Not painful. Just wrong.

We flung the doors and split. Bri and Kendry went left, and I went right. My shadow stretched under a dead charter bus. A prickle climbed my neck. I slid beneath the undercarriage as claws raked pavement inches behind my heel.

The bus lifted. Not all the way, just enough. One creature shouldered the frame while the other folded itself to slip under. Teamwork. Not instinct. My model of them cracked and reformed mid-crawl.

Creeping out from under the bus before I could be caught or crushed, I escaped from the side toward the end being pivoted upon. Processing everything while fleeing, I slid over the hood of a car and bolted right before dropping out of sight and heading left. I wasn't sure if the creatures relied on sight, but I slipped into a nearby van out of their line of view while they dropped the bus and searched for me.

Making the most of this brief reprieve, I began searching the van, using chaotic noises from outside to mask my movements. Shifting a bag of clothes, my hand brushed against something unexpected: martial arts equipment. The bag contained a few boards and some bamboo swords, which were of no use in the immediate crisis. However, beneath the bag was a long box. I opened it, expecting more training gear, and found a full-size katana, sheathed.

Unsure if the forty-inch blade was in usable condition, or even how I'd managed to discover it, I picked it up and began removing the sheath. Visually, the blade looked pristine, perfectly sharpened. It felt light, and the deep red tones of the metal gave it an almost majestic quality. The blade came out clean, edge true, oil scent catching in my throat. Just as I picked up some clothes from the van to test its sharpness, I sensed the creatures drawing closer.

The sword, I decided, would have to do. Figuring it might fare better than bullets, I readied myself to exit the vehicle. Pushing open the back doors of the van, I burst out. The searching monsters immediately noticed me, a couple of cars ahead of the van. As I moved to another vehicle for cover, I sensed them approaching, one gaining on me with alarming speed.

Channeling my prior martial arts training and days at the airsoft field, I understood their velocity and was confident I could match it. Distancing myself from the vehicle I'd used for cover, I waited until I felt the presence of one sharply, distinct pressure on my nerves.

I didn't backflip. I let it overshoot. As it lunged, I pivoted on my front foot and dropped, blade vertical. Its spine met steel in a clean, sliding draw, our opposing force doing the work. Tar-black hissed. It collapsed in a boneless twitch, clear foam stringing its teeth.

Seemingly unfazed by what it had witnessed, the creature that had initially trailed me stood motionless, staring directly at me. I maintained eye contact, assessing its intentions. Just as I formulated my next move, the monster emitted another ventilated shriek. The noise then ceased, and the holes closed, fading back into the fleshy mass of the creature's body. Sound without a mouth meant pressure sacks, not lungs.

Continuing to hold its gaze, the creature then burst toward me with speed far exceeding anything I'd seen prior. It closed the fifteen-car gap between us before I could fully react, leaving me exposed. Quickly raising my arms to defend myself, the creature rammed into me, sending me flying twenty feet backward into a nearby vehicle. Unsure why it hadn't gone for a killing blow, I gathered myself enough to pick up the sword I'd dropped and returned it to its sheath, which I'd strapped across my body.

Pushing through throbbing pain and unsteadiness, I stood and looked at the creature once more. Though my body felt shattered and my lungs were relieved of their air, I could tell it was preparing to strike again. However, this time, its razor-sharp claws were fully extended, seemingly primed for a fatal blow.

Recognizing I was too disoriented to outrun it, likely from the impact, I prepared to meet this thing head-on. My training and countless moments of performing under pressure converged in that instant. I took a deep, painful, centering breath. As it began to sprint at me, I adopted a stance I'd learned long ago, planting my rear foot on my toes while my front foot remained steady, aimed at the enemy.

Gripping the katana with both hands, I unsheathed it, timing the decisive blow, gaze fixed on the monster. It pounced over cars, covering the five feet between us faster than any regular person could perceive. But I could.

It came again with claws this time. I centered, rear foot light, front foot aimed through it, and drew as it crossed that final yard. Steel met face. The follow-through stuck; my core lagged behind my intent.

When the creature turned, I saw my blade had cut it, splitting its eyes enough that it could no longer see. However, I looked down to see drops of red blood hitting the ground. Checking myself, I found the creature had also landed a blow, slicing my left side open about seven inches in length and up to two inches deep at worst, judging by the increasing flow of blood. I sheathed the blade one-handed and pressed a shirt into the wound, breath counting down from ten so I wouldn't black out. The creature bled dark and retreated, dragging itself off the road.

Unable to finish off the creature due to the sustained injury, I sheathed the katana, prioritizing finding the others before I lost too much blood. Looking back in the direction where it had landed, I noticed a trail of dark fluid leading away from my position and off the road. Although I didn't know much about these creatures at the time, I was piecing together their behavior and a seemingly growing sense of self-preservation. These killing machines, which once seemed emotionless, had now shown me self-awareness, strategy, and unity. All things I registered in the moment, but was in no condition to dwell on.

Looking back toward where we'd left the SUV, I saw Bri and Kendry against another vehicle, a mix of confusion and irritation on their faces. As I moved toward them, I noticed my left leg feeling weaker and heavier. Essentially dragging my left side by that point, I finally got close enough to see they were being held at gunpoint by three individuals in suits.

Unsure of their objective, I hid behind a nearby car and watched closely. By this point, Bri had recognized my presence and had subtly tapped Kendry with her shoe in a way the suited people couldn't see, but he knew what it meant.

Sensing he was once again in a precarious situation, Kendry's mind began to churn. Bri and I could almost feel his thought process. Before I could discern his plan or receive a signal, he blurted out my location to the assailants. "Kendry—" I started, but he was already talking loudly, eyes never leaving the main assailant. "He's over there!" he shouted, pointing in my direction.

Upon hearing his words, I saw two of the suited people running in my direction, guns still drawn, while the third, who appeared to be their leader, remained behind.

Feeling my adrenaline surge again, I managed to move well enough to lead these two on a chase through the chaos. Clenching my side as I ran, pushing a shirt against the wound, the bleeding had slowed, but not significantly. Placing my faith in Kendry, I decided to compel myself onward as long as I could and observe his strategy unfold. Although I was inherently faster than these individuals, my injury made the contest more even. I trusted Kendry's plan, but I knew my time was limited before they caught me.

By this point in my recollection, we had observed a wide range of human traits: resilience, resolve, adaptation, and now, trust. Seriously injured, I had chosen to follow Kendry's plan, deliberately placing myself at risk. In times like these, putting faith in others can be the difference between life and death. But when you're compromised, when you know your autonomy is about to be lost, the only rational action is to step into uncertainty with those you trust.

This understanding of human nature marked a return to the past. It was back to square one, where there were no systems, no comforts, and no promise of a better tomorrow. No one knew what was going on. The internet was nonexistent, radios barely worked, and now it seemed as though humans were hunting humans. How could this happen at the perfect time to band together as a species? This was yet another sign that humanity isn't what it seems. It exists in constant transition, catering to the beholder's eye.

Regardless of this, I knew we had to survive. If I were going to do anything, it was to put faith in those who had faith in me and forge a way forward. Not only us, but everyone needed to do what they thought would lead to their survival. While we hadn't resorted to extremes of murder or thievery, we understood we would encounter those who had.

Even so, there's a reason you're hearing my recollection and not theirs.

As I ran from these two individuals, Kendry focused on handling the boss. Given the ongoing chaos among other people on the road, leaving the situation unpredictable, Kendry capitalized. Recognizing a wildly driving car heading their way, he bought some time by distracting the suited leader, asking what they were after.

The oddly tidy and clean-suited woman said nothing, simply raising her gun and taking aim at Bri. Just then,

Kendry turned toward Bri as she turned to him. They pushed their hands together, sending each other moving to the side as the car flew in and struck the mystery lady, pinning and crushing her between the vehicle that Kendry and Bri were held against.

Looking at the woman who lay motionless between the two cars, they then moved to find me.

I had run and evaded the pursuers to the best of my ability, even landing a slash at one of their legs. However, the blood loss was taking its toll. With no choice but to slow down, I found a corner formed by two cars to take momentary refuge.

As I waited for them to arrive, my consciousness began to waver, disorientation setting in. The last thing I remember seeing was a shadow standing over me before being kicked to the side. The person who remained stood and picked me up, carrying me away, but that's where the memory ends.

The next thing I knew, we were back in the SUV, with Kendry at the wheel. Bri was in the back with me, vigilantly monitoring my condition. When I attempted to move my head to assess the situation, she gently stopped me, offered me some water, and eased me back onto my side. Bri steadied my head with two fingers at my temple. "Don't." Her voice stayed clinical, but her hand didn't move for a breath longer than it needed to. Heat flickered through the pain. "You're stitched. Don't make me do it twice."

"What happened? Is it nighttime? How long was I unconscious?" I asked, my head throbbing.

"After you ran and distracted the other two," Bri explained, "we were able to get the suit holding us hostage distracted enough not to notice a speeding car that then crushed her. Then, we went looking for you and found the last two suits standing over you. Before they could do anything, however, I was able to interfere with the one in front of you, kicking them out of the way into a nearby fire. Kendry took care of the other one using your sword, although we don't believe he killed the person." Kendry's eyes remained fixed on the road ahead.

"Yeah... I hope I didn't kill anyone. I understand things have quickly turned dire, but I'd like to continue my life without being a murderer," Kendry said, a hint of unease in his voice. "You can survive losing an arm, right?"

"As for our location," Bri continued, "we're now about five minutes away from Columbus and twenty minutes from where Auxi and her team were staying. We took a separate route that added a little time to our journey, but we didn't want to enter the city through any standard methods. Doing so may have led us into an even more perilous situation, as the world continues to lose its grip on sanity. Many people seem to be heading west rather than north, but we chose not to take that chance. The Midwest would make sense given its vastness, but there may be more of those things as well. Better to avoid it altogether."

She paused briefly.

During her pause, I had the opportunity to observe her from a different perspective. My head was resting on a roll of clothes in her lap, a setup I would never have expected. Although still Bri, seeing her care for me like this opened my mind to emotions I'd never considered before. I experienced what I thought was an authentic feeling of being genuinely cared for. Not that I hadn't received care, my parents cared for me, and my friends too, but this was different. It felt warmer and more personal, not someone fulfilling an obligation of their position in my life.

Not understanding what this feeling meant, I tried to consider the media I'd consumed, what this would mean if it were fiction. Nonetheless, before my thoughts could stray too far, she gave me a strange look, seemingly sensing my mind might be wandering.

Her actions remained a revelation to me, but I simply assumed she was genuinely concerned.

"I also would prefer not to engage in any additional fights since your wounds are still fresh, although already seeming to heal well, considering what happened. None of your vital organs were slashed, and I was able to stitch you up efficiently using our med kit, but don't move too much or you may cause the bleeding to return," Bri said as we neared the city.

I checked the dressing: gauze was stacked, taped tight, and steri-strips were pulling skin together where the cut was clean. The pain was more than noticeable, but it gradually subsided.

"What about the suits? Did you two ever find out anything more about them?" I asked, raising myself from her lap and leaning my back against the other window.

"No, they had nothing identifiable, nor did they say anything. They all had an empty stare and seemed unbothered by what was happening around them. Their focus was oddly centered on us, but it was for more than murder. I could tell they wouldn't kill us; otherwise, I would have stopped that woman sooner, but I wanted to give her a chance to speak," Bri paused to take a sip of water.

"One thing was strange, though. When we walked by where the first suit was pinned, she was no longer there, and there was more space between the cars that had collided than before. We thought it was odd, but with the state you were in, we couldn't waste any further time in that location," Bri explained with a serious look on her face. The steel bumper still bowed inward, a smear like graphite along the crease. The license plate hung bent, two fresh chips in its paint. Someone, or something, had managed to work itself free.

"No blood left behind or anything?" I asked.

Bri shook her head.

"Interesting. It seems that no matter what happens, there's no more sense of normalcy or logic. I don't fully understand the predicaments and challenges that face us, but we need to be ready for anything if we want to see another year," I said aloud as we slowed to a stop before entering the city.

Questioning our halt, I looked over to see that the city had been destroyed, but not by the monsters. This destruction appeared to be the result of earthquakes, and there were still plenty of people, offering a sign of hope that this monster takeover hadn't been completed there yet.

Entering the city, we drove as far as we could before reaching seemingly unmoving traffic. Upon realizing we weren't going anywhere and wanting to find Auxi without further delay, we pulled the SUV into a nearby side alley. We exited the vehicle, with Bri assisting me in my departure.

Taking what we could carry and deemed critical, we covered the SUV with trash to conceal it. With two miles ahead of us, we didn't know how long it would take to find her, or if she was even aware of the current situation. Regardless, we proceeded on foot, blending in with the crowd, vigilant for any more suited individuals.

Traveling through the street-lit evening, we surveyed the crowd around us. Many people had bandages and varying injuries that one might assume were from the creatures. Oddly enough, though, most of the injuries we saw didn't seem to be from an attack, but mainly from earthquakes, providing more evidence for us to believe the monsters hadn't yet made their way there.

We also noticed that, despite the chaos, a sense of organization wasn't entirely lost, and that soldiers and police officers were helping to guide people through the crowds and direct them to various destinations. Out of curiosity, I asked one of the soldiers where everyone was going and what was happening.

"Everyone's being sent to central state safety camps. The coasts were hit far worse, and the situation is ever-changing. Now, please continue, sir," the soldier said, guiding people along.

"What about the monsters? These creatures with the face of a bear, body of a frog, and legs of a wolf?" I pressed, wanting to learn what the military knew about them.

The soldier's face turned pale after this question, revealing his knowledge.

"That's not a topic I'm allowed to speak on freely. All I can say is to stay away, use cover, and pray that they don't want you," the soldier said, moving elsewhere in the crowd.

Considering what I'd just heard, I repeated it back to Kendry, who couldn't hear through the crowd's noise. As I explained my thoughts on how something larger was unfolding, and that the soldier knew more than he revealed, I felt that an even greater threat was at play. Although I didn't know what lay ahead at that moment, we knew it was more crucial than ever to find Auxi and get in contact with our parents. Bri's earlier logic about colder zones snapped into focus. If the ground itself were a throat, bedrock and frost lines might slow the burrowing. Or not. We needed data, not hope.

As we approached the hotel where Auxi and her team were staying, within half a mile, the crowd came to a halt. Curious, we had Kendry stand on a nearby trash can, where he saw people moving back calmly at first, then running. Avoiding the stampede, Bri helped me move to a small door entry on the street while Kendry hid in the next alley.

Not knowing what was happening, Bri looked down the street to see that a small hole had opened in the ground, just large enough for two or so monsters to fit. As the hole ceased to expand, the crowd stopped running, and soldiers pushed forward.

Aware that these monsters were using such openings to enter the surface, the soldiers immediately surrounded it, pointing their rifles at the edges and center. After waiting thirty seconds for something to happen, no monsters appeared. To confirm nothing was coming, one soldier cracked a glow stick and dropped it down the hole. As it fell, it seemed they didn't see it illuminate anything or hit anything besides the wall on the way down; their reaction remained calm.

Assuming the area was safe enough, the soldiers urged the half of the crowd that had stayed back to move forward with caution. As they moved the crowd along, avoiding the opening, I couldn't help but feel something was amiss. I noticed Bri also sensed something, but couldn't pinpoint the exact nature of the feeling. Convinced that something would happen eventually, we returned to the road. As the on-foot crowd continued to move, vehicles were strategically positioned at the very front and back to minimize the risk of injuries.

Moving onward, we began to see the hotel where Auxi and her teammates had been. Breaking free from the crowd, we headed in that direction a couple of blocks over. Upon arrival, we were shocked to find the building had partially collapsed, leaving a massive pile of rubble around a few surviving structures.

Not wasting a minute to assume she was inside when this happened, we looked around for someone who knew something, but everyone passing through was simply passing through, not from the area. Heading to the parking lot, we found a beat-up coach with our school's logo, an eagle flying at an angle in front of a blazing sun, on the side.

Going to the door, we found it was jammed, and I was in no shape to open it with my side still sliced. Switching me off to Kendry, Bri went to the door and delivered two solid front kicks before the mechanism gave way. Upon entering the bus, the putrid smell from the trapped boy's legs filled the air; rotten flesh. Although it was hard to see through the dimly lit bus, we could discern enough to tell that something malicious had occurred.

Looking for clues, we had to step around the mangled remains of whoever was there. We'd seen enough carnage to last a lifetime, but the chilling image of a face sitting in the corner with no body attached made it all worse. Body parts were everywhere and seemed to have been eradicated by something, but the space was too tight for the monsters we saw to attack.

Focusing back on finding Auxi, we examined the remains and faces to see if any were hers, but none were. We also took note of a human-sized hole in the ceiling, which burst outward, leading us to conclude that whatever had done this had left. Another observation was that the people on the bus were from Auxi's team, based on their clothing, meaning these weren't random individuals who'd run into the bus to hide. One corner held wrongness arranged like a choice, shoelaces coiled in four neat stacks, teeth lined up smallest to largest along the edge of a seat.

The silver lining was that only about ten people's remains were found, suggesting the other ten were somewhere else. Maintaining hope, we left the bus and went to the undercarriage compartments to find Auxi's bag, assuming they'd been placed or left there for swift departure if needed.

Opening the undercarriage, it was surprisingly clean and not covered in blood, unlike the inside of the bus. Looking through bags of spikes and clothes, we found Auxi's bag toward the back. As we opened her bag and looked for anything that could help, we found a note with some instructions.

"Hey guys, I wasn't sure if you'd find this note or if the bus would even still be here, but I assume you have if you're reading this. I'm writing this on May 15, right before what's left of the team heads toward the Midwest. Whatever attacked those on the bus was small and deadly. I couldn't get a clear view of it as the rest of us hurried out of sight, but it didn't seem to have any eyes. I would say more, but I'm short on space. Follow the crowd, if they're still there, and we'll meet again," Auxi's note read.

"May 15? They were just here then. No way they've gotten far," Kendry said, hint of renewed hope in his voice.

"Judging these bodies, it has to have been at least twelve hours. Meaning we have a chance to find her if we move quickly," Bri assessed.

"Yeah, true. But what about D?" Kendry gestured to me, still supporting me. "I think he's still a bit hurt to move at the speed you're thinking about."

Knowing he was right, Bri and I decided it would be best to continue along with the larger group, leisurely making our way toward Auxi. As it neared 10:00 PM, according to Bri's analog watch, we heard another sound of panic and screams as people ran forward. This time, the threat seemed more severe as gunshots followed behind the running and screams.

Not being in good condition to run and force our way through a crowd, we went to one of the buildings a couple of streets over and found it was located in front of a small motel. Recognizing that no one was inside the front desk area, we opted for the motel and tried to open the door, but it was locked.

With no time to find another place to go as the crowd continued to spread and people came our way, Bri kicked the door. Despite her strength, the door only folded, straining the motel's structure with each kick. Realizing people were getting closer, Bri broke the window and jumped in. As she got up to open the main door, lifting the heavy bars keeping the door shut, I could see she now had cuts on her face and some on her jacket.

Quickly rushing to grab a handful of keys, we hurried back outside and to the backside of the motel, making sure to go into a room that no one could see us enter.

Entering the first room that opened for us, halfway down the row of rooms, Kendry helped me inside, and Bri quickly locked the door while making sure the curtains were softly closed.

As we sat in silence, listening to the banging of doors and the shrieks of new small creatures running around, we couldn't help but hope Auxi was in a safe place. Taking off the katana I'd picked up by removing the strap, I unsheathed it and sat on the floor facing the door. Hearing the commotion and gunshots for the next ten minutes, we all remained low to avoid any undesired injuries.

Once that ceased, we remained diligent, as silence didn't mean everything was clear. Sitting for the next couple of hours, we eventually passed out and could do nothing but hope no one or thing broke into the room.

IX. COLLECTIVE

The next morning, around 7:00 AM, we woke still streaked with dirt and the tacky black residue from yesterday. We needed clothes, food, and water. Bri took the katana, its stealth beating out bullets, and she and Kendry slipped out toward the office. I locked the door and sat on the floor with my back to it, counting breaths until the knocks came hard and fast.

Through the peephole: Bri, blank-faced and blazing; Kendry, wild-eyed. I unchained the door, and they spilled in, dragging plastic bags. Both were smeared with a grim mix of red and black, the tar already seeping in where it touched warm fabric.

"You two okay? What happened?" I asked, clutching my side.

"Started easy," Kendry said between breaths. "The office was empty. First aid, water, wrapped sandwiches; it was a score. The laundry room had clothes in the machines, so we grabbed whatever was dry. Then Bri froze."

Bri's gaze stayed on a narrow crack in the curtain, tone unwavering. "Someone ran around the corner, being chased by one of the small ones. They dove into a room where others were hiding. An argument followed. The runner came back out bleeding from the neck with a knife slipping from the gash. The thing had their scent already. It was too late. Three of the people blocked us in the laundry room. One said we were 'already dead.' Another raised a gun."

"And she... bro... she just—" Kendry chopped the air. "Buddy had his hand on the trigger and then... no hand. It hit the tile like a wet glove."

"It was him or us," Bri said. "We ran. One of the small ones waited in the hall. I saw its fibers twitch and cut as it pounced. They're much faster than the big ones. They have no eyes, just a slick, hair-fuzzed head like a ball with too much mouth. Webbed feet. Four claws. It loses traction on slick tile if you sidestep, a short skid before it resets." She peeled a clot of black from her sleeve. "I took the legs as it landed on me. It kept biting on reflex. I cut between the head and the body and then pinned the head."

"Damn, so these aren't just baby versions of those other things. How many variants could there be?" I posed rhetorically.

"We'll adapt," Bri answered, gaze still on the curtains. "They're dangerous, not impregnable." She eased the fabric wider one finger at a time, listening.

We waited ten minutes; ears out, watching for any shadow that broke the slivers of light across the carpet. Silence held, fly-buzz thinning, then stopping, then nothing. We decided on showers, one at a time. Bri took the first; the bathroom door closed, and the pipes complained before steadying. The water flowed, indicating that the system was still alive to some extent.

She was in the bathroom for fifteen minutes before she emerged. When she did, I felt as though I was seeing her for the first time in weeks. Her hair was pulled back neatly, keeping her semi-curly strands out of her face. Her clothes, though not her usual style, worked well; she'd used a shoelace as a belt for oversized jeans and tucked in the flannel shirt just enough to create a slight puff around the edges. She made Kendry and me look like mud farmers fresh from a shift.

Bri decided it was best for me to go next, given my injuries, with Kendry being the least compromised. Stepping into the shower, cold water had never felt so good. It pained me to stand there as my body was shocked to life, but I'd grown accustomed to these types of showers during my mental conditioning training. It also helped to constrict blood vessels, preventing any additional bleeding.

As I washed away blood, filth, and tar, I watched them ribbon down the drain, clinging to the steel before giving up. The images hit between breaths: the world burning while rivers ran clean; green thriving through ruin; creatures moving like livestock through fields that didn't belong to us anymore. Right before each strip of vision arrived, my stitches tugged tight, a zippering pinch and a faint taste of hot metal at the back of my tongue; then it passed.

I tried to shake the images, but they persisted, pervading my thoughts and revealing truths I didn't want to see, or perhaps was scared to admit. While I managed to suppress the thoughts enough to continue cleaning my stitches, I couldn't help but delve deeper into what was happening. These creatures seemed to attack humans, yes, but they didn't destroy everything. Even the earthquakes had primarily targeted populated areas, leaving more natural landscapes untouched. I began to consider this connection further, building a bridge of understanding.

However, lost in thought, Kendry knocked on the door.

"Hey, man." Knock, knock, knock. "You all good in there? If so, I'd like to clean myself off too if you don't mind."

"Sure, Ken, just give me a moment," I said as I quickly dried off and pulled on the navy blue coveralls Bri had found.

Stepping out of the shower with the top of the coveralls down, Kendry rushed in and immediately jumped into the running water. I shook my head and went over to Bri for her to examine my wound; she'd always been my personal doctor in the rare situations I needed one.

As she checked the no longer bleeding stitches, she remarked on how well I was healing. Although we'd always healed quickly, this was the first time we'd seen such a rapid recovery from an injury this severe; even her cuts and bruises were almost gone. Capillary refill normal, clotting time normal; it was the skin that seemed to hurry, knitting as if it had a head start. The stitches remained, but the wound looked half as shallow as before and showed no signs of infection; a surprise considering all that had happened.

Bri found this especially odd but reasoned we were simply gifted in some way and learned not to focus on it. That was the best explanation we had for our accelerated healing and advanced physical and mental abilities. Not because we weren't curious, but because we had no means of testing anything. We could have gone to a doctor to have our levels checked and run tests. Still, the facts would remain: we were different from most, and in the chaotic times we lived in, it was a blessing more than anything. It also helped that Auxi and Kendry were both extraordinary in their own ways, making us seem less of an outlier in that regard.

As we sat there, Bri shifted the conversation back to the day before, to when we were in the car.

"D, what was that in the SUV yesterday? I know there were many concurrent events, but the look in your eye told me something. I want to know what that something is," she said, gaze steady, slightly less deadpan than usual.

"I don't know, to be frank. I think it was the moment that got to me, and my brain was still waking up. If I knew, I'd tell you, but I don't. But wait, I had this visi—"

"You're lying," Bri interjected, cutting me off. "I saw it in your eyes. After all our time together, you try to lie now. That proves my point without a doubt. I know you too well. Even if I didn't, you know how well I can read people."

"Bri, let's do this another time. I need to tell you what I saw." I kept my voice even. "I had a strange vision in the shower. Images from what felt like the future… or maybe the past. The world as we knew it was gone."

"This vision, did you see the creatures in it? I know what you're doing with this conversation, but this is more important."

"I did, they were—"

Bri cut me off once more. "Standing on the burning world we knew, while the environment around them seemed to prosper. Yeah, I've seen that too. Did you also see the figures with them? They looked human-shaped, but I couldn't make it out before it ended. I saw it last night and woke up around 3 AM after it ended."

"I didn't see that, but I wouldn't be astonished if there were. Who knows what else will show up as this thing gets worse," I said, referring to the overall situation.

Before we could continue our conversation, Kendry flung the bathroom door open. He stepped out, asking what the "thing" we saw was. After explaining it once more, he quickly responded that he didn't see that in his mind, but he'd realized something else.

It was our graduation date.

"We can't consider this graduation without Auxi," Bri stated.

"That's true; it seems we should hurry and find her," I said, pulling up the top of my coveralls.

"How's the wound, man? I didn't see a whole lot of blood in the bathroom, and you seem fine."

"It's healing great, better than I would have expected. It's almost healed enough to remove the stitches. I just had Bri help me wrap it up, but I should be one hundred percent healed in one more day. Bri is healing nicely, too; you can hardly tell she ever had those cuts."

"I don't know what's up with you two, but I should start eating what y'all eat. My hand wound is healing nicely, but it's nowhere near as fast as yours. I thought your recovery from a grade two ankle sprain in three days was quick, but this puts that to shame. You too, Bri," Kendry said as he prepared to leave.

"I can hardly believe it myself, but I've always been quicker to do things than others and never really got hurt as a kid. Maybe I just had a good diet growing up," I said as I stood up to stretch.

"What about the blood loss? I feel like that would affect anyone," Kendry added.

"I can feel the decreased energy, but since I usually have more than an average person, I may be demoted to the stamina and energy of an above-average man, at least until I can replenish completely."

Making sure we had the last of our things packed among three book bags they found, Bri listened again at the door. Positive it was clear, she opened and took point, me and Kendry behind her in that order. I'd usually run point, but she was still in better condition than I was. With a katana strapped to my waist while Bri and Kendry both had guns, we eased back toward the street we'd fled the night prior.

Outside, bullets and bodies of humans and monsters alike lay sprawled across the asphalt. The small ones were easier to study up close: enormous shark-mouths rimmed with razors; hair along the limbs; webbed feet ending in four distinct phalanges and claws. Their mouths were full of human flesh and blood; far more than one could consume alone. Here and there tar-blood had skinned glossy under the sun, and when a breeze passed the surface made a faint cooling crackle like lacquer.

Looking for new transportation, we found a smaller sedan. I couldn't help but notice numerous people hiding in nearby buildings. Although I could only see a few, I sensed their fear. I detected a vast presence of people filling the interiors of these structures. Unable to help them, we checked the car to ensure it functioned properly and had enough fuel before getting back on the now-clear road, continuing our search for Auxi.

As I drove I checked the rearview, the last place we knew Auxi had been, and saw one of the suits from before standing in the middle of the street. Blink. Gone. Bri gave me a look like she'd read my mind. We didn't say it. We headed west.

Halfway through the day, we began to pass through the outskirts of Indianapolis. Judging by remnants and signs of struggle, we could tell the crowd had passed through there. The situation must have gone dire based on the bodies that remained. Some were full of bullet holes, others were dismembered or had chunks bitten out of them, and some were contorted in unimaginable ways. It was a bloodbath of death and destruction.

Although these sights were painful to witness, especially for Kendry, who tried to look elsewhere, we remained diligent along our path.

The world wasn't tipping into madness anymore; it had submerged. Desperation was thick enough to smell even over rot and iron. A flock of birds coasted low over an empty freeway, unbothered. Green shot up through a heaved seam in the median. A culvert ran clearer than any city river I'd seen in my lifetime. People still moving acted like anyone would when the floor keeps vanishing underfoot. Those who couldn't move had been left, or were on their way.

To think that things had deteriorated that quickly was unbelievable. Not in a good way, but the fact that our systems and way of life, which we believed to be so superior, could be upended in such a way was mind-blowing. Although I was unsure how the rest of the world fared, I could only imagine it was no better than we were. Destruction had been all the same. Why wouldn't the aftermath be?

Pondering all of this as we drove down the road, listening to the low static of the radio, I heard a voice attempting to come through. I turned it up, and sure enough, it was the woman from before. This time, however, she sounded more fatigued and as if she had a dry throat. Turning it up a bit more to ensure we could make out words, we listened intently.

"Greetings to anyone listening. First, I would like to remind those listening for the first time in a while that this is a live broadcast. To help confirm this, I would like to verify that the current date is May 17, 2025. Our sanctuary remains a safe place; however, we have increased our efforts to gather resources and materials as more and more people arrive. I'm thankful for everyone who comes, but from this point on, we will have no choice but to confiscate weaponry upon arrival. I know this may not sound pleasing, given current circumstances, but after the incident involving a new member of the community, we have been left with no choice but to take action. New developments and changes are occurring faster than we could have imagined. However, the military remains active in a few areas around the US and is holding off the creatures. We're unsure how long this may last, but there is still hope.

"Additionally, networks may be down, but some radio stations, such as this one, continue to operate. We don't know how or why, but use this as a sign that we can recover. We can come back from this. Please be careful and stay alive;

I'll be back in two hours. Remember, we are eighty miles northwest of Minneapolis, Minnesota. Find us and join our resistance to this extinction attempt on humanity," the voice said as the transmission ended.

"What are y'all thinking?" Kendry asked as we finished listening.

"I believe we should keep listening, but it's the best line we have so far. However, this doesn't change any of our immediate plans," Bri said, eyes closed in concentration.

"I agree, we should keep an ear out for the radio and see what else they say. Although it sounds like it has potential, we have to fulfill our first goal and find Auxi," I said as I kept driving.

A highway sign informed travelers of a military camp eight miles ahead. Fifty feet short of the checkpoint, a loudspeaker crackled to life, telling us to stop. I rolled to a halt behind a Jersey barrier while four rifles leveled down the single-lane funnel. Heat wobbled off the blacktop.

That's when soldiers began to approach with their guns drawn. Trusting that these soldiers hadn't been corrupted, we put our hands in the air. This trust was more so the fact that Bri hadn't reacted as such, and I felt no sense of malevolence either. Once at my window, I made sure I had permission first and then lowered it.

"Hey, I apologize about doing this, but we have to make sure your vehicle doesn't have any bombs or monsters in it. I understand that may sound excessive, but these times have made people act in ways you wouldn't imagine. All I need you three to do is wait patiently, and we'll let you know when you're in clear," the soldier said.

He spoke to us much more informally than I would have imagined, but given the state of things, I couldn't blame him. By that stage, the chain of command was shattered, and everyone was trying to survive. Being human and personable meant more to some than being dictatorial, and we happened to come across one of the former.

"What about these guys?" Kendry asked, referring to five soldiers pointing guns at us.

"Them... they're there just in case. Assume everyone's a threat until proven otherwise. I just prefer not to be an ass about it," the soldier said, then hand-signaled more troops forward.

New soldiers arrived with mirrors on poles to inspect the vehicle, while we were instructed to exit. Standing on the side of the road while they examined the car inside and out, I noticed Bri sharply look back the way we'd come. Feeling the same sense of dread, I looked over to see a larger monster rapidly approaching.

"Sixty feet," the soldier I'd spoken to called. Four rifles came up, two kneeling, two standing, lanes of fire staggered. "Thirty." The thing accelerated. "Now." The volley slapped into its chest; black flecks spattered and landed on the pavement with a quiet hiss. It stumbled, slid, and collapsed three feet short, leaving a glossy streak like fresh roadway. The soldier stepped in and put two rounds from a heavy pistol into the head.

The sound rang in our eardrums; not much had been left unscathed in those few days, our ears included.

"Never hurts to give it a double-up," the soldier said, a small smile cracking his face.

"These things usually move in groups of two or more, so I imagine others aren't far behind. Go ahead and let them through," the soldier said as he received a clear signal from his search team.

Heading back toward the barricade and passing through the opening the soldier had created for us, he left us with a few words before our departure.

"Just keep going until you get through a bit more into Indianapolis. Once you arrive, you'll see another barricade similar to this one. A large group of people came through here yesterday, as well as some soldiers from another unit, so the route should be relatively clear."

"You wouldn't have happened to see track team or some young women with matching green tracksuits, would you?" Kendry asked.

"Not that I recall, but there were piles of people in the back of some trucks and buses, so I'm sure this group you're looking for is doing fine. Radios are a bit wonky, but communication with other locations has been reliable so far. I've yet to hear of anything too disastrous, but things are changing every day. Just keep going and you'll see the next station. From there, they should guide you to a safe area that we set up. It's still a work in progress, but it beats being out here. Stay there for a bit, and you should be fine; however, it may also not hurt to keep moving. There are only so many resources available to us; we're going to have to pick and go ourselves soon. You all be safe, maybe we'll meet again," the soldier said as he went back to the barricade and closed it off.

As we drove away, more shooting started behind us; closer, louder, at least two more targets by the rhythm. Boot soles would stick in the cooling, tar-like blood for a while back there. They sounded equipped to handle it, so we continued along our way.

With about an hour to go, we prepared for our 2:00 PM arrival time. Switching drivers to give myself a break, I sat in the back and looked out the window as Bri took over. In that moment, all I could think about was where Auxi could be and if she'd been involved in whatever happenings were not "too disastrous" as the soldier said. Remaining diligent and clutching my newly found katana, I sat in wait as we continued our search.

Looking back, it all felt alien and too natural at the same time. My existence was now defined by survival, not by mundane tasks. Carrying a katana and traveling with firearms we'd scavenged, soldiers didn't even question us. Witnessing the violent deaths of both humans and creatures. It was a new reality where I didn't feel out of place.

Perhaps it was elongated trauma or delayed shock, but I was just numb enough for the situation. While most twenty-year-olds might freeze or fracture, I adapted. I leaned into chaos to find a way to survive; I had to.

It wasn't just me, but the three of us. Kendry was still a bit shakier than Bri or me, but he remained fundamentally unchanged. He was still Kendry, now with an intense need to survive and developing skills to handle situations from a strategic standpoint. This talent would become vital later.

I don't think there was anything particularly unusual about us; who's to say anyone still alive would have their sanity intact anyway?

Keeping our goals and survival paramount, along with our drive to figure it all out, helped us stay on track.

We had no idle hands to become a devil's workshop. Unfortunately, we lived in an idle world that had become Satan's resort. Surrounded by hell and its spawn, we had to do what was necessary to survive. Up to that point, I believed we'd managed to get by without accumulating too many transgressions.

I never would have imagined being able to openly carry a sword or be armed, using the real world as we did those airsoft fields. I especially couldn't imagine this with how I looked and the hate that came with it. For the percentage of the population, especially where I was from, it's a fuel for nightmares.

Nonetheless, none of that mattered anymore. Anyone clinging to outdated grudges or rigid political views in a world under attack belonged there anyway. For the rest of us, we just had to forge a new path forward.

And that's precisely what we would continue to do.

The next checkpoint ran the same play. Search mirrors, weapons ready, a loudspeaker that clipped the first syllable of every sentence. This time, there was no attack. We rolled into camp and parked at an angle for a quick exit.

The camp was a surprisingly makeshift city, utilizing nearby buildings and shops for food, clothing, showers, and other services. Former homeless shelters housed travelers, as did a few other buildings that had been spared by the earthquakes. The area felt more stable than other places we'd passed through, yet it was clearly a temporary rest stop. A diesel generator coughed near the clinic; its note stuttered the same way the radio did between transmissions.

As we exited the vehicle, we saw buses and trucks, just as the first soldier had described. Using this as a starting point to search for Auxi, we concealed our firearms but kept my sword visible. With our goals in mind, we made our way to populated areas. Everyone we passed gave us curious looks, and we even recognized some faces from the day prior, before the monster attack.

Our exploration of the first zone didn't reveal Auxi. Still, we did find many people being treated for various wounds by a mix of military personnel and medically trained civilians. Walking through this part of camp, it was striking to see doctors and surgeons who'd been reduced to treating injuries as they arose, stripped of their former high-power positions. Some were seasoned, while others were visibly frazzled, forced to rely on their basic training to reconnect with their profession.

Thankfully, Auxi wasn't among the patients, and we continued toward what we thought was the exit. When we pushed open the back doors, we were met with a horrific sight: giant, man-made holes filled with dead bodies. The pits were deep enough to hold what seemed like hundreds of corpses. As we stood there, stunned by the gruesome efficiency of it all, a few workers from inside brought out the mangled body of a person they'd tried to save. They calmly set the stretcher down and rolled the body into a pile with the rest, then prepared to cover it to mask the smell.

A mixture of horror and dread washed over me as we watched the cold pragmatism of mass death. There was neither time nor place for a proper burial, so this was the next best option. The value of human life has always been high to me, but my understanding of humanity wavered at that time.

On the edge of a child's jacket sleeve, a friendship bracelet, blue and sun-faded orange, had been knotted tight by hands that weren't here to untie it. Nearby, a sergeant told a worker they'd burn them tonight to avoid disease.

This was the new reality: survive, or be part of the heap. From Earth we come, and back to Earth we go. It clicked quickly as we turned away.

"Hey, isn't that one of the track team jackets?" Kendry asked, voice shaking as he pointed to a pile of bodies.

"It is... we need to check it out and see who it was," I said, walking to the edge of the pit.

The body lay near the lip, recent enough that no one had to step across others. I reached for the sheet and my side pinched tight, as if the skin were zipping itself. Bri caught my shoulder before I folded. I cracked the coveralls and peeked. The wound looked closed. The stitches had worked themselves out. I kept that to myself, nodded that I was fine, and lifted the sheet.

Lifting it, I knew immediately that it wasn't Auxi. The body had been ripped open at the stomach by the same claws that had injured me. As I reflected on how unfortunate this was and recalled my former classmates, a putrid smell hit my nose with force. I quickly dropped the sheet and we vacated the area, returning to the main room.

Back in the central space, the air shifted, filled with heat, diesel, and steam, and then the smell of food cut through everything. Only then did we realize how long it had been since a real meal. We followed it toward a café line.

Once inside, the smells of beef stroganoff, chili, and other stews were overpowering. In addition to this sensory overload, Bri and I felt intense sensations pulling us in, but we couldn't quite put our finger on it. Even Kendry felt an attractive force.

Putting feelings aside, we lined up for various pot-based meals. After picking up bowls of cheddar broccoli soup, beef and bean chili, and some bottled water, we made our way to the eating area. I was first to enter and couldn't help but notice a large crowd sitting in makeshift arrangements of tables, floors, boxes, and whatever else they could find.

The pull grew stronger, much like finding your way north with your eyes closed. We threaded through bodies toward the back right corner. That's when I saw a dirty green jacket like the track team's. The hat on her head was snuggly down. I knew it had to be Auxi. We rushed, almost sloshing our bowls.

Reaching out to touch her shoulder, she began to speak.

X. FAMILY

As the voice I desperately hoped belonged to Auxi spoke, I pulled my hand back from the stranger's shoulder.

"May I help you?" the woman asked, turning to face us, expression a mix of curiosity and weariness.

"I apologize," I said, trying not to drop the plastic fork while quickly gathering my food. "Are you a member of the track team from Clear View University? We're looking for our friend, and we thought you were her."

"Track team?" the woman questioned, a flicker of confusion crossing her face. She glanced down at her jacket, then seemed to realize. "Oh, this is a track jacket. My fault, I just got this from one of my second cousins I ran into here. I don't know where she went, but she and her friends are around here somewhere," she offered, gesturing vaguely across the busy, despair-laden eating area.

"Alright then, thank you. We'll find somewhere else to sit, but enjoy your food," Kendry said, gently nudging Bri and me forward.

"Ken, what are you doing? We should ask more questions. Are you not concerned by that? What about our feeling of her presence? You know I'm never wrong about those things," Bri said, a rare note of genuine confusion in her voice.

"Look, I think I know where she is. She probably got hungry for seconds and snuck back in line. Let's just walk around again."

As we began to head back toward the food area, still disoriented by the encounter, I felt a familiar breeze across the back of my neck. The sensation, as potent as ever, made the hairs on my arms rise in anticipation. I turned, seeking its source.

As time seemed to slow, I saw her. Auxi stood there, beaming a grin too big for this day. Dirt, blood, and grime caked her cheeks. Unmistakable.

Without second thought, we almost lunged at her, eager to embrace, careful to keep our food steady. As we hugged, a gesture deeply out of character for our pragmatic group, we couldn't help but feel a profound sense of completeness. The emotional wave was likely amplified by the brief, unsettling confusion of thinking we'd found her, only to be momentarily misled. We quickly moved to a vacant table, settling in to discuss all that had transpired during our separation.

"Auxi... we found you. It was a hell of a journey, but we made our way to you," I said, finally starting to eat.

"Yeah... there were some tough times along the way. We witnessed some unique events that may take a lifetime of therapy to process. Nonetheless, those who are still alive are here. Not to be a downer, but we lost a good number of people. I'm sure you know this if you found my note, but I mean, hey, what can you do?" Auxi said. She rubbed at a brown smear on her cuff and missed it completely.

Auxi looked the same, but the burden of loss was evident in subtle shadows around her eyes.

"I understand, and I'm sorry for the loss of your teammates and coaches. The situation evolved faster than any of us could have expected, but I'm sure you did what you could to keep them alive. Even if you couldn't get the desired outcome, you know you always have us. We'll never die," Bri said, her words eliciting a weird look from Kendry and me. "Obviously, we won't live forever. I mean it as a figure of speech. Regardless, I knew we would find you here; there was no shot you'd let those things get to you."

I met her eyes, a quick apology passed between us, and I let it go.

The rest of us were taken aback by Bri's words and her almost-humorous tone. I guess finding Auxi did mean something more profound to her after all.

"I don't even know what to say... I knew you'd be alive and all, but to see you... It makes it real, you know," Kendry said, pausing to absorb the sight of Auxi alive and well. "These past few days have been interesting, to say the least, so tell us, what happened to you? What've you been up to? Only if you feel like answering; I know there might be a lot of emotions at play here," Kendry finished, smiling, careful not to overbear on Auxi.

"Yeah, Auxi, how have you been? It seems like all is as well as it could be, but looks can be deceiving. Let's hear it," I said, leaning back against the wall.

"C'mon, guys, can't a girl eat before she tells the story of how she almost died more times than she'd like? Let me get some food, and I'll be back," Auxi said, heading back for what was likely her second serving. I assumed this was her second visit because the servers looked annoyed when she arrived, but they may have been tired themselves.

Although things were far from stable, we had completed our first immediate goal: finding Auxi. Reunited once more, we did our best to savor the moment before the inevitable return to madness.

In that time together, it felt good, natural, and for a fleeting moment, it felt like the world wasn't ending. Though the chaos around us was undeniable, we were fortunate enough to experience what it was like to be together again, something we'd come to appreciate far more. While I could elaborate on how our views and appreciations had changed, we prioritized Auxi's story: how she got here, what she'd learned, and what our next steps were.

After we gorged ourselves on our much-needed reunion meal, a meal that felt both like a desperate necessity and a ghost of celebrations past, the first thing we asked her was about her teammates and how many had survived.

"Well, some of my coaches and teammates were on the bus while the rest of them were still preparing to approach. I had gone back to help the others get there safely through rubble and flames from the earthquakes, but when I reached them, I heard screaming from the bus. I wasn't sure what was happening since I looked back and didn't see one of the monsters, so I decided to check. Running to the bus from the corner we were at, I got close enough to the doors to see blood spurring across the interior. I saw... I saw the limbs of my coaches being flung around like toys while they screamed in terror. No one else in the area came to help; they either watched or ran. Thinking as quickly as I could, I entered the bus through the open door and looked down the aisle. All I saw was a tube dripping red, and chunks of flesh spewed about. I even saw one of their faces... but the body was elsewhere. It was... horrific," Auxi said, pausing to take breath.

"Still, I yelled to see if anyone was alive. That's when an arm reached out from above one of the seats. Although it looked off, my mind was racing too much to think about it in detail. I made my way to it, but that's when that small creature poked out from behind the chair with a severed arm in its mouth. I could tell it belonged to Coach Jack by the watch; the silver dial with the cracked crystal. I'm surprised I even picked up on that in the moment. Either way, I saw it get ready to come my way, and I quickly ran off the bus as I heard it rushing toward me. I held the doors closed until it stopped biting at them and ran back to the remaining people from my team before the thing could exit through the hole in the ceiling it made to escape." She flexed her jaw. Somewhere in the quiet, I imagined a second hand ticking.

"I'm sure it could have gotten me through that door or chased us again if it wanted, but it didn't. It was almost mocking me in that way. Like I was prey for it to harvest at any time. It was sickening."

"Auxi... I'm so sorry you had to experience that. I can only imagine what that was like for you," Kendry said, leaning in to hug her.

"I appreciate that, truly. To be honest, it did shake me, and I'm still not sure how I'm processing it. But surprisingly, seeing that only pushed me to be better and stronger for my team. I don't know if something's wrong with me, if that's my trauma response, or if it's a product of spending too much time with you three, but I kind of felt that fire again. I mean, I always feel it when I'm running or doing something risky or athletic, but this was different. It was almost as if I were back on that airsoft field for the first time. The stress, the direness of the situation, it all just reignited something in me."

Auxi's eyes began to spark with teeming energy.

"The others think I'm a bit off for it, but I can't change myself any more than I can change the situation. So I figured, I might as well lean into it. Be some sort of modern-day Joan of Arc or Tomoe Gozen. Crazy, I know, but it beats letting the horrors build in my mind," Auxi said, a faint smile gracing her lips.

"Does that mean everything feels natural? I can't get read from you otherwise, but I want to clarify with you," Bri asked, her analytical mind at work.

"Yeah, I'm fine. Like I said, those first few minutes afterward were sucky, but we couldn't sit around and die. I quickly wrote that note for you guys and threw it where I knew you'd look. After that, we joined the crowds heading west and managed to hitch a few rides along the way. Those monsters kept popping up here and there, but I kept my team safe. Whenever they showed up or I had a hunch, I instructed them to either hide to the side of the crowd or use military vehicles for cover. There really wasn't too bad an attack on the way here, and holes weren't much of an issue. Combining all that, we got here around this time yesterday. Not bad, but definitely a stop along the road. I was hoping you guys would find me here; if not, I'd just have to find you."

"Well, I'm glad you and whoever else made it are okay. At least, I would assume so. Where are your teammates anyway? Twenty of you embarked for the tournament, and I'm not sure how many perished on the bus. Still, I know you had some of them with you, so I figured the rest would be here," I stated, looking around the crowded space.

"They're around here somewhere, but they should be fine for now. As for how many of us started, you have the correct number of people with twenty," Auxi replied. "Before the earthquakes and everything began, they had us on the seventh floor, two to a room. Although they said the building would hold up, and to be fair, it did for the first wave of earthquakes. Unfortunately, when that second wave hit, it was too much, and the building collapsed.

"They attempted to evacuate us in time, but four individuals became trapped in the collapse after the split wall blocked their path with a beam. I had hoped they would make it out through the back or side exit, but as I ran to meet them, the entire building caved inward, sending dust and debris flying my way. I tried to find them, hoping they were still alive, but with all attention on those they knew were alive but injured, I was forced to stop my search... That one stung, but I can't beat myself up over it; I can only improve," Auxi said, taking a sip of water.

"I think you did all you could in that situation. I know we've practiced and trained to remain calm in these circumstances, allowing ourselves to perform at peak efficiency, but this is beyond anything we could have expected. We can expect it to be challenging at first, but as long as we stay alive, stay together, and keep improving, nothing will prevent us from getting through this," I said, resting my hand on her shoulder.

"That means a lot, but it still sucks knowing half of my team is dead between those two incidents. We didn't even have time to mourn the first losses before the next ones came in. I think that sparked my energy, though. It just compounded, and somehow, two negatives made me right. Although... I still feel that feeling of despair. I think we all do to a certain extent. But hey, as long as you guys are safe, it's just like D said."

Bri then spoke, her tone cutting through lingering sentiment.

"I don't mean to speed through things, but we don't know how long we have here. Your teammates' tragic deaths were extremely unfortunate, but would you happen to have seen anyone wearing a suit? Oddly put together, out of place, and seemingly emotionless?"

"For you to say someone is emotionless must mean something; I'd be horrified to see them," Auxi said, offering a friendly jab at Bri. "But no, I don't recall anyone... Wait... I do remember seeing someone outside the window when the earthquakes stopped. They were just standing there, in these shades, and what I believe could have been a suit. They were somewhat difficult to see, since they were hidden behind some destroyed cars. I went to grab my phone to take a picture, and when I returned, they were gone... I'm not sure if it's related, but it was odd and sounds in character with these 'suits.' Did they do something to you guys? Other than freak you out, I mean."

"The other day, we came across three of them trying to capture us or something. We were already being attacked by larger monsters when they came out of nowhere. We didn't even see what happened to the other monster; it must've been the second one that attacked D," Kendry said.

"That does make sense now. I guess I hadn't thought about the other creature; I figured you two killed it and a third joined in," I mused aloud.

Kendry continued. "The three of them didn't even say anything; they just pointed their guns at us and moved like a single unit. Their muzzles tracked us like one metronome. It was strange. We stood there, waiting. Bri said if they meant to kill us, they already would have. Then the leader spoke: 'The other. Where is he?' Boss lady had a voice like she smoked a carton of cheap cigarettes a day. I didn't want to answer, but then Bri gave me the go-ahead, and that's when I saw him out of the corner of my eye. I told them, and the two flanking the boss went for D.

"Long story short, we saw the boss get slammed between two cars and handled the other two. We looked back, and she was gone. Already hurt and D bleeding everywhere, we said screw it and got back in the SUV."

I replayed the moment; their shoes never scuffed. All three shifted their weight in the same heartbeat.

"Those people are some freaks, man. But I can't even say I'm surprised anymore."

"I'd agree with that sentiment. There's no such thing as normal right now," Auxi said, leaning back on some boxes. "So... what's the plan from here?"

"We should probably get some sleep first. Then maybe we can head to that camp we heard about," Kendry suggested.

"The one in Minnesota? We overheard some people talking about that. That's what we're doing?" Auxi asked. "You didn't want to go find our parents first?"

"Think about it, our parents raised us, and we're doing just fine, relatively speaking. Since everyone who's still alive has been slowly getting pushed toward the center of the U.S. or further north, where fewer holes were created, it's logical that they would be in that area as well," I explained. "We've been receiving updates from them when we've been able to, so they are alive. We also know they left Maryland sometime after the second wave, at least. If anything, they may be ahead of us and already there."

"Yeah, our folks are smart. They may not be as young as we are, but they're beyond capable of defending themselves if need be. They'd also want us to prioritize safety before searching for them. The whole 'make sure you can breathe before you help your child' thing, but reversed," Kendry added.

"That makes sense to me; my parents are fine, I'm sure. If they can handle raising a daughter like me, I'm sure they can maneuver their way around this scorched Earth," Auxi said with a wry smile.

Just as she finished, the remaining televisions began to show colors instead of running static. Although no reporters were speaking, we could make out programmed emergency banners for each news station, signifying that the network was coming back online. As those with devices that still held enough power began to receive notifications, the room erupted. From sounds of laughter and joy to muffled cries of mourning, the world had been allowed to reconnect again.

As I was about to check my phone, which was barely clinging to life after everything that had happened, a figure appeared on television.

The figure slowly became clearer, identifiable as a soldier. Not a high-ranking official in a pristine suit, just a man in full combat uniform, tired, dirty, and broadcasting from what looked like a bunker. The room quieted in layers as he spoke; someone near the generators killed a rattling fan, and the captions flickered, then caught. Units running the camp turned the television to maximum volume and activated closed captions, ensuring everyone could participate.

"Citizens... survivors... we've been trying to get this running for a while, but we have an update," he said as images began to flood the screen.

"The world at large is under attack. We are fighting back, but we can't guarantee an outcome. What you are seeing is what's left of our news sources. The United States has lost almost all of its coastline on both sides, with the West Coast being hit considerably harder. Those along the fault line in California, Oregon, and Washington were decimated; ninety percent of the population perished in the second wave of tremors.

"We've also suffered mass casualties from a mixture of human-on-human violence, these abominations, and natural disasters. None of us knows what these things are, but we have teams working on a solution. Stay alive until then... As for everything else... I don't know what to say... The president is dead... The government has fallen... the total estimated loss of life in America alone is one hundred million, but those numbers could easily be greater... People, we are in unprecedented times, and we need to stay together to figure this out. We have bases throughout the Midwest and the Northern United States, extending into Canada. Find one of those, and we will do our best to protect you. Creatures do not thrive in cold environments and are significantly slower there. Get there, and your odds of survival increase. All of you are now survivors, and each of you has a responsibility to protect those around you. Use what you can, but we've found that 7.62 mm caliber is what works best, specifically on the larger abominations," he said, continuing his grim report.

"Battle rifle rounds. If you can't aim, don't waste it; pair a shooter with a spotter."

As TV played in the background, everyone was glued to screens at the sight of the total damage, barely coming through. Many news crews were in hiding or on remaining high structures, but it was clear that things were not going well. New York was utterly devastated by floods, left in ruins. What remained of Los Angeles was a flooded, broken wasteland where monsters seemed to roam freely, searching for any survivors. Washington, D.C., was a mess, with the monument standing as half of what it had been before, the Capitol overrun with people seeking shelter, and White House empty, its front gates destroyed and littered with bodies of humans and monsters alike.

The scenes were not sights for sore eyes; however, the Midwest and nearby areas seemed to be faring better, suffering fewer earthquake catastrophes and monster attacks. People there seemed to be struggling just as everyone else, but there were places for them to go and solid defenses against these monsters, more so than on coasts.

Continuing to watch and listen to the news, they eventually showed us scenes from around the world. China had been hit with devastating accuracy, as its estimated death count rose by tens of millions every few hours. Many countries in Africa had been devastated by earthquakes and monster attacks. However, those who could survive on water found themselves safer, as larger creatures struggled in aquatic environments. The smaller ones could make the trek, but they were easier to kill if you were quick enough.

Around the world, we saw large death tolls, immeasurable damage, and uncertain futures. The only continents that seemed to have suffered minimal damage from monsters were Antarctica and Australia. Although these places were not immune to the earthquakes, no confirmed holes were found in Antarctica, and only a few were found in Australia. The lack of damage in Antarctica could be attributed to the extremely frigid temperatures the continent experiences. Given that these creatures come from underground and are likely unequipped for those environments, they presumably could not survive there, making it a doubtful destination. As for Australia, the continent was dealing with a monster issue, but for some reason, it was not as severe; the cause was unknown.

"In sub-freezing zones," the soldier added, "we're seeing neuromuscular stalls, short windows where their joints seize. Think crabs out of water. Use those seconds."

As everyone continued to stare at the screens, I glanced at my dying phone, where notifications were popping up. Seeing that I'd received a message from my parents earlier that day, I took the opportunity to go outside and attempt a phone call. The setting sun felt good on my skin. For the first time in days, we were united, and I didn't finish the day any worse than I'd started.

As I called my mom first, the phone rang until it eventually stopped. When I called my dad, the phone rang for a few seconds before he finally picked up.

"Hello?" I asked, eager to hear the response.

"Hey, son, how are you?" my dad said.

Relieved to hear his voice, I began to ask them about their situation.

"Dad, how have you guys been? Where are you? Did anyone else's parents make it? Is Mom with you?" I asked, aiming to gather as much information as possible.

"Well, son, after earthquakes started, we stayed at home in the basement for a bit before we eventually lost all access to technological services. Gathering some food and water, we made our way to Tudwrig's, as it was closest. On the way there, we could see the destruction caused by everything, but we had to keep going because we were unsure of what else could happen. Once we arrived, we saw that their home had survived better than most, likely due to its sturdy foundation and somewhat remote location.

"That's when we had those couple of days of peace, where we waited to see what else would happen since none of us believed it was truly over. After those two days, when earthquakes returned, we checked their cameras and noticed that some creatures had begun to attack their neighbors next door. Understanding that they were heading our way, we grabbed what we could and ran for vehicles to head toward Alvars. That journey was treacherous itself for a plethora of reasons, but I can spare those details for now," my dad said, just as I interrupted him, the connection beginning to drop again.

"Dad, I need to know these three things quickly. Who is with you? Where are you going? And are you all safe from injury?" I pressed.

"All of us parents are here, together, with each set speaking to their kid. We are currently traveling through the woods near East Wisconsin on the way to that camp in Minnesota. No one has been injured badly, but Kendry's father rolled his ankle pretty severely in our last encounter with the creatures, naturally. We may be older, but we're still pretty capable, you know. Where do you kids think you got it from?" my father said as the connection began to fade.

"It sounds like the connection is going out again. Please keep in touch when you can. My phone is considerably damaged, so if it dies completely and service returns, reach out to Bri," I said, voice strained against a struggling call. "We will meet you at camp in Minnesota. Keep Mom safe. Also, I'm sure you're aware of this already, but don't trust anyone along the way. If you see anyone wearing suits and looking unusually clean, move away from them as soon as possible; they're dangerous."

"Sure, son. We'll see you soo—" my dad said, the dying connection severing his words.

Heading back inside, the emotions from before were amplified. The connection had gone out for everyone, meaning the television was off, and a potent mixture of heartbreak, happiness, and anger now filled the room.

Bypassing the understandably mixed emotions, I sat back down with my friends and filled them in on what I'd discussed with my father. As it turned out, every one of their parents had relayed the same message: the plan was to head toward camp up north, and each of our parents had played a pivotal role in the group's survival.

Bri's parents were eerily similar to her; two cool heads counting risks while everyone else counted steps. Apparently, they vetoed a bridge because the echo under the span was wrong.

My parents were the backbone, the driving force, and the morale. Mom stopped a dispute by making a decision that everyone had to follow.

Auxi's parents were the doers. When a two-lane highway was jammed with dead cars, her mom had them off-road in sixty seconds, using fence posts as traction.

Kendry's parents didn't say much, but they saw angles no one else did. His dad had rolled his ankle doing a stupidly brave detour to draw a creature away from the water carriers.

Sitting back with the others, we shared nothing but silent appreciation for our parents. It wasn't something that needed to be said, but we could tell by the look on each other's faces that things were going well. Choosing to discuss this amongst ourselves, we shared how none of us lacked faith in our parents' ability to stay alive and well. We had our own survival to focus on, which our parents would prefer we do, so we put it on hold in the back of our minds. Our faith was proven to be well-placed, which we already knew.

Although we were a mixture of physically and/or psychologically gifted compared to most people, our parents were the ones who aided in our cultivation. If you were to take a person with all the talent and ability in the world and leave them to grow without guidance or a proper source of knowledge and experience, their gifts would be wasted. Not to say it's impossible to do it alone, but I know that I would have turned out differently if it weren't for my parents.

I naturally lacked some of the characteristics that made a person human, as I've mentioned before. I struggled to connect with others, identify with what other kids liked, and even show interest in what normal children would do. This led to struggles making friends, dating back to when the concept first formed in my mind. To manage this, my parents introduced me to how they operated and allowed me to flourish in the ways that best suited me. They showed me how to lead, excel, and stay busy, ultimately finding satisfaction in myself and my accomplishments. This may not be considered healthy by many, but they assured me that what was meant for me would find me, and it did. Their trust and teachings allowed me not only to meet Bri, someone very similar to myself, but also to learn from her and grow alongside her. Finding an equal who wasn't intimidated by my natural intellect or bored by my geological fascinations, I saw their teachings manifest.

Although I was very young when Bri and I first met, they had already discussed everything with me, and I was more than capable of understanding. It was after I met Bri and we began to develop that I saw teachings truly form, putting more of my faith in them. They first introduced me to sports, training, hunger for knowledge, and genuine leadership, which is likely why they encouraged me to keep advancing early; however, I did not see eye-to-eye with them on that. These learnings only continued to grow as I met Auxi and Kendry. Despite my initial reservations about them, I was quickly proven wrong once again, as Bri showed me that I needed more faith in others.

The people in my life have taught me the importance of having others around. I may not always agree at first or see where they're coming from, but that's the point. I had to be open to other possibilities and opportunities. They allowed me to grow and showed me how to truly develop. Those teachings were why I was still alive, and I had no choice but to come to this realization over the years.

After that call with my dad and sitting back inside with my friends, all of these thoughts swept over me as I finally had the chance to think clearly.

The world had gone to hell, but my people, my family, were still alive. Bri found my eyes across the table. We counted each other and kept listening.

XI. DREAMS

After wrapping up our time inside, as the dining hall gradually transformed into a loud, makeshift dormitory, we made our way outside and located a clear patch of grass. After setting up our secluded sleeping area, slightly distanced from the main shelter and random clusters of people, Auxi went back inside to find her teammates and bid them goodnight. We'd briefly seen them earlier, but they were more her circle than ours, and she'd been their unwavering moral support since the ordeal began. Her stepping away for the first time in days was akin to a father leaving his small children for an overnight business trip.

As we lay there in a makeshift circle on our mats in damp grass for what felt like an eternity, we gazed into the lit-up night sky. Widespread destruction had created perpetual fog in many places, so being in a relatively less-impacted area allowed us a slightly more transparent view of stars. Continuing my gaze, I once again found myself lost in thought about the pervasive uncertainty of the future. The larger, existential threat that remained.

Pondering this for a while, I began to drift off to distant sounds of soldiers and vehicles running their perimeter routes. It was noisy, yes, but it offered the most secure and peaceful rest I'd experienced in days.

As I slumbered, I dreamed of a perfect world where we had all graduated and explored what life had to offer. I'd become a successful leader in geological engineering, creating optimal tunneling systems to increase human efficiency. While I was vaguely aware of what the others were doing, the dream centered sharply on my life, my particular existence within this idealized future.

After a long day at work, I arrived back home to discover my wife and two children at the dinner table, patiently waiting for me. It seemed a bit more cliché and standard than I would have thought my life would be, but I walked over to the table and saw that my wife was, indeed, Bri. A wave of confusion washed over me. We'd never shared any thoughts or feelings alluding to even remotely finding each other interesting in that way, beyond our recent, odd interactions that I still didn't fully comprehend. I confusedly sat down.

"Is something wrong, D?" she asked, her voice soft.

"No, I, uh... I just missed you all at work," I stammered, struggling to grasp why my brain would conjure such an image.

"Daddy," both of my kids chimed in.

My oldest daughter continued, her voice innocent, "What is that thing behind you?"

I turned to look at what she was referring to, and all I saw was a dark corner by the door.

"What are you talking about, dear? I don't see anything," I said, a growing sense of bewilderment adding to my confusion.

"D, you don't see that? It's coming closer," Bri said, standing up and pulling the children closer as she stepped back.

"I don't see what you're talking about. What's going on?" I said, rising and walking toward the seemingly empty area.

Certain that nothing was there, as I'd just checked, I turned back to the table. My family had gone dead silent. The dimly lit room had grown even darker. The single room, with its four white walls and lone light hanging from the ceiling, now had no doors, and the light itself had a sickly, increasingly yellow hue.

Attempting to speak to them, there was no response. Approaching closer, their eyes looked glossed over, and they stood frozen in time. As I continued to approach, determined to free them from whatever was happening, I stopped in my tracks. Their mouths slowly opened, releasing a groaning noise. The sound wasn't normal or natural; it was like a creaking floorboard being perpetually stepped on, amplified, and distorted. The noise grew, and their eyes rolled to the back of their heads, revealing not the sclera but taut, crimson cords that kept their eyes attached to their heads. They didn't stop; their eyes slowly rolled and rolled, continuing until the cords snapped and black blood spilled from their sockets, pouring into their open, synced, creaking mouths.

Shocked by what I was seeing, even after all that I'd already witnessed, I stepped back, moving instinctively until I hit what I believed to be the wall.

The creaking paused.

The three of them lifted their right arms in unison, pointing directly at me in profound silence, their detached eyeballs accelerating in their gruesome roll. Standing there, utterly frozen by the spectacle, they began to make another noise. This time, it was the piercing shriek I'd heard from the monster the day we were first introduced to the smaller ones. It was deafening, hitting my ears with the force of a sonic boom.

Covering my ears in a desperate attempt to protect them, the center of the room began to spin as a vortex-esque hole ripped open, swallowing up the plain, square table we'd sat at. The hole only grew as the walls around me shrank, forcing everything inside, including my family.

The air thinned the way it does when ground lets go; pressure dropped, edges chewed inward. The physics of a sinkhole pretending to be a dream.

Digging my hands into the wall, desperate to hold onto something, I noticed it felt warm and fluid-like. Looking up to see what it was, I saw the bearish, plain face of a larger monster, halfway merged into the wall, yet present enough to cover my hands with black blood as I clung on.

Recognizing that the creature had realized I saw it, the claw I assumed belonged to it began to sweep in, directly for my head. In an attempt to survive, I let go and plummeted into the vortex, catching a glimpse of what looked like the 'suits' appearing above the hole as I fell; now pale and wearing the skin of what seemed to be a fish-scaled hybrid corpse.

Falling into the unknown, unsure of what happened next, I embraced my potential demise and prepared to die. As I fell into the bottom of the vortex, facing death, I awoke in cold sweat back in the real world to screams and chaos surrounding me.

Lost as to what was happening and why I was just waking up, I reached out for Kendry, who was still lying down beside me. As I grabbed him, I felt warm and sticky fluid covering my hand. Rolling him over through the sliminess of substance, I found his chest had been ripped open, his rib cage nearly separated from his body. My eyes then darted to his blank face, seemingly holding the emotions of his final breath within it as his mouth lay wide, filled with deep red blood. His eyes glossed over with remnants of tears that had streamed from his face. Startled and perturbed by this sight, I turned and retched, fighting the urge to throw up.

"How? Kendry... I don't get it... Where are Bri and Auxi?" I thought to myself, realizing I had no time to mourn.

Quickly grabbing my sword, I moved toward the rest of the panicked crowd, searching for them. As I ran through flames, bullets tearing through the camouflage of smoke, I passed through throngs of terrified people and heaps of corpses alike. As I witnessed the military doing their best to fend off the creatures, the fires seemed to burn brighter, and the gunshots grew louder, disorienting my senses. Seeing that the crowd I was in was heading directly toward an onslaught of monsters, both large and small, attacking and ripping people apart, I ran back inside the shelter to find another way around.

Once inside, I saw Auxi in the same corner we'd been in the day before. This time, however, she was fiercely defending her teammates from three of these smaller monsters and one of the larger ones. Standing tall, she held her mangled left arm tightly against her body, likely to keep it from falling apart as her flesh and bone were visibly ravaged. She looked at me once more with that wild, almost manic look in her eye. Her glance wasn't one of fear; she looked excited, ready.

My adrenaline went into overdrive now, and I burst into the area. Just as I was a few feet away, the monsters all attacked simultaneously, and the corner where Auxi once stood, defending her teammates, had been reduced to a grotesque goulash of flesh and blood splattering the walls.

Realizing that I was too late, too slow, I felt a sensation that I could only describe as pure, untamed rage.

I moved with efficiency and speed that I hadn't known to be possible. Before I even knew what I was doing, I'd sliced off the head and arms of a larger monster and completely halved two of the smaller ones while decapitating the third. I then stood amidst a scene of meat chunks, blood, and that wretched black fluid these things had for blood. As I stood there and looked at what remained of Auxi, only her hair, portions of clothes, and what I assumed to be a mixture of her flesh, a sense of profound dread fully encapsulated my being.

Standing there, lost in overwhelming chaos within my head, I felt a sharp pain in the back of my thigh. Looking down, I saw that the larger monster I'd decapitated had somehow retained enough nerves in its lower body to kick and stab me through my leg. Unsurprised that I hadn't anticipated this, given the deafening noise and utter chaos, I swallowed my pain and simply cut off the claw. Figuring that I was as good as dead soon enough and not wanting to speed up the process, I left the claw embedded. I reasoned that hobbled movement and continued bacterial exposure were preferable to removing it and risking an arterial spray that would add to the existing blood on the floor.

Turning from this horrific scene and looking to find Bri, my last remaining hope of companionship, I stumbled toward the kitchen to exit the way we'd first come in. Unsteady and bleeding enough to make my foot feel as though it were in mud, I pushed through doors and saw a horde of monsters running through the night. As they chased everyone in sight, my gaze paused when my eyes landed on Bri. She was holding back a group of children, using an armored Humvee as a wall, defending them from encroaching creatures. She was holding them off well enough, but no single person could protect a group of ten children on all sides by themselves.

As she shot, fought, and stabbed creatures getting close to her, using every ounce of her training and experience, I hobbled over. Getting within twenty feet, more monsters began to attack her; she had to hold off two large monsters at a time and performed remarkably well, dodging blows as they came. Despite her efforts, children began to be picked off one by one, with smaller monsters bypassing Bri and quickly chomping off limbs and heads with no discretion. Before I knew it, I was fifteen feet away, and only three whole children remained.

Bri, doing her best to hold off two new large monsters, now using the armored Humvee door as a shield, was suddenly attacked from behind by a third. She must have sensed it coming as she moved to the side slightly, sacrificing only her right side to a deadly swipe instead of her entire body. As she stood there, three gashes deep enough to see through to the other side, using a military vehicle door to push back on these two monsters, I couldn't help but feel utterly useless. I could hardly move, feeling my energy drain rapidly.

In a last-ditch effort, I yelled to grab the creatures' attention, hoping to give Bri and the remaining kids a chance to escape. However, when I yelled with all of my strength, all I did was distract Bri long enough for one of the monsters to reach around and slice deeply into her throat.

Realizing the profound horror of what had just happened, I witnessed deep red blood pouring out of her as she desperately tried to hold on a little longer for the kids.

Looking at me, she gave me the most earnest smile I'd ever seen from her. Odd for the moment, but knowing her... knowing us... It made strange, terrible sense. Succumbing to pressure and force, creatures pressed past her and slaughtered the remaining children while smaller ones came and pulled her apart, limb by limb.

Wondering how I was still alive and how much longer I had, I collapsed, completely defeated. As I lay there, waiting for inevitable darkness, I saw the suits appear once more. The leader was the same dreadful woman. She just looked at me and walked close to where my head was lying. As she squatted to get closer, she reached into her eye and removed a colored contact lens. Doing this revealed black eyes with green pupils and no visible iris; a sight I didn't believe to be possible.

Not wanting this to be the last thing I saw, I used my dying strength to reach for my sword. Just as I was about to press the blade into her chest, everything began to fade, and ultimate darkness consumed the world.

The next thing I knew, I woke up again, drenched in sweat. I shot upright into the air, which reeked of wet grass and diesel. Generators droned along the fence; authentic sound, real stench. Soldiers were still doing their rounds, boots crisp on the gravel, and people lay safely asleep.

Unsure if what I was experiencing was real or not, I looked over at Kendry and saw his ribcage compressing and expanding rhythmically. Good. To ensure I was truly in reality, I glanced to my side and saw the still, freshly healed, miraculous scar. Not knowing if this was enough to prove where I was, I lay back down and braced myself for something insane to take place.

"Having trouble sleeping?" Bri asked, her voice a quiet murmur as she lay next to me in our semi-circle, on the side Kendry wasn't on.

"Yeah... I think I had a dream within a dream. They were both horrible experiences bordering on terror, but they showed me a few things," I responded, my voice hoarse.

"I understand. I would ask you to share something about them, but we should probably get some rest; who knows what the day holds for us," Bri added, ever practical.

"You're right... We should," I said, closing my eyes.

"I also had a dream, and you were in it. Although I'm not entirely sure what happened, I think we should try to get to know each other better. We've come a long way in speaking more naturally, and I try to be more informal, but there's still room for improvement. We don't know how much time we have left, so why not keep it flowing and honest?" Bri said, her uncharacteristic openness a stark contrast to her usual guarded nature.

"Do you ever... dream of what it's like to have your own family? To have a partner in this life?" I asked, the words feeling foreign yet urgent on my tongue as I cracked my eyes open.

"I'll see you in a couple of hours," Bri said simply.

Somewhere in the half-circle, Kendry twitched; just once. His hand pressed briefly to his left side before settling. Dream scrap, I told myself, as his breathing evened out again.

Thinking of how I could have approached that situation better, I let the dreams and thoughts of our new form of interaction spread through my mind like wildfire. The hole from the dream kept turning in my head; pressure dropped, walls leaned, air grew narrow. That isn't just fear; that's flow. That's a sinkhole chewing its edges.

As I dozed off, I realized that life is more than success and pursuing my professional aspirations. Nothing is more important than the people you spend your limited time with. If anything, these dreams revealed a side of myself I thought was nonexistent: something more human.

Waking up, I looked around once more to see that everything had been fine throughout the night; a fact that felt nothing short of miraculous. The others had just woken up as well. Despite the early hour, we were ready to get on the road and ensure our parents' safety. After gathering our belongings and heading to the nearby gym for quick showers in a secure bathing area, we made our way back to the dining hall, walking past sleeping survivors. Picking up some water and food for the road, we prepared ourselves for the journey ahead.

As Kendry and Bri went to fill the car and our gasoline canister with reserves, I accompanied Auxi as she searched for her teammates. Finding them in the corner of one of the rooms they'd designated for sleeping, she woke one of them up and began to share details of what was to come.

"Hey, wake up. Can you hear me?" Auxi said as she gently shook one of her teammates.

"Auxi? What are you doing? It's 4:00 AM," she mumbled, looking at her charging smartphone.

"I'm going to head out with my friends to go and find our parents up north. Do you think you're awake enough to remember some things to share with others?" Auxi said, speaking softly.

"I figured you would leave us eventually; you were always too fast to catch up to. But yeah, I'm up. Let me hear it," Auxi's teammate said, sitting upright.

"Hey, I wish you wouldn't say it like that. I'm not leaving y'all behind; I just have to take a questionable trip, and I think it would be better for you to stay with crowds and the military until we figure out what's going on.

"But here's the plan. My friends and I will head to this camp in Minnesota that keeps getting mentioned, as that's where our parents are headed. From there, we will assess the situation and determine whether to stay or proceed to the camps you are all headed to. Things change frequently, and this plan can easily fall apart, so maintaining contact whenever possible is the best thing you can do. I understand that I've helped the crew to stay alive, but I trust you will do right by them.

"These past few years as team captain and just being around you guys in general have been amazing. I trust I will see you again, but if not, just know that I've truly enjoyed it... Follow your gut and pay attention to the signs. If it feels wrong, it probably is," Auxi told her teammate, her voice laced with bittersweet sincerity.

Her teammate began to think about the last few years and the possibility of never seeing Auxi again. Leaning in to hug her, Auxi comforted her teammate, assuring her that she was only a call or text away, should the connection allow it. Not wanting to fall behind schedule, Auxi gave her teammate one final hug and told her to tell the rest of the team that she was sorry she couldn't be with them, but that if things went well, they would see each other again.

Heading back outside, I found Bri and Kendry sitting in the car. We explained the plan Auxi had laid out for her team to follow. While we knew plans were promising, anything seemed liable to happen in those days, and we had no clue what the road ahead really held. As we prepared for the worst, we made our way to the gate for departure, with Bri and Kendry up front while Auxi and I were in the back. Just as soon as we were all back together, it was time to hit the road back into the unknown once more.

Exiting the security gate, the soldier from the first gate the day before stepped out of the booth he'd been in. Surprised to see him, we spoke, and he asked for details on our plans.

"So, that haven up in Minnesota that I keep hearing about? Interesting. I was thinking of heading up there myself, but they say we've got to stay in the mid-Midwest. Crazy to me when we know these damn things are less common where it's cold. But who am I?" said the soldier, speaking cordially.

"Yes, sir, our parents are heading there, and we really think we could get ahead on these things if we had the chance. We're kind of geniuses in our own way," Kendry said, smiling back at the soldier.

"Well, you 'geniuses' are gonna need more than a sword and some pistols if you're gonna make that trip. You've got about seven hundred long miles ahead of you and a whole lot of unknown. Let me suit y'all up with some gear before you go," said the soldier as he went into the nearby tent with the word "ARMORY" crudely written on the side.

Coming back out after a few minutes, he loaded us up with duffels and ammo bricks. He also handed us a SCAR-H for reach, a Mossberg 590A1 for power, smoke bombs, flash bangs, grenades, and Beretta M9s. He also provided us with bulletproof vests, boots, and combat uniforms, among other essential survival tools.

"Are you sure about this, sir? Is this legal? Even if that doesn't matter, are you sure y'all won't need it?" Kendry asked, visibly surprised by the sudden generosity.

"Sure, why not? Yeah, it would be nice to have more for us, but if we start running that low, there's gonna be no point. We still have eggheads somewhere producing this stuff and trying to make a more potent version of 7.62 mm for larger ones. It'd be nice if small calibers did trick, but that's just not the case... Anyway, there's a map, some MREs, and other things in there too; don't use them all at once. For the record, my name is Captain Eric Burks, your favorite army connection. If y'all need anything else, now's the time," said Captain Burks.

"Thank you, sir. I think this is plenty, and we'll be on our w..." Kendry said before being cut off.

"Captain Burks, do you know what a BRR is? I had one before, but we lost it a few days ago. We could use that to understand what these things are and perhaps even how to kill them," Bri asked, her gaze fixed on him.

He disappeared into the tent.

Captain Burks came back out a few minutes later, much to Kendry's annoyance, who just wanted to leave.

"You talking about this thing?" Captain Burks said as he pointed to the same machine Bri had when we went to the initial hole back in Maryland.

"Yes, sir. Thank you," Bri said, reaching across Kendry to take hold of the machine. Even powered down, the casing held a whisper of vibration; the same register as that creak from the dream, only contained and sane. I didn't know if that made me feel better or worse.

"Watch your left flank," Burks added, habit more than omen. "They favor it."

Pulling away from the first barricade, Captain Burks tapped the roof of the vehicle. Although we were leaving, I appreciated the place for helping us find Auxi and providing us with more protection. As we approached the second barricade and were let back out into the open land of death, we all prepared ourselves for any unexpected situation that might arise. Looking through the back window one more time, I was certain I was going to see a suited, green-and-black-eyed person standing there. Thankfully, land was as clear as it could be; only destroyed cars and remnants of disaster remained; no standing freaks in suits.

As we embarked on our next journey, I mentally prepared myself for what was to come.

Unfortunately, nothing could have truly prepared me for the wake-up call we were all about to receive.

XII. OPEN EYES

About thirty minutes into our journey, as damaged roads stretched endlessly before us, I began to ask Bri about the BRR, curious if she'd gleaned any information.

"I'm still trying to log in," Bri replied, brow furrowed in concentration as her fingers danced across the device. "The last one was already loaded with the proper credentials. I believe my information should work, but I have to see."

"Yours? Why would yours work? Does this have something to do with that project you were part of?" Kendry asked from the driver's seat, expertly maneuvering the battered vehicle.

"Maybe," Bri said, attempting a casual tone that didn't quite mask her underlying intensity. "I didn't know everything they were working on, but I recall there being a discovery that sent shockwaves through the organization. Everything was quickly shut down and moved to a need-to-know basis. However, I found a way to patch my information into the next level, marking it as classified access. I could have tried this before, but I didn't necessarily have the time. If what we need to know is beyond that, there may be more effort required."

"Okay... that's cool, I guess," Kendry said, hint of unease in his voice as he returned to driving in silence.

"How close are you?" I pressed, noticing Auxi silently gazing out of the window, lost in her own thoughts.

"I'm nearly there. This login is more in-depth than a username and password; it requires almost as much detail as the initial security clearance... I'm two steps away, though... I've entered," Bri stated plainly, a faint click audible from the device.

"Are you able to view any key information?" I asked, my attention shifting to Auxi, whose quietude seemed heavier than usual. An obvious question, given everything, but I was curious nonetheless.

"Auxi, is everything okay? I know a lot has happened recently, but you seem... dejected."

"I think I'm fine... I have to be. As I mentioned earlier, I'm doing well and have a new spark keeping me going. I think the peace is starting to get to me, though, letting my mind run freely on everything I've seen and heard over these past few days... That doesn't matter, though. I'm sure we'll run into trouble or something soon," Auxi said, her voice a low murmur, as she continued to stare out the window.

"I know I'm not the best person for this, but you sound like you need to let something out. I know the quiet bothers me as well, but that's why we have to stay busy. It occupies our minds so we can't focus on everything else," I offered, attempting to ease her burgeoning emotions.

"Oh, I know, D. We're all like that; well, all of us except maybe Kendry. Perhaps, in the end, it impacts him as well. But when you've lost so much and had to stand strong, being the person you are meant to be and need to be for others, it catches up... That's why I'm just going to never stop thinking.

"You think I've been over here sulking and feeling sorry for myself, but I've been planning out my moves and attacks for the future. I know I'm not as fast or strong as you or Bri, but you can bet I'm no slouch. I can only think of what we're going to do to end this whole thing. The battles, the glory, the redemption... I need that to come so I can give the dead the proper honor they deserve. I need it to feed my spirit. I need my vengeance on those hell-spawned creatures that think this is their playground," Auxi said, turning to face me.

Her face wasn't etched with sadness, but instead glowed with unsettling fire and energy. Words she spoke sounded like something ripped from an action movie, a bit dramatic, perhaps, but if that's what kept her going, then we could all break down together later. Despite all this, I could see right through her, and I was certain Bri could sense it as well. She was hurting inside, but to be honest, I think we all were.

"I found it," Bri said, slightly more excited than usual, pulling us from our internal struggles.

"Using the scan I completed last time, as well as the security access of my account, I can see what it was. It appears that what I scanned was the DNA of these creatures, and they already have a profile. It says that the most recent update was completed today, listing off known weaknesses and detailing what they are."

"What does it say they are? Do they know where they came from?" Kendry asked, momentarily diverted from the road.

"They have officially called them Feralgehns, meaning 'savages from hell.' A fitting name, based on our interactions. It says they are slower and less deadly in colder climates, have thick skin penetrable by large caliber bullets or a high volume of smaller calibers, have a heart on its right side, and a brain, both of which will lead to its death when destroyed. They hunt using their sharpened senses and possess thermal vision, enabling them to be effective hunters at night. They remain effective during the day due to their sensitivity to movement and sound. Still, they lack our version of standard vision," Bri said, reading from the screen.

"They also are said to be susceptible to sharp objects and slashes, which we've seen firsthand with D."

"Interesting, it makes sense if they come from below the surface. Though their eyes aren't useless, it would explain the lack of movement in their faces. Does it say anything about the blood?" I asked, morbid curiosity taking hold of me.

"The blood is described to be what we have experienced it as; nothing deadly or concerning about it," Bri added.

"There are also some other listings here in related subjects. The smaller ones we have encountered are called Subterros, meaning 'gnawers beneath.' Weaknesses remain the same, but they are not as pronounced and can be defeated with ease using smaller-caliber bullets. It states that they are faster and use their mouths instead of claws to kill, but they also can't move at as high speeds in cold temperatures.

"It notes 'not great swimmers' overall, but clarifies the webbing offers stability, not speed; they fatigue fast in water despite the feet. Although an island was never on the table, we should note that water cannot save us... As for the third one, I see that it is called an Umbrorex, meaning 'king of the shadows.'"

"Third, and it's called 'king of the shadows'... we're screwed, man. I know I'm supposed to be some great thinker, but if these monsters we've fought are just the muscle, then that means these Umbrorexes are the brains; I'm not sure I can compete with that," Kendry added, his usual calm cracking with genuine concern.

"Yeah, what else does it say about them? Is there a description or something?" Auxi chimed in, suddenly engaged.

"I'm unable to access any farther than this. They must have added another layer of security. I have a feeling what those are, but I have no way to prove it. I recall hearing talk of life being discovered underground, but I didn't know what it was. If I had known, I would have told you all and we could have gotten ahead of this thing," Bri said, voice tinged with regret.

"You knew about life and didn't tell us? Why? Why did you think that was something to hide? Clearly, it was more than a worm or a single-celled organism; they added an entire layer of security!" Kendry said, voice rising in frustration.

"Yeah, Bri. I know you were doing top-secret stuff, but that's something we've trained on for years. You know, we could have performed much better than that sorry group of researchers and whatever organization was behind it. Clearly, there was government involvement, but look where that got us," Auxi said, sounding irritated.

"You don't understand. I wanted to say something, but every time I tried, I had this sensation of dread. It was as if I was picking up on something that no one else could feel, not even D. That's why I have a feeling of what I know the third creature to be. I know this sounds illogical, but remember who you're listening to. I've never been unsure about anything in my life. Even when I'm wrong, I'm right; there just may be another way to go about the solution," Bri said in a plain voice, her eyes fixed on me.

"I know that I'm certain because last night, I saw it in my dreams."

"Bri, I don't know how to say this, but I think you've lost your mind. I mean, I don't think you have, but these feelings and senses of yours can't see what we don't know. C'mon, you can't dream something you've never seen and arbitrarily call it the missing piece," Kendry said, appealing to the logic of the situation.

"I think she's right, Ken. If she's thinking about what I believe her to be, then we've had a run-in with these Umbrorexes before... Did they have black eyes with green pupils?" I asked, a chilling familiarity settling over me as I felt I had indeed seen what she had.

"They did... They were also the people we saw in suits. There was something different about them, though; their skin was akin to that of a frog or a snake more than that of a human, similar to the Feralgehns. I must ask, though, where did you see this dream? What was the situation?" Bri asked me, her eyes widening slightly.

"Auxi, you hearing this? I know they're more than likely right and all, but we're getting into supernatural territory now. Of course, these two have always been a bit above average people in many ways, but this takes it to a new level. How about you and Bri switch seats so they can discuss their dreams? We can listen in from up here and get a synopsis of the story," Kendry said, looking at me in the rearview mirror. His look wasn't one of speculation, but almost as if he was wanting this to set up something.

"Sure, I could use some up-front leg room anyway in this tiny thing," Auxi said as Kendry briefly pulled the car over.

After switching seats and getting back on the road, Bri and I continued our conversation. I'll spare you a repeat of my story.

"While I had no dream within a dream of having a family, I did have a dream with the same events unfolding just as you described them. Kendry was dead, Auxi died while protecting her teammates, and monsters slaughtered you. While a suited woman approached me in the same manner, in my dream, she spoke to me before everything went dark. All she said, in her slithering and warped voice, was, 'Your time is upon us; we await you.' I have no clue what she, or rather it, meant by that. That's when I woke up in cold sweat myself. I noticed that you were also awake, so I took a moment to ground myself in reality before speaking to you. I know we could have discussed this while it was fresh, but I wanted to think on it myself and get more rest," Bri said, looking at me plainly, her usual composure unyielding.

"I wonder what this could mean? I presume this can't be a coincidence, but is there some larger theme at play here? Something beyond attack from subterraneans?" I said rhetorically, gazing out at the passing landscape.

Before I could continue, Kendry and Auxi interjected.

"It sounds like we're all dead, no matter how you slice it. Suppose these visions of yours mean something, which can't be applied to that shelter, because I will never return to fulfill my sleeping fate. In that case, we should use this knowledge to get ahead of it," Kendry said, his voice flat.

"Agreed. However, we've been on the road for a while now, and I think a real stretch and restroom break are in order," Auxi said, stretching her arms with an audible groan.

Neither of them seemed particularly worried about what Bri and I had just shared with each other, but I couldn't blame them at that point. We'd survived a plethora of attacks, death traps, and made it out of Indianapolis with each other; what could possibly stop us now?

Agreeing to stop near Hammond, Indiana, something ironic due to my last name, we found a relatively low-population area that wasn't destroyed to kingdom come. We pulled into a gas station and went to the outdoor stalls in pairs, making sure that someone was always in the car. While Kendry and I went first, Bri and Auxi filled up the car and obtained more fuel to keep our resupply strong.

The place had been relatively deserted, with all nearby people keeping a distance. However, when I went to the restroom, Kendry and I used separate single-person rooms, and the door was initially locked. Banging on the door and listening for a response, I heard nothing. But as I began to pick the lock with some thin pieces of wire, I heard a faint rustling noise. Stopping, I spoke once again and received no response. Thinking it was an animal and not knowing how dangerous it was, I gripped my katana and kicked the door open, prepared for anything.

To my surprise, the opening in the ceiling that led outside was crumbling, allowing materials to drop into the restroom. Not wanting to take too long, I hurried to use the restroom and kept my eye on the opening, expecting a raccoon or similar animal to emerge.

Back outside, Kendry and I watched the car as the ladies went to handle business. As we waited, Kendry tapped me on the shoulder and pointed to an alleyway about fifty feet away.

"Hey, man, you see that? Looks like someone's watching," he said, and I turned to face what he saw.

Looking closely, I saw the person he was referring to. Not only that, but they had been the suited people from before, the boss.

"Damn it, Ken. You see her? That's the suited woman from before. The one from my dream."

"Wait... Yeah... That's her, alright. What do you wanna do?" Kendry asked, opening the car door to grab one of the rifles.

"I know this isn't smart, but I don't think she wants us dead. I'm going to see if she wants to talk."

As I made my way over, a foolish decision, even in the moment, Bri ran out of the restroom. She'd likely sensed or heard something taking place, so she tagged along.

"Are you insane? What are you doing? We just shared how this person or thing was in our dreams last night," Bri said, her voice laced with disbelief, as we continued to approach the person standing still.

"I understand that, but wouldn't you like to know what it is and what's going on here? We've been on the run; maybe it's time to take a step toward a solution. Besides, you and Kendry saw the other two bleed when you injured them; their blood was red, the same as ours. If this person is indeed something else, then perhaps they can explain this to us... I know you feel it. The lack of tension in the air; they don't want to harm us. Not yet, at least," I said, as we neared within ten feet of the woman.

The woman stood where the shadow ate the alley mouth. Wearing the same suit, same tilt of the head as in the dream.

Remaining in silence, Bri stood beside me as we stopped to look at the woman. She now had on shades, and her skin seemed different. Not quite like what we saw in our dreams, but it was apparent that something was abnormal.

Out by the street, a man froze mid-stride with a bag of chips in his hand, eyes glazed with a stare that never quite found us.

Just as I began to speak, I heard the voice of what sounded like ten people speaking in unison.

Dion... Abrial... Are you ready to communicate with us? said the voice, echoing in my mind, not my ears.

"What is this? Where are you?" Bri asked, looking around, unable to see anyone but the woman, who remained still and silent.

It is I, the female in front of you, it said, a multitude of voices resonating in our thoughts.

"Name it," I said. My mouth was dry. "Say what you are."

We are the habit your lungs learned from the first breath. We are the pressure in stone you built your cities on. We are not interested in your ending; endings bore us. Pets are interested in ending. We open doors. They run.

Bri's fingers brushed the back of my hand and then were gone.

"What about the roadblock, the grab?" Bri asked the creature, cutting straight to the point.

You misunderstand. If we had wanted to capture you, we could have done so at any moment. That was more of a planned introduction and test for the other two who were with me than anything. Those failures have proven themselves useless here and have been sent back.

Our methods may not be most understandable to your species, but do not be fooled, for we are one. You hear me, you see me, and in due time, you will understand me. We will meet again, and when that happens, you two will be ready... Your companions are approaching; ideally, they will not attack; remember, we are everywhere, said the suited being. Slightly dropping its shades just enough to show me the black eyes with green pupils from my dreams, before turning the corner into the alleyway where they initially stood.

The suit pivoted, one fluid slice of motion, and slipped into the alley's wet glare.

Just as that happened, Auxi and Kendry showed up on the other end of the alley and tried to box it in. Following suit, still stunned by everything that had transpired, we saw that they had begun climbing walls up to the roof. Seeing this, Kendry and Auxi opened fire, hitting the creature five times. Although it did not slow, Bri and I heard its voice one last time.

We will allow you to reach your destination and reunite with your families. However, you have two months from then to meet us at the location you know as Rosebud, South Dakota. See you soon, said the creature, voice echoing in our minds.

As it spoke, it let out an openly audible shriek, the same as those from monsters. Hearing this and being caught off guard, we all covered our ears until it abruptly stopped after fifteen agonizing seconds.

"What was that thing? Was that suit from before that you guys told me about?" Auxi asked, her voice tight.

"Yeah, it was. I see its blood up there, and it's that tar-like stuff, same as the Feralgehns and Subterros... What the hell was it saying to you two? I'm assuming it spoke telepathically or something, unless you've both lost your minds," Kendry said, looking at us, his eyes wide.

"You're right about it speaking to us telepathically, but it explained itself to be one of the beings that have been attacking us. Specifically, it said the monsters are their pets and that their species does not want to eradicate all human life. It said that Bri and I weren't ready to communicate, but that it would allow us to make it to the safety area in Minnesota with our families.

"That thing also said the creatures were acting on instincts and seemingly targeting indiscriminately;

something I don't find to be true," I explained, looking around the alley.

Bri squinted up at the smear on the brick. "The viscosity's wrong for blood," she said softly. "Looks like coolant, not hemoglobin."

"Alright then... let's go," Kendry said, abruptly turning.

"What? You don't have any questions or remarks?" I asked in confusion, caught off guard by his sudden acquiescence.

"No, man. The situation is worsening by the second. I'm tired and want to get to my folks. From what I can tell, we're dealing with some sinister alien species that lives under the surface of Earth and has some infatuation with you and Bri. You two had an entire conversation while Auxi and I were figuring out what to do.

"Not only that, but if they are allowing us to make it to shelter, then they can choose when we die, right? Sounds like we're ass out here. That said, I think we'd better get back to the car and keep moving," Kendry said, resting his new rifle across his body.

As we turned to follow Kendry back to the car, I felt hairs on my neck stand on end, and before I could react, Bri had yelled for Kendry to duck.

Quickly listening, he dropped to the ground as one of the Feralgehns dashed out of nowhere, slashing deeply into Kendry's back.

Kendry immediately went limp, as if his body was shut down. I asked Bri how many there were and prepared to sprint for Kendry.

"I don't know, I'm still learning to sense these things," Bri said, her voice strained.

"Try harder, Bri, I can only feel when they are close and attacking, and we need to get Kendry now," I said as I leaned my back against the brick wall of the alley.

"Two large ones, I think, and a few smaller ones. D, we should think this through, Kendry will be fine," Bri said, attempting to slow me down.

Looking at Kendry lying motionless in the street as blood began to puddle around him, I waited no longer to rush to his side.

Sprinting from the alley into the street, sword in hand, I saw the Feralgehn, who had attacked him down the street.

Looking at it as I stood over Kendry, the surrounding people hiding in their shops and homes, I focused in and took one breath of calm before sprinting at it full speed.

I felt as though I was faster than before. Perhaps fueled by rage, as I was in the dream, my muscles felt firmer than ever before, and I made it to the monster before it had a chance to charge me. These things thought and behaved like wild animals, but they were not completely clueless.

Just as it twitched to lift its arms to claw at me, I brought the sword up from where its legs met its body and dragged it all the way through to the top of its head. Wasting no time and realizing the direness of Kendry's injuries, I then sliced off the creature's arms and legs, butterflying it open and making sure it was dead.

Turning my attention back to Kendry, I saw that Auxi had come to pick him up and was carrying his unconscious body back to the car. Slowed by his dragging feet as she supported his weight under his shoulders, wearing him as if he were a backpack, she was slow to react to the two Subterros that leaped from the roofs of buildings and chased her.

As I sprinted back, Bri seemingly appeared from nowhere and used a tactical knife from the military equipment to slice open the brain of one and axe-kicked the other. Her kick turned the monster into a pile of twitching flesh as chunks of black brain matter spilled out, and the other one kept chomping through its paralysis. Ensuring that it would die, she picked up a nearby rod and shoved it into the body and through the heart of the monster, so much so that she penetrated the concrete and pinned it to the ground.

Making sure Auxi had enough time to reach the vehicle, Bri and I turned to face the final two. There was one more Subterro and one more Feralgehn, both perched on roofs of buildings overlooking the alleyway we'd just left. Looking up at them, waiting to see what they did, I noticed that the Feralgehn had a scar on its face similar to what I did to one that vanished from highway attack. Judging by the sensation I felt, I was sure it was the same one, and I sprinted at it out of sheer, blinding anger.

As I did so, Bri followed suit, and we both leapt from nearby cars as we met creatures on their descent toward us. As Bri took the Subterro, I lunged onto the Feralgehn with my sword ready to deliver a killing blow to the heart. As I was doing so, it used its right claw to dampen the blow, causing the blade to go through its claw and partially into its body. The creature then let out a shriek in response, almost as if it were calling for backup.

Overcome by rage, I used all of my strength to grip onto the large beast and push off the wall as I slammed it back into the exact car I'd just launched off of. I pinned it across the hood and kicked its knees backward until joints went with a wet pop. As I had it pinned down, I began pounding it in the face with my left hand. I punched and punched with all of my might.

My God... I'd never experienced such blind rage before in my life. I continued and continued, feeling everything that had happened catching up to me. I went so far that I no longer felt resistance from the creature, but even so, I held it to avoid the chance that it could be faking its death.

As the car became more and more crushed, the creature stopped squirming and felt limp. Not caring, I kept going, this time using both hands. I didn't stop until Bri said my name like a command she'd never needed before. In that moment, all I wanted was vengeance, an emotion that I was feeling for the first time.

Pausing and looking at the black dent in the hood of the car where the monster's head used to be, I rose and shook as much of that gunk off of me as I could. Jumping down from the car, I looked around to see that survivors had begun to exit their shelters and were recording me using various devices. Although everything was happening so fast, I knew that this was not a good sign. I'd exhibited most of the strength and speed I possessed my entire life, but that... that was something more than I knew I was capable of.

Being brought out of my trance, I was grabbed by Bri to go to the car. Pulling my sword from the Feralgehn's corpse and running to the car, I looked back one last time to see people crowding around what I'd done.

I quickly jumped in the driver's seat and got back on the road toward Minnesota. Bri and Auxi were in the backseat, Auxi fighting back tears as she worked to stop the bleeding. Bri stayed calm as she cut Kendry's shirt free, flushed the wounds with the cleanest water we had, and used hemostatic gauze to slow the bleed. His lack of reaction is what truly highlighted the gravity of the situation.

As she packed the wounds and applied steady pressure, she loosely approximated the edges with suture strips, leaving room to drain, and readied a stapler if the bleed wouldn't quit.

Driving onward while Auxi applied pressure and Bri began closing what she safely could, I couldn't help but think this was somehow my fault. How could I have let one of my best friends, my brother, end up in this situation? From then on, I was no longer the same.

I haven't added my current interjections in while, but I figured this was as good a place as any. You might have questions such as how I let my emotions get the best of me, why Kendry suddenly walked away, or maybe why Auxi, an aspiring trauma surgeon, was applying pressure while Bri completed field care. All of these things were just products of the moment. Products of four 20-22-year-olds facing an impossible situation and somehow beating the odds enough to keep going. While we were more adept than the average person, regardless of age, we were still young and inexperienced; who would have been prepared for that? The world as we knew it had collapsed, and we were running on fumes, no matter how much we wanted to deny it.

Bri and I were likely holding up best, but as I told you, I had a moment of collapse, and Bri's solidity had begun to fluctuate. Kendry, arguably the most significant thinker known to man, had been in such a state of disarray that he hardly had a chance to collect himself and process any of the situations. In a matter of days, he'd sent an assumed killer after his injured best friend, heard of himself being killed in two separate dreams, and was constantly reminded of his physical inefficiencies compared to the rest of us. How could someone not crumble under that?

Although our lapses were nowhere near as severe as others, possibly not even apparent, we simply needed time to reset. Auxi was embracing her war-mongering tendencies in an attempt to cope with the losses of her teammates and then having to leave them shortly after. And while her coping mechanism worked for a short time, her walls began to flood as she was forced to sit over an unconscious and badly bleeding Kendry. So distraught that she could only apply pressure. Thankfully, Bri was more than versed in first aid and medical practices, enough to treat Kendry for the time being.

Although I had no idea what was going through Bri's mind in that moment, focusing on collecting my own thoughts and getting us to our next location safely, I could tell that everything was piling on her. Her cold and matter-of-fact demeanor could only take so much, and I feel like I could have done more to stop it. Of course, there was only so much I could do about everything going on, and it's not all about me or what I think or feel. However, I can't help but say that I hated myself in that moment, and it is still one of my darkest times. I let my friends and family down, and in doing so, I discovered weaknesses I hadn't realized I had. I should have been a better leader and friend and kept my mouth closed in more situations than I did. In that moment, that day, the reality of what I believed to be the truth was shattered, and I vowed never to let it happen again. I needed to grow in every aspect, opening up parts of my mind and abilities that I hadn't realized to their full capacity.

I knew I couldn't do everything, but I knew that I could do better. Making that my mission, which I still carry to this day, I continued working toward becoming the leader and friend that I needed to be, that they needed me to be.

For all that Bri, Kendry, and Auxi could do. For all the similarities that Bri and I had. I didn't need to think that everyone was capable of doing it alone, as I'd become accustomed to. Even though I had Bri, I never pushed the boundaries of our relationship, nor did I try to mesh our powers. I never did so with others either. Everything was deeper than surface level, and they felt like family to me, but I knew there was more there. I could count on them for things beyond responsibilities and accountability. I never knew what it was like to cry, feel sadness, or experience anger. But all of that changed, and it made me realize the importance of emotional pillars.

Just as I'd become faster and stronger in the face of stress, I'd also become more aware of my own existence and its impact on the lives of those around me.

As for Bri, there was much more we needed to discuss when the time was right.

That was something I had to wait and discover.

XIII. HOME

Leaving the Indiana state line in the rearview, the sun felt almost dishonest; clean light, no monsters. Heat pooled on my forearms, and for a minute, I drifted into a version of life where this road just led home. Then Bri's voice cut through the glass.

"D... D!"

"Y...Yeah! What's going on?" I responded, exiting my mind and returning to reality, unsure of what I had been thinking. I was two steps away from losing my grip entirely.

"You have to find somewhere to pull over. I need more room to work on Kendry," Bri said, calm but laced with a tension I'd never heard from her. "Somewhere we can lay him flat. Now."

"Yeah... I'm on it," I said, surveying the land around us.

I banked down a tree-snagged exit toward a small, secluded home nestled deeper in the woods off the highway. Curtains gone. The front door ajar. People on porches watched us with their arms folded, eyes hard, calculating what trouble we were bringing to their street. Not my problem. Getting Kendry help was.

Once we arrived, I told Bri and Auxi to stay in the car while I checked the house. Going through the open front door, the place looked abandoned. Good for us. Katana ready, I cleared the rooms fast. Drawers were dumped, mirrors missing, but there was a bed frame and, in the dining room, a thick, scarred oak table; good enough to be a field table.

I went back to carry Kendry in, holding his arm around my neck while Auxi continued applying pressure to his back. Bri gathered the necessary equipment. As I lay him on the table and positioned a pillow under his head, Auxi was shedding tears; not sobbing, but in that silent, painful manner where water simply flows from the eyes. I felt useless.

When I asked if there was anything I could do, Bri told me to get water from a nearby lake she'd spotted.

"Water? We have water. How can I help?" I asked, confused.

"Don't argue. We have drinking water and enough to keep the wound clean, for now. We need more for everything to come... trust me," Bri said, gaze firm.

Looking at the map, I saw the closest lake was half a mile away. Not wanting to waste time, I grabbed a plastic tub left behind in the home and headed out.

The jog was easy; my head wasn't. The dreams, the suited creature, what happened to Kendry; everything replayed. I analyzed every decision I'd made, trying to understand how it led to that point. As I dissected every mistake and missed step, I recognized the truth I'd been dodging. I saw myself as a failure, like I was becoming the turning point I'd feared.

Lost in thought, I reached the lake in minutes. I skirted the warm scum and dead biomatter along the edge and found a ribbon of clear water. No point saving Kendry only to seed an infection.

I filled the bin and started back. Without a lid, every step sloshed weight onto my wrists and boots.

When I returned, I saw Bri holding an emotionally wrecked Auxi on the couch. Kendry was breathing, but weakly.

"He's lost a lot of blood, D. Strain that water twice and boil it," Bri said, her face pale. "Given that you and I are both O negative, we need to be prepared to give."

"Sure, let's do it. Auxi, could you keep an eye on the water? I'm going first with Kendry," I said as Auxi got up.

"Auxi... I'm sorry. You too, Bri. I don't have words for this right now, but I will do better, and we will get through this," I said, looking at Auxi passing by and at Bri, who was now prepping Kendry for the transfusion.

"Just because I'm a little emotional doesn't mean you get to go soft," Auxi said, taking the pot to the stove, voice raw but firm. "You messed up, yes, but I know you, D. It's been a wild two weeks. Keep Kendry alive, and I promise you, all is forgiven."

"I agree with Auxi; you could have done better, but so could I. Can't blame it all on you. Right now, we need to keep Kendry alive," Bri said as she stuck the needle into my freshly alcohol-prepped vein.

She taped the line, looped the tubing up to a curtain rod for gravity, and counted off a slow drip. "If your lips go gray, we stop," she said. "Auxi, watch for a boil, then do a second boil." She pressed Kendry's nailbed. "Cap refill three seconds, slower than I like."

Looking at blood flowing from me to the bag and into Kendry, who was alarmingly pale, I looked at Bri as I clenched my fist repeatedly.

"Look, I know this isn't the time, but I wanted to truly apologize to you. These past few days have made me realize how important you all are to me, and I want to do a better job showing that. I know our relationship has always been goal-oriented, blending enjoyment with learning and improvement. But something is missing. I'm missing pieces that make me human, and I don't want to continue like this. Witnessing such losses of life, surviving these close calls, seeing how it affects us, it's unlocked emotions within me that I never imagined. I've recently felt anger, anxiety, self-doubt, and even fear at the thought of losing others. All things I thought I could never feel...

"I know we've discussed it before, and you've always been more level-headed, the most level-headed person I've ever known, but I know you've felt it too. No matter how much you may want to deny it, we have more in common with the others than you think. Why would we fight it? Why not adopt this new and healthy way of life instead of harboring it and letting it fester?" I said, looking Bri in the eye, speaking in a way I'd never spoken to anyone. "I keep thinking about dying last in that second dream. How we both did. It feels like a nudge."

"Dion...D...I..." Bri seemed lost for words, gaze unwavering.

"Before you continue and possibly shoot down my idea, I wanted to let you know that in my dream, the one with the family, you were the other half of the creator of my children. Not to make things awkward between us, but I just wanted to be honest. Honest, because I know you had that dream too. No chance we both dreamed the same second dream and not the first. Even if you hadn't, the gaze we shared, the time together, the fact that we both died last in the second dream; it all means something. We've been seeing things we never have before, all with hidden meaning. Though I don't know what this means, and I'm not familiar with relationships beyond friends and family, that's still a gray area for me; I just need to know your thoughts. Please, help me understand what I cannot," I said, stopping breathless.

As Bri looked at me from across the table, I studied her face to see if I'd tried to go too far too quickly. Seeing her gears turn through her eyes, I prepared to speak once more to let her know I didn't need her response immediately. Once again, trying to talk too much.

"D, I'd be lying if I said I didn't share those same dreams or recognize the gazes we've shared. I've seen it in your eyes, but I know that's not something you've really taken time to explore. Contrary to popular belief, I understand those emotions and have learned to fully experience them, as much as I can, at least. While you continuously poured so much of yourself into endeavors and activities to keep your mind busy, I've taken my quiet time to try to become more understanding of those around us. That's part of why I can sense more and read people better than you. It wasn't that I was simply born more observant; I was cultivated differently and focused my energies in other ways.

"So yes, I've seen what you've shared, and I agree that we, as a collective, need to discuss our emotions more openly. Not asking how each other's days are and breaking down every minor inconvenience, but being able to share without feeling off about it. Being able to talk about how it feels to lose friends, to stare death in the face, to find out that your differences from others are growing, and not know why. We deserve that, and that's what I want moving forward.

"As for what's going on between us, I tried to talk to you about it before, but you just shut me out. Even before all this, you never let me get close... I've tried, Dion, but I don't think

I tried hard enough...or maybe I didn't care to. Relationships, love, lust; they've never been high on my list of things to think about. However, in my study of them, I found parallels between us, and I wanted to pick your brain to see if you saw it too, without even realizing it.

"I'm not sure what it all means; it may mean nothing, but it could mean everything. All I know is that I care for you, I care for all of you. But when it comes to you... There's this feeling I just can't shake. It was as though since the day we first met, we were meant to be together in some capacity... I'm still trying to figure out what that is," Bri said as she came over to remove my needle.

Without realizing it, I had already given Kendry more than I should have, but still not enough. Not thinking of my own blood loss a few days prior, I stood to provide Bri with the chair and fell onto the floor. As Auxi came over with the cleansed water, still warm from the boiling, I drank what I could and ate some rations to replenish my strength.

Finding enough power to stand and shakily make my way to the couch, my body growing colder, I looked at Kendry and hoped he would make it through. Reflecting on everything Bri had said, watching Auxi hook Bri up with a new needle, I could see why people prayed to God. Life was hard.

As Bri sat squeezing her fist, I looked at her and attempted to speak before my eyes started to dim. Bri, realizing what was happening, called to Auxi to help. As she rushed toward me, I only remember the room going dark and hearing food hit the floor from my hand.

Waking up later that evening, I found myself stretched out on the couch where Bri had been holding Auxi earlier. The tiny home was moonlit; Bri kept the lights off to avoid detection. Quiet pressed in.

Looking first at the table, I could see Kendry still lying there. Though I couldn't see much, I could see his back rise and fall as he lay stomach down with a pillow under his head. Relieved, I looked for Bri and Auxi but couldn't find them. Assuming they were out of sight, I tried to call out but quickly realized how dry my throat had become. Grabbing the cup of water Auxi had filled for me from the floor, I downed the entire lukewarm cup with gratitude.

Feeling more refreshed, I figured it would be better not to call out, realizing the risks of that approach. Even though

I thought my body would be weakened from blood loss, when I shifted to put my feet on the floor, I felt... fine. Nothing numb, dull, or heavy; I felt almost better than before. It was wrong and welcomed at once. Edges in the dark looked crisp, like the room had negotiated a truce with night. The real challenge would be standing. I braced for wobble and stood anyway. No wobble.

Confused by this, I considered the possibility that I was dreaming, but it felt different. Dreams for me had a haze, a thin film you could sense if you looked sideways. None of that. Assuming reality, I went into the kitchen and found Auxi sitting on the floor with her back against the wall. She was breathing normally and wouldn't have wanted to be moved, so I let her be and went to find Bri.

Remembering she had given blood right after I had, before I passed out, I made my way down the hall to the bedroom. It was pitch black, and my senses were still waking up, but I could tell she was there.

As I went to where I'd seen the bed when we first arrived, I peered into the room, expecting to see her coiled up on the mattress, covered with some layer to protect her from dirty sheets. I wasn't sure if I had seen anything, but upon entering the room, I could tell the bed was empty. Puzzled, I looked around and noticed a figure in a corner, just behind the moonlight that slipped through the cracked blinds.

Making my way over, I heard a voice.

"Dion... What are you doing?" Bri said, sounding fatigued both physically and emotionally.

"I just woke up and wanted to make sure you were okay. I briefly checked on Kendry and Auxi, not wanting to wake them. I planned to do the same with you, but I see that hasn't gone so well," I said as I approached the corner.

Once closer, I noticed she was wrapped in a few blankets and sitting as if holding her knees to her chest. From what I could see through the poorly lit room, she barely had her eyes open, but she was awake. Sitting down next to her on the wall, she gave me some of her cover; something very odd.

"Before you say anything, I'm doing this to conserve heat. Two live bodies are warmer than one, and you seem to have recovered exceptionally well in the last eight hours," she said with her eyes still closed. "Also, you always wake me when you move at night; maybe a habit, but it happens enough for you to have noticed."

"That's a good point. I think I've noticed it, and maybe that's what I was hoping for... Bri, what you said before I passed out... I've had time to think about it more in my unconscious state. I heard everything, and we don't have to talk about it tonight, but..." I said before Bri interrupted.

"D, we need the rest for tomorrow. Auxi won't want to hear us talking about these things anymore, not until Kendry is back up, but we will have time when we get to the Minnesota camp.

"You're right. Would it be fine if I stayed here? I can leave if that would be more desirable, but to be honest, I've gotten somewhat comfortable under this blanket," I said as I prepared to go back to sleep.

"Sure. Just don't think this will be a common occurrence. I may have shared some important thoughts with you, but there's still much to discuss. Not to mention saving what we can of this world before anything else takes precedence," Bri said as she remained still, allowing me to get more secure within the covers. "You're warm," she added after a beat; too warm for someone who'd just donated.

"Thank you for this. I'm not sure what this sensation is right now, but after hearing what you said, I want to conclude this night by sharing something with you. I understand where you were coming from, and honestly, I think you have helped me decode some of my own emotions. While I'm still figuring them out, there is something I'm reasonably confident in. I care about you a lot, too, not just in my dreams, but here, in the real world. I identify with your sentiments, and I pledge to do everything in my power to keep you and the others safe. Something like this will never happen again... I would like to clarify that you are the most important person to me on this planet. I hope you can provide more information so I can accurately identify my feelings. Thank you, Bri."

As I said this, I placed my arm around her and held her closely. I'm not sure why I did that or even why I said what I did, but I think it worked out for the best. To my surprise, Bri accepted this and rested her head on my chest as we fell into the night.

This seems sappy to me in retrospect. Regardless, I was discovering a new facet of my humanity. The Bri I had always known was beginning to evolve in my eyes, and so was I. I had no clue what would be awaiting us in the future, but I knew that my new dynamics and promises would make us more prepared than ever to face it head-on.

At first light, Bri was gone from the corner. In the kitchen, she and Auxi were over Kendry, this time on his side. When Bri saw me, she waited for me to enter the room.

"D, look who's awake," Bri said, rare joy in her voice.

"Ken? You're awake? How is this possible? How are you feeling?" I asked as I jogged to the table to face him. Auxi looked better as well; she seemed to have recovered from the emotional weight of the day prior, and I'm sure seeing Kendry conscious played a role in that.

"Yeah, man. I'm still amazed at myself based on what I remember happening and how much blood they said I lost. I mean, look at me, I look like I fell into a raspberry bush and rolled around in it," Kendry said, a wry grin on his face.

As he sat up, I could see the three deep gashes that had lined his back, centered and angled to match an invisible line from his left shoulder to his right hip. They looked horrid; yet the stitches lay in a neat lattice, and the tissue between them had a faint graphite sheen, like skin deciding to be scarred sooner than it should. Bri noticed it too, but didn't call it out.

"Look, Ken. I'm sorry about yesterday. I know Bri and I were talking about outlandish things and basically predicting our deaths, yours especially unfortunate, but that won't happen again. The sight of you on the ground, motionless... it helped kick something into motion for me. I always knew you were going to make it, but seeing you alive, sitting up, and talking here has shown me that faith was well placed," I said, genuinely happy my brother was alive.

"Ken... I was so worried about you. Seeing you out there, I just couldn't stand to watch you die... not after everything else that happened. I thought I had it under control and that I just needed more conflict, but if anything, I see that I needed you and the rest of my family," Auxi said as she looked at all of us, her eyes still a little red.

"I know I can't go back and change anything, so I want to be better going forward. My hunger to win this thing remains as strong as ever, but my desire to share those moments with you guys is just as strong. We need to be a team, a unit. Not just when it comes to battle and survival, but in expression and communication... Dion, you'd better not let this stuff get to your head again. Your actions almost got Kendry killed, albeit indirectly. We don't necessarily look to you for guidance, but we have a great deal of faith and trust in you, whether you're aware of it or not. Your morale, our morale; it's linked, and that will always be the case. Keep your head together and stay away from the clouds," Auxi said, looking at me sternly. Not with hate or contempt, but disappointment. She had every right to feel that way, and I nodded in silent agreement.

"As for you, Bri, Abrial, you're my best friend," Auxi said, turning. "But we need more mindfulness under fire. Your sensing system helps, but I need you next to me in the thick of it. You could catch up to D physically if you put in the effort. I watched him grow for years; he's accelerating now. We need that from you." She swallowed. "Yesterday, when I cracked, it felt like drowning with everyone watching. I'm not doing that again. I'll train my mind and hands.

"And Kendry... You know I care about you, right?" Auxi said as she rested her hand on his leg.

"Well... yeah. I think I know," Kendry responded, sounding slightly confused.

"Then don't ever do some mindless act like that again!" Auxi roared as she pinched his thigh, and Kendry winced.

"If Bri hadn't yelled to save your sorry ass, we'd be burying you instead of getting you ready to see your parents. You're the smartest guy I've ever met, the most caring person I've ever met, yet you do some BS like that... I don't care what

Bri and D were saying or what was going on; you need to think before you act, it's your specialty. You also need to use your brain more. Perhaps the world being in turmoil has altered your flow; it has for all of us. However, we could really use some game planning from you if we're going to have any chance of winning this thing... You're our secret weapon, so re-weaponize your mind and don't make silly mistakes that would lead to you being a foot shorter," Auxi said as she leaned in to hug the still-aching Kendry.

Unsure of what to make of what I just witnessed, I followed Bri's lead and went in to hug everyone as well. Although this felt like some cheesy moment in a horror movie just before the young cast goes and gets themselves killed, I'd be lying if I said it didn't feel good. As we embraced, I felt compelled to say something I wasn't sure I knew the meaning of at the time. It just felt right.

"I love you guys," I said in the group hug, the words surprising even myself.

Shocked by what they heard, the hug quickly dispersed, and they all stared at me.

"Something really is going on with you two. I never thought I'd see the day, but here we are," Kendry said in a joking manner, breaking the tension.

Preparing to leave, we helped Kendry to the bathroom and used the remaining water to clean his wounds. By this point, the clarity in his healing process, how he was conscious and mostly back to normal, other than some pain, was too great to ignore. We briefly discussed this and chalked it up to something possibly being from my blood or Bri's, as we both had naturally fast healing; however, this was even faster than my own healing, which was nowhere near as severe. Still unsure what to make of the situation, Bri and I left to get more water for everyone to bathe as Auxi stayed and helped clean Kendry's back.

We moved quickly to the lake and filled one bin each at the same spot I used the day prior. The sound of birds worked at my nerves like balm; violence felt far away for a minute.

"You remember what you said to me last night?" Bri asked as we knelt, filling the bins.

"Of course I remember. I meant every word... You amaze me, Bri. Not just in what you're able to accomplish or how you've pushed the limits of what we understood to be natural between the two of us, but for how you've been these last few days. You've held it together, even in times when I wasn't able to. For that, I thank you," I said as I finished filling my bin.

"Thanks, really," she said as she stood up as well. "I appreciate you, too. I know none of this has been easy, but you've handled it better than most, trust me. That's why we're moving around and most of the people we see are frozen in place... However, beyond the exchange of thanks and admiration, I would like to discuss this further. Now that we have some time."

"Sure, I hope I didn't freak you out or anything," I said, stupidly, as a pivotal moment crept up on me.

"No, not at all. Quite the contrary, really. The words you spoke resonated, and when you held me, I felt a new sensation, not something I had been able to extrapolate from books or other media. It felt sincere, honest, and pure in intention... Not to sound feeble, what I said about ending this thing remains, but I think I've realized what this nagging feeling I've had for all these years is," she said as we headed back toward the small home, still on a time crunch but able to talk while moving.

"Years? So you've felt something for a while? You've always intrigued me, too, and I've had an odd sensation for a while, but I never quite figured it out. And you know what it is?" I asked.

"I believe I have, D. It's something I wanted to see if you felt as well, but I never quite knew how to express it to you. It's changed over time, but as we grew and I looked at you differently, I had to come to some hard realizations with myself. I realized I wasn't some emotionally blocked machine, that I was capable of feelings, and that there were things I desired in this life that I couldn't achieve by myself. While I've known this for a while, our brushes with death have all but confirmed these feelings in me, and I see that something greater has connected us, almost through fate. The dreams, the situations, the fact that I cared so much more for you when you were hurt than I believed I was capable of. It all showed me that I can't lose you. Whether because of these strings between us, linking our very existence since the day we met, or because I grew up around you. You were the first person to ever make me feel like I didn't need to lower myself to be challenged by; you were always the one...

"Dion, I don't know whether today or tomorrow or next week could be our last day together, and I truly hope it isn't, but there's just one thing I need to tell you... I love you, Dion Hammond... I don't know what that fully means, and my statement on ending this global attack still stands, but I have no other word to describe the sensation and bond I have with you... I understand if this is not something you can share with me. Still, I felt like I had to let you know before I no longer had the chance," Bri said as we began the purifying process for our water back at the house.

Caught off guard by what had just happened and witnessing the emotional vulnerability expressed by Bri, I was at a loss for words. Forced to confront the situation in the moment, as Kendry and Auxi were still in the bathroom, I tried my best to respond.

"Bri, I... I'm not sure what to say. It's all so new to me, but if the things you have been describing are symptoms of love, then... I love you too. I've never felt for anyone how I feel about you. I hardly remember a life without you. You are my other half, and that's always been the case, always will be. Even going back to when you first brought in Auxi and

Kendry, I initially felt betrayed, and I had no reason other than thinking our tight bond had been infiltrated. But looking at it now, I think it was because the thought of losing you to others was so painful that I couldn't even process what it was... That pain is what led me to be so quick to accept them and eventually learn to view them as family. The competition you provided me with is what led to my success in so many areas, at least in the eyes of others. Your support and care have kept me alive during this entire ordeal. Even in the dreams where I die, it's with you.

"I know everything may feel rushed, and we're crossing roads we just discovered were there, but I'm ready for it. Abrial, I wouldn't be here or the man I am today without you, and for that I am grateful. I only hope we can live long enough to explore this further... I know I said I loved everyone earlier, which I truly do, as it accurately describes how I feel about our collective, our family. But this, this is different. Regardless, I couldn't be more affirmed in my emotions than I am about you right now," I said, letting my mouth speak faster than I could think about the words.

As we stood in the kitchen, watching the now multiple pots of water boil as they purified themselves, Bri looked at me with a gaze I had never seen before. Stepping toward me,

I found myself stepping toward her and resting my hands on her waist.

Note from my present self.

It felt like something from a movie; that's how young love works for first-timers gearing up for a first kiss. It was new for both of us, as far as I knew, so the moment was awkward in its honesty. Regardless, Bri and I had internalized enough cinema to understand the beats. Eyes closed. Then contact.

It wasn't the best first kiss; we still needed a bath and a toothbrush. Given the circumstances, though, I'd score it high for technique and effort.

Back to the recollection.

As we were just getting comfortable and used to the feeling, we heard footsteps and quickly separated before a freshly bathed Auxi and Kendry appeared.

"What's going on here?" Kendry said with his eyes wide, wearing his new military combat outfit.

"For someone who shouldn't be able to walk by themselves right now, you're pretty nosy," Bri responded, a slight flush on her cheeks. She wasn't necessarily embarrassed, but she was experiencing a slew of new emotions very quickly, as was I.

"Sure, bro," Kendry said as he chuckled and went to sit on the couch, seemingly gaining energy by the second.

"Don't worry, guys, you're not the only ones exploring those fields," Auxi said as she went to sit in Kendry's lap, a playful smirk on her face.

"Whoa, whoa, whoa! You're going to tell them now? Like this?" Kendry said, confused, as he tried to adjust to Auxi in his lap.

Puzzled about everything going on and feeling overwhelmed by the emotions, I took some of the warmed water and handed it to Bri to clean herself. Waiting in silence outside the bathroom, I yelled out to Auxi and Kendry.

"It seems as though we have a lot to talk about before we get to the Minnesota shelter. You two should pack everything up so that we're ready to hit the road when we finish. It's already almost 7:30."

"Yes, sir, Mr. Bossman," Auxi said in a mocking voice as she and Kendry made their way to the car, still chuckling.

Finishing up my shower and strapping my sword to my back, I made one last sweep through the home to make sure we had everything. Sitting in the back with Bri while Auxi drove and Kendry sat leisurely in the passenger seat, I couldn't help but think of everything that had happened: the changes, the realizations, and, most importantly, Kendry's miraculous recovery.

We ventured into the unknown, armed with limited knowledge and a radio that refused to work. Nonetheless, I found peace through a new understanding. I was finally learning more of what it meant to be human.

XIV. HEART

As I approach the final portion of my recollection, it is essential to note that the months that followed the small house were nothing short of amazing. The world continued to crumble, and the war only grew as our defenses slowly dwindled to small populations; every last-ditch effort to seal our victory was doomed from the start. However, I was allowed to learn more about myself and apply my knowledge in the most effective ways possible. I had been given a new purpose, a new reason to fight, and most importantly, a chance at redemption. Those months of daily struggle to survive and doing what we could to maintain momentum in our favor were stressful, but they were liberating.

The noise dimmed. The performative striving fell away. We measured value in clean water, intact mornings, and those who showed up when it hurt. Among those who remained, the field felt, if not equal, then at least reset around what mattered.

While life vanished in masses, the people left clutched it harder. Some cruelties paused. It felt obscene to admit any upside, and none of it made the bargain moral, but catastrophe re-leveled certain parts of living.

This opinion may be one that most would disagree with, but it is an opinion. I'm not saying it was the only way, but it was a way to achieve this. A clean slate for all who remained and the chance to prosper.

Given that I learned to see it this way, you may ask why I write this or why I would continue to fight back. However, just because the world was improved in some areas doesn't mean it was perfect. We had clean air, yes, but our very freedom was at stake. Those of us who remained in the rebellion were lucky, so much so that we grew to rather die in battle than kneel in defeat.

I digress.

I find myself far too advanced in these events compared to where I left off with my story. Zooming back in, I will now pick up in the car on the way to Minnesota. To the place where we would make our final push.

The car ride toward Minnesota had been quiet and peaceful for the first hour or so as everyone did their best to mentally prepare for what was to come. Although the roads were still covered in slaughter remnants, the chaos had mainly settled.

There were hardly any people on the roads, except for the occasional convoy of civilians mixed with soldiers making their way North toward the safer zones. There were also occasional holes, ranging in size. But one thing stood out to me the most: the lack of recent earthquakes and monster attacks. Sure, we had just been attacked the day prior and were still recovering in multiple ways. Regardless, there were usually a few roaming around or trying to attack. This isn't to say they weren't around or still attacking. It was hard to miss the jets that flew by every now and then or the sound of bombs and gunfire in the distance, but even that had significantly decreased. Perhaps it was primarily due to our location, but it seemed like things were calming down, for better or worse.

Sitting in silence, I looked over at Bri as she began to speak aloud.

"I know I'm not usually one to care, but I'm trying to turn over a new leaf," Bri said as she leaned toward the middle of the car. "What was Auxi talking about earlier when she jumped on your lap, Kendry? And how were both of you able to come back out clean?"

"Well... we're sorry to hide it from you guys, but Auxi and I have been seeing each other for a few months now. We would have told you, but we weren't sure how you would take it, so we planned to wait until after graduation.

"As for the shower situation, we didn't do anything in there; we're not crazy enough to let our guard down or dumb enough to swap all that filth, but she did jump in the shower while I prepared myself in front of the sink. I told her to come out a bit longer after me to avoid suspicion, but I guess she sped up when she heard the commotion," Kendry said as he leaned his head on the window, a faint blush on his cheeks.

"Really, now? If you two had been together for months, why weren't Bri and I able to tell? Even if you had somehow figured out how to do all of this behind our backs and stay platonic when around us, we should have been able to feel something off, especially Bri. Even so, I don't recall Kendry being particularly worried about Auxi when everything was happening," I said as I tried to piece it all together, remaining diligent in scanning the environment around me.

"It wasn't easy, but we basically had to act like we weren't interested in one another. It was tough at times, but Kendry always made sure to let me know I was on his mind. Even when all this was happening, he was in contact with me when possible, which is likely why he wasn't stressed to the point where it was noticeable. As for when the whole situation with my team happened... I would like to think he had faith in my ability to survive. But after all of this, on top of hearing you two talk, since you're not as quiet as you think, we figured we may as well just come out with it," Auxi said as she gave us a half-baked smile while maintaining her focus on the road.

"Yeah, we re-agreed to do it, but not exactly how or when," Kendry said, making sure to remind Auxi of his stance on how that was handled. "I've had my eye on her since high school, but I just never had the chance or knew when the time was right. I definitely didn't know if she'd go for me either. I thought D was more her type, with the physicality and all, but I guess the tortoise really can win the race."

"Me? I'm still comprehending all of this, and the fact that we're even talking about this right now is mind-blowing. I'm trying to turn a new leaf too, but you all have to understand how much of a shock this all is to me," I said, trying to comprehend, but truly confused by it all and how quickly it piled up. It was as if I were learning a new subject and had never encountered it before, but this time, I had no bridging knowledge of the topic. I felt like a rookie for the first time in a very long time.

"It's a bit strange and new to me too, D, but the trip has been clear so far, and my mind feels sharper, so try to comprehend it a bit more. If anything were approaching, I'd know with more than enough time to react, meaning you can expend more brain power. I've even come to better sense the monsters now; it's like I've unblocked some things I didn't know were in the way," Bri said calmly, her eyes focused yet distant as she changed the topic.

"Like D and his advanced speed and power? It sounds to me like there's not only something up with you two, but that as we've been forced to develop recently, you've unlocked hidden features," Kendry said before continuing. "I know I've been off my game recently, and maybe my deep concern for Auxi was to blame, but I feel it coming back and am more in control. I'm starting to see things differently already; the way we travel, the options ahead of us, even how we could perhaps win this thing. I'm not sure what's bringing on this sudden onset of opportunity and insight within me, but I also don't know how I'm even able to walk and talk already... As much as I would like to delve into the relationship between the two of you and help you both understand and navigate it, I think we need to think about our game plan for when we arrive at this location and all the scenarios that may arise. It also might be crucial to think about what you two are capable of, considering your blood is what has likely given me these gains," Kendry said as he addressed everyone, but was particularly speaking to Bri and me.

"I agree, but as for the blood and abilities, we're just as lost as you. As far as we know, there's nothing inherently special about us in a way that could defy what we understand to be basic human physiology. Of course, there may be side effects from repeatedly being covered in the blood of these creatures, but since this is not a widely known topic, we can't be sure. There's also the prospect that something happened to us at birth, since we've been like this our whole lives, different and all. However, the likelihood that both of us experienced some experiment or other changing feature is extremely low. I assume the same for D, but my mother clearly remembers having me and nothing occurring to change me from birth. I share their DNA, their characteristics, and more importantly, I'm human through and through.

"I know I'm covering multiple topics and possibilities, but I truly don't believe anything has altered us in some way.

I must say, it's peculiar that D and I share similar attributes, such as being able to quickly recover and possessing above-average intelligence, but we're not too different from you two. Knowing this, there's no way to definitively say that something is necessarily afoot, just that some people are more advanced in some areas than others, causing a lack or complete gloss over of areas deemed less significant by one's genetics... As for the blood, I can only say it's a side effect of years of priming ourselves for peak human performance. I know it's still not much of an explanation, but I know just as much as you about that. Trust me, when D healed, I was taken aback, but with our history of quick recovery, it's only natural that it would grow stronger as we did," Bri said, trying her best to make sense of everything happening.

"I agree with Bri. We don't know what's happening, but maybe our genetics are some form of early human evolution. History is riddled with anomalies and people who shouldn't have survived certain situations or displayed extremely high intelligence from an early age. Given that these events have occurred in various forms throughout history, it's reasonable to say that the stress of the situation has altered us. It's also been a great help, unlocking more power, healing, and our natural abilities, such as enhanced brain function. I want to understand the truth and how everything fits together, but this might be something we revisit once everything is over. For now, let's hope these effects continue for you and you don't suddenly revert or need more blood. As much as it intrigues me about what humans are truly capable of, it would be much worse if this were only temporary," I said as I attempted to level the situation, trying to ease the collective confusion.

"Yeah, I wasn't trying to prove a point with you guys, but those are some great arguments. I do feel great and like my mind is becoming clearer, but I don't feel any faster or stronger. I guess that rules out the possibility that your blood is some form of super soldier serum, but it piques my interest nonetheless. I'll think on it more as we travel and continue to see how we all respond to the challenges, but I think we should focus on something we can do something about... I have ideas, but I wanted to open the floor first before I share them for how we approach this shelter," Kendry said as his mind began to noticeably turn, a familiar spark returning to his eyes.

"Listening to y'all talk would make someone insecure start to really feel bad about themselves," Auxi said in a joking manner. "I know I'm not the most talented person in the world, especially on a planet with you three, but I do feel as though I've gotten faster. Of course, I'm not as fast as Dion exactly, but I think I could give anyone here a run for their money... I know it sounds random, but since we're all talking about abilities and features, I just wanted to remind y'all, just in case I'm needed. Also, I hope to inherit a portion of the magic blood that you all have in your veins, if need be. I've been healing and doing just fine, but just keep that in mind in case I ever require a boost."

"Of course, Auxi. We'd do anything to keep you alive. Also, we haven't forgotten about you in the slightest. There's just been a great deal of revelations amongst us," I said in an attempt to reassure Auxi, a warmth spreading through me at her words.

"Yeah, I know. I don't really feel hurt or left out, I'm just happy everyone can move and is happy. You both gave significant amounts of blood yesterday, and now you're here as though nothing happened. Y'all continue to amaze me, and I hope that this persistence endures... Now, what are we doing about this shelter?" Auxi asked as she went back to Kendry's initial question, bringing us back to the task at hand.

Looking at Bri, expecting her to have something to say, she looked right back at me. Her gaze instantly reminded me of my new vows and my desire to provide my team with the best possible help as a leader.

Sharing these thoughts, I explained my plan to stop five miles out and send one or two of us to the entrance of the shelter, while the other two went a long way around to enter from the flank. Unknowns stacked: no verified status, no map of the structure, no guarantee it hadn't become a trap. We'd use the handheld transceivers Capt. Burks gave us. The boxes that bragged "35 miles," which meant three to five through timber, ten on clean line-of-sight; if the shelter ran a repeater, maybe more. Rendezvous on failure back at the split point.

Kendry listened and nodded, then drew a line in the air. "Standard pairs say Auxi with D, me with Bri. Breaking our pattern is risky, but the geometry favors voice and restraint at the gate. You two, "he flicked a glance at Bri and me, "talk us in if talk's possible. Auxi and I go long to keep our options lethal. If the comms die, we get the hell outta dodge. How's that sound?"

Auxi rubbed her forehead once. "So we separate our two best hitters and put me on babysitting duty with the thinker?

Okay. If a voice on a wall makes the difference, I'll take the long way and keep that difference alive."

"We move pre-dawn," Bri said, already scanning the clock. "Four sharp. Fewer wanderers and fewer witnesses. I'll call heartbeats if they mass near us."

It was far from our best idea, but it was the best we could do with what we knew. In retrospect, I would have suggested another plan, but clearly, I'm still alive to write this, so it couldn't have gone too terribly.

Continuing on the road to Minnesota, we arranged to stop twenty miles away from the intended location. It made sense, as we could make a move early the next morning and still avoid detection if they had teams out scavenging. The roads were clearer than what we had seen, a sight that made the entire situation feel eerie. It was almost like they had made a path for us. Despite this, Bri could only sense the movement from the monsters in the distance, not particularly following us or exhibiting any herding behavior. Although my sensitivity to them was still growing, I felt something else. It was almost like a weight sitting on my chest that only grew as we approached. Unsure of what to make of it, I kept my eyes peeled and surveyed the land we traversed until it was my turn to drive.

Thinking back on this time frame, there were multiple things going on that we were not prepared for. As I navigated an unfamiliar situation, I found myself grappling with new group dynamics. I couldn't help but wonder what set Bri and me apart (or even just one of us, given that we both donated blood to Kendry), a weight that weighed heavily on my mind.

While I would eventually come to learn and understand what it all meant and why things happened when they did, I was stunned in the moment. Even more so, I was still mentally battling the words from the suited person-creature that haunted our existence. The way she, or rather it, had explained that they knew everything and were allowing us to travel and live. The sudden stopping of the earthquakes for a few days, and how they could seemingly begin at any time. The way we could only ever hear about the shelter in Minnesota, and none of the others. How our parents were heading to the same shelter. Everything seemed to be out of our control, yet it aligned with their plans.

Although I would find myself more correct than I had hoped, it was all part of a larger plan. The world ending brought out more of my speed and strength; it brought Bri and me together in a different way (somewhat), and it forced all of our families to be in the same location. It was off-putting, but in the moment, I went along with what led to our survival since that was priority number one.

The dreadful weight that was building on me was also something I had to ignore largely. It wasn't the same as the feeling when the creatures were around; it felt larger and more demanding. It was as if I were being called by something that wanted to kill me. I couldn't explain it.

Despite all of this, I continued onward with my team. Knowing that Bri and I both had two months from when we arrived at the shelter, we did our best to conceal the underlying concern. We would eventually tell the others, but until we knew we could make it there safely, we kept it to ourselves. There was already enough worry to spread as it was.

As I continue to look back and write down my memories, I understand myself and what has led up to the present day all the more. Zooming back into the recollection, I now take you to the small wooded area that we found for the night. Lying in wait for whatever the next day would present us with.

"We couldn't find anything better?" Kendry said as we created a makeshift tent out of tarps and string from Capt. Burks. The ground was wet, the rain still drizzling down from above. It wasn't an ideal location for anyone, but it provided more space than being in the car.

"I agree that it is unfortunate, Ken, but this is the most strategic location for our plans. You're the one who said so," I said to Kendry, trying to keep a straight face.

"Yeah... I did... but that was under the assumption there'd be someplace out here to stay. I know I can't complain about much, but sleeping in a soaking mound of earth was something I only planned to do when I die," Kendry responded as we laid down another tarp to separate us from the ground, shivering slightly.

"C'mon, Ken, it's just for a night, and we'll be moving early anyway. We don't know what tomorrow holds, so we might as well make the most of today... Who knows, maybe I'll finally get to quench my fire for some action; the buildup is almost too much... Of course, I would be content with some more peace, though," Auxi said, her voice a mixture of anticipation and weariness.

After setting up camp for the night, we walked around the campsite and rigged some wiring to trigger a press whistle in case something slipped by that we didn't notice. After this, we sat and ate some of the rations we had.

"Beans and anchovies... not a combination I would have pursued if I had the choice," Bri said as she scooped her first bite of the mixture, a slight grimace on her face. It was far from the best thing ever, but it beat starving, and some of the food we ate in the earlier days of the fall.

After we ate, we reviewed our game plan one more time. Bri and I would get out of the car with nothing but our weapons and the handheld transceivers that we had tuned that evening. Moving through the woods for the five-mile distance, we would let Kendry know when we found it, and he would begin his and Auxi's journey around through another way that flanks the main entrance. Once there, depending on the situation, we would either speak, fight, or run, hoping for a smooth interaction. From that point, we would simply have to assess the situation and determine the following steps to move forward.

With our semi-baked plan in place, we turned in for the night and rested for the next day.

As I lay next to Bri on our half of the small tarp, as Kendry and Auxi shared theirs, I slowly slipped away into slumber. The soft ground and sound of water dripping from leaf to leaf soothed me, but I should have known the night wouldn't be as peaceful as I was led to believe.

At some point in the middle of the night, too late for my eyes to see what time it was, I was woken by the sound of wet leaves compressing; light, then lighter, then still. The forest held its breath. Jet thunder, far away earlier, didn't echo here; the dark swallowed it.

On alert for what might have been an intruder, I turned to look at Bri as she lay behind me, facing the other direction. Almost certain that she was awake and heard what I heard, I reached out to touch her side. Just as I was about to reach her, she grabbed my hand and rolled over in our shared blanket.

"What is that sound?" I whispered to Bri, not wanting to wake Auxi or Kendry.

"Three steps. Then two more," she breathed. "Fast, staggered. Not them."

Knowing that I also didn't feel that dreadful feeling that let me know when one of those things was close, I lay still further to avoid drawing attention. Listening closely, I heard what sounded like more steps. I wasn't sure how many there were, but I knew there were more. Not wanting to wait any longer, Bri and I got up and slowly raised ourselves from the ground. As Bri went to quietly wake up Auxi and Kendry, I did my best to look around and find what was making the noise.

Remembering that we had received night vision goggles in the bags of equipment and tools from Capt. Burks, I went toward the bag. I quietly searched until I found them and ensured they had enough battery. Now with the goggles, I turned my attention back toward the direction of the sound and peered into the night.

At first, I only saw small animals such as owls and squirrels. However, upon closer inspection, I was able to see that about 50 yards away, a deer was present. Following along the path, I noticed another, and then another, until I saw the entire family of deer. Thinking this to be the cause and not hearing anything else, I decided to go back and tell the group.

"I think it's just deer. I looked around and that's all I saw," I said as Kendry and Auxi had begun packing up the few items they had out.

"You sure?" Kendry asked, his brow furrowed in skepticism.

"I'm pretty sure. You can look around if you'd like," I said as I handed over the goggles.

As Kendry looked around, I went to consult with Bri.

"You feeling anything else around?" I said as she leaned on a tree, her eyes scanning the darkness.

"I do, but I don't know what. It's almost as if something is close, but not large enough to portray its presence. Either way, I think we should leave the area. It's already 3:00 AM, early for our plans, but not too early to get started. Everyone's awake, anyway," Bri said as she looked at her watch.

She had a fair point. Although I felt somewhat bad about causing this minor inconvenience to everyone, it was better than ignoring it and letting a real threat exist.

After getting Auxi and Kendry to agree on the early start time for the plan, we returned to the car to prepare everything. As we did so, I fully expected to find a footprint, some clear slime, slashed tires, or anything that indicated we weren't out there alone. However, to my surprise, there was absolutely none of those things and nothing wrong in any way. Everything was going smoothly. Perhaps it was my response to the situation, since nothing had been going smoothly up to then, but I had no choice but to continue with it as it was.

Prepared for our five-mile journey toward the shelter, Bri and I headed off with nothing but one weapon each and our transceivers. We prepared for the unexpected. Following Kendry's idea, Bri and I moved in a mirroring zig-zag motion with one another. At the same time, he and Auxi began their drive around to enter through the back side of the shelter. Bri and I would run at an angle from each other and then angle back inward, each moving swiftly as I carried my katana and she held her tactical knife.

Once we broke canopy at a half mile, the trees thinned into a bald scar of dirt and floodlights. A fence rose out of it; ten feet, metal-backed, welded like it meant the last word. Beyond that: a mouth in the ground. Not a monster-bore. A bunker. The main door was a slab with a man-door set inside it, scored by black tar-like smears and handprints scrubbed to ghosts.

We lost cover and excuses. I keyed the transceiver. "Ken, half a mile. You two?"

"Swinging wide," Kendry replied, steadier than yesterday. " The geometry's clean. If it's a trap, it's at the center."

We agreed that one of us would stay unseen. Bri went visible. I slid obliquely to the fence and went to ground; dry grass with mud under it, iron on the air. Guards patrolled the catwalks. Not military. Training bled in from movies and former jobs. Still, turret mounts at the corners, one manned, one cold. Tower light pivoting.

A horn cracked. "Identify yourself," a voice ordered; the timbre said ex-cop, not soldier.

"Abrial Alvar," Bri called, palms up. The tower lamp knifed across her face. She didn't flinch.

The horn squawked back: "No entry during active contact. Hold position." A second voice, lower: "Weapons stay sheathed. Move and we ventilate you." A policy, not a panic.

The hair on my neck rose. That weight on my chest, the one building for miles, dropped like lead. Bri felt it too; her hand hovered off her knife and settled again. The lamp jittered. "Hands where we can—"

The treeline ripped open. Five Feralgehns burst from our backtrail; wet hide, climbing claws, amphibian stink you taste before you smell. Thirty yards and closing.

I ran. No shout, no warning. Just the angle I'd mapped while we waited, an intercept that put me in their teeth first. The nearest vaulted; the katana took the head clean, and the body didn't know it for a step and a half. I slid under the second, spine to belly, opening it like a zipper. Black spray hit the fence and boiled on a floodlight housing.

"Hold your fire!" Bri's voice cracked through the tower. Not pleading, but commanding. She sprinted the catwalk, shoving a barrel up and away. The guards froze. Their training wasn't built for us.

The remaining three circled, reading me. I feinted, drove steel through the boldest, and found my blade stuck. Bone locked the blade. My grip slid on their blood. No time to curse. They pounced. I dropped flat, scrambled up a back like a ladder, hide dry and awful under my hands. My fingers speared the neck seam; cartilage gave with a wet pop, and heat flooded my wrist.

The third sprang and caught its own. The shriek was teeth on foil. I ripped a claw free from the dead one, jammed it into the soft seam of the attacker's flank. The scream cut short. I wrenched my sword loose, split it clean, turned to the last; jugular half-torn, a hose under skin. I pinned its foot, climbed again, and pulled. The spray painted everything. When it stopped moving, I took the head. You always take the head.

Silence lands differently after violence. The tower lamp trembled on its bearing. I sheathed the blade. "We're not your problem," I called, steady. "We're your assets."

The man-door unsealed with a sigh. A woman stepped out wearing a badge on a gray lanyard and a look of calculation.

A low mechanical hum under the threshold pressed faintly against my ribs; the same pressure that had ridden my chest on approach.

"Are you in charge, ma'am?" I said, trying to be polite.

"Yes, yes, I am. Did you do this?" She looked around at the carnage, eyes wide with horror and awe.

"I did?" I said, still covered in black blood.

She glanced at a guard by a panel. The gate began to lift.

As I radioed Kendry to let him know it was safe to come now, Bri dropped to ground level.

After wiping my right hand on a post, I stuck it out to greet the woman.

"My name is Dion Hammond. Pleasure to meet you," I said, giving her the benefit of the doubt as to whether this was a good place or not.

"Dr. Aisha Ibezzi. Pleasure to meet you as well," she said as she took my still bloodied hand, a faint smile on her face.

"This here is Abrial Alvar, and the two people arriving by vehicle are Kendry Rainer and Auxiliadora Tudwrig. This is our group, and I hope we can work together to resolve this issue. I do hope that is a goal of yours," I said as I stood next to Bri while Kendry and Auxi pulled into the gate, the car lights now on.

"Absolutely. I don't know what it is, but something tells me you four will help us do just that," Dr. Ibezzi said with a hint of excitement. "Follow me inside, and we will get you cleaned up and fed. There is much to discuss."

"What about our weapons?" Auxi asked, ever practical.

"Keep them," Dr. Ibezzi said. "You're more skilled than anyone we've seen yet."

As the inner door cycled, the hum deepened, familiar, unwelcome, and the weight on my chest eased by a hair. Not the creatures. Something else. I filed it for later.

It might have been a touch performative, but we made it inside. It was time for the real challenge to begin.

BOOK III.

TO THE

LIGHT

XV. SHELTER

Now inside the shelter, I could see that it was more of a facility. The long walkway tunneled forward, thick walls swallowing any trace of the outside world. After a gentle descent of about fifty feet, the corridor opened into a cavernous hub.

The main room was lined with high-tech consoles and lab coats, the whole place running like a research lab. It looked sterile in its operation, but was clearly sharing this technology with people who were much in need of refuge from the dangers of the outside world. The computer screens were filled with data and what I assumed to be local research, given the limited internet access and radio waves. With the net and radio mostly blind, every screen carried local feeds like a nervous system learning to feel again. It was a shock to feel like we were back in school, continuing our various research projects and studies.

"What is this place? I thought it was just a shelter, but it seems like much more," I said as I wanted to learn more from Dr. Ibezzi.

"What you're looking at is an abandoned underground quarry that was retrofitted decades ago after the first subterranean inconsistencies were recorded. It is 50 feet below the surface, with another 100 feet of rooms, food, recreation, and, most importantly, the possible keys to how we end this. I usually spare my guests this speech, but you four have proven to be different; no standard individuals could do what I witnessed from you," she said as she looked at a screen of cameras watching the exterior, a flicker of something unreadable in her eyes.

"We've been attempting to gather more people to this location to build our forces and prolong humanity's struggle for survival, but we've only managed to gather a few hundred. What you may not know, due to the mass media outages, is that a true war is being waged, and we stand no chance in it. These creatures, their species, are much more complex than we could ever imagine. Around the world, we have seen humans erased clean off the face of the Earth, not just in recent history, but for centuries.

"None of it was ever truly understood until we began to make these discoveries about what really lay beneath our feet... I would like to continue speaking with you all, but I can tell you may require a shower and a proper meal. We also have fresh clothes if you would like, even though they may not be as trendy," Dr. Ibezzi said, even though she was only in her forties herself. A monitor to her right blinked, then steadied. A fine dust thread floated in the light and vanished.

"A shower, you say... Not with hot water, right?" Auxi asked, a hint of desperation in her voice.

"Absolutely. The system utilizes naturally warmed water through a geothermal loop, boasting energy efficiency and regeneration capabilities that will sustain it for the next century. Feel free to bathe as long as you'd like. The showers are just down the hall, straight ahead, beyond the dining area. After that, it should be time for the food to be ready, and you can help yourselves to anything you'd like; the food quantities, however, are restricted. Once you're all finished, meet me back out here. I will share my knowledge with you," Dr. Ibezzi said as she went to a table by the computers, and we made our way to the showers.

Absorbed in everything she just said, hearing that everything happening was likely connected to some larger investigation, my mind wandered. While I could tell that the others' minds were turning too at the thought of this information, and perhaps how much damage the world had truly sustained, I could tell that no one was more shaken than Bri. She wasn't literally shaking or showing any signs of nervousness, but I could tell something was off by how she began to walk a little differently, just a slight bit of tenseness that the average eye wouldn't see.

As we approached the bathrooms, the corridor split into two large restrooms, military style, filled with shower curtains and sinks. Although the two separate sections didn't indicate whether they were for men or women, it was relieving to see two functional restroom areas available. Looking at Bri, a touch of worry was evident in the look she gave me. Despite this, we all entered the same bathroom and collected our share of showering supplies. Finding our own showers, Kendry and I were next to each other, while Bri and Auxi did the same. We were grateful to be early enough to avoid the packed bathroom.

While showering in the makeshift stalls separated by curtains, I thought about what the suited thing said to me. According to the timeline, based on when we arrived, I had a two-month countdown starting from that point. By the end of July, Bri and I needed to be ready to go face them in whatever meeting they wanted to have. It wasn't an ideal setup, but that likely meant two months of peace, at least enough to not kill us. The thought of having to go, as bad as it may have been, was silver-lined by the chance to prepare for two months before that. I wasn't sure if it was an oversight on their end, but these beings beneath us claimed to have power over the Earth, yet they led us here and allowed for this facility to exist. Although massive holes were less common in the North, they could have very well made one there and doomed that place to death. They could have either told us to go there immediately or taken us, but they chose to give us time. What for, I didn't know. If they wanted us erased, why steer us underground, to one of the few places we could become harder to kill?

As all these thoughts played through my head, I found myself reluctant to get out of the shower. This wasn't an uncommon thing, but I was actually using warm water, something I hadn't used in years. I don't know why I didn't go for the cold water like usual, but maybe it was part of my evolution to be different. Either way, I began to see why people enjoyed them so much and why they risked their skin health for the brief moments of warmth. It was soothing, a feeling I can't say I'd ever truly known. That wasn't just me, though; Kendry was having a ball.

"Oh man, this beats the dorms or that old beat-up apartment any day. This is the best shower I've had in ages,"

Kendry said excitedly, his voice echoing slightly in the tiled space.

"The dorms weren't that bad, and our apartment was nice. I think it's just the fatigue talking," I said in response, a small smile playing on my lips.

"Shoot, man, you're even taking a warm shower, I can feel the heat. It must mean something's really up; maybe you really are changing a little bit. Even so, I've just gotta enjoy these moments while I can. We never know how long they'll last," Kendry responded, a sense of fleeting pleasure in his tone.

"Sure, I agree, I think..." I was saying before another voice cut me off, gruff and annoyed.

"The world's already gone to hell. Now you're telling me I have to listen to you bums talking in the shower this early in the morning! C'mon now, give me a break," said a voice sounding like it belonged to a middle-aged truck driver. "It's the apocalypse, not open mic. Wrap it up."

"My apologies, sir. We'll let you shower in peace," I said as Kendry tried to hide his snickering.

Once we had all finished, the girls having somehow evaded the trucker guy in the showers, we met back at the café. Upon receiving our food, we each had our allotted portions from the breakfast menu. Although it was an upgrade, we were still left with only three medium-sized portions, which was plenty, considering the state of the world. The choices were turkey sausage, regular sausage, oatmeal, powdered scrambled eggs, toast, and potatoes. Selecting my choice of turkey sausage, oatmeal, and potatoes, I joined the group as we sat at one of the tables. I slid my toast onto Bri's tray and nudged her potatoes back toward mine, the kind of quiet trade we did when she was up to it.

Sipping on my water, as I had had more than enough sun recently to drink their hyperconcentrated orange juice, we began to discuss the place we were in.

"What do you all think? I know they allowed us to keep our weapons and have this unrealistically nice and prepared setup, but I'm still unsure. I have a bad feeling, something that has persisted and grown as we've reached closer to this destination. Though I have no justification as of yet," I said as I tried to keep it down, my gaze sweeping over the bustling room. A guard's hand checked a holster by habit. Overhead, a pipe ticked as hot water moved.

"It is all strange, yes, but I think we should give it a shot. We've been on the run, and this place looks like we really have a chance to do something about what's going on outside. They know things we don't, which means we can work with them to understand and gather the history of what happened here and why this species chose to strike now. Not to mention that our parents are still on the way as well as other possible survivors from our school and travels, assuming they decided to go here," Auxi said as she finished cleaning off her plate in record speed, her usual optimism shining through. She still sat with her back to the wall and eyes on the exits.

"I agree with Auxi, we should give it a try. I think we should check it out and see everything for ourselves, but it's not a bad start. Plus, I think it's too early for people to have lost their minds to the extent that this is some human death trap or sacrificial grounds for whatever those things are," Kendry said as he looked around, a glimmer of excitement in his eyes.

"I understand those views, and I also would like to learn more about what we could really do to make a change, but we do need to make sure this place is as it seems. Why don't we ask Dr. Ibezzi to give us a tour of the entire facility before we speak on the situation? I know we need to work toward a solution, if one exists. Still, we should address any concerns here first," Bri said as she tried to find a solution working for everyone, her gaze steady and thoughtful. She rubbed at the base of her skull once, distracted, then folded her hands again.

All in agreement on the choice to request a formal tour, we made our way over across the large entrance room to Dr. Ibezzi. As we approached with our donated clothes, which were slightly too large for Bri and Kendry, waiting for ours to be cleaned and disinfected, she turned to face us. As I saw information about the Earth on the screen, my mind was immediately fascinated by the views of data and structures I had never seen before. Nevertheless, I kept my focus on the topic at hand and requested a formal tour.

"A tour? We have finally found you, the people who have survived in the new world we live in and now have access to critical knowledge that has long been hidden from the government and society at large, yet... You want a tour of the facilities? Is that correct?" Dr. Ibezzi said to us, her expression slightly confused, with a curious tilt to her head.

"Affirmative," Kendry said as Auxi slightly elbowed him for his dramatized vernacular.

"Well then, I guess we really have found the right people," Dr. Ibezzi said as I assumed she appreciated our thoroughness. "Follow me, and we will walk through each of the ten levels."

Walking down the large, dark hallway where the shower entries were held, we came upon a slight slope in the walkway that would bottom out after 10 vertical feet had been traveled. Each flat portion of the level was approximately 40 yards in length until the next slope, creating adequate space for the features she said were present when we first entered. So far, a good sign.

"The first two levels, heading down, are where we house our scientists, researchers, volunteer soldiers, and other key staff members. As we pass by, look to the left and right, and you'll see that each entryway is connected to a large room filled with cots that stack upon one another and line the walls. This leaves space in the center for a small restroom area containing three toilets and four sinks. It's not much, but it's more than being outside, using leaves, and sleeping on rocks.

"Although these areas hold around one hundred persons on each side, the three levels beyond this are fitted to house two hundred persons each in a more compact design. These areas are designed this way, as this is where the survivors come. It is not that we deem them to be less deserving. However, when you don't contribute or have a key role, we prefer to keep you further from the top levels so that you can access the recreation areas and our staff can easily go to their stations when necessary. The sleeping spaces all have adequate room for one person, so the difference lies in their setup. The larger space also helps our staff to stretch and whatever else they need to do as they prepare to leave," Dr. Ibezzi said as we continued our descent, her voice echoing slightly in the vastness of the underground facility.

Walking past the rooms, I peered in to see the state of the place. The rooms were occupied, as she noted, with half of the people asleep and the other half preparing for the day in various ways. The spaces were clean, the cots looked somewhat comfortable, and the people appeared much calmer and healthier than those we saw at our last stop, which was crowded with strangers. In total, the people's situation seemed as presented, and I didn't get the feeling of ill intentions from anyone while there; instead, I likely encountered more confusion than anything.

As we continued past the sleeping quarters and various guards walking around the facility, I looked to see if anyone I recognized had arrived. While I couldn't tell at first, Bri confirmed this later, and I had a feeling that it was a solid location to reconvene, with our parents likely to be there sometime that day or the next. Unsure of exactly when they would arrive, I just knew they would, and I paid attention to Dr. Ibezzi as she continued explaining.

"On the next level down, sub-level six, we have our local doctor's office and pharmacy. As you would imagine, this area is heavily guarded and designed for non-emergency situations and treatments, provided we can offer them. We originally had our emergency room and trauma center here, but when someone is bleeding out, you don't want to waste time dragging them down six stories. Having that in mind, we moved it to floor zero, or the base level, where you first entered after our initial descent into the shelter. Here, you have free, but limited, access to stitches, medicine, and more that will help keep you and our community healthy. We place an emphasis on health here, as even a single outbreak of an illness can spread rapidly and undo all that we have worked to accomplish. Our Faraday shielding around the ER also reduces outside interference, so communications can become strange."

"On the next level, we have our gym on one side and a training facility on the other. The people who built this place must have foreseen what was to come, so they created an area where everyone could be close enough to survive. Although it was long before my tenure, I agree with that addition, as we never know when we might need to leave, requiring decent physical conditioning. It's not much, but it has everything you need to stay ready, and the training area for our soldiers has even more equipment. As the world only worsens and people eventually become desperate as their resources run out, it is critical to know how to combat humans and Manslayers alike," Dr. Ibezzi said as she continued, her voice gaining a more serious edge.

"Manslayers? Is that what you call those creatures?" I asked because this was my first time hearing the term.

"Yes, although they have specific names per creature, which you may know already, we call them Manslayers as a collective, at least the ones that we see slaughtering humans. It's fitting and dehumanizing, not that it requires much to do so, but it serves to remind people what's out there in case they've been lucky enough not to have direct contact with one... At this level, specifically sub-level seven, we have a gaming and snack area with limited options and quantities per person. While I do see this as frivolous, it is one of our most popular attractions, as the option to play board games or video games is available to help alleviate some of the reality that is setting in. As much as I would like to turn this space into another work area, we have plenty of those on the base level, and this helps to keep our people from wiring themselves too tight, especially when you're living underground for most of the day," Dr. Ibezzi said as she continued with the tour, with an evidently rare hint of a smile on her face. A fluorescent tube buzzed, then settled.

"Further down from sub-levels eight to ten, we have equipment, vehicles, and our armory; not in that order. These items are under special supervision because they are our most critical resources, which we cannot regrow. We have everything from armored vehicles to weapons that will easily take down twenty Feralgehns when manned properly. There's not too much to say about this area. Still, I'm sure you have questions about this," Dr. Ibezzi said as she placed her hand on a set of massive, solid steel doors that were at the end of the tunnel, a stark contrast to the earlier levels.

The corridor ended at a set of steel doors big enough to make the hallway feel like a throat. Cold radiated off the metal. When Ibezzi laid her palm against it, the skin on my forearms lifted, the way it does before thunder. "One of the original entrances the Manslayers and their masters made, to our knowledge," she said. "Discovered in 1934. Buried and sealed. We built around it." A guard's radio hissed, carrier only, no voice. Overhead, a pipe shivered; a drop of condensation fell and burst on stone. "With the recent activity from the Manslayers, I keep special precautions in place to ensure this thing does not open any time soon," she said, but her eyes held the door one beat too long.

As we analyzed the facility, we believed we had seen enough to understand the situation and didn't get the feeling that any of the monsters, or "Manslayers" as she called them, were around or had easy access. We agreed to stay for a while. Heading back up to the base level, we prepared to receive all the information that was to be shared with us. On the ascent, the low vibration in the ducts returned for a breath, then vanished.

Once back at the base level, the place was buzzing with the sounds of people showering and talking as the general populace had begun to rise. Sitting far enough away to drown out the noise with my own thoughts and conversation, I listened in as Dr. Ibezzi told us what she knew.

"Here's the condensed version: after the early 1930s discovery of the giant hole that I showed you earlier by some of the workers in the underground quarry, and subsequent research interests, a privately funded organization swept in before the government could get eyes or ears on what was happening. While this place was not always this large or expansive, things quickly changed when they found a dead Feralgehn inside a cave not too far from here. Piecing the story together as best they could at the time, they attributed it to some underground species emerging to the surface. Now, for what reasons, they had no clue. Back then, instruments would often fail near the holes. They thought it was the equipment. It was them."

"Fast forward fifty years, and things got interesting. The company behind this establishment was aware of similar discoveries made around the world. Holes were appearing out of nowhere in remote areas and various biomes, with reported sightings of humanoid figures wandering around and evading detection by major governmental agencies.

Despite their ability to make areas go dark and avoid mass detection, the company was able to keep track of them and follow their movements. We didn't yet know it at the time, but this species we believed to be emerging was collecting information on our technology, networks, behavior, weapons systems, and about humans as a whole. Although we wouldn't know the extent of it until much later, we suspected they were plotting something. Still, we needed more information before taking action, more knowledge about what they were and how to defeat them, should the need arise." A nearby monitor's spectrogram twitched, a brief comb of lines that flattened as quickly as they arrived.

"As time went on and we continued to monitor them, just as we assumed they monitored us, this trend continued until the 80s, when a sharp increase in human disappearances was observed in areas where these holes had appeared. We weren't sure what they were doing, but we knew they were behind the disappearances. That was around the time my father took control of the company, succeeding his father and completely reinventing our approach. Instead of simply watching and following, we began building systems and devising ways to defend against them, should they ever attack. The only issue was that we still lacked the necessary information. To fill in the gaps, we began sending devices equipped with cameras into these holes, a project that had grown over the decades. Although the first few didn't reveal much as we underestimated the depth of the holes and underestimated the interference by this mystery species, a few of them were able to be recovered, supplying us with these images," Dr. Ibezzi said as she pointed to the screen, her voice grave.

On the screen, I saw what appeared to be hundreds, if not thousands, of Feralgehns lying completely still along the hole walls as if they were sleeping. Looking closer, I could see there were even more Subterros that lined up between the Feralgehns. As she continued to show the grainy images of these creatures, she displayed one that revealed one of the humanoid figures. It wasn't very clear, but I could see that it had an elongated head and a humanoid body that was covered in skin similar to that of the Feralgehns.

Realizing an entirely new frame of reference had been opened to us, I began to ask questions.

"We have seen these Feralgehns and Subterros, but what about the Umbrorexes? Is that what that is?" I asked with a serious tone, the revelation of the suited figure from before clicking into place.

Dr. Ibezzi paused, her eyes narrowing slightly. "How do you know that name? We just recently shared that information with the military, and it was through our Biological Residual Readers only," she said as she seemed genuinely confused, her gaze sharp. The spectrogram did that quick shiver again, as if the word itself plucked a wire.

As she finished, however, she turned her attention to Bri.

"Abrial Alvar... why does that sound so familiar... You weren't working on a private underground research program, were you?" Dr. Ibezzi said as she looked at Bri, a sudden realization dawning on her face.

Bri took a second to respond before calmly replying, "Yes."

"Then it was you. I received word that someone unauthorized had added themselves to the list, but we had larger concerns at the time, as this species displayed power we didn't know to be possible... I heard about your achievements within our organization. I apologize for not being transparent about the true purpose of your work. We just didn't know who to trust," Dr. Ibezzi said, a flicker of something akin to respect in her eyes.

"I understand that the information was sensitive, but why would you not know whom to trust? It sounds like you mean that in a way where there was some sort of breach. Would that be a correct understanding?" Bri said as she fished for answers, her voice even despite the weight of the revelation.

"That would be somewhat accurate. Although there were no breaches that I am aware of, we discovered that the masters of these Manslayers had devised another project to support their efforts... Among the samples and corpses we collected, we came across one that appeared to be a mixture of what Dion assumed to be an Umbrorex and a pure human. Upon closer examination, we discovered that what we were observing was indeed human, albeit in a manner that defies our conventional self-perception.

"The internals were similar to ours, and the bodily functions seemed comparable, but it had the distinctive black fluid that resembles blood. The skin was also identical to ours, but it began to break off as it decayed and split in unnatural ways as we dissected it, behaving more like an outer layer than actual flesh. This is what we call the Umbrorex.

"That revelation was bewildering, yes, but it displayed the true power and goal of the underground species. Not only had they evolved to create geological changes, interfere with electronics, and somehow survive on the surface with no known repercussions, but now, we saw they were making attempts to blend in with us. They were trying to walk the Earth and only do what I assume to be their main goal: take back what's theirs," Dr. Ibezzi said, her words carrying a chilling finality.

"Wait, let me get this straight so I can understand what you're saying... You and your family have known about these 'Manslayers' and their mysterious masters for years, yet have done nothing to stop them. They have demonstrated destructive capabilities and the ability to take down our methods of communication. They have studied us for a known period of approximately 90 years, likely much longer. And you believe they stole humans for experimentation to create some sort of hybrid being that will speed up human extinction so they can reclaim the Earth... All that sounds about right?" Kendry said skeptically, his face a mask of disbelief.

"Yes, Kendry, that is the gist of the matter," Dr. Ibezzi said as we could do nothing but watch on as she spelled out the death of humanity, her voice calm in the face of such grim facts.

"Great, amazing, fantastic... So what are we supposed to do? All this time... what's the plan?" Kendry said as he waited to hear something positive; we all were.

"Well, we are trying to synthesize a biological weapon to defeat them, but there is still much we don't know. Their DNA is complex; they possess regenerative abilities that enable their cells to repopulate more quickly than we can eliminate them. The danger they pose also makes it difficult to obtain proper samples, plus we have yet to gather a decent sample from one of their leaders. The dead Umbrorex we found was too decomposed and early in its developmental process to provide any data in that way; it was clearly far from perfection. To combat this lacking side, we have been working with what remains of the military to coordinate air strikes on the creatures, which likely keeps them too occupied to cause any more natural disasters as of late, but that can only go on for so long... We're essentially approaching the end of the road and about to fly off a cliff as humanity takes the backseat to its own downgrade... If that happens, then at best we will be their slaves and at worst, we will become more stock for their experiments as they attempt to alter or improve their species.

"This is where I hope to learn from you four. Have you seen anything that could possibly help us to learn more? Anything that could serve as assistance? I witnessed what you did out there at the gate. I'm not sure about what the rest of you are capable of, but that was more than anything I've seen a soldier do against any of the Feralgehns... let alone five of them. So please, if there's anything you can do for us, we will guarantee you will have it your way, within reason. We need your help to save humanity," Dr. Ibezzi said as she seemed to earnestly want our support, her composure finally cracking to reveal a desperate plea.

Taking a moment to think before I spoke, I looked around the table at the others before looking back at Dr. Ibezzi and her associates. Unsure whether to fully trust them, given their past shaky ethical decisions, I could tell that the team was waiting for my response. Realizing that this was our last chance and I only had two months before it all might come to an end, I made up my mind.

"Dr. Ibezzi... we realize the predicament you are in and that humanity is in as well, and we would like to help. However, there are a few things I would like to agree upon before we get started, if you deem them acceptable terms," I said as I looked at her intently, reading her behavior as I spoke, trying to discern any hidden motives.

"Within reason, and if your information is beneficial, I don't see why not," she said as she leaned back, a flicker of hope in her eyes. Her gaze cut to a monitor and back.

"Good. I would like all survivors, regardless of their status, to be assigned a role to help keep this place going. A continued outward reach as we expand the areas under our control. Guaranteed protection for our families when they arrive. Lastly, I would like to secure guaranteed positions within your ranks, with Kendry serving as your lead combat strategist and commander. How does that sound?" I said as I looked for a reaction from Dr. Ibezzi, pushing for what I believed my team deserved.

"Sure, consider it done," she said as she let out no visible reaction to what I said, her face a mask of control.

Pleased by this, I finally provided her with the piece of information she was looking for, in the form of a question.

"Would you like to know what they sound like?" I said as her eyes grew wide with a new realization, and a faint, almost imperceptible tremor ran through her.

A new future was here; this was my opportunity to ensure it made it to fruition.

XVI. PREPARATIONS

Explaining everything to Dr. Ibezzi, I thought she would stop me at any moment to call my bluff, effectively ending our agreement. However, to my delight, as I explained the observed strategy, behavior, and communication methods to her, she continued to listen attentively, while her peers took notes. Intentionally leaving out the fact that Kendry had a remarkable recovery and that I also had an inexplicable recovery from a deadly wound, I told her about everything relevant to the situation. As part of this sharing, I also shared the two-month deadline that we received.

In retrospect, I should have told Kendry and Auxi sooner, but due to our prior engagements, the opportunity fell in that moment. The sharing of key information also meant that the dreams and visions were left out, as those had not been explicitly useful or telling in what was happening or how to defeat them.

Although I lacked specific information on defeating the creatures, I was able to share the thoughts they shared with me: how they knew all we were doing, how they controlled when the signals would work, and even how they could cause disasters anywhere on Earth. Hearing myself say it out loud was bizarre. Still, she absorbed the information and began to ponder its meaning. One thing she was especially stuck on was the fact that Bri and I were the only ones who could hear it speak. Initially hesitant to share that it was both of us, I decided to be completely transparent; my newly developed strength and senses would not allow anything to happen to Bri.

Upon completing my explanation, the area around us was fully awake and bustling, with people walking around, waiting for something to do. Dr. Ibezzi began to speak.

"You had contact, multiple contacts, with one of these Umbrorexes? And it spoke to you, saying, 'We are one'... Never in my life would I have imagined it had grown this bad. You made contact and communicated with the most comprehensive form of Umbrorex we have encountered. Not only that, but it also targeted you two to communicate through some form of telepathy, at least I assume so, since Auxiliadora and Kendry were unable to hear the conversation from their end. It also had Feralgehns and Subterros on standby to protect it as it departed, a strange find indeed. It seems to have followed you, but it gave you a two-month warning, meaning we have time to prepare, and a reminder that it may be watching our responses in real time.

"Whatever these beings are, they are a force to be reckoned with, a force that grows stronger by the day in its plans. Although we will work together to devise a way to combat this and upend whatever they have in mind, I can only think of what my father considered for all of this, as he may have been correct...

"My father had a few suspicions about what their species was, but he was not around long enough to see much of the ones with more mind than instinct. He believed they were either aliens who arrived on Earth long before humans and hid underground to avoid the harshness of the surface, which I find far-fetched. However, he had another theory. He theorized that the beings and their Manslayer pets were some broken branch of past human evolution. He figured that, while Homo sapiens were the preeminent species that had prevailed on the surface, another variant of human had developed just as much as we had, if not more. Many people dismissed this theory, but a few considered its plausibility, and so did I. Having been raised in this ideology and aware of the dangers that lay beneath, I considered his idea and attempted to test it. Now, perhaps it is because he was wrong or because evolution has diverged too much to show resemblance. However, when I was able to collect a rare DNA sample with sufficient material to test, it showed less similarity to what we share with chimpanzees, indicating it was too distant to be a human hybrid.

"However, I have only been operating from what we understand to be possible. What if this species possesses technology and genetics different from what we currently understand? We could be applying our limitations to a species that knows no bounds anywhere within our spectrum of thought. No human has the power or knowledge to create the massive holes and earthquakes that these beings have, so why would this be any different?

"My understanding of the situation has shifted rapidly, but is there anything else you would like to share with me as we process this information?" Dr. Ibezzi said, already switching her focus to the future of her research and plans.

"Knowing all of this, I would assume that this species is not too different from us. Given that they communicate and are trying to convey something to us, my best guess is that they have a civilization beneath us as well. I may be wrong, but if I am correct, then perhaps we can create something to counter their attacks before they launch them against us.

The holes they create are where the creatures originate, meaning that they must return to a specific location. I would also bet that the holes are all connected, forming an interlocking maze that centers on a central location. We may not know where the central location is, but since the Umbrorex told us to meet it in Rosebud, South Dakota, I would like to think that this location is where we can make our entrance to try and nip this in the bud, at least for this region," I said as I tried to think of what to do.

As I finished, Kendry began to comment and demonstrate his strategic thinking.

"While I agree with D's plans, I do have a few tweaks I would like to suggest to better shield us from any potential backfires or traps. Keep in mind, this is coming from a conversation that he and Bri had in their heads... Firstly, I need to know how many people you have here, how many are able-bodied, how many on average arrive per day, and what the total death toll is for the United States, if you have an estimate," Kendry said as he sat with a notebook they had given him, poised to write.

"Jeffery, bring me the data that this young man just requested," Dr. Ibezzi yelled as she faced one of the office areas.

"Yes, ma'am," Jeffery responded, his voice clear and immediate.

A few seconds later, Jeffery returned with the data and read it aloud.

"Just as requested. We have approximately 500 collected survivors, 200 staff, and 100 soldiers here. As for those who are able, we have a 90 percent healthy, able staff, 300 able-bodied adults, including 100 children over the age of 15, and the rest are elderly, injured, or too young. All of the soldiers recorded are able-bodied, with only a few having minor injuries.

"As for our daily numbers, we calculate that we receive an average of about 50 people per day, with that number expected to drop as the death toll rises with the attacks, as well as with earthly disasters based on our seismic readings. Lastly, although we are not sure, we estimate that the total US death toll is at about eighty percent. This means that there are approximately seventy million people left, but the exact number is uncertain. Also, I know you did not ask for global numbers. Nonetheless, the Earth as a whole is estimated to have lost 75 percent of the human population," Jeffery said, as the people in the area let the quantity of those lives lost sink in, a low gasp rippling through the room.

"Thank you, Jeffery," Kendry said as he rubbed his hand on his forehead, absorbing the grim statistics. "I understand that the situation is bleak, beyond that, actually, but we still have a chance to save what is left of the world. Not with a nuke or some other suicidal detonation at the center of the Earth, but through precision-based attacks to lure out the enemy and get a sense of what they are truly capable of," Kendry said, before being interrupted by Dr. Ibezzi's second-in-command, Dr. Edward Sharpton.

"What makes you so sure this is possible, young man? I get you must be some great strategist, but why is your plan better than continuing to work on a biological weapon?" he said, his tone condescending, clearly wanting to make an example of why Kendry's plan was unintelligent.

"Well, sir," Kendry began, unperturbed, "I see it as a game of chess. And before you jump to any conclusions, just think for a minute. If these beings have the capabilities we believe them to have, to open holes in the Earth and reshape the terrain, they could have easily killed us by now if they wanted. Not to mention the monsters that are constantly hunting humans around the clock. I know you think those soldiers you have outside are enough, but if they rushed the gates and kept piling on, it would only be a matter of time until they were inside. Thinking about it that way, there is either something they don't want to destroy or they are not as capable as we believe them to be," Kendry said, and Dr. Sharpton relaxed and kept quiet, a hint of grudging respect in his eyes.

"See, these creatures said that we were one, meaning that they see something in us that we overlook in them, some form of connection. This is not stopping them from killing us, but it gives us insight into their minds. Think about any time people have gone to war in the past. Usually, it's for some resource or to claim land, right? So, how many times have we seen the attacker destroy all of the land it wanted to capture or all of the resources it wanted to control? They didn't. Because that is the end goal. Now, I don't know if humans are the resource and they want to experiment without kidnapping people, or if the land is what they want and they feel as though we have ruined it, earning ourselves a swift replacement in the food chain. Regardless, we have the protection of being, or being around, something they want, so let us attack them before they change their mind.

"Yes, continue working on the bioweapon, as my plan may not be foolproof. But we still need to build an army that goes out not only to fight, but also to capture these things, save other survivors, and anger them enough that they might show their hand. No battle is won without sacrifice. And right now, all I am seeing is the human race losing. Does that make sense to everyone?" Kendry said, looking around the area at the staff members, his voice resonating with conviction.

"We understand you, Kendry. What would you like us to do?" Dr. Ibezzi said as she prepared to follow Kendry's instruction, her earlier confusion now replaced with determination.

Once again, this time without needing to be in an agitated situation, Kendry's abilities shone bright. Although it was not necessarily his ability to strategize that worked well, it was his mindset and the way he made others see situations from his perspective. It did not require fancy words or empty threats; it appealed to the logic within most people and left them no room to rebut. It was as if I were watching a master at work, further cementing Kendry as the true force he was.

Over the next few days, Kendry convinced the soldiers, who were not military personnel but rather mercenaries and security types hired to protect that place, to begin training all adults and teens sixteen and older in how to use weapons and overall battle tactics. Everyone who was not interested in that was either assigned to assist the scientists, perform chores around the facility, or sent to contribute to the larger effort of expanding the facility's real estate.

While the surface had been used to store personal vehicles that did not need indoor protection, the area was relatively small. Seeing this as a weak point and an opening for a concentrated attack, Kendry helped guide the workers in creating makeshift walls farther and farther out, using whatever they could find. Of course, this had not gone far in the few days since his influence took effect, but he was still able to make an impact.

As for the rest of us, we each prepared for what was to come in our own way. Given that Bri and I were the main ones summoned to this location, we began a practice regimen in which I focused on sharpening my senses. While I did this, Bri began developing her physical attributes and becoming more comfortable pushing her limits. Although we knew that everyone could only improve by so much within the two-month time frame, we figured that Bri and I would be able to develop the most, given how much we had accomplished in the days leading up to our arrival at the shelter. It also helped that we had all unlocked something at the time when Kendry was gravely injured. Due to the emotional strain of the situation, I broke through my physical limitations, growing faster and stronger with each situation or training, proving that stress and adrenaline gave me a momentary boost as well as a lasting increase in ability.

As for Bri, the moment that everything truly changed for her was when we shared our emotions with one another, finally clearing the air. Although we still explored this arena, taking the time to expand on it when we were afforded the opportunity, we were still learning. Despite this, it strengthened our bond, our understanding, and cleared Bri's mind, allowing her to discern even more. I could tell she was growing stronger by the day when she could feel a breeze ten seconds before it arrived. The fact that she could do that meant that I could too if I tried hard enough, so that is what we did. We devised a plan to train both inside and outside the growing facility, preparing for real-world situations we might encounter, while also utilizing the shelter for more hazardous or vulnerable practices.

When it came to Auxi, she may not have had some great awakening or rekindling of an ability like the rest of us, but she wasted no time in expanding her expertise otherwise. In addition to continually pushing her own limits in speed and strength, developing at a rate more comparable to Bri's and mine than anyone else's, she partnered with the medics, working to educate everyone on first aid and emergency tactics. From staying calm under pressure, something she had mentally trained for after the Kendry incident, to performing miniature surgery to save a life, she began a program to train everyone in the facility. For those interested in learning more and potentially becoming a medic, she dedicated additional time to teaching them how to assist. Two months was nowhere near enough time to train someone to be a doctor, but she and those she worked with did what they could to ensure the new learners were prepared with the basics.

While doing all of this, Auxi still had time for Kendry, and we all still had time for each other. Although Kendry was the busiest with his military regime and strategic planning, we made sure to stop by each other's areas to see what was going on. Bri and I had the most free time, as the only specific things we did outside of training were helping with scouting missions or other ventures, as well as working with Dr. Ibezzi and Dr. Sharpton to discuss the plans at large and retrieve samples for the chemical agent they were creating to fight the creatures.

Although not all volunteers were grateful or on board with the changes, as some did not fully understand the situation's gravity, the shelter experienced rapid change and immediate growth during those first few days. We even found the young woman making the announcements to be Dr. Ibezzi's daughter, who, while only eighteen, was already picking up the slack and following her mother's command. Everything was working as it should.

However, a few days after we began, a group of vehicles came racing toward us, accompanied by an entire wave of twenty-five Feralgehns and multiple Subterros behind them. Given that it was midday, fortunately for us, the guards sounded the alarm, and everyone immediately assumed their positions. Kendry's plan was simple: rifle team up top, Auxi and an infantry unit ready to flank, Bri and me in the center lane. With everyone in position, we waited for Kendry's signal. Waiting anxiously, excited to see how much Bri and Auxi had developed, as well as Kendry's general skills, I got a weird feeling. I looked at the vehicles, locking eyes with a set of familiar peepers. Instantly recognizing who it was, I looked at Kendry and burst through the gate opening just as he instructed his soldiers to fan out.

Our parents had finally made it.

I broke into the open field as Kendry had instructed the first set of soldiers to begin firing at the creatures. They aimed high for the head, taking semi-automatic shots to efficiently use ammunition while not harming any of us on the ground. Although running alongside flying bullets was nerve-racking, even for me, I have to admit... they had good aim.

Taking advantage of the cover fire distracting the slowing monsters, I ran past the vehicles. As I did, I saw our families within one of them, their faces pale in the windshield glare, confirmation enough. Knowing they were approaching the gate, I ran for the back row of monsters to begin taking them out and working my way back in.

As I slid and glided around the speeding creatures, I could tell my abilities had grown stronger in just that short amount of time. Not only that, but I was able to sense the monsters to the point where I was confident enough to do that with my eyes closed. While I didn't take the risk, I took advantage of the situation and sliced off a few legs as I made my way to the back. Once there, I noticed Bri had kept up with me as I turned around. She, too, had built up her abilities and was now dual-wielding gladii and creating her own path of damage, a feat of strength and skill in itself.

As she reached me, we both stood looking upon the creatures that had been surrounded by not only us, but also Auxi and Kendry's ground forces.

By this point, Kendry's riflemen had stopped shooting to avoid hitting anyone, and the creatures no longer made attempts to advance. The monsters seemed paralyzed by a fear that I could feel emanating from their bodies; the first time it had ever happened. Even more astounding was that Auxi and the others were capable of surrounding and standing their ground with these creatures so soon. While they were by no means prepared for full battle or one-on-one combat, their bravery and readiness to fight were more than enough to serve as an example for those still inside, watching on the camera screens. As we prepared our continued assault on the injured and standing monsters, Bri and I looked at Auxi, who understood what that meant and waited for us to break the circle. Attacking the fully healthy monsters and leaving the more injured ones to the survivors who were facing off against these creatures for the first time, some of the survivors were visibly shaking as they were forced to fight or die.

Absorbing the moment and not letting the danger posed by these creatures go over our heads, Bri and I sprinted toward the healthy Feralgehns, leaving a cloud of mist in our wake across the moist terrain. Although I was still faster than Bri, the past few days and increased mental clarity had done her well. She fought beside me as we each went for the Feralgehns' weak points and joints, disabling them as we dodged their relentless attacks. Sliding, jumping, spinning, and diving, we employed every tactic we could to reduce the numbers and strength of the fifteen or so remaining Feralgehns.

While in this frenzied yet strategic attack, we had to be mindful of the Subterros that surfaced in the seams of our movement. Despite being unable to rely on Kendry's still-training snipers to shoot with enough precision to kill a sprinting Subterros individual without hitting one of us, he used his radio transmitters to coordinate his soldiers on the ground. They followed his command by listening for the assigned number each had been given. He could have called them by name, as he knew all of them and continued to learn about new recruits, but referring to them by number was ideal and avoided confusion caused by duplicate names.

Working as though we were a well-oiled machine, Bri and I carved our way through the monsters and moved with such speed that it was difficult for the viewers to keep up. The strength it took to cleanly slice through these creatures was intense, especially for Bri, using a single weapon per hand. Yet, our developments and training made it look almost supernatural. More questions about our skill would likely have been raised if more people had successfully attempted to cut through one of those creatures with a single slash, but many never got close enough to try. Regardless, we kept moving, but found ourselves at one point surrounded by five more Feralgehns as we finished off one each. Realizing that we had to get out of this ourselves, as the others were killing off the ones we had injured or fighting the smaller Subterros, we prepared to make something happen. Just as the creatures' muscles began to twitch, as did ours to move, I felt a new sensation approaching the area. Familiar, yet stronger than what I could have imagined.

I turned to see that Auxi had made her way to the Feralgehns surrounding us and used her own blade, a recently acquired kukri, to slice at a few of their Achilles tendons, reducing the number that could attack. As she did this, the ones she couldn't reach sprinted toward us. Dodging the first one, Bri and I dashed back and narrowly missed a claw swipe that would likely have opened a few new holes in our faces. Unable to land a strike, we turned our attention to Auxi as she worked to finish off the ones she injured, basking in the glory as she was visibly overtaken by her energy. However, as she did this, the monster we dodged targeted her while the other two that had been surrounding us charged. Silently deciding that Bri would go and help Auxi, I stayed to fight the two that charged us.

Isolated with the two monsters, I patiently waited for them to get close enough for the hairs on my neck to stand. Although I was able to sense and feel them better, the hairs on my neck rising warned me that they were about to attack. Using this sign, I took the first at the elbow creases as it reached for me, then drove my blade through the second one's torso. Pulling myself close to the one I had just stabbed in an attempt to avoid being slashed, I planted my feet and used all of my strength to lift the heavy creature and slam it onto the one that had just lost its arms. Now sandwiched and still writhing, I removed the sword, lined up my blade, and decapitated them both as the ground began to turn black with their spewing blood. Observing the scene, I looked at Bri and Auxi to see that Bri had disemboweled and dissected the attacker. At the same time, Auxi removed her blade one final time from the second of the two she single-handedly killed.

Amazed at what our group accomplished and improved on in such a short amount of time, I couldn't help but shed a genuine smile. The world was still burning as the military continued to fail and run out of firepower, but seeing how much our hard work paid off was something I was proud of. Even more so, the other people around us had developed as well, successfully fighting and killing the smaller Subterros and wounded Feralgehns that Bri and I had left in our initial sprint. Looking about the carnage, dead corpses everywhere, leaving almost every fighter covered in the creatures' blood from head to toe, I was pleased to see that there were no significant injuries, only a few bruises and cuts from the struggle. Facing back to Kendry, who was now standing more relaxed as the danger subsided for the time being, he gave me a smile, signifying the success of our young force in its first real challenge. In just those few short days, our plans and regimen, combined with our knowledge from surviving, had paved the way for a change. A change that could shift the momentum of what was happening.

Heading back to the base, excited to see our families and whoever else had been in the entourage, we thought of how much brighter the future had just become in light of our advancements. We figured we might have actually stood a chance.

Once back inside the gate, we made an attempt to wipe some of the blood off of us as others went out to collect samples from the corpses and dispose of the rest.

After cleaning off what we could, we turned our attention to the three vehicles. As the doors of the first one opened, I was delighted to see my mother and father step out from the front seats of the SUV. It wasn't the SUV my friends and I had started with, but one similar to it. Feeling a new sense of warmth and relief, I made my way over and hugged them, trying to avoid smearing the black blood. As most parents would react, they didn't care about the blood. They were happier to see their son alive and well in a scenario that seemed like the end of the world. Standing with my parents, I watched as Bri, Kendry, and Auxi's parents also exited the SUV. It was a tight fit for them all, but thankfully, we had all been only children and they had traveled lightly, doing well scavenging for what they didn't need to carry at all times.

As Bri's parents stepped from the SUV, I could see that they looked exhausted, but something was different. Their usual cold and calculated demeanor was still present, but they seemed genuinely happy to see Bri and the rest of us. Standing and looking at Bri, who was unsure of how to respond since she had been changing and didn't want to project too much of this onto them, they began walking toward one another. They then embraced in a three-way hug, likely the first time they had ever done so. It wasn't that their household was unloving or lacking familial tradition, but everyone within it had always been so focused and driven that there was hardly any time to step back and look at things from an emotional standpoint. The world coming to an end seemed to affect that dynamic, but there was no guarantee it would stay or that there was time for it to remain if they desired.

Auxi and her family had less emotional strain than Bri's and mine. Although I had seen her parents plenty, it was an interesting sight to see them emerge from the vehicle with the same burning look in their eyes. Although all our parents, except Kendry's, were exceptionally fit and athletic for their age, her parents were on another level. They didn't look like bodybuilders or have packed on weight, but they looked lean, strong, and agile, clearly passing that on to her as well. As they embraced, I could see the overflow of emotion as they could finally reunite. For such a war-mongering and adrenaline-filled family, they had a massive soft spot for one another and seemingly anyone they cared deeply about.

Kendry's parents' reunion was nothing special, but it was calm and peaceful. Kendry, now acting as the general, had tapped into the sources of his great strategic mind, and it was evident in their immediate comments about his ability to lead, witnessing it from the moment of their arrival. Instead of exchanging an emotional hug or another gesture, they simply stood close and began speaking quietly, looking at the other two vehicles that had arrived with them.

As we prepared to go back inside to clean up and sit down to speak with our parents, we looked on as stranger after stranger emerged from the vehicles. Just as we turned to go inside, I turned once more, expecting someone else we had met or known to exit the cars. Instead, as the vehicles emptied, I saw that they were being prepared for parking, with no familiar faces exiting. Not knowing what to make of that, if anything, I went down into the base and quickly cleaned myself off before sitting at a table with our parents and Dr. Ibezzi, prepared to explain the current situation and plans.

After exchanging greetings and introductions, we began discussing the plans underway to reclaim our freedom. Although our parents weren't thrilled about their children engaging in these risky acts, they understood our capabilities. They trusted us to make it happen. It also helped that we were all college graduates, technically old enough to make our own decisions and live with them. As for what was to come, neither of us had a choice in the matter if we wanted to prolong humanity's survival. Although we had no idea if what we were doing would make a difference on a global scale, local success would reveal the extent of the damage and the reach of these creatures, providing us with crucial information. Upon sharing our plans and information, we waited for their response.

"I am sure you four, plus Dr. Ibezzi here, can understand why we would not be so excited about these plans. However, we understand that you have a duty and feel a responsibility to perform that. That said, I have no choice but to provide my blessing and support toward fulfilling this goal. Anything toward the cause is something I am willing to do," said my father, Carter, his voice firm but laced with quiet concern.

"Absolutely, son. We know we can't speak for everyone, but we are confident we understand the gravity of the situation. We had to make it through a few different predicaments just to get here, nowhere near what you all went through it seems, but still enough to see the danger and acknowledge how bad this has gotten and will continue to grow," said my mom, Jasmine, as she rested her hand on my father's, her eyes reflecting the weariness of their journey.

Thankful for this, I felt a renewed sense of assurance in my decision-making as my parents supported my plans. Although we were still awaiting the other parents' decisions, my parents' quasi-leadership gave us a strong start on how we were to move forward. That said, the most logical and observant parents of the group, Bri's, had information they would like to add.

"I appreciate all that you plan to do, and no doubt have a great appreciation for how you all made it here. Even a blind man could see what you all, especially our Bri and Mr.

Dion, were able to do out there... That said, we can see that changes have occurred within the group," Mr. Alvar, Andrew, said as he folded his arms in a cold demeanor, his gaze unnervingly piercing.

"I agree. Something is happening between you and Dion," Mrs. Alvar, Adriana, said as she looked at Bri, her voice devoid of inflection. "We can tell the same with Kendry and Auxiliadora; however, that is nothing new to us. Although we see no issue with what is going on, the timing could not be worse. You have made it here and remain effective, but we want to ensure that these bonds do not cloud your vision when it is time to make decisions or read the situation. It is critical to remain open to everything happening around you. While our Abrial tends to retain that aspect, we will see how these changes impact decisions when the air thins. Would everyone see that as fair?"

As Mrs. Alvar finished, all the parents seemed to agree, although they were not pleased with the coldness of their responses. Even factoring out the coldness, there was much truth to these statements that we simply could not ignore. It was almost like they had read us like a book, but before Bri or I could form a response, Auxi began to speak, her voice steady.

"I understand your concern, Mr. and Mrs. Alvar, but we have already ironed out these issues. While it is true that our dynamic with each other and within ourselves has changed, we have adapted to make the most of these changes and have greatly improved since then. Just to provide you with proof, I would like to shed light on the situation with Kendry's injury and scars," Auxi said, a determined glint in her eyes.

While she spoke, the rest of us were quietly, though very well hidden, concerned about what she might say. Even though we explained a version of what happened to Kendry to our parents earlier, since he has three large scars on his back, almost completely healed, might I add, we did not divulge the full extent of what happened in an attempt to keep anyone from growing too much concern or having questions about his recovery. This was something we had kept to ourselves, which Auxi was well aware of, so we watched silently as she continued to speak.

"Those three large scars on Kendry's back, while obviously not that deep due to the extent to which they have healed, had an impact on me that initially made me lose efficiency in the field. Yes, I did not completely shut down and freeze, but I lacked key elements that would have otherwise been helpful in a tough situation. Although his injuries were non-life-threatening and he was still mobile, the thought of losing Kendry, or anyone at this table, suddenly hit me all at once. After watching my teammates and coaches die in front of me, my mind was not in the best of places, and that was the straw that broke the camel's back.

"Recognizing this, conversations were had and changes were made. We realized that we needed not only to improve for ourselves, but also to understand that this was something none of us wanted to experience again. We were motivated to protect one another. In a time when anything can happen at any moment, we need not freeze; instead, we need to improve, even in the most dire of times. So yes, we have not been in a similar situation yet, but I have been offered clarity that has changed my entire perspective. I believe we all have. That said, we are more than ready to proceed with our plans and save what we can of the world," Auxi said with confidence as she looked at the Alvars, her gaze unwavering.

As she said this, the Alvars' expressions did not change, but it was clear her words carried weight. As they and the other parents absorbed this information, Bri began to add to the topic.

"I agree completely with Auxi. We all gained clarity during the situation with Kendry and explored the impacts and value of our relationships. For a short time, when we first met with and struggled against this species, my senses were dulled against them. I am not sure what it was, but perhaps it was because I needed an adjustment period. Yet, at no point did they recover and improve as much as they did when our shifting dynamic reached its peak. When Kendry was injured, it opened a new window of possibility that we had yet to confront, even for me. It forced me to view life and our situation in a different light, causing me to aspire to be different. The doubts, thoughts, and realizations that I had come to before that event were slowly seeping out, and that was the moment it all happened; after we knew he was going to make it, of course. Since that moment and since I have allowed myself to enjoy more of the life I have, while still understanding the risks associated with having such a life, my vision has never been clearer," Bri said as she calmly made her case, something we hardly saw.

"I second that, well, third, I guess. Either way, that moment and those realizations allowed me to reopen my mind. Not that it was closed before that, but it was almost as if something had been lifted. My strategic planning and overall problem-solving and preparedness have been expanding nonstop since that moment. Although I am still myself and rather unathletic compared to these three overachievers, I can feel the changes taking place within. You two think trust and cordiality mean vulnerability, which is true to a degree. On the flip side, one could argue that keeping those emotions pent up and only releasing them in acts of violence, love, or any degree of extreme will only provide a brief reprieve. All we did was create a healthier circle for us, which is working," Kendry added as he turned his attention to me, as if I had to speak.

"Mr. and Mrs. Alvar, I have known you two for a long time. You know you can trust us, even if you try to act like you can't. You know Bri well enough to have faith in her abilities; she is your daughter, and therefore, everything you have poured into her and much more. She has brought out the most in us and continues to empower our growth and contributions to this day. None of us would even have been here right now if it weren't for her; so why question her judgment now? Although I can see you are satisfied, I would like to reassure you that we are improving every day; we will be more than prepared when the time comes to take the fight to these monsters and their leaders. I guarantee you, we will not leave empty-handed," I said as I looked at them with respect and confidence, holding their gaze.

As all of the parents looked back at the Alvars, Dr. Ibezzi sitting in silence, likely wondering how long this would take, they silently acknowledged our comments before Mrs. Alvar responded.

"We appreciate your responses and support for one another. While it was rather dramatic and assuming we lacked faith, it is appreciated. Let us know what is required from our end, and we will ensure it is provided," she said as she and her husband gave a signature Alvar stare.

"That is all rather difficult to follow, but just know we support you all. We have plenty of gas left in the tank and would love nothing more than to fight alongside our daughter," Mr. Tudwrig, Leo, said as he looked to his wife, Aurelia.

"Affirmative. Truth be told, we did a good amount of the battling on the way here. It got messy at times, but we loathed every minute longer we were away from our Auxi. Obviously, she is a growing young woman who makes her own decisions, especially with Mr. Kendry here, apparently, but we know that she has a bit of a drive. That energy, which can be destructive at times, wraps a big heart, and we would love to join in to guide it all. Besides, we can't let you kids have all the fun," Mrs. Tudwrig said, the same fiery look in her eye as Auxi's, as if the fate of the world was not on the line.

"I guess you would like our blessings as well, right? Interestingly enough, I have nothing much to say other than congratulations on surviving, congratulations on your relationships, and congratulations on getting injured, just like your old man. I love you, son," Mr. Rainer, Arthur, said as he looked proudly at his son, a rare display of paternal affection.

"Same here. We also know a thing or two about strategy and quick decisions, from the safety of a control room, of course. Kendry is a brilliant young man, but you cannot always beat the original. Count us in," Ava, Kendry's mother, said as she excitedly wrapped up the parents' conversation.

After the conversation, Dr. Ibezzi sat in silence for a moment, then began to speak.

"Fantastic, I hope that covers everything. Now, I would like to continue my research on this possible chemical agent and explore ways to eliminate these Manslayers. For the rest of you, try to determine where to place everyone so they can make the best contributions. I am sure that will be easy, given how oddly similar you are to your parents; it is quite peculiar. Also, be mindful of these Umbrorex beings. We do not know much about them, but if Dion's statement is accurate, we have approximately seven weeks before they become a threat. Either way, I am truly grateful to you all. What you have contributed to the future makes it much brighter.

"We still have food and resources, but feel free to hunt game as we continue to expand our population. It would not hurt to have reserves. I will be with the scientists and my daughter in the research room. Radio if you need me," Dr. Ibezzi said as she clipped her short-range radio to her waist and made her way to the room.

As we began meeting once more to discuss the plans for our parents, which were ultimately up to me but guided by everyone, particularly Kendry, I began to feel a slight tremble. Yelling for everyone to get down, the Earth started to shake violently once more.

The quakes and tremors that had been happening across the United States and the world had finally returned to us, in what felt like a targeted attack. Preparing for what might happen, Bri and I ran to the surface to better understand the situation, leaving the others to take cover.

The false peace we were provided had come to a pause.

XVII. COUNTDOWN

The ground shook violently with a strength even greater than when they had first returned. The structures on the surface began to lose dust and any loose material as the Earth seemed to want it gone. Staying methodical, we examined the underground shelter and did our best to assess its condition. Thankfully, it was built solid enough to withstand the tremors, though fresh shear lines laced a few columns and a fire door no longer closed true; however, the same could not be said if one of the signature holes opened in the ground and swallowed the place whole. This was primarily a concern, given that the facility was built around one of these holes, which provided easy access and the opportunity to recreate the hole.

We thought through the possibilities, rocking with the aftershocks while restoring what order we could. Instructing the guards and volunteer soldiers to come down to ground level, in case the center structure collapsed, we noticed some children had been getting fresh air. Although they were not unsupervised, the parents and guards with them struggled to return to the stability of the underground base.

Assisting them by maintaining our own balance, growing ever more comfortable with the unsteadiness of the ground as if we had sea legs on a ship, I noticed that some of the vehicles were not parked with the parking brake engaged. One SUV jolted and rolled a foot, taking the next nudge like a dare. I shouldered into the bumper, jammed a wheel chock under the tire, and felt the frame settle. Holding back what cars I could, I watched as Bri continued to guide everyone back to the underground base.

While things had been going smoothly, I felt another change occurring and yelled for Bri to come and activate the cars' parking brakes. Just as the last of the children and parents had made their way inside, we felt the ground rip as cracks appeared about 500 yards from the facility, on the back side. As the prolonged shaking continued, we watched a clearing begin to form as foliage collapsed into the Earth. The hole that soon formed was not massive, but it was large enough to let out multiple Feralgehns at a time.

Looking on, we expected those creatures to appear or even to see one of the Umbrorexes; however, none came. A few minutes later, the quaking stopped, but the damage had been done. While the watchtower in the center had not completely crumbled, it had sustained structural damage that required attention to prevent it from becoming a hazard. Spalled concrete dusted its base like ash, and the ladder cage looked a degree off plumb. There were also damages inside the facility, with items being knocked over, food spilled, and slight damage to the interior walls. Thankfully, the structural integrity of the entire base was intact, being extremely well-built. Still, this event seemed more like a warning than anything else. They knew we were within their grasp at any moment they chose; it was merely a reminder for those who may not have believed. From the new opening, a damp updraft rose, smelling of metal and mushrooms. Somewhere, a toddler started crying without knowing why.

After waiting a short while to ensure the shocks were complete, everyone began moving again. Standing outside, waiting for the others, Bri and I had a small conversation about what had happened.

"Are you thinking what I am? Was that a warning of some sort?" I asked as I wanted to confirm my thoughts with Bri.

"Absolutely, but I question their motives. If we are so within reach to kill or otherwise maim, then why wait? What purpose could that serve in allowing us to build our defenses and strength as we plot their defeat? Although we have no idea if they can hear what we speak about in person, it would be a well-educated guess to picture that they know what our goals are at a fundamental level based on our radio chatter," Bri said as we continued to watch the new hole.

Sitting in silence, leaning on the cars as we thought, Kendry and Auxi emerged from the shelter.

"Is that a new hole you two are looking at?" Kendry asked as he made his way over.

"It sure is, but nothing came out of it. I'm sure they will eventually, which is why I think we should strengthen our security and perhaps not expand that far out," I said.

"I concur. I believe the progress we, as a community, have made is nothing short of amazing, but this changes everything. We need to remove the training wheels a bit earlier to better prepare for potential challenges. That said, what are your thoughts on reducing our available time to six weeks instead of the seven we currently have? Not to just go catch them off guard, but to ensure we're not strolling into some death trap," Kendry said as he looked at Bri and me, his expression serious.

"That works for me. I was going to intensify my training anyway, so that will only feed the fire. Speaking of which, I wanted to ask: what was the plan for that exactly? I know Dr. Ibezzi looks to me for leadership, which I am more than happy to oblige, but from your strategic perspective, how are you picturing this doomsday meet-up going?" I asked to gauge Kendry's thoughts on the topic.

"Although I've been focusing on the army we've been building up, I have put thought into that day as well. Even though there are many ways these creatures could be planning to screw us over, I think that the reason they haven't killed all of us is because of you two. They requested that only you two go and have only directly communicated with you both, not anyone else. Sure, they may be keeping people alive to be slaves or some other tool. Yet, I don't see them taking us for that, not with our defiance and the damage we are capable of causing to them. Having that in mind, I have a strong feeling they will attack or completely destroy this place when you arrive at the location. They would have you by that point, being the big showdown, so even if you came out victorious, you would return to a hole in the ground where your friends and family used to be," Kendry said as Bri interrupted him.

"We understand that they will likely go for everyone here, but what is the solution to get around this? Clearly, everyone can't go with us; we would be walking into the worst situation for anyone to be in," Bri said as she looked intently at Kendry, her brow furrowed in thought.

"Exactly, Bri. I'm proposing that we all leave this place, but those who are not going to South Dakota head farther north to get away from these things. We do not know whether they can really go that far, but it's better than walking into formerly densely populated areas and hoping for the best. I still need to work out the kinks, and we need to speak with Dr. Ibezzi about it, but if we do it this way, at least someone survives," Kendry said as he explained his idea, his voice firm with confidence.

"I agree with Kendry on this. We obviously have no idea how everything will unfold or if any plan we make will work. However, we want to ensure that you both arrive safely and that we can provide you with the necessary support. Whatever we have to do to stay alive and stay together, we will.

"I know this may not go over well with everyone, but it makes more sense than waiting here. Not to mention the dangers that everyone will be exposed to without us. Even if

Kendry and I stayed, there are things you two can do that we simply can't; it is just the truth. You two are our greatest weapons and are currently the reason this entire place isn't a lake of dust and blood; so we would all be better on the move sooner rather than later," Auxi said as we all came to an agreement, a shared resolve in our eyes.

"Alright, I can't say I am happy about having to convince everyone to move and what that comes with, but it makes the most sense. When we discuss this with our parents and Dr. Ibezzi, we need to make sure Dr. Ibezzi's daughter doesn't expose these plans on the radio. Even though the creatures may already know what we are doing, broadcasting it to an audience that may or may not be alive or have access to a functional radio would only ensure they are aware. That said, when should we do it?" I asked, knowing I could be too ambitious at times.

"Well, there is no time like the present," Auxi said as we turned from the hole that was just created, a new urgency in her voice.

"You three go ahead, I'm gonna stay up here and watch this thing. I have some updated instructions for my volunteers," Kendry said as he radioed for all of his forces to come to the surface, already shifting into command mode.

Heading back inside to the base, we maneuvered through the still recovering survivors to find Dr. Ibezzi and our parents. Finding her in the research room, deep in experimentation as if she had not stopped working during the earthquake, we requested her to meet with us. Although she was less than enthusiastic about leaving her work again, we managed to get her to the table with our parents, and I began to explain the plan. As she and our parents listened, it became clear that not everything was going as we had hoped, but more than we had expected.

"You are proposing that we leave this place a week earlier than your scheduled meeting and split off into at least two groups? Is that right?" Dr. Ibezzi said, clearly flustered, as she unbuttoned the top button of her shirt to relieve the constriction she felt.

"Yeah, Dion, I don't know about this one. What did Kendry say?" Mr. Rainer said as he looked at us concerningly, a frown on his face.

"I know this sounds concerning, but have faith that I would do something different if I saw another way; however, this is the plan we have at the moment. Kendry conceived most of this plan, but we all contributed to its implementation. Consider this: this place will eventually be overrun or depleted of resources, necessitating expansion or relocation. Even if we were wrong and this place wasn't a particular target, if Bri and I were to unfortunately not make it back, how long would you all last? Especially without bullets," I said as I was interrupted.

"What do you mean, not make it back? You are both coming back, and I will personally guarantee it if necessary. We understand that there are things you cannot share with us, which is entirely understandable given the uncertainty of this situation as a whole. However, we believe there is more to the story than what has been shared. You two are special, for whatever reason that may be, which is why they want you.

"Keeping this in mind, we will follow your plan and ensure it proceeds as smoothly as possible. Dr. Ibezzi, do what you will, but we, along with the other parents, will stand behind them. They have made it this far in life without having their hands held, especially over these last few weeks as they fought all sorts of demons, so why would we go against the grain now?" my dad said as he looked around the table, his gaze firm, daring anyone to disagree.

As my father finished and everyone else remained silent, he looked toward Mr. Alvar for support, as he had known him the longest.

"Come on, Andrew, you know I'm right. Help me out here, this is not the time to start changing the narrative with one another, not now," my dad said as Mr. Alvar sat with his arms crossed, eyes closed, a picture of deep contemplation.

Breathing out sharply, Bri's father began to speak in response to my father.

"For as much as I personally agree with Dr. Ibezzi, not wanting to split our forces and leave anyone unprotected, I must also face the logic in the solution of our children. I do see that there is more to the story, Carter; you know that I do. I just want to make the best decision for our families and for our future. However, I understand that this decision is not mine alone to make, and I also see the responsibility that our children have. That said, if I agree to support this plan, I need you three and Kendry to train yourselves mentally and physically until it is maddening. Never underestimate our enemy; I want you all calm and collected in this fight to finish them.

"I also need the parents to train as well. I know we are a bit older and our health may not be what it used to be, but that is no excuse to place all of that weight on the youth. I am not saying that you need to become killing machines, but we all need to grow and be better for the sake of our children, our future, and this community. If we agree to this, we need to do everything in our power to help them succeed. Does that sound fair?"

He scanned faces. No one argued. Someone at the back asked, not accusing, only tired, "Where is the line, then?"

"Where it always was," Alvar said. "Protect the most people you can without lying to yourself."

The truth is that the line in question was lost long ago, before the end of the world began. For generations, the line had been blurred. Blurred with the cynicism and greed that had long taken over mankind, plaguing our minds to think we were doing what was for the greater good when all we did was serve ourselves and leave the world behind. Now, being forced to face the music for our dreadful nature, we were compelled to face our fears and take a risk. Seeing no other way out and realizing that the solution was trust, relatively blind trust, but the path that had to be decided on by Dr. Ibezzi and the survivors. We had been the difference-makers for the community; this was their opportunity to make or break that benefit.

Breaking the silence on this to announce that they were on board and completely understood was Auxi's parents.

"We understand that there is no other way to solve this problem, at least not yet, so we will do our absolute best to make sure this mission is completed to perfection. Let us know what to do, and we will take care of it. We have more than enough experience to train and help Kendry with his units," Mrs. Tudwrig said, her voice resolute.

"Completely. If we are going to take a chance and vacate this place, the people here could use a bit of improvement. My time overseas, living off the land for days during missions, taught me a great deal. It is hard out there, but it certainly beats being dead or dissected by these creatures," Mr. Tudwrig said as he tried to bring some energy back to the room, a wry smile on his face.

"Screw it, let us get planning," said Mr. Rainer as his wife nodded in agreement, a renewed sense of purpose filling the room.

Realizing she now had practically no choice, as her best hope for survival had all but agreed to leave that facility within the next six weeks, she decided to accept the plan and informed her staff. The situation remained tense, but preparations had to be made, and research on the chemical agent intensified. Knowing this, I was tasked with producing an announcement to the facility's general population. A task that I knew would fall onto someone, but I had figured it would have been Dr. Ibezzi herself, her daughter, Dr. Sharpton, Jeffery, or anyone else who was officially in charge of that place. Either way, I prepared to make my announcement soon after that conversation so that the training could commence immediately.

After a few minutes, my friends and family went outside to inform Kendry of what was happening and to work with him on strategic planning for carrying out our new mission. As they did this, I finished curating what I had planned to say to the survivors, incorporating a bit of creativity to avoid a significant public backlash or disapproval. Ready to make my announcement, I hoped that the enemy wouldn't hear it. I calmly grasped the intercom mic and pushed the speak button.

"Hello, everyone. Hello, everyone. This is a critical announcement that requires your attention. I am sure you all know that we have been preparing and training for a fierce but necessary battle. While that will continue, with the intensity increasing as we progress, the enemy has once again demonstrated its capabilities. Though this sanctuary protects us now, we realize the dangers that come with being stationary and complacent. The food and resources will eventually run out. Our ammunition and generators will also eventually deplete, leaving us with nothing. This is not a matter of overpopulation, so do not think that denying entry or removing survivors is an option here. Anyone who attempts this or is found planning anything of the sort will face repercussions for their ignorance.

"All of that said, some of you may have known that a mission was going to take place in seven weeks, taking some of our most skilled combatants. This mission will now occur in six weeks and will be at the same time as our mass exodus from this location," I said as the noise level of the survivors began to rise, what I assumed to be fear or frustration, a murmur spreading through the assembled crowd.

A voice rose from the floor. "So you leave and the rest of us get eaten?"

"We run toward the thing that wants to eat you," I said.

Tuning out any additional direct complaints, I stayed focused on my message.

"I understand that many of you may not agree with this or understand it yet, but do not worry, you will not be forced to leave. The leaders of this place and all their resources will be vacating the premises, as we believe an attack will occur after the top combatants leave. However, you are free to stay behind in the shelter. We may be wrong, but we believe the earthquake and the Manslayer hole that opened 500 yards from here were a warning or preparation for completely obliterating this place, either through an attack or by simply creating a hole in the ground large enough to swallow it whole. Even though it is not guaranteed, that is a risk that none of us is willing to take.

"Please listen carefully to what I have said and make wise decisions. You can speak to anyone in charge if you have questions, but please ensure you rest so that we can continue our training and preparations. Consider who you are doing this for and what they would want. Be better for yourself. Be better for your future. Be better for the fate of mankind. For all we know, this is it, and we carry the weight of that responsibility. Do your best to meet the demand and go down in history as a hero," I said as I finished speaking to the population, my voice resonating with quiet intensity.

As I looked around the room full of people, I couldn't help but feel a slight sense of disappointment for them, but I still had confidence in our decision. Waiting for the words I said to sink in, most of them quieted down their complaints. They seemed to understand the gravity of the situation, and whether they planned to leave or not, they were aware of what was going to happen.

Continuing to look around, I noticed a group of survivors who seemed different from the rest. Not like they were Umbrorexes or anything like that, but they seemed relatively unfazed by my statements. If I hadn't been practicing my perception with Bri, I likely wouldn't have been able to feel it; however, since I had, I could tell there was some form of malice. Three mid-twenties, skater-thin, moved like a habit. One had a black-ink sigil half-healed on his throat. Later, I caught them lingering by the generator room door, counting beats between flickers like they had done it before.

Figuring that they would sooner or later become a problem, I watched until the three of them faded into the crowd, going back to the sleeping areas. Taking a mental note of this, I made my way back outside to the rest.

Finally back in the sunlight and surrounded by my friends and family, I approached them as they spoke.

"Good speech, man. I would have tried to drop the hammer a bit lighter, but for you, that was great," Kendry said with a hint of sarcasm, a smirk playing on his lips.

"Sure," I said in response, shaking my head slightly. "Just an FYI for everyone, I saw these three people down there who looked especially unapproving of my statements and seemed to harbor some form of hatred inside them towards me. It was a group of two gentlemen and a lady, all in their mid-twenties, with skater-skinny builds. I haven't taken any action at the moment, as they haven't technically done anything wrong, but I will keep an eye on them. I can only assume they will become an issue sooner or later," I said as I leaned against the car, a new concern adding to the existing pressures.

"For sure, D. We got you," Auxi said as she looked my way with her arms folded, her expression serious.

"Kendry here was just telling us his plan to fix this place up from the earthquake damages and how he planned to prepare his soldiers to be ready for our new task. He also had something in mind for breaking up the forces when it was time to leave," said my mom, her tone a little lighter now that the initial shock of my announcement had passed.

"I assume there is some concrete mix lying around, and you will reinforce it with other materials and provide it with a better construction to make sure it can last for the next two months. Would that be correct?" I asked Kendry, already anticipating his solution.

"Yes, sir," Kendry replied, a confident nod.

"That is a solid plan. Although I am curious to see your travel plan. I figured we would have to split our group, including the parents, to ensure adequate protection. Of course, Bri and I could go it alone, but that wouldn't be ideal in the case that something happens," I said. Bri's father gave me a look of light judgment, his usual stoic demeanor momentarily hardening.

"It sure as hell isn't ideal," Mr. Alvar said, his voice flat but firm.

Jumping back into the conversation, Kendry re-explained his proposal to me.

"So, basically, I was thinking that I would send volunteer soldiers with you two and save the medical staff for the larger group since you are both more than capable. Not just that, but they would be traveling alongside you to make sure someone had your back if needed. It'll be like they're not there, but they'll be in radio range in case they are necessary. I also figured we could do the same thing for your parents if they wanted to go. They're still deciding, but I proposed that Mr. Alvar and Mr. Hammond also go and travel separately from you two to avoid alarming the creatures. Odds are they would know people were with you, but at least this way it is not like they're right there, so they may think you're alone enough to speak to or whatever they are planning.

"Now, back to why I said your fathers. I chose them because this journey is about 600 miles and would require a solid amount of resources; the fewer people, the better. Given that you both have competent mothers and fathers who will only improve over the next six weeks, I thought it crucial to keep at least one of each with the main group; otherwise, we would be completely missing one of the signature Hammond or Alvar skill sets, something we can't afford. Of course, these are just suggestions, but they make sense to me. You following so far?"

"Sure, I'm following," I said as Kendry went back to explaining, his plan unfolding with impressive detail.

"Great. As for everyone else, I propose that we continue heading northeast until we reach Akimiski Island. I know this is a stretch and will need more planning, but it's colder, and it is an island. I know these monsters can't swim well, and I'm sure they won't open any huge holes in the ocean and risk flooding their entire civilization, if they have one. It's just the thought I have for now, but it's something solid. Realistically, not everyone will make it; I think we all know this. Still, we can surely set ourselves up to limit those losses and, hopefully, keep everyone in this circle alive. So, with that in mind, how are you feeling?" Kendry asked me as everyone looked my direction, awaiting my verdict.

"I don't like it much at all, but why would I not listen to the greatest strategic mind I've ever met? I know you will find a way to make it work, even when it doesn't seem possible. That said, let us get back to training so we can save the world."

After that meeting, we immediately resumed preparations and training for the new journeys ahead. Kendry had enlisted his parents' assistance as his advisors and to help lead his new efforts to expand and gather resources. Bri's parents joined mine in our latest group training to sharpen our minds and physical attributes. Although our parents were older, they were by no means slow or holding us back. Adding them to our training quickly proved to be a great decision, as it helped us identify holes we had not realized were there and pushed our limits even further. Auxi's parents spent their time between helping with the medical side of things and training Kendry's soldiers in survival tactics. They also provided general training to everyone on how to survive in the wilderness and what to do if they found themselves in a tricky situation. Their all-around knowledge and experience became one of the most valuable assets, which often kept them busy, but they had to maintain the pace.

We all trained together from time to time as well. Kendry and his family would physically contribute when possible, but usually acted as coaches for those training. As the population continued to grow and we kept our eyes on the hole that had appeared, I observed the three people I had seen at the announcement. Over the next few days, they slowly added to their group and began to walk around in steadily increasing numbers. While they contributed around the base and showed no overt signs of ill intent, I remained diligent in my thoughts and practices, sure that one day they would strike. Until then, however, we all stayed the course and continued to improve. From field exercises, resource runs, hunting, wound simulation, and mental and perception training, we only improved as we grew closer to the final days before our attack.

During those weeks leading up, Bri and I grew closer as we began to discuss what would happen after. All that time together, even when our parents were there, was time that was made better than it should have been. The clarity it offered only grew as we explored our emotions, seemingly learning what love truly felt like. The small moments, the meals, and the times at night where we would walk the premises or go to the edge of the gate and lean over from above as we spoke all added up. As we grew closer during that time, we also pushed the boundaries of what we considered normal for us. We found ourselves hugging more, holding hands, and even kissing in situations that weren't prompted by a deep conversation or a tragic accident. Although light for many people, for us, it was something that we could never have imagined just two months prior. In all its glory, it was terrific, a time when I felt blood flow differently within my veins, revealing a side of myself I had never known existed. As we learned more about that side of us, trained harder, and grew more powerful, we began to explore a new form of training. One that neither of us had ever thought would be something we looked forward to.

Once, during a spar, Bri corrected my stance and our breathing synced for a few quiet seconds. The radio crackled, pulling us apart. Stakes had a way of reminding us which love came first.

Looking into what Kendry and Auxi were doing, I obviously only knew so much. However, they spent a lot of time together when they could and even worked alongside each other at times, without losing any efficiency. They seemed to be doing great, even sharing some tips and tricks with us. It was as if they were the perfect fit for one another, something that their parents had appreciated since both Kendry and Auxi were extremely talented in different areas. Still, once combined, they could be an unstoppable force.

As for Dr. Ibezzi and our parents, they continued to do their best to contribute to the cause. Dr. Ibezzi would find success in her chemicals, only for it to be short-lived due to another realization.

"Above eight degrees Celsius, efficacy falls off a cliff," she said one afternoon, pinching the bridge of her nose. "UV hits it even harder."

It gave us a window and a deadline: cold, shade, speed.

Her daughter spent a lot of time with her to help, but was still learning about it all herself. Our parents would offer Dr. Ibezzi support when they could, but all she would ask for was more tissue samples from the creatures.

Everyone had seemingly found their niche, but as the time to act would wind down, so would some of the survivors' patience. Either way, we had a duty to fulfill and a world to save; nothing was going to keep us from that.

As I recall this portion of the events that have taken place, I have nothing but a deep respect and gratitude to those involved. Dr. Ibezzi and her staff welcomed us with open arms from the very beginning. Yes, her seeing what we could do likely heavily influenced that decision, but she still took a risk. Within one short week of our arrival, she handed us the keys and essentially gave us complete autonomy over the shelter. While she still oversaw the overall operations, it was up to us to ensure that every plan was working as expected and to prepare the survivors for what would come next. The weapons rule was still in place inside the facility, except for us. Regardless, we made room to address their ignorance. We shed light on what was really happening, and much confusion was cleared for us as well. It was a synergistic relationship that reached its peak when she, while not fully invested, had faith in our plan to evacuate everyone from the facility. Even though she had gained more time to work on her research due to our involvement and her acceptance of us, our parents, and our plans, everything became much smoother and allowed the entire survivor community to keep growing.

As for my friends, their ability to lead and take charge was something we needed but didn't know how badly. Yes, Kendry and I made a hefty number of decisions. I was usually in charge of the more consequential ones or having the final say, but all of us were needed to make it happen. From Bri taking the time to teach me as well as learn from me, to Auxi being busy day in and day out with a variety of key tasks, to Kendry, who had come in command of a rugged, consistently growing force that needed to be battle-ready in less than two months. They faced impossible odds and were still people I relied on, adding even greater pressure to their duties. Even so, they gave nothing less than their best, pushing me to go even further as I witnessed the sacrifices they made.

Bri, in particular, warrants all my respect because she unlocked something in me that I didn't know was there. Outside of the mental and physical training, she helped me to realize that I had a metaphorical heart and was capable of more than completing tasks. For a long time, I had become accustomed to being robotic. Completing task after task, only basking in the sun when I was grateful enough for a success or completion, but not too bored to find another thing to take my attention and effort. By risking her most sensitive side on me, a risk that I'm not sure too many would take in any situation, let alone ours, she opened my eyes to an entirely new world worth fighting for.

This is not a sap story, and our relationship was far from anything like that. Nonetheless, by opening herself and both showing and allowing me to do the same, I unlocked energy that could have been a game-changer for me the entire time. Although I believe that everything happens for a reason, even after surviving all that I have, I realize how different things could have been if Bri and I were able to express ourselves sooner. Having that fuel and energy release could have made me an even better student, professional, and athlete, but everything happens for a reason. Never underestimate the power of an outlet and having someone in the world who truly loves you for who you are, not just what you bring to the table. (I write this in retrospect; obviously, I didn't have too much time to realize this in the moment. Bri and I did have a great time, though).

Lastly, I must commend our parents, not only for finding us through it all, but also for having the faith to follow our lead. All too often, when I was growing up, I would see parents refuse to listen to their children. They could be entirely correct, successful, and have done all the right things, yet their parents would still doubt and deny them. As for ours, they raised a proper bunch of kids, and they knew it. Even with the shifting dynamics among us, it didn't become an issue; they trusted our judgment to let us make our own mistakes and live with the consequences. Of course, it helped our case that we were not only extremely capable of defending ourselves but also demonstrated a strong desire and ability to defend others. Our judgment and character created a strong foundation that they only added to, never tore down. Even when they had doubts or concerns, they wanted details to understand our thinking rather than pressure us to change our plan. For that, I am grateful and have eternal respect.

As I reflect on this time ten years ago, I am filled with a mix of emotions. It feels as though so much time has passed, each day growing longer. Although I still have responsibilities and situations to handle, looking back and reflecting on these thoughts brings me peace, reminding me I am still human. Every detail, conversation, and activity is forever seared into my mind. Each passing day is only another chance to regrow my roots.

Two weeks from the journey, we had schedules taped to bulkheads, sectors sprayed in scavenged paint, and a radio code for everything from "latrine clog" to "Subterro sighting." A ring of motion sensors and tripwire chimes circled the hole's rim, and an orange flag meant "seal the south corridor." Kendry's drills held. The soldiers moved as one thought, sweeping clean and returning with samples and scrounged items, calm under pressure. Bri and I only drew our blades outside the wire, turning the Feralgehns and the Subterros into training partners that didn't learn. The hole stayed quiet. Quiet, not meaning safe, so we watched for the flicker that meant wrong.

Although it had been business as usual for the weeks I had glossed over, a few notable happenings both improved our situation and reminded us of the times we were in. Early in the arrival and partial leadership of Kendry's parents, it became clear that while Kendry respected his mother and father, their leadership styles worked better for different tasks. They decided it was best to divide our forces into two groups. Kendry would take the main force of skilled, motivated soldiers. His parents would lead a second group of soldiers who wanted to help but might be more of a liability on the field than an asset. Not wanting to create a rift, they made the two groups flow as one, with Kendry's set completing the high-risk work and his parents handling security, support, and mid-range defense. It wasn't groundbreaking, but it could have spiraled into a full division and fractured what little structure remained.

Additionally, we were able to check broadcasts and news from other military bases whenever the signal returned. Most of what we heard was that larger bases had exhausted their resources trying to deliver a strike strong enough to kill the monsters. Although they fired what remaining missiles they could, it had no lasting effect. The creatures kept coming and eventually took over. Smaller bases still existed, such as the ones Auxi's teammates and Capt. Burks were heading to, but we could only hope those would fare better as the situation grew more dire.

Slowly, fewer survivors showed up. Helicopters and planes turned into relics, and news networks around the world went dark. We could only imagine the damage done to the rest of the planet. As the stories worsened, we increased security to counter nomadic groups seeking to steal resources and desperate survivors seeking entry, sometimes as scouts for others. The human mindset devolved fast, mirroring the apocalyptic shows my friends and I used to watch. Our interactions with these people were brief and never led to vendettas, although a few sustained simple injuries. Sometimes I saw a figure at a distance, too far to read, which could have been an Umbrorex or a person watching us. Each time we checked, they were gone, leaving little to no trace. I assumed it was the Umbrorexes, a reminder of our duty, and kept preparing.

As for the three people I had sensed with ill intent, I realized it had not been aimed at me or what I said. Since that incident, they had spread an ideology that the creatures were demons from hell and that it was their divine duty to slay the demons walking the Earth. Feeling called, they joined the volunteer soldiers and quickly rose to the elite levels of Kendry's ranks. After a string of successful runs returning material for Dr. Ibezzi, their leader, Jackson, proposed an idea. Since he and his comrades had a strong desire to punish "hell spawns," they wanted a unit that actively hunted the creatures. Jackson said his unit would be protected by God and more than capable. Kendry hesitated, rightfully. He told Jackson to prove they could operate alone and sent them to capture a live Feralgehn for Dr. Ibezzi to test the chemical agent. He expected them to balk. They did not. They planned a fifteen-person mission. Realizing how far in over their heads they could be, Kendry sent me to watch over them. This mission took place four weeks before our mass departure from the shelter.

Jackson and his self-titled "Angels" moved before first light, slipping through the woods toward the highway. Time of day still mattered, since the creatures ran thinner at dawn in that sector. I left thirty minutes later to keep a shadowed gap. We had cleared a one-mile radius around the shelter, which meant the Angels would need to travel at least a mile before finding Feralgehns.

The first mile stayed clean. The air ran warm and wet under the canopy. Following at a safe distance to avoid detection, I began to feel a knot of Feralgehns and a few Subterros moving along the road ahead as the Angels reached the highway. I waited to see their choices, climbed a nearby tree to keep my signature away from the fight, and watched as a car tore through, engine screaming. Behind it came a tide of bodies, about twenty Feralgehns with an equal number of Subterros. Jackson read the play in an instant. He split his team with a two-finger snap, half to each tree line, prepared and out of sight. Their timing aimed at the rear of the horde.

The sedan passed. Jackson let three beats go, then burst from cover and swung his machete into the Achilles of the last Feralgehn. Tendons parted and the beast pitched. The others flowed in, cutting hamstrings and pinning wrists, binding the snout before a potential bite could land. They had it muzzled and tied in seconds.

The pack noticed. One Feralgehn and three Subterros peeled off and angled back toward the ambush. "Angels, formation three-five-three, now," Jackson said, and shields lifted together, a moving wall that brought breath. "The Subterro demon variant will strike first. Between the eyes. Conviction, certainty, and the power of God that flows through you. Do not fail me, for you fail the Lord."

The Subterros hit low and fast. The wall braced. From behind the shields, five blades flashed up into the triangle between the eyes. Bodies shuddered and dropped, blood pattering the white road paint. The Feralgehn lunged. An angel on the right caught a claw through the forearm and kept his shield where it belonged. I had my sword in hand, then Jackson slid under the beast and opened its belly from sternum to hip in one clean pull. He popped up in the spray and hacked through the front claws. The creature tried to run. He took the legs at the knee, black blood sheeting across the cracked lane.

"Two for the sleds," he called. Ropes went tight. A second Feralgehn, the one that had overshot the car and doubled back, wounded by the Angels' bite-line, staggered into view. They tied that one too, hobbles on the ankles, figure-eight on the wrists, clean wraps like in drills. I stayed in the tree and let them work. It wasn't our kind of beautiful, but it was competence, and competence keeps people alive.

Then the cold found me, not a breeze, an absence. My skin pebbled, and every hair stood. I unsheathed my sword and scanned. Nothing moved. Pressure climbed in my inner ears like a deep dive. I stayed put. If this was a lure, I was not leaving the Angels bare.

Dion. One voice built from many, speaking inside the bones. *You held position. Sensible. Your friends would not have fared as luckily.*

I barely moved my mouth. "How many of you are there, and what do you want? I still have time."

Quantity does not matter. We have enough for all of you. We are aware of your plans to travel and how you intend to deceive us. You may try, and we will not stop you. Give us a word. You are almost ready, close to realization, and still far. We will open your eyes to the truth, to what you are meant to be. The sound came from around me and nowhere, echoing from places that did not exist. A metallic taste hit the back of my tongue, and my shadow lagged a fraction behind my motion.

"You already said you are watching. I am not what you think," I said, voice low, the sword the only warm thing in my hand.

We shall see. As promised, you live until then. We will meet you in two weeks, at your planned arrival time instead of our agreed hour. These insects live, as long as they do not strike us. The dogs are yours to play with. We have plenty. Leave us out of it. You call us Umbrorexes, but we are perfection. There is nothing you can do to stop what is happening. Learn quickly, and it may end better for the species that calls itself almighty. Ensure that you continue to learn and understand your circumstances. Come with your partner. When you arrive, clarity will come. The pressure bled away. Sound rushed back into the world.

I sat in the branches until my breathing steadied and the Angels started home, two sleds dragging, one shield strapped over the injured man's arm. I watched them every step back, then dropped from the tree and moved in parallel for their return.

Back at the shelter, they walked into a sea of gratitude and applause from Kendry. After my report, he approved their request and created the Angel Task Force, Angels for short. Jackson had his wounded comrade patched up, and they celebrated within ration limits, proud of the two captured demons. Dr. Ibezzi was more pleased than anyone. She had created a chemical agent harmful to the Manslayers and possibly to the Umbrorexes. The catch was delivery, time, and effectiveness. Although the agent could slow them down, its effect was very short-lived, taking almost an hour to activate, which was far from adequate.

As she continued to analyze the blood from the tied-down Feralgehns on the surface, I met with my team to discuss what the Umbrorex had told me. We sat outside at one of the new tables in an expanded area, and I explained. They weren't excited, no surprise there. With the situation newly confirmed, we talked about the next steps.

"Great, so as expected, they know everything we are doing. Big shock," Kendry said, running a hand through his hair. "What bothers me is that they are allowing it. Why? They have a plan for you and Bri, so what are the rest of us going to be, food for the pets?"

"I'm not sure, Ken, and I'm sure D does not know either. Whatever the reason, we need to capitalize on it," Auxi said, rubbing her face, frustration creeping in.

"Precisely," Bri said. "The Umbrorex said it will allow us to complete our plan as long as we do not attack them. Given that we saw one crushed by a car and it appeared days later as if nothing happened, it is safe to assume enhanced healing, possibly beyond what Dion and I can do."

"What about the one whose arm I cut off? I remember the blood being red, not black. We haven't seen the newest evolution's blood up close, and Dr. Ibezzi told us Umbrorexes had black blood and false skin. I didn't see any of that. Unless..." Kendry said, pausing as something clicked.

"That could be one use for the humans they were kidnapping. What if they are mixing lines and raising humans as their own, without the special features and biology? Regular humans, but useful to their evolution through behavior and cover," I said, picking up his thought.

"Wait, if you two are right, what does that do for our predicament? Do we follow instructions and back off from the plan or not? We never discussed what happens next. What is that plan?" Auxi said, pulling us back from the edges, practical as ever.

"Auxi has a point. What are we doing?" Bri asked, eyes on me.

I weighed it and landed where I liked least. "We proceed as planned, no changes to strategy. Kendry, move the main group to a new location, only you and your trusted people know, to avoid another leak. When we arrive, everyone keeps a distance from Bri and me, stepping in only if it is absolutely necessary. We are not positioned to make demands or push back, so we go along to get inside. They want us for a reason. We find out the reason."

"I hate it," I said before they could. "But logic says this is the way to keep most people alive. We use it to collect intel and, if we can, strengthen the agent. If we run, more people die. With what they can do, why choose that fight? I'm not saying we cut a deal. They claim not to want the death they cause, which makes no sense. So we think differently from what we have."

They looked at me, puzzled. I looked to Bri, and even she seemed unsure. I let them process. After a minute, Kendry spoke.

"D, man, listen to how this sounds. We can train people and keep many alive, but without you two, we won't last long. Even if you come back, we don't know who will be here to see it. We never planned to attack them directly, but maybe we can give you tools to take them out before they take you both. I already have some ideas."

"Where are you going with this, Kendry? If it is a weapon, they will check us before letting us near anything worth destroying," Bri said, calm and sharp.

"Yes, so not a simple bomb on you. These beings have to use machines for what they do. We've seen evolution, not magic. They don't make the Earth grow holes with thought. The language problem could be technology, or some frequency we don't hear unless targeted. If you see machines or meet the leader, you could sabotage systems and seed defeat from within. Risky, yes, but the two of you keep breaking what looks unbreakable. So you go peacefully, and your travel aids wait five days. Your fathers won't like it, but who knows where you come out if they lead you into a hole in their society. Anything could happen. We can also coat your blades with poison if it's ready, and give you a last resort in case you need to kill the leader. It's just a thought. We don't know any of this until you get there, but hey, it beats saying yes and walking to your certain death," Kendry said, hope and fear sharing his eyes.

"I don't have a better idea. Until I do, I'm fine with this. I will do my best to keep us alive and to keep everyone alive. Any objections?" I asked.

No one objected. The mood said enough. Tough decisions grew tougher by the day, but at least we had a plan. We stood to tell our parents when my hip-clipped radio buzzed and Dr. Ibezzi spoke.

"Dion, are you there?" she asked, her voice ragged with static.

"Yes, ma'am. Everything alright?" I said.

"I am ecstatic. I need you and your friends in my lab. I think I made a breakthrough," she said, excitement overriding the fatigue.

We put off the parent talk and headed below.

The lab was a wreck, as if she had not left it in weeks. We found her in a chair at a desk by one of the machines. For a second, we thought she might be passed out. She turned, and the truth of her exhaustion showed, eyes bagged, skin pale and bloodless. Her energy did not match her face. She pointed at a monitor.

"Look. Do you see that?" she said.

"It looks like the cells are dying, then multiplying, then dying again. Are they repopulating slower than they die, even by a small margin?" I asked.

"That's exactly what's happening," Auxi said, already explaining. "The cells regenerate quickly, but the rate tilts toward the agent. It looks like apoptosis, the body killing its own cells."

"Precisely," Dr. Ibezzi said. "At this concentration, the curve is slow. Forty-five minutes to an hour for a Feralgehn. If I can concentrate it and tie it to serum proteins, a cut that draws blood should be enough, and we are talking minutes. The micro-capsules rupture on contact with hemoglobin."

She tapped a second graph, where a shallow slope steepened after the catalyst spike.

"That's great, truly," Kendry said. "How soon can you reach that stage, and how effective would it be against an Umbrorex, if you know?"

"Given viability, a week and a half to something more potent," she said.

"Very close," Kendry said, sharp.

She gave him a look and kept going. "I want enough quantity and strong enough dosage that it matters. As for Umbrorexes, I can only hope. They share some human DNA, which could be lethal to them and dangerous to us. Old samples are useless, per Dion's report of their upgrades, and also gone. Their bodies deteriorate faster than ours, perhaps due to the false skin or a compromised cellular structure. That may have changed, which means we need a fresh sample. Capture or kill one in the next week, and we can test; although, I am fairly certain that will not happen. I do not doubt you, but they are elusive and waiting for us. Why would they risk coming here?"

"Wait," Auxi said. "D, did the Umbrorex mention this poison specifically? They claim to know everything we do, but this is something I doubt they would allow unless they were immune."

"It didn't say anything specific. I wouldn't be surprised if they knew, though. Assume they do. If we get a chance, I will use the agent to see the result. It may be one of our best shots," I said.

"You spoke with one again?" Dr. Ibezzi asked, caught off guard, turning from her work.

"Yes, ma'am," I said, steady.

"Anything new, or is it the usual?" she asked, eyes back on the screen.

"Usual for everyone else, different for us, especially Bri and me. To keep it simple, they know our plan and claim not to want to kill everyone. They want Bri and me to come peacefully. Another reason we need this agent to be functional. Who knows what they have planned?" I said as we stepped aside for her daughter to slide in a tray of food.

We headed to the deep blue table where we usually met. We laid out the plan. The questions came again, harder this time, and we had fewer counters. Our parents were right on safety and logic. They also knew when self-preservation had to bend to the larger good. None of us knew what this meeting could mean. We took their concerns into account and kept our course. They arrived at the same unpopular decision, optimism pinned to any crack in the enemy's armor. No one disliked the circumstances more than Mr. Alvar.

Distrust had been his baseline before this. Now it climbed. He knew that any violence against Umbrorexes could mean casualties on site or back with the larger group. He asked Kendry for safety mechanisms or plans to keep them out of harm's way. Total protection was impossible, but he wanted a fighting chance. Kendry answered.

"Mr. Alvar, you know the severity here. I'm not being smart when I say this," Kendry said. The two of them watched each other, steady. "We will let them talk and hope they get led to a base. If there's an issue, and only if, they will give the balled-fist signal for intervention. That's an option, not ideal. The area would be surrounded and defended, and a direct engagement would be suicide, even with our full force. To give them a last line, we'll coat their blades with the concentrated poison and give them additional vials once Dr. Ibezzi finishes."

"Additionally," he said, "I'm working on a special device with what we have here. Binary gel, stable apart, inert to most scans, low EM signature. Mixed, it's strong enough to vaporize targets within a half-mile radius. It would require an immediate clear-out if used. The fuse is two minutes. That window should be enough for Bri and Dion to escape, should they have to use it."

Mr. Alvar worked through it before speaking. "Reactive. If it must be used at a base, how do you get it there without detection on Abrial or Dion? And are there other ways to ensure their safety?"

"That is the catch," Kendry said. "We split components. Torso wraps, canteens, and whatever other methods we can think of. If they find one piece, we play it off as something else. If they find both, they still need to be mixed to be dangerous, so it shouldn't have any immediate red flags. If it comes to it, a water-bottle swap is enough to arm it. If they're listening now, they know all of this, but I'm choosing to believe they aren't."

"Other safety," he said, "is speed and judgment. No elaborate extras. You two make the final calls. The soldiers with you will follow. Don't be rash. Stay sharp."

"It sounds like we somewhat have a plan. Andrew, we can dig into this later. For now, back to training and drills. Agreed?" my dad said, pushing back his chair.

"Agreed," Mr. Alvar said. He looked at Bri, then at me. "Abrial, I will make this as smooth as possible. Dion, make sure you are ready. I need you more than ever. Can I trust you with that?"

"Absolutely, sir," I said, letting the weight settle where it had to.

Heading into our training area, while Auxi and Kendry began work on the device, the reality set in. What we had to do felt more real than ever, pushing Bri and me to new levels. As the weeks closed and everyone prepared to step back into the world they had escaped, terror and excitement mingled in the shelter. Regardless, we needed to win and come out as the victors in some way. No matter what.

XIX. CROSSROADS

The final hours leading up to our departure were marked by a range of emotions on all sides of the shelter. The survivors who had not become soldiers or medics were the most shaken and unhappy about it all, but only slightly behind the others. The soldiers, although ready, did not want to leave their shelter and warm bed to embark on a trip on a hunch that the place would be under attack; nonetheless, they followed orders. The medics had been in a similar mental state, having to pack the supplies they could to be best ready to treat what injuries, illnesses, and other problems arose while the group was on the road. Taking into account all the information we had and understanding the actual danger of these creatures and their leadership, most survivors were determined to leave, ensuring they played their part in packing the essentials and collaborating with us to plan the journey. I say most because a few decided against going, choosing to stay back and take the risk. This group consisted of only about twenty people, unfortunately, with children. It represented less than 4% of the total survivor population, yet it was still considered a loss. As they kept their fair share of rations and protection, they hunkered down further rather than preparing to leave, an act that we assumed to be their last.

As for Bri and me, we helped Kendry and Auxi pack up their items and strategically place the necessary gas cans throughout the vehicles. For a little under 500 people, the transportation methods required were substantial. Still, we had collected enough materials to ease that process. Using military trucks, coach buses, and every available car, we planned how to pack everyone in so we could use fewer vehicles rather than more. Of course, after a while, the automobiles would run out of gas reserves and break down, so they prepared a plan in case they had to travel on foot. Despite this, the initial plan to combat these situations was to pick up any functional vehicles along the way and have one to two soldiers drive those. At the same time, the main body of survivors was transported in large-capacity vehicles. We knew problems would eventually arise as they traveled the 700-mile journey northwest, under the assumption they were still heading that way, but we had to make something happen.

After spending time working with Kendry and Auxi, Bri and I prepared ourselves for the journey ahead. We didn't need much, considering we had no clue what awaited us, so it was easy to pack. Extra clothes, food, water, and those gel pouch explosives that Kendry and Auxi had somehow made, though we weren't sure of their efficiency since they were such a risk, and we had all we needed. As for our regular weapons, we didn't bring any firearms, as they would only add weight and be loud. So, we carried our signature weapons as usual: my katana, freshly cleaned and strapped across my waist, and Bri's dual gladius, one on each side of her waist. Before we left the room, Bri tested a blade's edge against her thumbnail; I pressed the mekugi pin on my katana flush; quiet rituals that made the steel feel ready. As we made our final sweep through the base to confirm we had all our belongings, we realized we had more time to spare. Bri came up with an idea.

"Hey, D," Bri said in a way that she didn't usually, her voice softer, almost hesitant.

"What's on your mind, Bri?" I asked as I was sure she would say something about the journey ahead of us.

"I know we're about to leave and enter into an unknown situation that ends with us either dead or forever changed, but how do you feel about one final shower? Just to remember what proper warm running water feels like," Bri said as she looked at me strangely, a nervous smile playing on her lips.

Finding this entire thing weird, but feeling there was more to it, I played along with a bit of skepticism.

"A shower? Now? We need to leave in an hour and still have to run over a few things with Kendry and our parents."

"We do. I'm not denying that. However, the showers are empty since everyone is focused on leaving, and you know we'll be fast. Besides, I have an idea that I think you might appreciate."

As Bri pressed herself against me while saying this, I found myself in slight discomfort, not because of what she was insinuating, which I could pick up on since I wasn't that blind to human emotion, but because it was eerily timed and seemed out of character for her. Thinking through this as I naturally responded to her action, pulling her in close, I figured that this weird sensation was because of an unknown arena we were entering, seemingly opening an entirely new door in our relationship. We had been close for what felt like our entire lives and had grown even closer over the last few months, changing our dynamic in ways I could never have imagined. Realizing that she had likely made this move because I had been far too focused on the next steps of our plans to think about it (she was always better at multitasking), I decided to go along with it.

"I think I understand... Are you sure you want to do this? I mean, there's so much going on, I don't want this to be something you're only doing because we might not make it out alive. Even though these things have only become a part of my thinking recently, I still know the difference between right and wrong and don't want you to feel bad about anything or pressured," I said as I wanted to make sure this was what she really wanted, my voice gentle.

"D, you're overthinking. Coming from me, that means something. I'm not trying to do this because I feel like we're doomed to death or because of some invisible pressure. I want to do this because I love you, I always have. I know that until recently, we were only ever friends, closer than siblings in our bond, but that's because I never knew how to work with emotions. I have taken the time to learn from and study others, but ever since that day in kindergarten when we first spoke, I have seen in you something I still haven't seen in anyone else. After years of trying to understand it and watching the world around me, I found that I had grown to love you in a way unlike anything I had experienced before.

Once I recognized that feeling, I realized I had been experiencing it for a long time and that it had been a driving force behind my efforts. I would have been perfectly fine going under the radar and completing college as a typical student, but your drive to excel pushed me to do the same. As we interlocked in the race to be great amongst each other, as well as Ken and Auxi, I saw the things we were both accomplishing and how much we could truly change the world. So, as I learned to outdo you and push you, in ways similar to how you did with me, whether intentionally or not, I realized our potential if we were together as a single force.

"Though we have been doing that a great deal lately, growing in ways I could never have imagined, I still had to figure out how to share this side of me with you. It was a critical moment when you shared your thoughts and gave me those looks when this all started, showing me that what I felt may have been reciprocal. Acknowledging this possibility, I first had to confirm that you understood what it meant and give you a chance to learn for yourself before I mentioned it. But once you knew and we shared that, our world changed... So, as we prepare to leave and finally have an indoor moment to ourselves, I wanted to try to open another door of opportunity and truly become one. While I am still working on my informalities and breaking them, I have one statement to propose to make sure we are clear," Bri said as she paused for me to capture all of what she said, her eyes searching mine.

Though this was all mind-bending to me, I went through my memory and could clearly see all that she was talking about. We did grow closer, she did push me, and after a while, I realized that I had loved her, unlike anyone else I had "loved" in my life. Considering all of this and seeing that she was correct, I put myself in her shoes and thought about the courage it must have taken for her to do this. The strongest and most gifted woman I knew was willing to risk everything and share her most vulnerable sides with me. Knowing that I too felt what she felt and shared the same desires, even if I had just realized it, I knew I had to be vulnerable as well.

Not wanting to leave her hanging on her thoughts, I began to speak.

"I know what you're going to say, and the answer is absolutely. I will become one with you... You are the most talented, beautiful, caring, and intelligent woman I have ever had the pleasure of meeting. You complete me in ways that I can't even understand, yet I know are relevant. You have shown me new ways of thinking and acting without ever leading me astray; for that, I am thankful. I've never been an enormous emotion guy, and I still have much to learn, but as long as I'm learning, living, and loving with you, everything will work out as it should...

"Abrial Alvar, I love you with all of my being and understanding of the thing that is. So as we prepare to go out into the unknown and face death, I would like to spend this moment with you and you alone," I said in my best attempt to be romantic and deeply emotional, my voice a little rough with sincerity.

Although I was still a rookie, clearly what I said worked as she leaned in to kiss me in the most aggressive way possible (in my mind). Not being one to back down, I matched the intensity and even took it to another notch.

What followed belongs to us. We closed the door on the world and let the water drown the noise.

Back outside, with thirty minutes remaining before departure, Kendry and Auxi were guiding people to their designated vehicles. Seeing that Bri and I were making our way to our dads' and the soldiers they had assigned for us, Kendry and Auxi came over. Just as they arrived to speak, Kendry immediately gave me an odd look, looked at Bri, and then smiled before speaking.

"You ready to slay out there, tiger?" Kendry said, grin a shade too bright, nerves leaking through.

Picking up on this, Mr. Alvar quickly came over and asked Kendry what that meant, clearly sensing something more to the comment.

"Nerves, sir," Kendry said, palms up. "I cover nerves with dumb jokes. Working on better habits."

Sneering at Kendry, Mr. Alvar turned to head back to the car, which he and my dad were packing to make sure they had everything.

"I know you're lying. Be grateful that the world is ending; otherwise, I would find out what's so funny," Mr. Alvar said as he walked away, his voice low and pointed. Kendry gave a slight, chastened nod and busied himself checking an antenna coupling.

"My apologies for that. My father is truly a nice guy. I think he acts that way because he doesn't know how to be any other. To be fair, when you see the ugly in the world through constant observation, what else can you do?" Bri said as she looked at Kendry, giving a slight shrug.

"Sure, I guess that's one way to put it... Either way, I hope you two are safe," Kendry said as he gave us a funny look, a knowing smirk.

"I'm not too sure what he's on about, but I think he was going to explain the plan. But since he's clearly not wanting to discuss the most important matters, I'll share with you the plan once more," Auxi said as she pushed Kendry to the side, taking charge.

"Your dads will travel together on one side of you, and the soldiers will be on the other, moving in parallel about half a mile apart to ensure they don't get mixed into what's happening. Although they are at that distance, they will come within 1000 feet during the meeting so they can act quickly if needed. We understand that four individuals can only do so much to help you, so their primary task is to assist and report on the situation. To do this, they've been fitted with a specially configured HF radio with a 1500-mile range, directly linked to one of our own, so we should always be within talking distance. It's a high-frequency set with a long-wire antenna spooled under the roof rack; night skip will carry your traffic. The only issue there is that we don't know how well it will work with the monsters' frequency blocker, so if you can find a way to shut it down or destroy it, that would greatly help with your chances of finding us.

"Since no one really knows where we're going other than Kendry and me, I have circled a general area on this map where we should be. We understand that this trip may take some time, and anything could happen between now and then. However, if you have power, please try to use your radio to reach us. Otherwise, we will leave signs of where we have been that only you could pick up on. They may be small, but they will be noticeable to you. Even if that doesn't work, I have no doubt that you two can find us.

"If you both feel trapped or find a way to attack their central controls, you have the gel packs to use. We don't know how efficient it is or if that two-minute countdown is accurate, but we did our best to create something that could blow them away, so please try to be smart with it. It's just a little bit in each, mainly so you can keep it on you or put it in a canteen if necessary, but you should have enough to incinerate a medium-sized house. Although this is just an estimate, as it activates with oxygen in the air and likely causes more damage, we only had a limited time to understand its capabilities. Also, here are two small vials of the concentrated poison created by Dr. Ibezzi. She's taken what she could to continue working while on the road, but this is the best she could do right now. We've already given your dads and the soldiers some of their own to use if necessary, but you can try to kill them with this if you're stuck in a situation. Bloodstream contact works fastest through a cut or puncture. Don't waste it. Other than that, I don't think there's much else to cover," Auxi said as she looked to Kendry, signaling she was done.

"Yeah, Auxi broke it down pretty well for you guys. Everything you need should already be in your car, except for any items you have with you. However, be careful and use it wisely. The soldiers you have with you aren't extremely elite or like the Angels. I kind of need them with us. However, those with you can manage on their own. There shouldn't be too many hiccups on the way, but we never know. In any case, making it there alive and healthy is your priority, so make sure that happens. I would also appreciate it if you could come back to us and assist us in creating the new world, assuming you have eliminated these threats. However, I know that's not something we can directly control. Either way, I know you can do this, just be smart. If they wanted you dead, I'm sure you already would be,"

Kendry said as he stood and looked into the falling sun, his voice filled with a mixture of hope and grim reality.

Wrapping up the final checks and ensuring everything was in order, our parents convened with us one last time before what we hoped would be the end of this nightmare.

"I know we've all just got back together, but I want to say that these last two months have been amazing," Kendry's dad said as he looked around, a sentimental tone in his voice.

"Absolutely, we've seen so much growth from you four, and it has been a joy to watch. Bri, Dion, please be sure to end this. We don't know how much more humanity can hang on, but even if it can't, find your way back to us," Kendry's mother said as she hugged Bri and me, her eyes welling up.

"Absolutely, Mrs. Rainer. We will do our best to prevent the situation from worsening. We can't make any promises, but we guarantee we will try our best," Bri said as I nodded in agreement, a shared determination between us.

"Do great things," Mr. Tudwrig said as he cuffed my hand and gave Bri a hug, his grip firm with reassurance. "We'll watch over these folks here. Come back with stories worth the pain."

"And come back whole," Mrs. Tudwrig added as she hugged Bri and me in a soft embrace. "We'll keep a place warm for you."

Thanking them both, our parents had walked up to speak. Our dads then said goodbye to Kendry and Auxi's parents as the four of them walked back to the convoy of people ready to leave. Recognizing that our parents wanted to speak to us privately, Kendry and Auxi stepped aside to give us the space.

As Bri's parents spoke to her, my parents talked to me. In the most emotional conversation we've ever had, my parents finally told me how they felt.

"Son, I know we always pushed you to be the best and to be more, often letting the other aspects of life fall to the wayside, but I want to apologize for that. Of course, we can't change what we've done, but I want to share how proud I am of you for the man you've become. Despite our harshness and ambitions for you, you went on to create an amazing circle of friends and develop the qualities of a leader worth following. The growth and development we've seen from you over the years have been astounding, even beyond the physical and mental aspects. We recognize your character development, emotional maturity, and even how well you treat Abrial; yes, we are aware of the full extent of what's happening, and we're proud of you. Although this isn't goodbye, I just wanted to let you know how proud I am of you... I love you, baby boy. You better come back to me," my mother said as she began to cry and brought me in for a hug, holding me tightly.

Stepping back and leaning on my father, who had already spoken with her, he began to talk.

"Hey, son. I know your mother mentioned how hard we've been on you and how we recognize our mistakes. However, I wouldn't go back and change it for a second. I'm not taking credit for your actions or your accountability, but clearly, we did something right. So even though we may not be the most tight-knit family or have the strongest emotional compass, I couldn't be prouder of the decisions you've made and the people you've brought into your life. You took our push for development and ran with it, creating your own world of possibility. This world allowed you to develop and grow, even helping you to combat our decisions when you felt unaligned. You are strong, brave, and more of a man than I could ever be, truly. As much as I wish I could be helping you move into your first real place, I am still glad to help you in this final act... Even though I'll be right beside you the whole way, I know it's only up to you what happens. Thank you for the opportunity to be your father, and thank you for being the perfect son. I love you, D," my father said as we embraced in a hug, a rare moment of profound connection.

"I appreciate everything you both have done for me, and I promise to do right by you. As much as I could go into history and my feelings, I want to save that for later. You both mean the world to me, and I will be back to tell you just how much. I love you," I said as I hugged both of them, tears stinging my own eyes.

As they turned to go talk to Bri, my mother, still wiping tears from her eyes, Bri's parents came to me. Not knowing what to expect, I prepared for some form of criticism or strong remark about how much I need to protect their daughter. Instead, they surprised me.

"Dion, we had the opportunity to watch you grow up and become the young man you are today. Ever since Abrial came home and told us about the boy whom she could actually talk to, we knew you were a good kid. Not once did you ever do wrong by her or by us, and we've only seen that continue in your relationships with others and in your responsibilities. As you prepare to leave and fulfill another duty, I must say how proud I am of you and how grateful I am that she found you. You've truly changed her, and I see she has done the same. Hopefully, you both can continue to do that and bring even more greatness when you return to the rest of us," Bri's mother said to me as she hugged me, her voice filled with warmth.

"I second everything my wife has said, and I truly am proud of you. I know I can be a challenge, but you have earned my respect, and I wish you nothing but blessings for your efforts. As for your relationship with my daughter, my baby girl, I expect that you will continue with the respectful ways you treat her and honor her as an equal," Mr. Alvar said as he gripped my hand and leaned in, his usual stern demeanor softened by the gravity of the moment.

"I am more perceptive than you think. I understand you are both adults, consenting adults... That said, you better not disappoint me, son," Mr. Alvar said as he whispered in my ear. Although this message sent chills down my spine, something that rarely happened to me, I can appreciate his stance and was thankful for his support. All I had to do was not mess it up, simple enough.

As Mr. Alvar stepped back and gave his wife a hug and a kiss, I assumed my dad did the same with my mom; our moms then made their way back towards everyone else.

Seeing them for possibly the last time for a while, I couldn't help but feel some sorrow as I had learned what my emotions were. For as much good as those feelings can bring, it seems to hurt even stronger when they turn against you, one of the double-edged swords detailing what it means to be human.

Seeing that our parents had dispersed, Kendry and Aux returned to us. Given that we had little time to spare and wanted to get on the road before sundown, our interaction was brief.

"So, my friends, this is it?" Kendry said, trying to lighten the mood with a nervous smile.

"Absolutely not. Besides, you have our blood coursing through your veins, so we're always with you," Bri said as she, too, was feeling the emotions of it all, her voice soft but resolute.

"Yeah, I guess so," Kendry said as he leaned in and hugged us, a genuine embrace.

"Don't forget to come back in one piece, for me. Your moms will kill me if you don't. Auxi, I'll be waiting for you back at the lead car... Thank you for saving my life more times than I can count and for providing me with the best memories a guy could ask for; I truly appreciate everything.

I love you guys," Kendry said as he walked back to the vehicles waiting to leave, his voice thick with emotion.

As Kendry walked away, it felt like we were breaking apart once more. However, we had to complete this mission and then return; that was the only way.

As Auxi stood there, fighting the emotions of being separated again, she began to speak.

"I don't think you two know how much you mean to me, really. Not only did you risk your lives to save me, but you pushed me to become the woman and warrior that I am today. I could thank you for so much more, but I just want you to know how grateful I am for both of you," Auxi said as she leaned in for a hug from us both, dropping tears on our shoulders.

"We couldn't have done it without you, Auxi," I said as we embraced, a comforting squeeze.

"Never. Without you, we wouldn't have the burning fire within us that drives us to continue. You showed us the way and made us believe that anything was possible. We'll use that energy to save the world and come back," Bri said in an attempt to appeal to Auxi, her voice firm with resolve.

"You guys don't have to lie; you would've done this stuff anyway. You're both incredible specimens of the human race, and I'm grateful to call you family," Auxi said as she began to walk away, a bittersweet smile on her face.

"D, keep my girl safe. Bri, make sure D keeps you safe," Auxi said as her final parting words, a playful but earnest warning.

Smiling in happiness from the friendships and family bonds, yet in pain from having to possibly say our final goodbyes, we got into the small sedan we all arrived in and prepared to make our leave.

"All good and ready to go?" One of the soldiers said on our handheld transceiver frequency, his voice crackling.

"Ready," said my father as he looked at us from the car next over, a silent prayer in his eyes.

Looking in my mirrors and watching the convoy leave our shelter, I saw a glimpse of those who chose to stay going inside, while a couple waited for everyone to leave before closing the gates. I was unsure of what would happen to them, but I could only hope that I was wrong about the attack. Although we were entering the unknown, I couldn't have done it with a better group of people.

As the hinges moaned and the gate slid toward its post, a kid in a doorway clutched something small and soft, watching until the metal met metal. Looking around and feeling Bri's hand rest on my leg, I shifted into drive in preparation to go into the sunset.

As I uttered the words "ready" into the transceiver, we all went off in our own direction, Bri's father watching until no longer visible. The gel pouch at my hip felt faintly warm through the sleeve; a reminder that even our tools were alive on a timer.

As those gates closed, the people dispersed, and the noise of the night took over, I remained hopeful that this final trip would mark the end of this disaster. We were going to save the world.

XX. TOGETHER

Entering the trek with the sun setting, we planned to drive for two to three hours, making up part of our estimated nine-hour trip. The first portion of the trip was relatively quiet for Bri and me, as we were still processing the bulk of what had transpired that day. We took in the surroundings as a means of reflection. The grass and other greenery had begun to grow out into the remains of the roads, as human intervention had not kept them confined to the sides. The air around us held a crispness and clarity that I had never experienced before, as if it were freshly filtered and prepared for my lungs. The sunset also had a clearness that I don't recall seeing before this all happened. Perhaps it was because we were in a new location, but the Earth seemed to be healing from the damage caused by humanity.

Thinking through this, realizing and seeing the correlation to my visions and what the Umbrorex had said, I couldn't help but agree with the idea that humanity was a problem on Earth. Humans destroyed, pillaged, and poisoned the Earth throughout our short reign. We caused more damage in a few short thousand years than had happened to the Earth in the billions of years it existed, but was extinction the answer? Although I was sure that all humans were not yet gone, it crossed my mind that it could be an objective. We still had no clue about what these things wanted, but the plan was to find out once we made it. Deciding not to think much more about the topic, I paid close attention to the road and what was in my way as the sun set fully.

Riding through the night, about an hour from a location we planned to stop, Bri began to pick my brain on a few topics. We discussed the upcoming challenges, our thoughts on what might happen to the central group and to us, and even practiced a script of what we might say to the creatures. While all of this was interesting enough to pass the time, I couldn't help but ask about what happened earlier at the base. It was all so new to me, yet it was a welcome and exciting aspect of life. Having that on my mind, I figured it'd be worth a conversation, particularly if we lived long enough to try it once more.

"Bri, I don't mean to shift the topic so abruptly, but would you like to talk about what happened back at the base before we left?" I asked as I paid attention to the road and glanced at her.

Making sure that our transceiver was off, just in case her father was listening, she began to respond.

"What about it?" Bri said casually, a slight smirk playing on her lips.

"Well, other than how the whole experience was for you, I'm just curious about how you feel. I'm still trying to wrap my mind around these feelings. Do you notice any changes or any clarity at all? Kind of like after our conversation in the kitchen of that small house a couple of months ago," I said as I tried to pry for more information, my voice a low hum.

"Clarity... yes. I would say that there is a new layer of that, but I'm sure more will come as we continue to bond. More than anything, though, I learned of a deeper side to you and gathered a sense of you that I've never seen. I can't fully explain it, but even though we didn't literally become one, I feel a sense of closeness and understanding with you that wasn't there before, even beyond our emotional familiarity. I'm not sure if you feel it at all. It's something I'm struggling to identify, but that's all so far. We'll see how much clearer and smoother things feel the next time we have an inevitable conflict.

"As for how I felt about it in a more standard sense, I can see why everyone makes such a big deal out of it. It was nice to experience something new and refreshing. Although I'm not sure if we'll live long enough to find out, I hope we can try it again sometime," Bri said calmly as she gave me a softer look, her gaze steady.

Reflecting on what she said and being grateful for the experience, I quickly tried to determine if I felt anything different. Unsure of anything in the moment, still having most of my focus on the tasks coming up, and in the moment, I began to respond with what I could.

"Firstly, I'm glad you enjoyed yourself and would like to do it again sometime as well. I share the same sentiments. It was an experience that I couldn't say I had sought out, but I'm glad it happened. Most importantly, I'm glad it was with you. There's no other person for me, and you've only brought out the best of me; this was no different. Although I can't say if anything has been cleared or reevaluated regarding my abilities, I believe that we have grown closer and stronger together. As you said, when we eventually have to fight, we can see just how much stronger we've grown and evaluate our performance from there," I said as we neared our stopping point for the night.

Although we could have taken the main routes through Minnesota on the way, we decided to take less popular routes to avoid potential issues or significant damage in those areas. We also figured that any humans still living in the city would have tried to fortify their surroundings. Having this in mind, we radioed our accompanying vehicles on different roads going in the same direction. Looking for a place to stop, we found a suitable spot. It wasn't necessarily a house or shelter, but it was an opening in the tree line that was on stable enough ground to drive into.

"Team, this is Dion checking in. We're approaching a suitable stopping point and were thinking of calling it a night. We plan to refuel before continuing at about 4:00 AM tomorrow. Does that work?" I said as we waited for a response.

"That works for us. We'll pull into this empty gas station and park here for the night. There shouldn't be any trouble, but I'll radio if there is," my dad's voice crackled through the transceiver.

Next to speak were the soldiers. Although they took longer to begin their reply, they eventually talked.

"Roger that, we'll go ahead and pull over."

"What was the reason for the delay? Are there any issues?" Bri asked, her voice sharp with concern.

"None at all, ma'am. We received a communication from Kendry that they were stopping for the night as well. He also wanted to know about our situation, so we provided an appropriate response. He expects their journey to take them another day or two, which would place us at our destination before them. We will likely arrive early tomorrow afternoon, assuming no delays, so he will be waiting to hear what happens," the soldier said as he went off mic.

"Great, I'm sure they will reach their destination safely. As for us, keep your eyes open and be watchful. We have no idea what we're getting into. I will hear from you all tomorrow," I said as I released the speaker button.

Upon checking the surroundings, we ensured that we kept the handheld transceiver with us. Given that it was our only line of communication, we had to keep it on and charged at all times. This meant we would risk draining the car's battery by constantly charging the transceiver, but we had to take that risk. Keeping this in mind, upon checking, we found the area to be clear and safe enough for us to rest for the night.

Getting back in the car, Bri and I shared a few more conversations before calling it a night. As I watched the stars through the windows, reclined in the driver's seat as far back as possible, I couldn't shake this sensation. I had the feeling of the monsters running around me, just close enough for me to sense, but not close enough to be a threat. I couldn't tell if they were doing this intentionally, but it was an occurrence I had never experienced before. Unsure of what to make of it, I did my best to rest while maintaining a level of awareness for my surroundings.

For all that had happened, I was grateful to spend what might be my last day alive with Bri.

The next day, at 3:55 AM, I radioed everyone to confirm they were awake and ready to go. To my delight and surprise, everyone was not only prepared, but there had been no instances of attack or manipulation through the night. It was as if the creatures had gone into hiding, waiting to attack when the time was right. They could have tried to kill or stop us at any moment, but they didn't. Although we all found this peculiar, we had no choice but to continue our journey.

Back on the road, driving through the changing terrain, the ground became less green and more dirt; we were passing into South Dakota. Watching the rising summer sun for perhaps the last time, we rode in a quiet sense of peacefulness. Everything had led up to this. From the moment we first met to the present, we have somehow survived the most confusing and tumultuous moments in human history, making the most of life. It had to be for a reason. We didn't believe that we had survived and learned from all of that to go and die when it was finally time to do something about what was happening to us. As we went down the road, the hours ticking down and the grip we held onto one another slowly tightening in anticipation of what was to come, we had nothing but peace building within us.

There was no fear, no doubt, and no confusion about what was going to happen. We knew that these beings would not stop until they achieved their goals; otherwise, they wouldn't have created so much damage and death. Even where we were in South Dakota, we saw the remnants of human corpses and encampments that at one point were lively and considered a safe place. They destroyed everything, clearly aware of the damage they had caused to the Earth, yet they told me that their communication methods were different. All of it seemed hypocritical and like an attempt on the world as we knew it. Tired of this and ready for it to end, we found ourselves about an hour out from where we expected to find the creatures.

Getting back on the radio, I spoke to our fathers.

"Hey, Dad and Mr. Alvar, how's it going for you?" I said.

"We're ready to see what all the fuss is about," my dad said over the crackling connection, his voice resolute.

"I agree, it's time we put an end to this. I know we originally made this move a week early to gain an advantage. However, given that the element of surprise is out of the window, we'll have to find another way to make this successful," Mr. Alvar said, his tone grim.

"We do, and we will," I said. "If they get a hold of you, you become leverage. If they press us, you can't help from half a mile away. Stop here. Wait for five days. If we don't return, you know what to assume."

"D, this is crazy," my father said. "You want us to stop an hour out?"

"Think about outcomes," I said. "All of us being dead is useless. If you were to live, you can share with the others."

"I've spoken to Kendry," a soldier cut in. "He doesn't like it, but he understands. We'll align with the fathers and keep the line clear."

Silence.

"Dad, you know Dion's right," Bri said, voice steady but softening. "You trained us for this. Don't switch your logic now. Stop the car."

Another silence, longer.

"...Dion, you keep my little girl safe," Mr. Alvar said, emotion hanging on the words.

"Thank you," Bri said, and for the first time in months, her voice shook.

Given that my dad was driving them, I wanted to ensure he was on board. It was also likely our last time speaking with them until this was over, since the range of the transceivers only traveled so far and was impacted by the creature's jammers. Reaching out to him one last time, I began to speak.

"Dad, are you on board?" I said as I continued to drive.

"Yes, son... I am," my dad said, his voice a quiet resignation.

"Good, we'll be back. Meet up with the soldiers alongside the road we're currently on, since it's between the two of you. Once you're there, wait for us along that road to come back, and we'll be there. I'm not sure how long this will be, but if it's longer than five days…"

"Then what?" my dad said, with a desperate edge to his voice.

"Then assume the worst has happened… I can't guarantee anything, but I will do my absolute best to get Bri and me back safely," I said, heart aching.

"You better be right, son, we're pulling towards your road to meet with the soldiers now… I hate this, but you'd better get back to us. Just make sure you—"

"You're fading out, Dad," I said as the connection started to thin and warp. "I'm not sure if you can hear me, but I love you and Mom more than you know."

"I love you and Mom dearly, Father," Bri said. The transceiver answered with static, the silence sudden and total.

Realizing that that was our final time speaking to them, we placed the transceiver into the cup holder and focused on the journey ahead. A mile marker ticked past; after that, there would be no signal and no turning back. Having about another thirty miles to go, a sense of dread began to loom over both of us and only grew in intensity. It was a perfectly sunny day, but this feeling made it seem like a dark cloud had swallowed the world, turning everything we thought we believed to be correct upside down. As we embraced this, not wanting to show any fear or doubt, and not believing we harbored any, we mentally and physically prepared ourselves.

As Bri dropped dabs of that poison on our blades, just to coat them enough to leave a residue in the event of any slashes to the enemy, I handed her my water bottle. Pouring extra water into her canteen, she pushed the gel pack inside and did the same with mine, masking our final fail-safe plan. She squeezed my right hand once; I squeezed back.

Fully prepared and sitting in silence, we began to see where we were supposed to meet. As Feralgehns, Subterros, and multiple Umbrorexes lined the opening of a hole in the ground, standing completely still, we prepared for what was to be our final battle.

The conclusion of the end of the world.

As we arrived, I stopped the car thirty feet away, just in case the monsters tried to lunge at us. I had a feeling that we would be crushed in a real fight at that moment. The sense of creatures all around us was overwhelming; it felt as though there were hundreds of them using the surrounding hills and thin tree lines. Realizing we were greatly outmatched, I continued to stand by the car and watch as the main Umbrorex we had interacted with began walking forward, with three more following behind.

As they approached, the black suit and shades of the female-looking lead waved in the wind, human-like hair in a short fade at the top. The other three wore black trench coats and shades that made them look very conspicuous, but that wouldn't have mattered anyway, as they weren't as evolved as the first. Their skin looked more leathery and not as natural. Their faces held the human shape but had features that were overpronounced, such as prominent brows that pushed them farther than standard. In addition, they gave off the sense that they were beings other than humans, more similar to the creatures than to the lead Umbrorex. The lead, while not perfect, seemed to fit the human build more, even covering its monstrous intentions well and remaining calm and collected. Seeing this and watching the monsters behind them stay still as though they were loyal pets, all heads held at the same angle, Bri and I began to walk in front of the car and come closer together, unsure of what the next steps would look like.

Closing the distance, I imagined an opening slash: throats first, then bodies, pivot right, sprint for the car, and drive a wedge through the line. The plan collapsed when the lead Umbrorex stopped in front of us and extended its right hand.

Shocked and caught off guard, I stood frozen, unsure of what to do. Realizing that Bri, too, was stuck, I waited to see what would happen. As we waited, the Umbrorex kept its hand out and began to open its mouth. Fully expecting a shriek of some kind, the creature started to communicate verbally.

"Hello... Dion... Abrial," the creature said as its voice pushed out the slimy and labored words, each syllable thick with an unsettling wetness.

Although Bri had heard the creature speak before, I could tell by her reaction that something was different. Taken aback by what I was witnessing and curious about how the creature used an audible voice, hearing it myself for the first time, we stood frozen. The other Umbrorexes around it remained still, but the main one that had just spoken kept its hand stretched towards me.

"Why... do you hesitate?... Take my hand... It is a human gesture... correct?" the creature said as it stepped closer to me, its head tilted slightly.

Feeling trapped and forced to oblige, I took the risk of leaving myself open to an attack by taking the creature's hand. As I gripped its somehow five-fingered hand, I could feel that the skin was different from our own, despite the attempt to make it appear otherwise. The slightly moist and grippy skin wrapped around my hand like wet shark leather, a faint solvent smell rising from it, and I felt it begin to shake its arm as it poorly mimicked a real handshake. Although it was a weird feeling, I didn't feel an increase in malice from the creature; it was as if it brought me a sense of peace. Unsure of what the reason for that was, I assumed it to be a sign of genuine friendliness, but of course, I wasn't going to believe that thought.

Letting go of its hand and looking to Bri as she also shook its hand, I could tell that she, too, was confused about the sensation. Outside of the creature feeling completely repulsive, it wasn't an experience that bothered us too much. Now, standing there, waiting for the creature to speak again, we looked into its eyes as it lowered the shades slightly. The black and green colors of the eyes were off-putting, but I didn't sense any malice within them, not at that moment.

"Attempting to read me... There is no purpose," the creature said as it tried to push the words out, a faint hiss accompanying them.

I let a test thought bloom. *If you can read this, look left.* The creature looked left.

"I... can read too... You know... I see you... I see your thoughts... I know your secrets..." it said as it stepped back and kept its gaze upon us, its voice gaining a subtle, unsettling clarity.

Finally, I found it to be a time to speak, and I began to form a sentence to understand more.

"What are we here for? What do you want from us?" I said, keeping my voice firm despite the underlying tension.

"Want?... All we want... is what is ours... I see... You do not yet... understand," it said as it stretched its words through its strained voice box, a slight rasp in its tone.

"You have grown... yes... You have learned... but still know... nothing... Thank you for... for completing your... duty," the creature said as it began to sniff around us as if it were a dog, its head darting from me to Bri.

As it sniffed, its eyes widened and turned its gaze to Bri. Recognizing this, my body must have naturally tensed, causing the other three Umbrorexes to quickly turn their heads to me and the monsters behind them to lower their heads in the same inch. Picking up on this quickly, I relaxed and went back to watching what this thing was doing.

"Ahh... yes... You have mated also," it said as it looked at Bri, its voice carrying an odd, almost pleased inflection.

Disapproving of these comments and the way we were being analyzed, Bri responded to the creature.

"What do you want from us? Answer the question," Bri said sternly, her hand subtly inching toward her right gladius.

"As I said... we want... what is ours... Come with us... you... will know all," the creature said as it continued to stare, its black and green eyes unblinking.

"What if we don't? Who's to say we're not walking to our deaths? So why not do it here?" Bri said as she rested her hands on her blades, the creatures responding accordingly with low vibrational releases and shifting stances.

"Do not... be foolish... Come now... and your fathers... live," the creature squeezed out painfully, a hint of genuine effort in its voice. "Besides... we have been... waiting... We will not... kill you."

Seeing that we had no more options, our fathers were unable to defend against whatever kind of wave would be sent at them. We reluctantly began to walk forward with the creature.

As we walked to the hole in the ground, the lead Umbrorex put its arms around Bri and me while the other three confiscated our weapons, ignoring our handheld transceiver in the car. While we still had our canteens with the bomb gel in there and the vials of poison, made to look like medicine, inside our pockets, we couldn't help but feel even more at a disadvantage as the creatures took our weapons. When they patted us down, they took the blades and the visible knives and missed the flat vials pressed into our pockets. Approaching the hole, the creatures moved to the side to allow us to pass, not providing the slightest bit of resistance. Standing at the edge, Bri and I stopped walking as there was no way down.

"How are we supposed to go in there? Clearly, we don't have much choice, but we'll die if we just go in," I said, my voice echoing slightly in the vast opening.

"I agree, we also won't be able to breathe down there," Bri said as she tried to get the creature to stay on the surface, her gaze skeptical.

"You have... not learned enough... Walk forward... know your nature... All will become... clear soon," the creature said as it removed its arms from around us and stepped into the abyss, disappearing from view.

Fully expecting it to fall down, it shocked us by walking along the wall, even in shoes. Under the lip, a soft industrial thrum vibrated through my boots. The air sharpened, ozone and cold metal, and a cool draft rose from below.

As it strode down, it used the mental voices from earlier and spoke to us more clearly, but still eerily.

Walk forward, you will not fall. Put one foot in front of the other, the creature said as it continued, its voice now a coherent, chilling whisper in our minds.

Taking the first step, I felt myself falling until my foot stuck to the side of the hole. Pressure gathered in my arches and shins, a magnetic tug. Confused but steady, I moved my other foot, and it did the same. Before I knew it, I had both feet on the wall and was walking completely normal.

Grabbing Bri's hand, I led her along as she did the same; the other three Umbrorexes and the monsters followed behind.

Walking into the unknown, we were utterly shocked by the encounter's peacefulness and followed the leader down to what we assumed was their headquarters. At intervals, vents exhaled cold vapor that shunted the heat away, and the machinery's layered hum dominated the shrieks and odd sounds further below.

Only a little longer until you know the truth. Everything you have done was for a purpose, and it is time for you to serve it, the lead Umbrorex said in its many voices as it spoke without speaking, its words a symphony of alien purpose.

Finally seeing the bottom of the hole, after being made to sprint for most of it, we were likely twenty kilometers down. The lights that illuminated it shone brightly, and the sounds of machinery dominated the other noises, including shrieks and odd sounds. Unsure of what would happen next, we walked into the most shocking situation of our lives.

Their civilization.

XXI. BENEATH

Before we entered that cavern, the world as we knew it, though changed, was still familiar. We understood the sun would come up, just as surely as it would go down. We knew that the survival of human beings depended on water, food, and other essentials we would attain throughout the days or weeks we lived. We fundamentally understood what it meant to be human and to survive on Earth.

That first day in the hole, in their civilization, changed everything we had ever understood.

Fully expecting to be greeted by a cavern filled with grotesque, murderous creatures and their long-skulled masters, we were met instead by what appeared to be an oasis-city, guarded by the lesser-developed Umbrorex variants. Although the settlement lay far from where we stood, it was clear this deadly and brutal species was more than the murderous monsters we had perceived. That didn't mean our interpretation was wrong; it meant it was incomplete. The sight of a city-like place with abundant lighting and ceilings high enough to mimic the outside world displayed intelligence and creativity typically claimed by humans. Animals and insects create shelter, yes, but this was more than that; it was an active attempt at paradise, or so it seemed.

Thinking this through, so focused I barely registered the figures approaching the gate, I turned to Bri. Her expression mixed amazement and confusion, more than understandable. This was something we could never have expected, but we had to stay focused on our purpose and the plan. Returning to the present as the cloak-wearing figures drew near, guarded by their own Umbrorexes similar to the one that led us down here, I stepped toward them. The ones beside me grabbed me instantly, their grips iron-hard. I knew I could break free if necessary.

The central cloaked figure of the three raised its leathery, five-fingered right hand. The Umbrorexes released me. Confused, I started to speak.

"What is this place, and why are we here?" I asked as the three figures continued their silent, unnerving approach.

Still wordless and now within a few feet, I asked again. "Why are we here?" Their guards stilled, and the air tightened.

They drew back their hoods. The faces beneath were humanoid with elongated skulls, like the creature we had seen with Dr. Ibezzi. Eyes jet-black and sunken gave their leathery faces a skeletal cast, as if covered in a thin layer of flesh. Hairless and tall, they resembled Feralgehns at a distance, but nothing about them was animal. They could think and choose. As I studied the leaders, their mouths, circular openings on their noseless faces, widened, but no sound emerged. Instead, one of the Umbrorexes with them, also cloaked, came around and stood close to Bri and me. When the leader of the leaders closed its mouth, that Umbrorex, the most human-looking of them from the skin I could see, opened his and spoke.

"Hello, and welcome, on behalf of the Supremes," he said in pristine, smooth English, the most natural we had heard from any of them. "They would like us to give you a tour of our main city, Thraxxundar. I can feel you have many questions. Do not be afraid or doubtful; all will be made clear shortly. That said, should I worry about you trying anything? I know you will, depending on how this goes. Still, the Supremes want me to give you a chance first, and that's what I'll do."

Shocked by a creature so clearly not human, yet more human-sounding than either of us at times, we agreed.

"No. You don't have to worry," Bri said. "We'll listen to what you have to say and see if a solution is possible." I nodded, mind reeling.

"Good. That makes things easier for now… Guards, lift the gate and let us pass. We have much to see and learn," the Umbrorex said, taking position between us and the beings the locals would call Supremes.

We moved forward. The Umbrorex who had handled us on the surface fell in behind, along with the Feralgehns and other escorts that had brought us down. This new speaker seemed to be in charge down there. As we passed through the gate and onto a long road toward the city, the place's liveliness and its inventions came into view.

"Just a warning," he said. "The first time can be… mind-bending. It will make sense soon, and you'll see why we were right. My name is Jax, by the way. You can stop looking at me like a mindless killing machine. Welcome to Thraxxundar." He lifted his arms from under his cloak in a strangely human gesture of showmanship.

Confusion deepened into shock. I took Bri's hand as we approached the city, our fingers tightening in a wordless pact.

If what I suspected proved true, nothing would ever be the same.

At the city's edge, the local rhythm emerged. Child-sized beings ran laughing, kicking a stone sphere that was literally a fist-sized rock. Each strike sent a chalky fleck across the path. They barely flinched when it glanced bone against their callused feet. Subterros lounged near their handlers, leather leads braided through plated necks, huffing warm breath that smelled like damp soil.

Parents and idle onlookers watched us with flat contempt edged by fear. They stared harder at Bri. Later, I would understand why: a human woman was myth made flesh. Umbrorexes, half-human in silhouette, less so up close, passed among them in layered cloaks, green eyes catching the furnace-warm light.

A draft kissed my ankles. Somewhere beneath the stone, air moved in a steady current, like vents pulling heat off a server rack. The place smelled of minerals and old steam.

Windowless stone cottages lined the lane, their edges worn smooth. Children played with devices that touched their temples, thin filaments sinking into hairlines, eyes tracking symbols only they could see.

Jax walked as if the avenue belonged to him, pausing to trade seconds of that soundless language with a child who offered him the rock. Feralgehns and Subterros responded to a clipped, trilled note; the beasts' attention snapped like a switch. The Umbrorex behind us kept pace without comment. If resentment had a temperature, I felt it at my back.

"So… friends," Jax said at last. "How are you liking it so far? Different doesn't have to mean worse. You adapt." He peered from behind his shades, mouth curving. Then he tossed us two rolled cloaks. "Wear these. The city center is proud. They dislike the human-looking among us. Better if you pass unnoticed."

I pulled mine on. It was heavy with old warmth, and the hood softened the edges of sound. Beside me, Bri spoke in the tone she reserved for specimens and liars.

"I can tell you're different. You read us too easily," she said. "If these cloaks hide that we're human, is it safe to assume you are, or at least can appear to be?"

He didn't answer. But something in him spiked, energy compressed and sheathed, as we crossed into streets where the stone gleamed like glazed basalt and the cloaks around us shifted to deep green. Foot coverings, stitched from Feralgehn hide, the pores still visible, whispered over the gloss. The buildings here had windows instead of open holes. Markets were active but orderly. Whatever fed this place, whatever power kept it stable, ran quietly and efficiently.

"Your perception is strong, Abrial," Jax said, not looking at her. "You're right about some of it. The rest... You already know. You're not ready to name it."

Ahead rose a tower shaped like an overgrown stalagmite. Red sigils crawled softly along its flank, heat shimmering above them without any visible flame. The crowd thinned. Space opened as if the city had learned to walk around the place.

"Keep your heads down," Jax murmured, almost kind. "The Founders here value purity. They find human resemblance... distasteful."

Two long-skulled guards waited on the steps, armor latticed with fused Feralgehn claws. They didn't speak. Their mouths opened in silent ovals, and a pressure pricked the air. The gate lifted. Sandra's pace hitched. Jax tugged a glove finger tight, lifted his chin, and led us in.

Inside, the space resembled a vast, archaic cathedral. Before we could absorb it, the floor shuddered, and the platform beneath us began to sink. No one else reacted; we stayed still as the mechanism carried us down into a chamber lit by the glow of a control center and by holographic screens mapping the Earth. The dark beyond felt enormous.

The larger Supremes rose from stations and came toward us. When they formed a ring, Jax removed his cloak and shades, slow and deliberate. The fear I had named with Bri was confirmed: he looked perfectly, unnervingly human.

He was not human.

The skin was an artist's copy, flawlessly imperfect. Hair, eyes, mouth, nose: all precisely wrong by being so right. His voice, his emotional mimicry, his thoughtfulness, human tells he had mastered. Even if he was somehow a human raised below, what was he doing here, translating for things that wanted to reshape our world?

"I know it's a shock," Jax said, voice smooth as polished stone. "It's part of the truth you came for. The Supremes would like you to remove your cloaks. They dislike guessing." He gestured, urgency barely veiled.

The elders' black eyes harbored something I could only read as intent. I lifted my hood. Bri did the same. The Supremes stepped back, conferred in silence; their mouths widened again, and a faint pressure combed the air. They looked to Jax. He moved to the console and brushed a sequence. The room brightened.

The rest of it was displayed.

Cages held bound humans, their throats clasped by chrome collars whose inner plates showed circuitry; devices that turned breath into silence. Many had been slashed and sutured and slashed again, left alive but removed from choice. Beyond them, Umbrorexes and Supreme-looking technicians worked at black tables. There were no glowing tubes, no film clichés; only machines and bodies and a tireless, clinical pace. Rigs held headless pregnant torsos in place; peristaltic pumps pulsed like throats to maintain perfusion, and laryngeal stumps were sealed by hush collars. There were hundreds. The stench arrived late but total.

My head swam. Jax watched my eyes, and he smiled.

"Things a little much, Donny?" he asked softly. "You've seen nothing. Get yourself together so I can show you the rest. I want you to see what we are, where we come from; where your particular abilities come from."

"Abilities?" I said. "What the hell are you talking about?" I pressed my palms into my scalp as if I could hold my mind in place.

"Spare me the performance," Jax said. "You have always felt apart. You mistook separation for virtue."

Bri's hand settled on my shoulder and steadied the spin. Tears shone in her eyes. "D... I think this is where we come from," she whispered.

Jax clapped once, softly. "There it is. Recognition. Origin always lands like a fall. May I assume you're ready for the rest?"

The floor met my knees. It wasn't wise, but the collapse felt inevitable. If he was right, my life was a lie. Everything was a lie. I didn't even know if I was human. Bri knelt with me as the Supremes watched, measuring how minds bend.

"Since it's sinking in, and because the Supremes approve, let me give you the truth," Jax said, hands resting on his knees, eyes amused. "Ready?"

He paced, casting gestures like a lecturer.

"Three hundred thousand years ago, Homo sapiens took a recognizable shape. Your story paints a straight climb. But there is a fraction you refused to see. When a rift formed, a branch of developing humans and a swath of fauna were cut off and left to die. They found a way instead, deep in an isolated jungle, severed from the rest of the world. New diet. New threats. Rapid pressure. Evolution's hand on the throttle. Their skin shifted toward the amphibious; their features adapted to their needs; their intelligence accelerated because time and space allowed it. The surface promised only cataclysm, so they chose a domain of their own. Beneath, they found minerals and energies with leverage; the power to build, to influence life, even to mold earth. They learned. They grew. They spread."

He paused. Machines whispered. Somewhere, a pump exhaled a slow, warm breath.

"They left the natural caves and expanded the network, sometimes visiting the surface but finding it increasingly intolerable. Oceans posed challenges. So did their own growing pains; miscalculations causing shifts, quakes, and accidents. But their rise was relentless. They learned what it meant to be of Earth, not merely on it. Pain and stormy emotion hampered progress, so they selected them out. Bodies strengthened. Beasts like Feralgehns and Subterros were shaped to survive and serve. Their blood blackened with the nutrients and compounds that made strength and healing efficient..."

I tuned him out just enough to think of the dead who had carried us this far, and the promises we made to the living. I started to plan. If I could get to a weapon—

Bri's fingers tightened, a warning: not yet. I forced myself to wait.

"Wise," Jax murmured without looking at me. His smile thinned.

"Humans made their own strides," he went on. "Mostly, you killed each other and stripped the planet. Parasites devouring a host while pretending to rule it. As your wars and extractive appetites expanded, the Founders sought a solution. Control of the surface was the only way to secure the planet and our society. We could have obliterated you.

That would defeat the point. The Earth had to live. So we captured, we studied, and we looked for vectors; eyes above."

He turned his head slightly, listening to a silence only he heard.

"The first plan tried to transform humans. You proved fragile. You can't breathe here for long. Hence, the devices on their necks." He flicked a glance at the collars. "The next plan spliced Founder genetics into offspring. Emotion was no obstacle for us. Results were promising but skewed; too Founder, not convincingly human. That research produced the Umbrorexes. Mute, most of them. Eyes wrong. Blood occasionally red. The most successful from that line is the one you met topside, Sandra. She has mastered our language and yours and can pass in certain light among Umbrorexes, but not humans."

Sandra made a sound like a breath dragged over broken glass. Resentment lived there.

"Which led to the final plan," Jax said. "You see the maternal rigs. Bodies kept viable, heads removed to simplify control. From those, the purest hybrids: beings human enough to embed, Founder enough to thrive." He pointed at himself, then at us. "The outcomes vary, but the goals align. You think you come from your Earth mothers and fathers, and in a way, you do. It is grotesque, yes. But both of you carry Founder blood and responsibility. Your Umbrorexes selected healthy hosts, avoiding the approach you see here, made minor interventions, and watched. You found each other on the surface; that was an accident, a useful one. You've been observed ever since. Your inclinations toward the Earth? Genetics, enabled by imagination. You are here to realize your strength and put it to use. Questions?"

"If any of this is true," I said, "we're still human. And what about you? If you were made the same way, why choose them?"

"Human?" He tilted his head. "Partly. You are of the most innovative species on this planet, not the bumbling apes you protect at the cost of everything else. Founder genetics mixed with yours early and were concentrated, meaning you are no longer just them. Those genes kept you alive. Be grateful." His gaze didn't soften. "As for me, I recognized myself when Sandra found me. I recognized the truth when the Supremes, the Founder species, showed it. Humanity never learned. It called itself sovereign while poisoning its home, while never understanding its home's capacities."

He looked us over, almost wistful. "They saw more in you than in me. That stung. It also made sense after Sandra's reports. You are exceptional. Stronger together. You read and feel and still adapt. I lack the telepathic capacities of a few rare hybrids, as I assume you do too. But we can learn. You are the proof of the future. You mastered empathy for humans. You scaled your abilities. And... Sandra mentioned procreation. That should be instructive."

"You don't know what you are," Bri said, voice calm and cold enough to cut. "You talk about Founders and humans as if certainty makes a soul. I see your fear. Your doubt. Your shame. If you believe we are beyond you, what grants you that certainty you wear like armor?"

Jax's smile flattened. "Your insight means little. In a few generations, you will be a relic. I am at ease with my mortality. I am a step in a process. Are you?"

He let the question hang, then smoothed it with contempt. "It annoys me to be near those deemed more crucial. But bonds are your advantage; bonds I cannot make. You win goodwill. You generate life. That is your leverage. As you watch the world you fought to protect burn, and the world you were born to serve rise, remember this: you are experiments. Unnatural. But with the act you have performed and will perform until deemed complete, you will seed an army of perfectly adapted Founders who will master this planet above and below. You will help build an oasis on a healthy Earth."

Rage broke my stillness. I lunged.

The floor sigils flared, thin lines of red sliding awake beneath the translucent stone. Cold laced my calves. My knees locked, tendons humming like wire. Umbrorexes unfolded from shadow, surrounding me; dozens, incomplete like Sandra or worse, enough to tell me the truth: I wouldn't win like this.

I forced myself back to Bri as the figures melted away. My skin crawled. I waited for Jax's judgment.

"Brave," he said. "And blind to the room. You'll come around. I don't intend to babysit you into it." He turned past us. "Sandra."

"Yes... Jax," she replied, voice stretched and pained.

"Take them to the holding area. One cell. Together. I'll check on them shortly. They need time."

"Will... do."

We were led to a far corner away from the control center and the Supremes and shut into a dark, slick cell. Bri met my eyes. We didn't need to speak. We would plan here and act.

It was time to make headway on our objective.

XXII. LIBERATION

Sitting in the cell, we held each other tightly at first, in silence, as we watched the many Umbrorexes and Supremes traversing the area. The sight of them made me sick, but we had to find a way to escape and still accomplish what we came to do. I glanced at Bri, ready to pick her brain about an exit plan. Certain Jax and the others could hear us, we kept our voices low and made it look like we were just holding on to each other.

"How're you doing?" I whispered into her ear.

"I'm not worried about these things," Bri murmured back. "We have a task to do, and while they creep me out, there's nothing here we didn't suspect. The revelation that we're one of them, if that's even true, wasn't the reason behind our abilities that I thought, but it tracks. As for their comments on our 'procreation'... I still don't know what they mean, and I don't care to right now. We need to learn more and then kill them with certainty."

"I agree. Everything he's said is shocking, but it's time to keep moving with the plan. You thinking what I'm thinking?"

"If it's that we speak up and try to get out to gather more information, then yes. We need to communicate with Jax. He's the only one dumb enough to share details, but we have to be careful. Our deflection worked, but he'll see through it if we slack. I'll ask the questions; you sell some fear to distract, but not so much that he clocks it. That work?"

"Sure. Ask about other colonies, how they move the Earth exactly, and whether we can get out to walk around. His hubris might be his demise; funny, considering his comments about humanity."

"Yeah. Let's get it over with," Bri said, standing and moving to the cage entrance.

Thinking back on this, I still don't see how we didn't do something sooner. We wanted information and needed to know our enemy, but at some point, the odds were clear. Jax and his army were monsters, but they were also flesh and blood. They bled like we bled. Some were worse off, hybrids not fully developed or mixed with the proper ratios to improve on the founder DNA. Flawed beings clinging to the past, convinced they had a claim to the Earth's resources. Their technology, their society, their drive to alter life were formidable, but not enough to stop us. We knew that, yet we kept asking for one more piece of understanding before we moved.

Jax was the anomaly that showed how dire it could get. We had no clue if he was unique in his treachery or if others like him were spread across the US and the world. We didn't know if more enhanced people like Bri and me existed, ready to help humanity. We weren't even sure how much time had passed; our watches had failed, and we had no sense of how our people on the surface were doing. Only this much was clear: the threat was massive, and we were the ones primed to act. The military had been all but defeated. Other camps were a mystery, communications failing, silence spreading. Resources were likely running thin, and power had to be self-supplied. These creatures were healing the planet while laying waste to humanity as if we were a parasite to be burned out. Bri and I had to intervene.

Humanity, though still a blur to me most days, has always pushed at my understanding of living things. How could something so primitive and so biologically complex climb its way to running the Earth? Humans were not rightful rulers, maybe not even dominant, yet they had built traits you don't often see in the wild. The range of emotion and self-awareness, the stubborn vitality, became the root of much good and much evil, constantly shifting what "human" meant. Some would argue that humans would be better without emotions, that pure rationale would bring prosperity. Maybe, for a short time. But that would flatten us into founder-like machines that only work toward goals and miss the connective thread. Emotions are contagious; they move person to person, intentionally or not. For years, I lacked that whole side and still racked up what most call extreme success. I felt something was different, and I worked anyway, always chasing a version of fulfillment that stayed just out of reach. If that's the ideal, I felt closer to the real thing here than ever. My family, my friends, and Bri together made those feelings possible. They enriched my life and widened my understanding of what "human" meant to me.

When I replay these events and all that could have shifted, I'm still grateful for what did happen. I may not be where I want to be, or with whom, but everything has its reason. We waited to move because we needed to see one more thing and hear one more tale.

It wasn't pretty, but we knew what to do to end this.

At the gate entrance, two hybrid Umbrorexes stared at Bri in silence, spear-staves held at a relaxed, ready stance. She raised her voice to Jax.

"Jax... I think I can see where your mind is with all of this. We don't agree on everything. I can't sign off on the death and destruction. Still, I wanted to learn more about what's going on around the world."

"Abrial," Jax said, sauntering to the bars with that teacher's smile. "You seem to have come around quickly, quick enough to ask the right questions. Sure, it's been about a day since you've been in there, but you're fast learners."

"A day? What do you mean?" Bri asked. We traded a quick, bewildered glance.

"Twenty-four hours," he said. "You two were harboring malicious intentions, so to calm the situation, I had a colorless, odorless gas pumped in. You were out like lights. We didn't probe you. We're not savages. But we did search you, and found these." He lifted our poison vials and dangled them. "Not sure what it is. Given your prep, I'd bet it kills Feralgehns, since that's all you could study. We tested it. It kills the pets. Against founders and hybrids, results vary.

Either way, no chemical warfare. If you try anything else, you'll be the first to taste it."

My tongue held a faint metallic tang, my mouth dry as chalk. The stakes climbed a notch. We needed a way out of the cage.

"It's a shame you felt the need to do all of that instead of communicating properly," Bri said, cool as stone. "I can't say I blame you. I'd be scared too if I saw what we did and then tried to throw us in a cage."

Jax scoffed and waited.

"Since we're talking," she said, eyes steady on him, "how do you control the ground, the frequency bands, and the surface internet? I figure it's tied to that console. I want clarity."

"Happy to educate," Jax said. "But first, Dion should join us at the front. Pouting in the back won't help."

I came to the gate beside Bri. Jax's smile sharpened.

"That console is one node among many," he said. "Each can trigger a selective spectrum collapse that strangles communications and targeted devices. It looks like an EMP, but cleaner, and we can filter it. We chose to limit it to the internet and comms so planes wouldn't fall. The Supremes were merciful." He flicked a toggle on the console. The overhead lamps stuttered, then steadied. The floor gave a faint insect hum under my boots. "It can do more. Move land. Sing rock loose. We seed lithokinetic induction arrays and send thermal-acoustic drilling swarms to drink the debris. These machines have run for a long time. Human discoveries occasionally add materials we don't mine down here, and the founders use them. Humans had their uses. That drive to improve is part of why humans remain, and why there wasn't a hole opened under your shelter. You kept a few crucial individuals who could aid us. That's where we come in."

He gestured lazily at his own face. "The founders learned that working with humans goes smoothly when the messenger looks familiar. Hybrids like us retain human features, along with improved body function and adrenaline responses. It makes partnering easier, even while we reduce the population and quiet rebellion. That's partially why you're here. Going beyond your initial questions, we want you to help re-educate humanity and make the world healthier. The Supremes still struggle on the surface, despite evolving to survive the harsher environment down here. The resources topside are critical for further development and for eventual adaptation above and below. We would still require sacrifices to birth more hybrids, but it can be humane and let children remain with parents, similar to you two. The headless corpse process is not their favorite. Nor what happens to the natural fathers, many of whom are in the cage you saw. Personally, I think a complete, clean process would be better for everyone. Maybe that's the human in me... After some years, you will live to see that there will be naturally born hybrids that embody the perfection the Supremes want."

"When you say we'd be around to see it, what do you mean?" I asked. A knot tightened low in my stomach.

"The Supremes live three to four centuries," he said, bright with pride. "Based on that math and our data on healing factors in hybrids, we expect a natural life expectancy of about two hundred and fifty years or more. That is one reason the population needed a sharp reduction. The new society will be better and prosperous for all. Be happy you get to be at the forefront."

His plans showed a kind of promise that ignored the human cost. Humanity wasn't perfect, but the roles he laid out reduced people to co-authors of their own extinction. No one we loved would agree. Kendry's fate lurked at the edge of my thoughts; we didn't know what our blood had done to him, only that we would find out later when we had the truth.

I shifted toward the ask that mattered. "Jax, we understand what you're trying to do. We disagree with the methods, and we don't forgive what's happened. But we can move forward on a better footing if we understand more. We can't do that from inside this cage. Is it possible to let us out and speak with us? We don't have our weapons. Hand-to-hand would be pointless against these numbers."

"Are you asking me to let you out now?" He let out a small laugh and flicked his fingers. Guards moved. "Sure. I'll let you out. I still don't know what they see in you or how you advanced so much more than I have, but it amuses me that you ask me for freedom."

The cage lifted. We stepped out as the Umbrorexes watched, expressionless.

"Since you're free, let's go to the console and sit," Jax said. "The Supremes have been waiting."

We followed. A wave of adrenaline cut cold through me. On the way, Bri and I traded a look that said everything. We still needed intel, but the window to strike was opening.

At the table, the backdrop of headless corpses and caged humans framed the four Supremes, their Umbrorex guards, and Sandra, the pale, reptilian humanoid. We took our seats. Their black eyes held steady on us, an eerie quiet radiating off them. Jax turned to a Supreme and opened his mouth in their odd way, a silent exchange we couldn't hear. The creature replied in kind. Jax faced us again.

"Against my better judgment, the Supremes want to share more about life below," he said. "They will keep the full extent of your purpose hidden, but they want you to see what portion of your bloodline is worth protecting and will better serve the world. This site is one of many central locations, each run by its own Supremes. They connect through the tunnel apertures on the level above, tying our society together across the world. The network lets us travel quickly using efficient designs. The surroundings may not look high-tech, but they had time to build what matters. They don't care for the surface conveniences. The same technology underwrites the biological enhancements: durability and recovery."

"Durability and recovery," I said. "You mean the strength and healing we've seen."

"Yes. The exact strength and healing in your veins comes from generations of experimentation," Jax said. "The Supremes aren't helpless. Everything down here, including pets, has been enhanced over time. Hard to kill and good at killing, which is why humans struggle above ground. As for mental capabilities, adaptability, and mind-to-mind communication, those are natural traits refined over time. Those like us hear it but can't initiate it easily. Odd, but it works."

"You said 'those like us,'" Bri said, gaze narrowing. "How many more versions of us are there?"

Jax leaned forward in a comical little fold, eyes bright. The Umbrorexes at the table watched in forceful silence.

"That's for us to know and for you to discover. I'd love to tell you, but I won't. Some of the others aren't as nice as I am. We still have some like you who are undecided, but once we lower the population by a few more percentage points, they'll see we're right. Hopefully it won't take that kind of effort for you two, but I know how stubborn our minds can be."

Silence settled. The fly-buzz near the corpses rose, then faded. A slow drip from somewhere behind the cages kept time with a Supreme's breath. We were surrounded by headless, pregnant bodies used to build our enemies and by chained human slaves, and by hundreds of humanoids who looked at us and saw what they were supposed to be. If they could feel envy, it would live here. The founder-faced ones had to know their time would end, too. Even if they supported the cause, evolution would remake them. I looked at Jax, then at Sandra. Enough. I asked if they could retrieve our water bottles. Bri caught it and gave the slightest nod. Her hand brushed my thigh: the time is soon.

"Water?" Jax said, puzzled. "You know you don't need it like humans do. We can go weeks. It's part of being a hybrid. Wait... is this a trick?"

"We haven't had anything to drink in over twenty-four hours," I said evenly. "We're still learning ourselves. We're surrounded and miles underground. What trick could we play here?"

"I know something's involved. I'm curious. If it's to kill a Supreme, it changes nothing. There are thousands more. If it's to kill me, it won't work. Your hands will be off your arms before you're halfway across the table, and I don't think we can regrow limbs. If it's to kill yourselves, that also won't work how you'd like. If you had a tool, it'd be those vials. We tested them. Good on pets. Mixed on founders and hybrids. No chemical cheats." He looked at Sandra. "Any reason they shouldn't drink?"

"I see... no reason for... withholding," Sandra rasped. "They are... tactical... but we are greater."

"Well then," Jax said, eyes on us, "bring our guests their beverages."

The guards who carried our bottles were the same ones holding our weapons. A side instruction changed the handoff. The canteens came without the blades. Everyone watched, waiting for us to lunge. I didn't. I opened my canteen and took a sip, keeping my half of the mixture steady. Bri mirrored me. The air felt dense, mineral-rich. If oxygen ran higher down here, the bomb might amplify or dampen in unpredictable ways. We would need perfect timing. I capped the canteen and set it on the cold, foreign metal of the table. The tension eased by a hair.

"Sheesh," Jax said. "For a second, I thought you'd make us mutilate you. If we do, we still have ways to keep your bodies useful. Keep that in mind."

He smiled. "So, do you think you know enough to decide, or do you want the cage again? I bet your fathers and those other guys are still waiting topside."

"You make it sound like we could leave and go back if we agree," Bri said. "It can't be that simple."

"Sure, it can. We don't want too many humans to die, and you two are crucial. If we keep you here working below, we leave your genes out of the pool. You're already close to creating the first naturally born hybrid, even though it's far too early to tell. There's no benefit to keeping you here. Go back. Enjoy the time you have with your families. The world will continue to reset. The pets hunt well now, so they'll still be around, but you can count on a somewhat peaceful life. Eventually, we intervene for the next stages of our evolution plans. You may not like that. If you figure it out yourselves, we intervene less."

"What are you talking about?" I said, barely above a whisper. "You want us to make babies to replace us and these creatures and to test on natural humans. That only ends in the loss of life you claim you don't want."

"It can be different." He leaned back with a knowing smirk. "You've already done some testing without knowing it. We've mixed human DNA with founder DNA plenty of times. You mixed hybrid blood into a human. Kendry, specifically."

Cold flooded me. Kendry is like a brother. The transfusion was necessary. Maybe it was the lack of compassion in his voice. Maybe it was the triumph. Either way, I'd had enough. I kept my composure. Bri read me and set her hand on my leg again, a steadying pressure. I breathed, then let him continue.

"He was dying, huge slashes in his back, not what we intended to happen so soon, but you gave him blood tainted with the future of life," Jax said. "Don't worry. You likely extended his life in more ways than one. We want to see what happens to him over time, whether he develops our abilities. Eventually, we'll take him and test the full extent of changes, but that can wait years. Life created from two science-based hybrids will be the first step toward the perfect species, mixing the best of humans and founders. All of us will die eventually and pave the way for perfection. Once you accept that, everything gets easier. For now, you're not on board. That's unfortunate... back to the cage. We'll bring our delicacies from below to keep your strength up. You'll need it to meet the others."

The creatures stood, signaling the end of the conversation. As Jax and the Supremes remained, Sandra stayed as well. The other Umbrorexes gathered, spear-staves out, some gleaming with Feralgehn claws worked into their design. This was the moment. I looked at Bri, then at the guards holding our gear. We slung our canteens tight across our bodies and prepared to put our training to work.

The two guards with our gear stood ten feet to our right and left, respectively. Four more blocked the path to the cage. A hostage wouldn't help; Jax would never trade. Our intent bled through. Jax felt it. The room tightened. We didn't wait for his call.

We broke at once; Bri left, and I right. I hit the Umbrorex with my katana strapped across its chest, palmed the cross-strap, yanked it forward, and cut across the side of the neck fast and deep, through muscle into the bright artery. The skin folded oddly away from the blade as if eager to peel. Red sprayed. For a heartbeat, my brain shouted human, then I shut it down and moved. I slid to Bri's back-right corner. Her target lay twisted, head turned where it shouldn't go, femur shattered from a stomp and twist I'd seen her practice a hundred times.

We faced Jax, the Supremes, and the ring of Umbrorexes, with more shapes shifting in the dark edges. Jax stood at the center, irritated and smiling, likely pleased at the chance to kill us and repurpose our bodies. He lifted a hand, pausing the room. Weapons stayed trained, breath leveled, eyes black and without blink. Bri and I stood in a sheen of fresh blood, watching the herd of guards re-form and close.

The standoff held for a breath that felt like a minute. The lamps hummed. The console lights flicked in a rhythm I didn't trust.

It was time to make our escape.

XXIII. BLOODSHED

Standing with our backs against the rocky wall, our weapons in hand, we were in a stalemate that was fated to end at any moment. As Jax stood, all the creatures around us waited in silence; his face remained calm. I could see his brain churning as he thought of what to do. Although the situation was tense and it seemed we were all aware of it, no action was taken hastily; they had time on their side, and we were the ones who needed to make something happen. Figuring that we were only delaying the inevitable, I prepared myself to attack. Thinking of my route, I planned that Bri and I would split opposite directions along the wall, keeping the console dead center, and run along the wall as we held off the more elusive but weaker Umbrorexes and possibly steal a few slices at the Supremes. We weren't sure how strong they were, but given what Jax had said about their evolved abilities, we knew they were no easy task to handle. Imagining that we wouldn't make it out of that situation completely unscathed, I could only hope that our training and improvements were enough to get us out of there alive. As we both prepared to make our final stand, not siding with those horrible creatures, Jax simply turned his back to us and went toward the center console. On his walk back, he began to speak.

"I always knew you would be too attached to human flaws to fully accept the truth of what we were doing, but the Supremes wanted to give it a chance. Though I hoped for a different outcome, you both will help us one way or another. However, suppose this behavior is any indication of the rest of those you were with, one of whom is now sharing our blood. In that case, that is an infestation that I simply can't allow to spread," Jax said with a hint of glee in his voice, his words chilling.

"What do you mean you can't allow it? What could they do to you that we can't? Given the situation we're in and the resources available to you all, it's fair to say that their actions are largely inconsequential. Your plans to erase human nature will take place gradually," I said as I kept an eye on the still stationary Umbrorexes around me, keeping the rock wall at my left and the sanctuary doors behind the Supremes, my mind racing for an opening.

"That may be true, but defiance and terror are things that we have to nip in the bud. You two will aid us in our plans, whether you're sentient or not, so rest assured that you are on the right side of history and will be quietly remembered as the producers of the first natural-born variant of perfection. As for your friends and family, we will find more to take their place, and we can mix your blood with any human we choose to keep alive. They are insects and a prehistoric species that serve only as food for the cattle and as a precursor to the excellence that will ultimately rule this planet. Their time has been up, and you've only accelerated the process," Jax said as he reached the center console and prepared to do what I assumed to be opening another hole.

Not waiting to find out if my assumption was correct, I knew I had to act.

"Wait!" I yelled as I burst forward, Bri following closely.

Moving at a speed I can't recall hitting before this, Bri slid off my right shoulder like a thrown blade, and we made our way through the increasing horde of now-attacking Umbrorexes. By this point, many of them were attacking us and sneaking up from behind, but we remained quick and aware enough to tell what they were doing and where they were going. Though we didn't break any laws of physics, our strength allowed us to move our weapons with ease and contort our bodies in unnatural ways. I refused stabs; slashes only. Mobility over heroics. Blood found my eyes. Unable to clear them in the moment, I relied on my other senses and kept a clear view of the large room in my mind. Feeling where I was going and what my blade was doing, everything was with the intent to kill, not injure. In our frenzied blitz to the middle, I sliced at their throats, arms, legs, and eyes as we maimed these creatures.

Taking a quick moment to wipe my eyes as we made our way through, I saw that Bri had been killing nearly two times as many as I was with excellent precision. She sliced off the leg on one and, in the same motion, stabbed and ripped open another. Though her stabbing acts took more time, her increased speed made up for the delay, allowing her to remain one step ahead of the Umbrorexes around us.

As more of them surrounded her, she executed a move where she began to rotate rapidly while still maintaining control of her attacks. Her rotation was engineered, not pretty; she kept both blades between her and everything else, turning falling bodies into a moving guard. This way, she was able to defend, kill, and avoid being hit, all while retaining her balance on the floor covered in a mixture of black and red blood. The scene was grotesque, and we found no enjoyment in it, but these creatures had given us no choice. Through

Jax, they had even expressed their excitement at being replaced. They were essentially forcing themselves into extinction through their own creations, further highlighting the flaws in their thinking.

As we approached the center console, the Umbrorexes had slowly begun to back off. In the moment of space, I began to feel the damage that they had inflicted upon me. Though they didn't land anything potentially fatal, the group of cloaked humanoid creatures had been punching, kicking, and slicing at us during our push forward. Everything worked fine, and I felt no signs of slowing. Yet, the blood coming from my body and the somewhat shredded cloak over me made me feel as if I were a gladiator who survived against an army. Nonetheless, Bri had also taken slight damage and had noticeable cuts on her face with blood streaming down her cheeks and neck. The sight of this only added more fuel to my fire, so when three of the Supremes stood before us, the original one we came with behind us with the Umbrorex known as Sandra, I didn't bother waiting for them to remove their cloaks. There was no fairness in these things, so I refused to sit and watch as they stripped off their clothing to be better suited for combat.

Just as the nearly eight-foot-tall creature in front of me began to reach for its cloak, I quickly sliced at its head, knees, and arms to completely dismember the creature. Though my sword did cut through it, I felt a much greater resistance to my attack than usual, and the creature had not died immediately. While it was injured, its body splayed awkwardly as it remained upright and let out a noise only describable as air hissing from a deep cave. Black veining feathered out from the cuts where Dr. Ibezzi's poison rode the edges. Realizing what was happening, I looked at Bri.

"Get to Jax, you have to stop him before he pushes that button," I said quickly as she began her escape around the Supremes. Just as she was bolting past them, one of the other Supremes had shifted rapidly to where it was to intercept her. It didn't vanish; it loaded, then blurred, the floor hairline-cracking under its first step. However, I dashed to the location and split its grabbing hand right down the middle to where the elbow would be, allowing her to continue to Jax.

As I held the blade in the arm of the Supreme, I looked back toward the Umbrorexes behind me. I wasn't sure if the poison worked on them much, but I could see dark lines spreading from the cut areas on the corpses, meaning there had to be some form of reaction. Proceeding with this in mind, I pulled out the sword from the creature's arm, using much more force than I expected, as it had begun to heal already. Looking at the Supreme, I could see that in a few short seconds, it had regained full functionality in its arm, even though it was still halved. Despite this, the first Supreme I had engaged with was healing much more slowly, and I recognized the same dark lines forming around where I had sliced it. Seeing that I may not have had a strong enough poison to kill them immediately, I figured I could use the poison to slow them down and otherwise make them more killable.

Standing back in front of the three creatures, I saw the two in the back begin to remove their cloaks. Not wanting to waste time, I finished off the one in front that was still trying to heal by lunging up and fully slicing through its head area, effectively decapitating it at the mouth as its black blood flowed out like a fountain. To ensure it was deceased and bypass any other evolutionary or experimentally induced enhancements, I shoved the katana down its spinal cord. I then felt a strong twitch before I twisted the blade, and the body went completely limp. Removing the katana, I looked to see the tall and skinny creatures in front of me with only garments around their waist. Seeing them in full, their elongated skulls and leathery skin were complemented by sharp bony structures protruding from their torsos as if they were begging to break through the skin. They had similar holes on their sides to the Feralgehns, but unlike the Feralgehns, their legs were closer to a mix of human and wolf than just wolf. They had spread out humanoid feet that angled into a hind limb and a bony leg structure. They were lean, but all I saw was leathery dark skin, no hair of any kind, bone, and a surprising amount of muscle. Their narrow features and long skulls reminded me of an old film we watched when we were younger, but there was no time to reminisce. Before I knew it, I saw the one I had not fought yet swinging its long and sharpened nails at me, seemingly extending its arm to cause me to misjudge the distance. Though I dodged it, I had to remain careful as the Umbrorexes behind me were waiting for me to get close enough to grab without interfering with the Supremes.

Standing back on my feet from a crouched position, I was able to see Bri just past the Supremes in a duel with Jax. Though he had picked up one weapon and she had two, he was able to defend against her attacks and land a few of his own. It didn't quite look like she was losing the battle, but I didn't know how much longer she had before he landed something more serious or the Umbrorexes started to join in. Recognizing this, I acted quickly as I lunged to attack the Supremes in front of me. Unfortunately, just as I began my approach towards them, the one that swung at me was immediately in my face after a coil-and-blur step. Being caught completely off guard by the speed of this creature, I lifted my arms to cover myself in defense before being launched across the room into the horde of Umbrorexes and into the side wall, crushing a few of them in the process with the force of the impact.

Falling from the wall covered in innards, leaving a crater in the rock-like material, I found myself on the ground in a world of pain that I had never felt before. The bones of my back felt obliterated, and my lungs ached as everything else felt the shock of the whiplash. My chest felt as though it was completely fractured from the impact, leaving me nearly defenseless from any additional strikes. Writhing on the ground, I was somehow able to will myself into a sort of upright fetal position where my knees were on the ground and I was folded over myself. Not ignoring the deadliness of the situation or wanting to leave Bri to fend for herself, I tried my best to straighten my back. Though the pain was excruciating and it felt like I was pulling my spine from my body with each movement, I finally straightened my back and planted my fists into the ground to face the swarm of enemies surrounding me. While I somehow maintained the grip on the katana through all of this, I thought my survival to be limited given the sheer volume of assailants against me and the degree to which one blow from a Supreme had nearly killed me. As I sat there, coughing up blood as I tried to stand and prepare my body for a continued battle, I looked forward. Looking with the best of my blurred vision, I saw the sight of Bri fighting the Supreme, whom I hadn't injured, while also holding off Jax. While she seemed to be doing well, the truth was that they were working to slowly disable her. She fought off the key strikes well, but Jax was aiming for her joints and pressure points while the Supreme was more or less fighting to force her into a subconscious state. The sight of this gave me enough energy to stand on my feet as I released a visceral groan, signifying the nearing of my end and undying will to protect her, along with the rest of the human race. Finally taking my stance against the army before me, the Umbrorexes waiting, as if they were either stunned at my ability to move or wanting to give me a somewhat decent chance at survival, I prepared for my potential final offensive. Planning to slice my way through and get straight to Bri so that I could use the bomb Dr. Ibezzi made for us, I began to hear a voice.

Dion... said the same tongue from before that sounded like many of the demonic voices. *I have seen your determination and find it admirable. Although I am not the same as you, I truly have no place in either of these worlds and would rather work with the mightiest of them all. You are far from the most powerful in the room by your lonesome, but to watch your journey end here would be a disservice to my beliefs of attainable perfection. Truthfully, Jax was never a leader, and he views all of us as cattle aiding in the harvest of more superior beings through our sacrifice. If you will allow it, I would like to help you escape from here to see how much greater you become. Will this be suitable?* The voices said as they quieted down.

Shocked and surprised by this, I figured that this could only have come from the Umbrorex named Sandra. While I had no reason to trust it or believe anything it said, I felt a compelling emotion within me, one that overshadowed the pain I was enduring. In that emotion, I focused on the voice and its source. Unable to see Sandra, I did my best to respond to the signal that reached my mind, projecting the words *I allow it.* Upon doing this, it seemed as though all of the Umbrorexes around me had heard my message; they stood surprised and even more motionless in their confusion. Besides this, I felt a surge of aggression in the crowd and heard words being uttered back to me.

Great choice, my fellow hybrid.

Just then, Sandra flew in from an upper side wall of the large room and landed directly on the Supreme that was with it earlier. Without wasting any time, Sandra grabbed hold of the long skull. Sandra then twisted it once, then again, and pulled with great strength, fully decapitating the large creature. As the blood from the beast spewed out and covered the surroundings, discoloring the dark red cloak, the Umbrorexes around me were stunned at the act of betrayal, something I could only assume had not been a common occurrence. Betrayal has a sound; the room paused on it. Not wasting time in the moment, I took a deep and sharp breath and began to kill the Umbrorexes around me. Even though I was injured, I had more than enough strength to take them on, but I had to be careful, as I was considerably slowed by the attack from the Supreme.

Cutting through the dozens of enemies, every blow they landed felt like it had the force of ten times as much, but I had to keep going. Slicing off their heads and cutting through the bodies of their varied evolutionary stages, pieces of flesh and peeling pale skin flew around me once more, only adding to the difficulty I had seeing. Doing just as I had before, I took a second to wipe my eyes clear, but that's when one of the Umbrorexes jabbed me with one of their weapons. While it didn't stab me, it was tipped with a dense and sharp piece of metal that sent shockwaves of electrical force, forcing my leg to buckle and dropping me to the ground. Now surrounded, I made my best effort to stand and fight, but my leg was struggling to respond. Just when I thought it was over, the one that jabbed me was lifted from its feet and ripped in half at an angle, being pulled apart from the left side of its neck down to its right hip. As the two halves of the bodies were spread, I could see Sandra, with its black eyes, the green portion of it even clearer than before. As it looked into my soul, I realized that my leg was functional again. Getting back into the action, I cut off the legs of three Umbrorexes around me before cutting their heads off at the mouth, nose area, and eyes, respectively. As I did this, Sandra used the two halves of the body as a shield and weapon, explosively crushing other Umbrorexes until there was nothing but meat and fabric left in its hands. Seeing such carnage and realizing that the Umbrorex numbers had begun to decline, something I hadn't noticed until I looked around at the hundreds of corpses and the rising lake of blood that was forming, the others backed off and seemingly ran back to the shadows of the room. Though I wasn't sure if this was a form of retreat to them, I knew they had left me an opening to get to Bri. Taking advantage of this, I used my strength to run as fast as I could to the injured Supreme, only to see Sandra jump ahead of me.

Get to Abrial. I will handle this one... Your poison has made one of its arms useless. I will join you shortly, Sandra said telepathically as it wielded the freshly harvested bones of its fellow Umbrorexes as weapons.

Making my way to Bri, I saw that she was now leaning up against the control panel with Jax's hand seemingly forced inside her upper left shoulder, as if he used it as a blade. Leaning there, trying to stab him with her good arm while the Supreme prepared to strike, I used all of the energy in my body to lunge at the creature as hard as I could. Holding my blade out and gripping the end of it with my other arm, I flew into the back of the creature with the blade slicing halfway through its torso. Before I could finish the job, Jax had thrown Bri to the side and appeared next to me, similar to how the prior Supreme had done. Not wanting to face a repeat of what happened before, as my body would likely not withstand it, I dodged out of the way as he swung and kicked in his right knee as hard as I could. Clearly feeling the pain, Jax fell to the ground.

"You ungrateful bastard!" Jax yelled as he sat there, clutching his backward-facing knee, his face contorted in pain and rage.

Using the moment to finish off the Supreme before it could reach behind its back, I pulled out the sword. Quickly lining up my slashing angle, I swung it cleanly through the back side of its long skull, slicing its brain in half as the darkened matter fell to the floor. Ensuring it was fully deceased, I shoved my sword in the open portion of the skull and began to twist until I saw the brains start to flow out to the ground from its face. A disgusting and dirty sensation had covered me in that moment, but all things considered, I had to be sure it was dead.

Looking back at Jax, he was standing on his good leg and hit his fist into the back of his broken leg, straightening it back out with a sickening pop. Standing there, both of us battered from battle, I prepared to go for the killing blow. Waiting as long as I could to build up any usable energy, considering I kept spending it all, I assumed an attack position. Although this stance was proper, it was merely a bluff in the moment, as I needed at least a few more seconds to build up anything useful.

As I was prepared to fight, Jax raised his hand and faced it towards me as if he was telling me to stop. Looking at him sideways, I pulled back my sword. Keeping my stance and remaining aware of my surroundings for any approaching Umbrorexes, I listened to what he had to say.

"Damn, man... You really know how to ruin a party. I mean, look around. You may not have known it yet, but these creatures could have been your family, servants, whatever you wanted. But you went ahead and pissed all that away for nothing. How does that feel?" Jax said, standing awkwardly, holding his leg with his right hand on the front side, a bizarre mix of pain and condescension in his voice.

Although he was clearly buying time to heal, since we didn't have the healing speed of the Supremes, I went along with it to do the same.

"A party... You're a sick and delusional bastard. You creatures threatened to kill everyone and everything, offering reprieve only through staying alive long enough to produce your offspring and serve as slaves for your army. Death doesn't even set one free when it comes to you, so why would we be a part of this? I don't care for your reasons or how flawed you think humanity is; I still don't fully understand it myself, but this isn't the way... I mean, for goodness' sake, did you not have parents or a family, or anyone on Earth that you cared about? No one meant more to you than all of this?" I said as I tried to pick his brain, disgust rising in my throat.

While doing this, I could see that Sandra had defeated the Supreme; it fought for me and was now climbing around the walls toward the roof. As it did this, it spoke to me through the mental connection.

Should I take care of Jax as well, or is there something else I can do? The creature said in its many voices.

Responding, I tried to focus so Jax couldn't hear me and provided instructions for part of my escape plan.

No, go back to the level above this and secure a way out for us. I will handle Jax.

Will do. Stay alive, and I will help you escape, Sandra replied as it crawled toward the open exit in the ceiling.

As Sandra exited, I listened to Jax's response.

"I was never particularly emotional," Jax said. "Genetics, probably. But I understood utility. I came home early after Sandra told me what I am. I made a demonstration. Father first. I put a hole in his chest, and I lifted the body so they could see the future. Mother ran. I used what was in my hand. The trajectory was sufficient." He regarded his knuckles. "My brothers attempted a restraint they favored as children. I corrected it by meeting their heads together until the noise stopped. My sister watched. I set the house on fire and brought her here. She is useful now. Your fathers will be too. They are leverage until they are labor."

In disbelief at what I had heard, I took a moment to respond. In that moment, I looked over to Bri as she began to pull herself from the ground, blood flowing freely from her shoulder. Watching as she stood, I tried to communicate with her using my newly found telepathic abilities.

Bri... Bri, it's me, I said as she confusedly looked my way, clearly suffering greatly from the battle.

Listen, I have a plan to get us out of here, but we need to destroy that console first. Do you have enough strength left to do that? Nod your head to respond, I said as I looked at her slightly, trying not to draw Jax's attention fully to her.

Nodding her head yes, she hobbled to the console and grabbed one of her blades in preparation. Looking back, with 90% focus on Jax, I responded to keep him busy.

"You're worse than I thought. I don't think any part of you is human... Where is your sister now?" I asked in genuine concern, a cold dread creeping in.

"My sister... well... if you were to look around pretty intently in this room on the side where the corpses are... You know... the ones with the babies in them. You would find her somewhere in the middle, serving her destined purpose of fueling the future," Jax said as a wider, more maniacal smile grew on his face.

Filled with more rage and disgust, surpassing the levels of those emotions in a day more than what I had in a lifetime, I chose to attack just as Bri was lifting her blade to stab into the console.

"You'll pay!" I yelled as I lunged at him, feeling my recovery factor already taking effect and my energy increasing. As I lunged, fueled by my confusing care and compassion for humanity, I noticed his leg had healed enough to move, and he slightly dodged my attack as my blade pierced him in his side. To this day, I don't know why I went for the stab over the slice, but I can only chalk it up to a lapse in judgment during a stressful moment. Either way, Jax had seen what Bri was doing and tried to get to her. Seeing that I still had control over the situation, I twisted the blade in his flesh, inducing enough pain to keep him at bay and allow for Bri to shove her blade into the console. When she did, the lighting in the area began to fade in and out, but eventually stayed on enough for us to see what was happening. Realizing that the system was not yet down, judging by the still-lit controls, Bri reached for her other gladius. Holding Jax in place with my sword, we watched as Bri used her injured arm to somehow shove the second sword deep within the panel. As the sparks flew and the lights shut off, the place rumbled, and a set of darker emergency lights flickered into view. Somewhere behind the consoles, a caged man rattled weakly at iron; another didn't move at all. The stink of burned wiring mixed with rot. Assuming that the system had finally gone down, at least in that region, since it was the headquarters, we figured it would be time to get back to the surface, where we could radio our fathers to get out of there.

Seeing that Bri was low on energy, the hole in her shoulder requiring more healing time than what we had, I immobilized Jax by cutting his foot off at the ankle and slicing his patellar tendons. Sure, it was brutal, but I wanted him to be alive to burn when we used our secret weapon. Burning while he thought over his decisions and bad choices, I hoped that he would feel the same suffering that he had forced so many others into. The thoughts and feelings of revenge were something new to me at the time. Regardless, they felt completely natural and understandable in their source. So, as I stood and walked towards Bri while Jax angrily grabbed at my feet, all I could see in his face was a deep red and a sense of entitlement being stomped on. His ego was being crushed in real time, and there was nothing he could do about it.

Upon reaching Bri, I placed her blades in what remained of my waistband and wrapped her canteen around myself. Being cautious, I helped Bri move quickly to the platform that would take us back to the next level. While we promptly made our way to the exit, Jax was left surrounded by the hiding Umbrorexes, screaming at us and sharing his disgruntlement. Though he said things along the lines of revenge and that we're dead, I simply paid him no mind and raised the somehow still functioning platform to the next level. Although there were still humans down there, caged, there was nothing we could do to free them or bring them back to the surface. Besides, the condition they were in is one where death is a privilege.

Despite my thoughts and disregard for Jax's words, one thing in particular stood out to me. As we were rising up, the Umbrorexes had begun to reappear below us, and Jax's tone changed.

"No matter what, you will fulfill your mission. Once you do that, I will be there and end your wasted existence," Jax yelled as he sounded a mixture of excitement and pain, his voice echoing eerily.

Listening to this, I wanted to respond with a quip, as many of the characters had done in the movies we grew up watching. Nonetheless, my attention was quickly needed as we had arrived in a war zone. Somehow, Sandra's actions sparked a sub-surface conflict that quickly spiraled out of control. While many of the Umbrorexes were killing each other and the ones that looked more like the Supremes, a good number had taken notice of us and began to head our way. Wondering where Sandra was, I prepared to fight, as did Bri, as she grabbed her blades, one arm still requiring much recovery. Standing in the sanctuary, waiting for them to come in through the large doors, I saw them suddenly vanish from sight, leaving only a mist of blood in the air. Confused and unable to identify what had happened, I heard a voice.

Come through the doors. We must leave now, Sandra said in her many voices.

Given that Bri had also heard this, we made our way to the doors and found Sandra, along with a few other advanced Umbrorexes with green eyes. Unsure if they were as evolved as Sandra, we didn't speak, but I'm not sure they planned for that anyway. Guiding us towards something that looked like a wagon the farmers would have used with two Feralgehns in the front, missing the signature claws as if they were bred for other uses, we climbed in the back, waiting for Sandra and its companions to join in. Once they were all there, Sandra got in the back with us and two other Umbrorexes while two more sat in the driver's seat for the Feralgehns. Lying down to avoid the attacks and flying objects, I heard a loud pop as the cart began moving forward rapidly. As we were in the back of this seemingly old-school cart used by a supposedly advanced society, we heard much violence and watched as Sandra and the others would occasionally leave and return, covered in red and black blood alike, signifying the differences among the creatures that lived there. Racing through the city of Thraxxundar, I could feel all of the bumps as we rode over the bodies of these creatures. Alarms sounded just loud enough for us to hear, and they seemed to be pouring in from the distance and the holes in the walls as I peeked over the cart lining. Unsure about the situation, I prepped Bri for the worst-case scenario as we exited the city and approached the outer society we initially passed through when we first arrived.

"Bri, I need you to know that I'm going to use this stuff one way or another. It would have been ideal for us to use it in the main control center, but I have a hunch that the air density will cause it to spread like wildfire and kill everything, at least in Thraxxundar. That said, we're going to need to run like hell through this tunnel if something happens to these Feralgehns. In any case, I will ensure you get out of here and inform the others about what we found. You have to let them know there's more and possibly more like Jax. We've only scratched the surface of what these creatures are doing and how far this really goes," I said as I looked into her eyes, my voice filled with grim determination.

Looking back at me, clearly distraught at what I said and facing the challenges of her injuries, Bri responded. "What do you mean by 'you'? We're both getting out of here, D, and we'll tell them together. We have a better idea of how to beat them. We possibly have these five on our side. We don't need to die today to win tomorrow," Bri said as she felt my face through all of the blood and dirt, her voice cracking slightly.

"I know, but I made your father a promise, and I don't want us to escape only to be killed on the way back to the rest. Trust me, I want to get out of here with you, but we need to close this hole as soon as we can," I said back as we neared the exit and the assault grew stronger.

"D, I..." Bri said, but was cut off by the cart flipping over.

Reacting as fast as I could, I grabbed Bri and held her as we rolled through the dirt-covered rocky ground. Looking up to see the Feralgehns leading us had been punctured with a variety of weapons and taken a beating, I felt a hand grab my back and lift me up.

We have to keep moving, Sandra said telepathically, seemingly unable to show expressive emotion.

As we ran as best as we could, slowed by the injuries, the Umbrorexes that had been sent, along with the Feralgehns and Subterros, were gaining on us quickly. Two of the Umbrorexes that were with Sandra would rush into the crowd and return, each more damaging, but giving us time. Approaching the exit, we mentally prepared for the long trip to the surface, and I pushed Bri ahead of me as we began to run up the wall. Running, only just outpacing our pursuers by a couple of seconds, Sandra and the other two began to get more involved in the fighting as the swarm of enemies started to block the light at the bottom of the hole. The sensation of running vertically was one that we hadn't had time to get used to, or the rapidly thinning air, so we were disoriented during the ordeal, unable to join the fight. My ears pressed, and a metallic taste tickled my tongue. It also didn't help that my lungs were on fire and I coughed up more blood as I fought to push beyond my limits, still recovering from the earlier blow. Either way, we had to get there, and we were getting closer to seeing the exit of the hole.

As we neared thirty seconds from the hole, running with an insane speed given our injuries, one of the Umbrorexes with Sandra had been impaled through the leg by a Feralgehn and tossed into the horde behind it. Seeing this, the

Umbrorex that was with it, seemingly one of the ones that felt emotions, let out a shriek and sacrificed itself, killing everything in sight with reckless abandon and using its arms as if they were blades. By this point, I could feel the sadness within Sandra building, but I could tell she was holding it together and being logical. Keeping focused, we found ourselves approaching the surface when the horde behind us suddenly stopped in its tracks, letting us escape. Once at the lip, we flew out of the hole and clung to the familiar Earth, adjusting to the air and nearly unable to breathe after the twenty-kilometer sprint. Realizing that they were still in the hole and not moving, I sensed another group of monsters. I looked around to see the corpses of many Feralgehns, Subterros, and even a few Umbrorexes. Unsure of what happened, I glanced into the treeline and saw the soldiers that Kendry had sent with us hanging from trees by their feet, with their heads partially gone and their arms removed. Sickened by this, I immediately stood to my feet as best I could and tried to sense our fathers. Unable to do so with the overwhelming presence of evil surrounding us, I helped Bri up and slowly moved forward with Sandra and the other two Umbrorexes.

As we moved away from the hole, we could hear the creatures within slowly making their way to the lip, their sickening limbs and faces beginning to appear. Before we had a chance to face them, we were all frozen in shock as a Supreme exited the woods wearing some form of breathing apparatus that sighed with each inhale. In each of its hands, it held our fathers. They were both poorly bloodied, and Bri's father looked as if he had lost his left eye; they were breathing... barely.

Faced with this new situation, Bri leaned on me as I could feel the anger within her bubbling over. Just as I felt her beginning to get ready to expend what energy she could possibly have left, a familiar voice spoke from behind us.

"I told you... You will not succeed."

XXIV. SACRIFICES

Looking at Jax, a sense of defeat washed over me as we were placed in another impossible situation. I knew the crisis was not over. I had hoped for more time to prepare. Reality didn't care. We were trapped again, and this time, more lives sat inside our circle. Bri at my shoulder. The Umbrorexes, our unlikely ally, completing the ring. We waited for whatever ultimatum Jax would drop.

As they carried him from the hole to within twenty feet, I saw what I had done to him. He was less a whole being than a collection of surviving parts. His tourniquet leaked. The severed tendons where my blade bit were blackening, the poison still riding the metal's bite. Dark lines spidered his skin. The toxin was slowly and surely killing his cells. That also meant it was lethal to Bri and me. Still, I tracked what it did to him: the stab through his side, the limp, the labored breath. Given time, it might finish him. We didn't have time. We braced. Even the militant, robotic Umbrorexes panted.

I waited for the speech.

"You know... that little trick of poison you used was a nice touch." His forehead swelled with veins. "I can feel it spreading... limiting me. We will make an antitoxin. Even if not, my death will mean something. Yours? A flash of sunlight in an infinite abyss." His breath grated.

He lifted his voice. "For now, watch as we tear you apart and feed you to our pets. You have ruined enough of what we are doing for this planet, so you will not see the end. We will keep a few organs intact; useful ones. We will harvest what we need and replicate you in crystal vats and breeding beds. We will make enough copies to dissect, daily, so your failures instruct the future."

He turned to Sandra. "As for you and the traitors, you are recon and meat. You are already being phased out, you just don't want to face it. Your envy caught up to you." He lifted his right arm for a signal.

I tensed for the swarm. I looked at Bri. Looked past her to our fathers. Their faces pulled a feeling I hate into the open: failure. His arm came down.

Nothing moved.

Silence pressed in. Then the skin tore. A heartbeat pumped to the air. I swept the treeline for motion and found Bri's eyes. They were glassing over, going wet and wide. Time slowed. Her spirit, usually unbreakable, fractured in front of me.

I followed her stare.

The Supreme held Mr. Alvar. Same hand as before. Only now it was just his head. The rest of him lay in a collapsed suit of clothes and opened organs at its feet. His crooked face looked at us while blood trickled from his nose and ears. A thin strand of saliva swung from his jaw and caught the light. A soundless apology.

I froze.

Bri did not. Something old and animal took her. She moved as if her injuries were nonexistent. The Supreme swung my father by the neck like a club; she slid under, took both its arms off at the shoulders in one blur, and stabbed both Gladii into its midline. She rotated the blades vertically and drew them up through the skull. The creature stepped back on a brain still sparking, trisected, trying to hold itself together. It collapsed into black blood and organs.

She didn't stop. She couldn't. Her father was dead, and there was nothing in the world she could fix except the next cut. She became a storm, killing what she reached, poisoning what she nicked. Black lines bloomed from every slice. The poison did its work by forcing their accelerated cells to eat themselves, and mitosis turned cannibal.

Our chance is now, I sent to Sandra, the thought sharp and fast.

We broke the ring and joined. I carved my path toward my father, decapitating a Feralgehn, disabling an Umbrorex, then scooped him and ran him deeper into the trees. I made sure he was breathing, gave him some water, and thought of a plan for the bomb.

Back to the fight. Jax was propped up, the poison working. He still adjusted the Umbrorexes with clipped orders, and their patterns sharpened. Sandra's squad took pressure; Bri's speed finally paid its debt, and pain caught up. A Feralgehn lunged at her spine; my blade took its head. She pivoted on me, blades high, eyes red and wide. I ducked. Her tears kept falling, but inside, she was emptied out; a shell being puppeted by rage.

In that state, her injured arm moved like it remembered itself, not like it was healed; fresh blood still flowed when she cut. I looked into her eyes again and saw the buried sadness and the desire to kill. Revenge had hold of her, dragging her down into a pit even deeper than sorrow. I wanted to hold her. I had to fight instead.

We pressed palms and shoved apart. The space between us was filled with a Feralgehn claw that missed by inches. I used the shift in momentum and rose from the ground, taking the creature's head as the body toppled.

Across the field, a friendly Umbrorex was dragged down and ripped apart in a spray of limbs. The other was being surrounded. I moved to help, but Bri was already there, slicing the napes of their necks and burning black down every wound.

Sandra fought near Jax's entourage. A Feralgehn speared her through the side and lifted her. I cut the monster's face in half from ear to ear; Sandra dropped, ripped out the claw, and stood with me. Jax's supporters kept pouring from the hole. We stood together for the heartbeat between waves.

Take this chance to get out and work with Bri to find the others. I am not sure how much I can trust you, but if you get my father and her to safety, I guarantee your sacrifice will not be in vain. Understood? I sent to Sandra.

She nodded and sprinted through a seam in the line. I turned to Jax. I had both canteens strapped tight, my katana wet and heavy, clothes caked with blood, dirt, and sweat. The sun touched the edge of the world and painted everything bronze.

Jax made a small gesture, and the nearby creatures stilled. He raised his head and found his voice again. "What are you doing? Are you... Looking to God? Didn't know our kind could do that. You and your girlfriend surprise me more every day." He wheezed between words.

I tuned him out and used the beat of safety he had given me by accident. Sandra had reached Bri and the other Umbrorex. They were wounded but moving; they could make it to the trees. I let myself think about the word he had used. Girlfriend. It meant more now, after everything Bri and I had become and done. Maybe I thought I was about to die, and the word lit the fuse on whatever love I had been holding back. Perhaps I was just honest.

I pushed the link to Bri until a needle dug behind my eye. We had only ever held it across a few hundred yards. This had to be enough.

Bri... Abrial... I don't know if this will carry, but I want to apologize in advance. I know you wanted us both to make it home, but I only see one way out where you survive. You know what I'm planning. I felt the link tug. She turned, trying to reach me. Sandra and the other Umbrorex held her back with everything they had. *The past sixteen years with you have been nothing but bright. You unlocked things in me I didn't know were there. I hope I did the same for you.*

She fought them, strong, even when wounded.

I see you trying to get here, but that cannot happen. I told Sandra to get you and my father back to the main group. I don't know if the radios will work, but you destroyed the machine. Maybe you can reach them. Find the car and get out. I will find you again when I can. I love you. Tears spilled from her face. At that distance, I barely saw them. I felt them.

I turned away as the other Umbrorex lifted my father and slipped into the treeline. Jax was still talking.

"You were close... really close. But we are—"

"You never shut up, do you?" I said, and ran.

Katana in hand. The hole in front of me. Jax's eyes widened, and he tried to order a wall of bodies. I hit him before anyone could react. We went off the edge locked together.

His hand sank into my shoulder, fingers digging into the old wound the Supreme had punched through my chest. Pain flared white. I pulled my knees high and planted both feet on his chest, then kicked hard and launched away. A mouthful of his blood fogged the air between us. Flesh tore out of my shoulder with him as we separated. He grinned through red, and I hated that grin more than anything I have ever seen.

Umbrorexes and Feralgehns jumped between the walls of the hole, trying to reach us mid-fall. Some tried to net us with their bodies. I killed what I could; clumsy, falling, swinging in the air.

Jax mouthed something. The wind and the screams made him a nightmare for lip readers. I think it was, "We will never lose."

Below, Umbrorexes and a few Supreme-bodied creatures linked arms and torsos into a net. They meant to save him. They meant to break his fall, not mine.

I needed a strike that their flesh could not dampen. I could stab, but after all he had done, I wanted a certainty only weight could give.

I tightened the straps on the canteens and made sure the katana was sheathed. I pointed my knees straight down. I arched my back until it hurt and aimed for his heart.

For a breath, he kept that ignorant smile. Then he saw the line I had made. The smile died.

He hit the net first. It stretched and took him. I hit him a blink after and went through flesh and bone and into the ground. Stone cratered. Dust geysered. Everything rang.

I was still conscious somehow, but could not feel my feet. My knees had struck something that broke like dry wood. His spine, I think. I felt soft push out under my knees like toothpaste from a tube. The ground was six inches deeper where I sat. Jax's body twitched in two unhappy halves. Blood bubbled in his mouth, eyes leaking, nose leaking, ears leaking. He tried to say something, or breathe, or both.

The walls crawled with enemies coming down to finish it. I reached for the canteens. If my legs were broken, I would die here with purpose.

I pulled out the two inner bags. The horde circled. I opened the first and lifted the second to pour.

A hand caught the back of my shirt and dragged me. I got a look over my shoulder and saw an Umbrorex with half a body; one arm gone, hide flayed, face pale and almost human, green eyes steady.

Who are you and why are you doing this? I sent as stone and bone scraped my back, and the crowd followed a stride behind.

Do you not think a thank you is in order? The thought came in a single, smooth voice. *I am Etioch, Sandra's second-in-command. She left me to lead the conflict. We were severely beaten. I waited for your return. She said you would likely bring a weapon. Is that it? Those bags?*

Sandra was a she. They were all monsters in my eyes at the time, and still, some of them stood with us. Evolutionary zealots, yes. Also, pieces on our side of the board, at least for the time being.

I appreciate it. Yes. It is a bomb that will incinerate the oxygen down here and use that as the base for its explosion. I'm not sure how powerful it is, but if we are right, it could wipe out all of these things at once. Are you planning to help me use it?

Affirmative, Etioch said, and dragged me faster toward the city. The cathedral with the command center waited like a dark mouth.

Going into the same place we had escaped felt wrong. Not as wrong as staying where thousands of enemies poured in behind us. They filled the floor, the opening to the bottom level, and the air until distance meant nothing. Etioch slipped ahead of their reach and hurled me into a chamber in the far back corner; solid titanium and exotic lattice. It felt like it could take a small sun.

He meant to stay out. I could lock it from within. I mixed the two bags and threw them through the opening as he turned.

"Get in! I threw it out already!"

Etioch's pale face and green eyes flashed with something like joy. He shouldered in and threw the lock with his one good arm. The door shuddered as the flood of bodies hit. The transparent pane, some engineered crystal, veined with stress.

I waited for the bomb and tried not to picture the door bending. Three seconds. Nothing. The wall at my back shook with weight. Etioch leaned next to me and pressed the other wall with his shoulder. We braced for them to get in and end it.

Then... the light came.

Even with the chamber silent, the blast was a thing I could see and feel. An instant ignition took hold of the air outside and raced through the connected tunnels. The pane went from clear to white to fracture-traced and held. Where the blast touched, the horde melted into moving ash, then into nothing. Stone faces of the corridor shone like new glass. Holes collapsed. The door's color deepened, and the edge curled a fraction. Somewhere outside, whatever humans had still been alive at their hands were gone in that same instant. Mercy, in the balance of what they had planned for them.

When the light finally slipped, the heat still rode the walls. We stared through the ruined window at a world reduced to glittering soot.

You know you and I are the same... partially, Etioch sent in that steady voice. *So I have some advice. Close your eyes. We heal faster when we rest. Do not worry. I am about to do the same.*

He went out like someone had blown out a candle.

I could not walk. I could not do anything but listen to my heart and feel the room cool by degrees. I pushed myself against the wall and let the dark take me.

I could only hope Bri and my father made it out. I could only hope we had done enough.

I could only hope.

When the heat faded to a dull smear on the warped door, the old thought returned. Earth breathed easier without us. Air cleaner. Silence deeper. It is tempting to mistake that relief for justice. It is not. The enemy that rose was not the planet. It was a patient intelligence that learned us, then used that knowledge like a wire around our throat. If there is a balance, it is not made by killing Mr. Alvar. It is made by what we do next.

XXV. TRUTH

By the time I awoke, my mouth felt lined with sand and my joints crackled like they'd been locked for years. I'd gone to sleep the most beat up I'd ever been, and my body had taken the time it needed without asking. Peeling myself from the cold wall, I tested each hinge, neck, shoulder, and knee until the pops ran out. Pain didn't answer. Strength did. My legs looked new, regrown, and clean where they should have stayed ruined. There was a quiet promise in the way they held me: hydrate, feed, move, and you'll be stronger than before.

I glanced left. Etioch's arm was still gone, no miracle there, but the stump had sealed over in a way that made the synthetic skin look like a bad copy. His eyes snapped open: black pools with green rings that found me without blinking. I didn't feel surprised, only the thought that he probably hadn't slept as long as I had.

"Glad to see you're still with me, Etioch. I know you just opened your eyes, but do you mind telling me how long we've been in here for?" I asked as I eased into a crouch and pushed up the wall to stand.

Standing felt strange, like I was riding on brand-new parts, and I could tell by the way Etioch rose and set his feet that he was making the same calculation. We faced the door together.

"I am here with you... to make the future better... Not just for you and the humans... but for our people as well... I know you did not ask that... but I wanted to give you a summary... We are not enemies," Etioch said. His voice was more capable than Sandra's had been, but it still sounded like speech dragged over gravel.

"Thanks for letting me know. I'll ask more about that later. The entire side switch surprised me, but right now we need to get out of here before more come," I said, waiting for his answer to my original question.

"I see... You want to know about the passage of time... To be transparent... I am not too sure you want to know... However, you need to know... Judging by my estimates... seven to ten days... since the events you last remember," he said, looking plainly into my eyes.

His attempt to be more human was noticeable in his language, but none of it reached his face. Seven to ten days landed hard. I needed to move. Even if the others were long gone, I had to try to find them. Feeling energy return and the harm from dehydration right there with it, I crossed to the door and gripped the large rotating handle. Through the clear port, lights still burned on the other side; bioluminescent strips wired through EM-baffled conduits that had ridden out the surge. The blast had killed everyone, not everything. I turned the handle. It budged, then seized. Three of the five sliding bars pulled back; the bottom two stayed planted. The door had warped, and the channels had tightened; the pins had fused into vitrified stone.

"You do not want to... break the handle," Etioch said.

I ignored him and reset my grip; right hand high, left low, elbows tucked to keep the spindle from flexing. The mechanism complained a dry, crystalline sound, then stopped dead. I exhaled and looked at Etioch.

"Think you've got enough in that arm to help me get this open?"

"I will try," he said, stepping in and taking a stance that put his one arm in its best range.

"On my pace. Half-tooth turns. If it binds, we climb back," I said.

We leaned into it together. The handle shuffled a millimeter, then another, the cam riding past the warped spot. Veins rose for no one but us. At the sticking point, something inside the door cracked, less metal, more glass, and the last pins slipped. The slab slumped off its hinges and crashed outward into a shallow hill of bones and ash.

Air that shouldn't have been there hit my lungs; stale, charged, glass-smelling. I coughed until stars pricked the edges of my vision. The natural lighting they used in these underground spaces hummed brighter.

We stepped out into a space that felt sterilized by a god who liked clean lines. The glass beneath my feet was odd, slick, and squealing under my boots, but not odd enough to make me forget I needed water and new clothes. Etioch's clothes were barely hanging on. Mine weren't much better. We could scavenge before moving. I didn't fully understand their tech or its tolerances, but a sealed room could have survived.

We walked through what had been a breeding and rearing area. The human cage held only collars and shackles. Bones that might have survived had been cooked to ash. I kept my balance like a toddler getting its legs back under it. The regenerated cells were there in greater numbers than I expected. My shoes were in ribbons from the fight and from the impact with Jax that shattered my legs and ended him. Etioch's voice touched my mind.

I know a place here where we can find new clothes and resources. Continue toward the exit and turn right upon arrival, where the console used to be located. All the way by the far wall will be a chamber similar to the one we were in, and it will have all that we need.

I picked up the pace to test the legs. We reached the chamber; the door still closed, the seals unbroken. I planted my feet and drove my weight backward, feeling the new muscle learn me as I pulled. The warped metal groaned. Cracks formed along the fused seam. One final pull, and the door tore free and swung outward, revealing a dim room filled with clothing, food, and other supplies, all human-sized and human-made.

"Why do you have all of this? I don't see how these items are useful to the beings down here," I said, taking in the piles.

"They may not be... useful for most... but for us hybrids... they are essential to blend in... also—" he started.

"Use telepathy? There isn't anything wrong with your voice, but you're faster in my head. I still don't know how much time we have before more creatures come… if they are," I said, already rummaging. I found tactical pants, boots, a shirt, and clean undergarments. I dressed fast.

You don't have to worry about more coming, he said in my mind. *This is an unprecedented situation for the founder race. If they meant to be here, they would have by now.*

"Then why the stockpile?" I said, filling a pack.

We hybrids aren't the same as the founders. Our bodies fit human clothes and take to human foods better. We can live mineral-based, like the founders, and eat the occasional pet, but our genetics respond better to what you eat, he said, tying his left sleeve into a knot to keep it clear.

We packed what we could into large bags. I sat, drank a liter of water, and ate enough to wake all systems. The food was rough, prepackaged MREs and cans, but after a week asleep, anything would do. Etioch spooned from a large can of applesauce and nothing else.

"Just that?" I asked.

Pectin and simple sugars. Tissue repair fuel, he said, without looking up.

I strapped my katana at my waist and slung the pack onto my back. My body felt essentially normal, maybe better. If the near-death or the long sleep had shifted the baseline up, I'd learn it when a fight made me find out. Until then, the walk would be the scale.

We stepped back into the bone-and-ash space. Pregnant shapes lay as outlines in powder, most of them so thoroughly burned that even their bones had lost structure. It was a clean kind of evil. Their approach, vile and brilliant, was the sort of thing humanity might have collaborated on if we didn't hate what it said about us. They had known what prejudice waited for them up top and decided to force complicity instead. I kept moving. I had no clue what the surface looked like now.

At the cathedral where the control center rose, the platform was gone, its lift melted and fused into the wall. We needed to move. I dropped into a crouch, loaded ankles and hips, and jumped for the nearest edge, about a story and a half. My fingers caught stone. Forearms scraped glassy grit. I pulled through and rolled a shoulder to clear the lip, the pack dragging but not winning. That height would have stopped me before, and the pack weighed close to a hundred pounds, but my tendons answered cleanly, and the landing stuck. Etioch followed, one arm, same weight, using a shallow toe-hold I'd scuffed into the floor as a launch point. He came up beside me with a thin, awkward smile, one corner of his borrowed lip hitching, eyes squinting like he was still learning which muscles did what. I didn't indulge it. I turned to the exit and stepped out of the ruined structure in the cavern's center.

The cavern spread sterilely around us. The rock-homes still stood, mostly turned to glass. The bodies were bones and particles. A part of me wanted to feel sorry for the ones who'd had nothing to do with the surface plans; some of them looked like children, but nothing landed. I stayed aware of the holes in the walls that hadn't collapsed and kept scanning. Something was wrong with the air. No draft. No wind sound from the shaft to the surface. Like the hole had vanished.

I burst into a sprint. Even with the pack, I moved faster than I ever had outside of a fight. The dust-glossed ground hissed under my boots. The bomb had been efficient. It had torched the air and vitrified the rock's pores, sealing everything it touched. It could have killed us, too, if we'd been slow. That same small mixture had wiped a city clean, leaving ash and glass where a world had been.

Near the exit tunnel, I slowed. Etioch matched me. The crater where I'd landed on Jax still marked the ground. There wasn't much left of him, but the face of his skull had somehow survived, a final, stubborn warning about how hard he was to kill. Indentations from my knees were still etched in the glass where the heat had sealed the ground. The main shaft had collapsed into itself. The chimney didn't breathe; the heat had glazed the pores shut. I pressed my palm to the wall and listened for empty spaces or a moving draft, any hint that digging would matter. Nothing. We were cut off.

Realizing how buried we were, I could only hope Bri and the others had gotten clear before the blast and the collapse. I had no clue whether they knew I was alive. I was too deep to feel for them. Bri knew we were survivors and that, if there was a way out, I would find it or it would find me, but there was nothing solid to hold on to. I sat and looked over at Etioch.

"Etioch," I said. His eyes met mine. "Can you reach Sandra or the others? I know we can both do telepathy, but you're better at it."

He closed his eyes. The prosthetic skin on his forehead folded as he worked. I felt a pressure at the edge of my awareness, ghost-noise, the way thunder feels before it sounds. After a minute, he opened his eyes and shook his head.

I tried to find Sandra, but I was unable to locate her mind. I could send a message out for all to hear, hoping she would receive it, but I highly recommend against that. Our foes may understand that we are still alive. Right now, they likely think we're dead, if they even know what happened. We should keep that advantage, he said in my head, still staring at the far wall like he could see through it.

I sighed and dropped my head. If we were staying dark, then I needed to understand him and why he helped me.

"I know you mentioned it earlier, but why did you, Sandra, and the others switch sides? I don't remember any of you when I fought to get to Jax. You didn't attack me. Why not?"

No tension came off him. No vibration of nerves. His answer landed calmly.

Sandra leads our kind, third-generation hybrids. The first were proofs of life and were killed once the data was collected. The second could think, bleed red, and speak in minds, but they are evolutionary dead ends. We are not. We speak. We heal.

We feel, imperfectly. We hid that from the founders because it kept us alive. Jax changed the calculus. He arrived, calling us inferior. The Supremes agreed. There was no problem with the next stage of evolution; only with the contempt that came with it. Sandra watched you, weighed Jax, and waited. When you could beat him, she acted.

While you went below, we sparked a fight up here; hybrid against founder, to pull bodies off your path. The second generation aided not because they loved us, but because new emotions had been brewing, and the founders responded with retaliation, not thought. It worked enough. Not cleanly. Not without a cost. My arm is part of that cost. My duty remains the same: get you out and back to Abrial, assuming she is alive.

He turned his face away at her name and then back, something like fear, or something close to it, passing over the bad copy of skin. He wasn't wrong. I had no clue whether she lived.

"Okay," I said. "I can understand that. We don't talk down to you like Jax, but your kind is an enemy. We can't forget what they did. I have to kill every last one of you to make sure my people survive."

He kept his gaze on the distance.

I understand, and I agree with you; we all do. We know that our original species must die for this, and any hybrid that is not with us. That is a part of the deal. We will focus on the proper plan and on keeping the bloodlines alive, especially you two. There are many more out there like you and Jax. We have not seen them, but we have heard of them. Some are extremely intelligent, some stronger or faster than we imagined, some with abilities we don't know. It is unclear how many were contacted and became like Jax versus how many chose humanity. No matter the ratios, your version of hybrid is alive and will help us create what this planet needs; something that grew from love, not from force. A future that forgets this strife and grows into what survives. If securing this means sacrificing ourselves or slaughtering our brethren, who are yours in a sense, so be it.

Humans can't exist with each other, and Founders can't exist with humans. Natural hybrids are the only solution, he said.

It made a clean kind of sense. He didn't plan to kill humans; he planned for us to make more of us until the numbers solved the problem. Hybrids would win that math. It would still mean the loss of human life and the end of humans as they were, leaving only a piece behind. But evolution doesn't ask for permission.

"When you and the others refer to Bri and me and the possibility of reproduction, what do you mean?" I asked.

Well, other than the fact that two people can reproduce, you two have already taken that step. Although we cannot know for certain if something was created from it, there is a high possibility that it was; our species is especially fertile. I have many offspring, but our culture's lack of empathy makes it easy to forget them and follow orders. It also makes it easy to kill those who look like me, as long as it is for the right reason. I assume you and Abrial did not use defense against reproduction, so there is a high chance you have begun the process we seek, he said.

A memory hit from nowhere; Bri's thumb circling once on my wrist when I overthink. It went as quickly as it came. I stood and shouldered my pack.

"I think it's time we go. Suggestions on how to get out of here?"

He looked toward the black mouth of a tunnel on the far side.

There. That tunnel links to a colony network with waypoints every fifty kilometers. If the glyphs still read, we can ride cold air until it rises again. Hundreds of miles.

"A few hundred miles? There's nothing closer?"

If there were, the founders would have used it to come for us by now. With the machine destroyed, this is our best bet. Unless you would like to dig.

I shook my head and headed for the tunnel. Etioch tried a chuckle. It sounded like coughing through a wall of slime. We entered a possible future. Darkness took the place of the old illumination. Rock replaced the glass. I didn't know what we were marching toward, where Bri and the others were, or whether I had just chosen to be a father without deciding. I made it simple. Survive. Find a way out. Kill every last one of these creatures.

I'm writing this from a lichen-slick rock above a green river that threads through what I think are the Coast Mountains of Canada. The wind carries cold. The last decade has been battles and revelations, and other days you don't forget, but those first months still hold the most weight. The world we knew ended in a way no one expected.

Humanity got a quiet death sentence that I helped write. The truth is, the cleanest end would be to kill every hybrid, myself included, and wipe the founders with us. That's neat on paper. Reality doesn't let you find every trace, and I believe what Etioch said, that this is the best path left. Not perfect. Best. There are hybrids out there, and whatever they've made since. You don't erase that. You work with what is.

For every person I lost and every person I found, I'll do everything I can to give them a life that ends when it's supposed to. Our enemies have grown stronger, trying to finish us. We've grown too. We don't sit back and die while the world burns. They took everything, but we're still holding reins. We decide what happens next, and I'll fight to my last breath to make sure of it.

So... as I sit here with cold air in my chest and river grit on my tongue, the people I'm responsible for behind me where they're safer today than yesterday, I won't stop until it's over.

To Bri... you are the heat that holds in a stormy wind. I'm not sure where you are, but I hear of you and I know you're out there. Maybe we don't cross again for a long time. Our lives will be longer. Even if I fail and the world burns, I'll still be here to find you.

To Kendry, Auxi, and my parents, I keep the promise I made ten years ago when Kendry almost died. That day turned something in me. I don't turn it back. You are my core. I will honor that every day I'm breathing.

To everyone else, have faith in me and in what we're doing. It will look pointless sometimes. It isn't. As long as we have enemies, we won't be safe. I don't know everything about being human, but ten years have taught me this: being human is resilience and courage and refusing to stop. We will prevail.

Through the humanity that runs my mind and the evil that courses my veins to give me strength, we will prevail.

As I close out this portion of my life and look to what the future holds, I hope you see a world where what we did meant something. I hope we saved enough. I hope you get a life worth living and fighting for.

I hope we showed you what it truly means to be *human*.

AFTERWORD

I started writing *Not So Human* during the fall semester of 2023. What began as a creative spark quickly became something more profound. At the time, I didn't know where the story would go, only that it *had* to be written. The first scenes came to me in moments between classes and long nights where the noise of the world made it easier to explore a quieter, darker one. I carried the idea into winter break, and while I took long gaps in between, the story never really left me.

In fact, space was necessary. Sometimes, distance is what allows clarity to emerge.

After finishing my first book, *Start From Something*, I returned to *Not So Human* with new energy and purpose. That first book taught me how to see a project through to completion. This one taught me how to wrestle with scale, world-building, and characters who feel *real enough to hurt*. Dion's voice took shape, and the world around him began to breathe. The more I wrote, the more I realized this wasn't just a story about war or survival; it was about identity, friendship, purpose, and the strange, humbling truth that we know so little about the planet we claim to rule.

This book asked a lot of questions. Some I had answers for. Some I still don't. But that's what I love about writing, especially science fiction. It gives you space to wrestle with the unknown and still make meaning from it.

If you made it to the end, thank you. Thank you for investing your time, your imagination, and your curiosity in this world. I hope you felt the tension, the thought, the care, and the possibility that this story tried to offer. And I hope it reminded you, like it reminded me, what makes us human... and what might not.

— *Thomas J. Freeman*

ABOUT THE AUTHOR

Thomas J. Freeman is the author of *Not So Human* and *Start From Something*. His work fuses propulsive sci-fi with human-scale heart, asking what endures when the world tilts. When he's not writing, he's exploring horror-centric creations, impactful projects, and hosting conversations that build community. He believes any story good enough to read should be impactful enough to alter your perspective.

Dion's journey will continue.